THE TRUTH UNRAVEL

SHERLINA IDID

ISBN:

Cover Designed by Miblart

Edited by Gone Roque Editing Services & Nevvie Ganes Book Editors

Published by: Shariffah Norazlina Idid

For Alisya

Chapter 1

I am going to die today.

The door of my room closes behind me, and a sudden tremor runs down the walls under my hand. I nearly lose my balance as the floor shakes again. I turn to the window, where I watch as trees uproot, a high-rise apartment collapses, and waves of debris and mud race down the slope rapidly toward my apartment.

Automatically, my hands cover my head, and shivers wrack my body. I turn my head, heart racing, and my gaze catches on the mirror trimmed with golden leaves hanging on the wall.

I blink and rub the heels of my palms into my eyes. *It is just my imagination.* Dizziness seeps through my body as I notice a dark bloodstain on the left of my black blouse. My mouth drops open, and my hands quiver. *How did I get that?*

I sneak a final glance at myself in the mirror, still freaking out about the blood, and grab my bag from the floor before running as fast as my legs can carry me.

I need to save myself before I can find out where this blood came from.

I fling open the emergency exit door and scamper

down the staircase, tripping on some steps as I run downstairs. My legs shake, and my heart hammers against my chest.

As I reach the last landing, the door for the lobby flies open, its hinge giving way, and the door falls, almost hitting my toe before it clatters to the cement floor.

'Jamie!' My heart beats hard against my chest as I stand eye to eye with my best friend. Jamie's shirt is spotted with blood around his waist here and there. Whose blood is smeared on his shirt? I shake my head to brush the last thought aside.

His hands tremble, and he has some cuts and bruises. His eyes open wide, then he reverses and speeds away.

"Wait, Jamie. Wait for me!" I move to follow him, but a shudder runs through the building. Dust debris falls from the ceiling. I look up and sigh in relief that the ceiling is intact. As I step further, a second stronger shudder strikes, and I clutch the railing tighter as I wait for the shaking to stop.

Once the shudders stop, I reach out for the door. I barely pass through the emergency door and step onto the ground floor when a loud gunshot echoes through the space.

I instantly turn my head in the direction of the gunfire, ducking and covering my head. My heartbeat quickens even more, and a trickle of sweat rolls down my temple. A spike of fear hits me as I frantically search the chaotic crowd for Jamie.

Several rushing steps ring in my ears, and two security guards with guns drawn take off in the direction of the gunshot.

A noise on my left causes my head to turn, and the glass entrance door is covered halfway with piles of debris mixed with brown and grey mud.

"How are we going to get out? Are we safe here?" A man in a blue blazer grabs the jacket a security guard is wearing, shaking him.

Another security guard standing beside him pats the man's shoulder, gently easing his grip from his co-worker.

"Kindly be patient, Mr. LeBlance. The apartment's surrounding area was hit by a landslide. The natural disaster authority is on its way to save us."

Other guests standing a few feet away from the entrance whisper tensely, worry etched onto their faces. There are two men walking to and fro and another man playing with his cigar in his hands, his left shoe tapping the floor incessantly. In the corner, standing tall with her Persian cat in her arms, my neighbor Mrs. Aminah fidgets with her small purse as she starts to wail, "All of us are trapped." She blows her nose with a tissue, and the crowd's chattering increases.

Two security officers walk toward the front entrance as the apartment manager says to Mrs. Aminah and the other residents gathered near the entrance, "Mrs. Aminah and all, please remain calm. Stay clear from doors and windows. I believe the authorities are doing their best to clear the debris quickly and save us."

One of the security guards holds out a hand to Mrs. Aminah and guides her to sit on a Chesterfield chair a few feet from the entrance, mumbling quiet reassurances to her.

I turn away from the entrance, facing the direction of the gunfire, and a small gasp slips through my lips. Two bodies lay on the floor a few feet away from the Italian restaurant opposite the entrance. I take one step at a time, slowly getting closer to the two bodies surrounded by a small group of people. Tension lies thick over the residents as they look over the scene, and my shoulders tighten as I reach the location and stretch my neck to look at the bodies.

Dear God, please don't let either be Jamie. I push aside a lady standing in front of me so I can reach the first body. It is an elderly lady wearing a thick knee-length red dress, a few steps away from the inside of the restaurant. I release a small sigh of relief. Luckily, it is not Jamie. One of the apartment personnel checks her pulse as I make my way over.

"Are you able to check whether she is breathing?" they ask as they glance up at me. I squat down beside the lady. Her chest moves up and down shallowly, and I reach forward, bending both her knees and hips to the proper angle and gently tilting her head back to keep the airway open. To everyone's immediate relief, she opens her eyes and starts coughing.

After making sure the woman is truly fine, I shakily get to my feet, my eyes landing on the other body. I breathe in deeply, my hands trembling, and I walk closer to take stock of it. A man's lifeless body lays in a pool of dark blood streaming from his stomach at the restaurant's entrance. I let out a wobbly breath as the fact it isn't Jamie registers in my brain. *Thank God.*

All around, there are residents fidgeting and biting their nails as more and more people begin to gather to stare at the body. Another apartment security personnel arrives to attend to the corpse, covering it from view with a dark cloth. It doesn't help erase the image from my mind.

I blink, trying to remove the scene from my mind. I glance around furtively, worry unfurling in my stomach again. *Where is Jamie?* My eyes dart from one corner to another while I bite my lip, and my jaw clenches. Anxious questions swirl through my head the longer I can't find him.

Suddenly, a scream tears through the chattering of the nervous crowd. A hush descends as we collectively turn toward the sound. A young woman in a yellow dress trembles as she points in the direction of the carpeted staircase, her mouth dropping in a horrified gasp. It only takes a moment for the crowd to explode into even more chaos than before.

The centerpiece of the luxury apartment, an expensive Parisian painting, is sprayed with graffiti that looks an awful lot like blood.

The End of Mrs. Smith.

Chapter 2

I skip around my room with joy, a bright smile never leaving my face as I stare at the email on my computer screen.

Unbelievable! I finally got my PI license. I text my WhatsApp group with Jamie and Suzanne. We have been best friends since we were in fourth grade. We were lucky to have been able to attend the same university as well.

It is already three months after graduation, and much to the dismay of our parents, none of us have been successful with finding a full-time position yet.

My mouth curves upward again. It feels like sunshine is engulfing my soul, letting a flower bloom brightly in summer.

I look through my bedroom window, an image of me wearing a long brown jacket with black boots, a gun neatly holstered on my waist, and wearing black trim spectacles while looking at evidence. My gloved hands thrusting bushes aside as I investigate. The sound of incoming messages arrives, and I blink back to reality. I brush aside the daydream as I open my phone.

Good for you, now you can protect not only your

6

mother but us too, Jamie sends with a laughing emoji.

"*You must thank your mother for experiencing a supermarket robbery at night three years ago. Otherwise, you would never have thought of taking the exams that lead to being a part-time PI,* Suzanne replies with wink emoji.

I will register myself as a trainee at a private investigator's office to gain experience. What do you think? Inside, my chest sparkles with joy.

Let's meet up to celebrate! Suzanne writes with broad smiling emoji.

Good idea. I need a cold drink to wind down too. Let's meet at Tinsel Café in an hour, girls. I just finished golfing, Jamie replies.

Right on. I just finished swimming, Suzanne replies.

Sounds great. I can't wait to celebrate with you both, I respond with a smiling emoji.

Suzanne arrives thirty minutes late, her long wavy hair, perfectly tanned skin, and curvy body making her look like a blonde version of Jennifer Lopez. She had lots of admirers in university, but her taste for guys is high, and she has never had a boyfriend.

"Sorry I'm late." She looks around, a small crease wrinkling her forehead. "Looks like Jamie is also late." Suzanne grabs a menu from the holder on the table as she slips into the seat opposite me. "I feel famished. Let's go ahead and order. Jamie can join when he comes." She starts flipping the menu, and I follow suit, unable to disagree with her logic. I am starving too.

After ordering our food, she looks at me and says, "I do miss our university days when we attended parties and went camping during breaks. I could take a peep at some hot guys. This town doesn't have many new ones for me to look at," Suzanne says with a wink.

I let out a short laugh, shaking my head.

"You and muscular body guys . . . You never stick with one after more than a couple of dates, though," I respond with a teasing grin.

An hour passes with laughter and food, and the waitress serves us dessert, but there still is no sign of Jamie. I chew my lip nervously and ring his mobile. "You have reached Jamie Henderson's phone. Please leave a message after the tone." I breathe in deeply as I hang up, looking at my wristwatch for the hundredth time. I turn to look through the window while arching my brow. "Where is he? I hope he's alright."

"We will drop by to check on him once we finish our dinner," Suzanne says to me. I nod and dig back into my chocolate sundae.

"Tell me about your work. I am dying to know since your work is totally different than my line, so spill the beans." Suzanne leans forward, curiosity gleaming in her eyes.

"Working in a small consultancy firm like my uncle's is tiring for sure. Not only do I have to do analysis, but I have secretary and receptionist work too." I roll my eyes and sigh.

"I guess the company does not have many employees; thus, the multi-tasking, Alyssa," Suzanne says with a teasing laugh. "On top of that, you will be a trainee PI soon. You will be busier."

I nod, a grin tugging about my lips.

"I cannot wait to start getting involved in a case to brush up my PI skills and experience." I rub my palms together, my eyes shining with the thought.

"I know, you must be excited. You can probably register at the nearby police station for any cases to rope you in." Suzanne and I beam at each other.

"That is a brilliant idea, Suzanne." I shoot her a thumbs up before we burst into a fit of giggles.

"How is working at the tailor shop . . . what's its name again? I can't seem to remember," I ask while tilting my head after our laughter subsides.

"I have learned a lot about tailoring at Small Bob's Tailoring Shop downtown. The owner is patient with my questions and while teaching me sewing. However, the styles are so outdated." Suzanne curls her lips and scoffs.

"My father is encouraging me to work elsewhere since it will provide better prospects for me in the fashion industry. This town is full of retired people, and there is no demand for new fashion," Suzanne adds with a slouch.

"You are lucky to have such a supportive father. I bet he can't wait to see your name on a clothes label soon." I chuckle, shaking my head.

"I have applied to branded boutiques like Armani, Dior, and Celine recently." She smiles while showing me her applications on her phone.

"That is a good move, Suzanne. I hope you land in one of them soon," I say while smiling and finishing off my sundae.

Suzanne gestures dismissively. "Let me show you the design I drew and submitted to them as part of my application," Suzanne adds. She twists, facing her bag beside her, unbuckles it, and digs through it before pulling out a block of sketching papers. She moves the plates on the table aside and places her drawings on the table facing me once she's satisfied it is clean.

She flips them to the second page of the sketchbook and waves her hand over them with a flourish. I lean forward in my seat to look at it.

"I like this dress and the two pantsuits. They look stunning and Parisian chic. I really hope you will get to work with them," I say when looking at her drawings and flipping front and back again, smiling.

Once we finish our dinner, Suzanne tries to call Jamie one more time. I chew the inside of my lip and tug on the end of my hair. He normally never misses an outing with us.

"His phone is ringing," Suzanne says and smiles at me.

My lips curve widely from side to side when I hear his ringing tone. But my shoulders slouch upon hearing the auto-machine voicemail. Unconsciously, I start tapping my right heel on the floor.

"Let's visit him. We have not gone to his father's house ever since he remarried his new wife," I suggest to Suzanne, my voice rougher than normal.

"They moved into a mansion when Jamie's father got a new bride. Remember?" Suzanne says as she gathers her things.

"What are you waiting for? Let's go!" Suzanne pulls her sling bag over her shoulder and gets up from her seat. I bump the table in my haste to follow her, almost sipping the leftover liquid in my cup. I steady it before also scooting from the booth. Suzanne waits for me a few steps away from the table before continuing to walk toward the entrance side by side with me.

Chapter 3

We arrive in front of a gated two-story mansion with a water fountain in front of the gate and lush pine trees surrounding the compound.

A security guard from his guard post walks toward our car. "Who are you? What is your purpose of visit?" the security guard asks Suzanne.

"We are close friends of Jamie; we would like to visit him," I reply.

"Please give me your identification card to check in the system. If you are his permissible friends, you will be in our visitor's listing."

We pass the cards over, and within a few minutes, he returns to us. "Please proceed to the entrance at the center and park at the designated guest parking place."

"Thank you, Mr. Security . . ." I trail off for a moment before reading his name badge, "Lee." I smile, tilting my head slightly as I take our cards, and Suzanne pulls forward.

"Wow, this house is huge compared to their previous cottage at the end of this street. You see the pool at the corner, right?" Suzanne exclaims excitedly.

"Girl, remember we are here to search for Jamie and

not for a house tour." I cross my arms after Suzanne sets the car in park. "I am worried that something bad happened to him. He never keeps us in the dark about his whereabouts when we're supposed to meet up. He will call or text one of us if he can't come." My right foot taps the car floor while checking my phone for any incoming messages from Jamie.

"Thinking of it, you're right on that point," Suzanne replies while driving into the widened lot.

Suzanne parks her Ford Focus beside a black Range Rover and emerald green Mini Cooper. There is also an empty spot with a reserved sign that reads "HEAD OF THE HOUSE."

When we step onto the edge of the marble stone entrance, the dark brown, detailed antique door automatically opens for us. Suzanne and I look at each other, shocked to see no one behind it; however, the door remains open. "I wonder if the security guy at the gatehouse can see us?" I say out loud, glancing back over at Suzanne. She shrugs and steps through the door.

"Hello, Mr. and Mrs. Henderson, we are Jamie's friends," I say loudly for anyone nearby to hear us as I follow behind.

Suddenly, a lady in her thirties wearing a white frilled apron set over her black and white working dress appears from a hallway. I whisper in Suzanne's ear, "Looks like there is a new helper. The previous one was an old lady." Suzanne nods at me.

"Hi there, I am Rosalind, the Head helper of Henderson mansion," the woman says with a polite smile. "Please, come in. I heard from security that you are visiting Jamie.

"You must be?" She waves her right hand toward us

and tilts her head.

"We are Jamie's childhood friends, Suzanne and Alyssa," I respond with a slight nod.

"You may proceed to his room from this staircase in front here. Once you reach the top, turn to the left and walk a few steps. His room will be the second door on your right. You can't miss it; his room door is pale blue with his name on a center plate," the helper provides while stepping back to let us further into the house before disappearing back down the hallway she had come from.

"Thank you," we reply together.

This place reminds me of one of my grandmother's villas. I glance over at Suzanne, and she gulps, her eyes darting here and there, awe clear on her face. I smile at Suzanne, place a hand on her arm with a quick squeeze, and whisper, "Let's leave our bags down here. "

We place our handbags on a long sofa in the living room just a few steps before the staircase Rosalind had indicated.

A plush sapphire carpet runs up the center of the staircase. Suzanne whistles quietly as she takes in the Versace trimming. "Mr. Henderson significantly upgraded the décor in this house."

I shrug. "Or maybe his new wife has higher expectations than his previous one in decorating." Once we reach the top landing, we see a lady's shoe mark on the carpeted flooring.

"Do you think he has a girl in his room?" Suzanne whispers to me with a wink. I shrug stiffly at her statement while frowning. Pain stabs through my chest at the thought.

Upon reaching the second door on our right, I knock. The door swings open at the pressure, not having been latched properly.

I glance at Suzanne before pushing the door open wider. His room is tidy, nothing noticeably out of place from the doorway, and his floor is carpeted in pale blue. As we step further, a two-door glass cupboard displaying his soccer trophies and a souvenir signed by famous footballers worldwide comes into view.

I look farther down the small walkway to see an armchair with a pale blue cushion at the furthest corner before the path turns left into the room proper. Suzanne walks in front of me as I trail behind and call out, "Jamie, Suzanne and I are here. We are worried sick. Why did you not . . ."

"Ah! Ah!" Suzanne shouts as loud as a speaker while her hand flies up to cover her mouth.

Jamie is lying on the carpeted floor in front of a curved loveseat sofa. Bruises are visible along his cheek, and his face is specked with blood. Beside him is a golf club, and a few feet away, broken glass is scattered among the carpet.

"Jamie!" I shout as I run to his side. My heart squeezes seeing him on the floor.

I kneel and instantly grab his hand to check his pulse. My breath comes out in a rush as I feel his heartbeat against my fingers. "He's alive. Call the helper or security to contact 911, Suzanne."

Suzanne runs as fast as she can, already shouting for help as she leaves.

"Jamie, Jamie, please wake up," I say as I shake his hands gently.

His head turns, and he groans in pain. "Alyssa, is that you?" he croaks in a shaky voice. Thousands of questions prowl in my mind as I squeeze his hands.

"Yes. It is a relief you are responding, Jamie. I was

worried sick. You are going to be OK. Let's get you on your bed." I place my hands under his neck, pushing his back gently, and help him sit up slowly. Security officer Lee enters the room, running toward Jamie, and squats down, placing his hand around Jamie's waist to help carry him to his bed.

"What happened, Jamie?" he asks after Jamie is safely deposited.

"I—I didn't manage to see the person's face. They were wearing a black mask. . . That I remember well." He starts rubbing his temple with a groan.

"I will check the CCTV for the intruder's where-abouts. They could still be in the house," Lee comments.

We both nod as he leaves the room, pulling out a walkie-talkie.

"How did the golf club end up beside you?" I turn to him while my eyebrows draw together.

"I can't recall bringing it to my room. They're always kept in a sports room downstairs."

I nod as Suzanne reappears from the hall and stops a few steps away, wringing her hands.

"We were worried sick when you didn't turn up at dinner." I sit on the edge of his bed, reaching out to grab and pat his hand.

"I owe both of you an apology. I was dumbfounded after receiving a call from Jennifer, my stepmom. She insists I work in my father's office branch in Amster-dam. But I refuse to be so far from you and Suzanne and in a strange country," he says as his eyes look directly into mine. I swear he can see all the way to my soul and feel my insides melting. "I took some liquor from the bar downstairs and drank more than two glasses to beat the stress and try to figure out the mess." He rubs the back of his neck with his free hand. "I must have forgotten to call you on my whereabouts."

Both of us smile at Jamie, and Suzanne lets out a semi-relieved laugh.

I get up and take a hand towel from his bathroom and fill a small glass with water before returning. I start to wipe some of the blood from his face.

"It is painful, be gentle," Jamie says with a wince.

Lee returns to the room with a grim expression, his hand clenching around the walkie-talkie. "Negative, Jamie. The CCTV footage showed nothing; no people or shadows are lurking inside the house or compound. No one entered your room from the afternoon until the time of the incident. Everything looks normal."

"That's impossible. How could this have happened?" Dennis Lamberheart, Jamie's old-time father's secretary, states as he enters the room and straightens his already pristine coat.

A loud bang interrupts further conversation as Jamie's door flies open, and rushing footsteps proceed his help-er's appearance. She stands a few steps from Jamie's bed, wringing her hands on her apron, and says in an anguished tone and a scrunched forehead, "Is Loraine safe? Has anyone checked on her in her room?"

I shrug, looking at Jamie with confusion, and he puts forward, "Loraine is my stepsister. She is from Jennifer's previous marriage."

Hearing this, I nod and say, "I will check on Loraine with Rosalind." He tilts his head in agreement with my suggestion and closes his eyes as he leans back against the headboard. Suzanne takes my place at Jamie's side as I get up. I scurry toward his door, closing it once I am out of his room, and follow behind Rosalind to Loraine's room opposite Jamie's.

When Rosalind twists the doorknob, it doesn't budge. She shakes the doorknob slightly to open it, but the door stays firmly locked. Her face crumbles, and I bite the inside of my lip. She quickly takes a bunch of keys from her pocket, inserts the correct key into the keyhole, and pushes the door open.

The room's layout is similar to Jamie's, with a glass cupboard facing the entrance door. However, it holds various types of dolls and a few trophies for winning a horse-riding competition instead of soccer memorabilia.

Once we turn to the left, facing Loraine's bed, the helper and I breathe deeply and smile at one another. Loraine is sound asleep on her bed, buried under a comforter and hugging a dark brown teddy bear. I signal to Rosalind that I am going to Jamie's room, and she nods. She lingers in Loraine's room, humming quietly to herself.

My gaze lands on the family room at the bottom of the stairs as I exit into the hallway. The crystal chandelier hanging in the center is not on, but it still sparkles beautifully in the light from the room next to it and upstairs. I pause and smile, and the side of my left eye catches a dark shape moving quickly across the space before I can turn away. I blink, and without any further hesitation, curiosity takes over. I close Lorraine's door, then lean against the wrought-iron staircase banister. I can't see anyone initially, and I brush it aside as my imagination. The only light in the room itself is from the table lamp near the corner, so obviously, the lighting and my imagination have me seeing things. A feeling of head-pounding tension slices through me, and I turn my body to face the opposite direction overlooking Jamie's room. A shadow flies by my periphery again, and I whip around. I notice a large dark shape that seems to pass behind the white antique grandfather clock in the guest room by the living room downstairs.

I momentarily tense, freezing in the spot I am standing, and turn my head and body slowly, following what I think are the movements of the shadow. It moves toward the sliding door at the edge of the living room like a bullet train. I drop to the floor and crawl as quickly as I can to keep the sliding door in my sight. I should get a better view of the person if I get closer. I crawl nearer to the shadow while peeking through the iron leaves on the railing. Suddenly, I stop, realizing that if I can see the intruder, then they can see me as well. Sweat trickles down my neck, and I stare downstairs from my current vantage point.

Seeing that the living room stays tranquil, I stand and speed walk to Jamie's room, tripping on the carpet near his door. I slam the door behind me, panting. Jamie and Suzanne look alarmed as I step into sight. "What happened? Has anything bad happened to Lorraine?" Jamie demands, his eyebrows drawing together.

My eyes widen, and I shake my head. "She is fine and fast asleep. I thought I saw a shadow. It was bulky and in the living room that has a fireplace downstairs. It ran away when I tried to follow them while remaining upstairs."

"Alyssa, please calm down and take some deep breathes." Jamie raises his palm in a calming gesture while he smiles. "Suzanne, go to the intercom on the wall opposite my bed and dial No. 1 for security. Put it on speaker, so I can talk to Lee," Jamie says. Suzanne scurries to follow Jamie's instructions. We all wait with bated breath as the machine rings.

"Hello, security here.'"

"Please check the video footage in the number one living room for the past two hours. My friend saw shadows walking past. Please report to me by tonight," Jamie says.

"Noted, Jamie." The intercom crackles off.

A few minutes pass before I sigh. "We better run along. We will check on you tomorrow. Meanwhile, Jamie, please have a good rest." Suzanne and I gather ourselves to leave Jamie's room, but we pause and look over at the sound of the door slamming against the wall.

A beautiful woman in her mid-thirties with wavy shoulder-length hair and a dimple on her right cheek appears in a sequined short silver dress and French stiletto heels, a clutch handbag tucked in her elbow. Her neck is adorned with a chunky diamond necklace.

Standing beside her is a man that looks strikingly like an older version of Jamie; six feet in height, grey hair visible at the corner of his head and eyebrows.

"Hi, Mr. Henderson,' both of us say with a small smile.

He just nods back, stoic as ever.

His one hand is clenched in a fist, and the other hand holds a Gucci brown leather handbag. I gasp as my eyes take in the sight. It is similar to mine. *Is it mine?*

"Jamie, I heard from Dennis about the recent incidents. Are you alright, young man?" Mr. Henderson walks closer to Jamie's bed, and Lee slips into the room and hurriedly stands behind Mr. Henderson.

Jamie shrugs. "I am fine, just bruised on my face, elbow, and forehead."

"Tomorrow, an investigator will come to scour the house. I cannot abide any intruders lurking around my house for the safety of my children," Jamie's father replies, his eyebrows pulling together.

Mr. Henderson shifts his gaze, looking at me, then Suzanne.

"Ladies, according to our security, there are valuable items belonging to me in this bag." Mr. Henderson raises my Gucci bag by the strap, making it swing. "I am opening this bag to show that those items are indeed inside your handbag as proof," he continues.

His left hand unzips the center before digging into the bag to reveal a sapphire blue velvet pouch. He starts shaking his head and winces, his sea-blue eyes looking straight into my brown ones, causing me to shiver. "It seems that one of your impromptu visitors is a thief."

My eyes widen and nearly pop out of the socket, and my mouth falls open. *What is that? How did it get into my bag?* "Who put that pouch in my handbag?" I cry loudly.

"Exactly what I wanted to ask you, young lady." He opens the pouch tie and places the items on his palm. Four diamond shirt buttons and four golden coins roll onto his palm.

"I—I—didn't steal it. I have been with Jamie most of the time we've been here, and then I went to Loraine's room," I stammer, trying to defend myself.

"The items found in your handbag are good evidence that you stole it." He shoves the items in his palm nearer for me to see.

"Father, she was with me the entire time, and she is financially stable. She doesn't have any motivation to steal from us!" Jamie says with a scoff, defending me.

"Lee showed me these items, which he found with his Niton theft analyzer machine. He checked it after you suspected an intruder lurking in the living room, and he saw your handbag lying on the sofa. We'll have security do a detailed review of the CCTV footage tomorrow morning," Mr. Henderson says with finality.

"Mr. Henderson, someone must have framed me." I clench my jaw. "Why would I steal buttons and old coins? As Jamie said, I have plenty of money, and Jamie has been my good friend since we were in fourth grade. I would never do such a thing to his family," I plead.

"We will discuss further once Jamie is better. Expect a call from my office tomorrow to settle this."

I nod in agreement, frustration bubbling in my stomach despite my calm exterior. My heart burns furiously at whoever framed me. I cannot brush this incident aside. It is a grave stain on my reputation and my long friendship with Jamie. "Mr. Henderson, I believe I saw a shadow or two lurking around your downstairs living room, which is the room that we left our handbags in, after I went to Loraine's room to check on her. Your security team should check on that area and its surroundings. I have suspicions that the culprit planted those items in my handbag to turn around their intrusions on me," I respond while looking at him.

"Very well," he says with a nod to Lee, who returns it and steps forward.

He makes a circle passing by both Suzanne and me with a small machine in his hands; his theft detector vibrates, and my heartbeat skips. Lee stops and walks past again, slower this time. This time, he stands next to Suzanne, and the detector machine vibrates, a deafening beep filling the air. "Show me your hands, lady." Without any hesitation, Suzanne opens her arms and shows her palms. Lee looks thoroughly at her fingers and wrists, both front and back. "Nothing on your bare hands. I see you are carrying a small pouch. Hand it over to me for inspection."

Suzanne quickly holds out her small pouch that is attached to her arm with a wristlet. "Here you go. This pouch I brought with me ever since I left my handbag downstairs."

Lee opens it and produces a pair of latex gloves from his pocket, pulling them on before rifling through the items in her small pouch. After a moment, he pulls out a pair of small ruby and diamond buttons and—

"My Graff ruby brooch!" shrieks Jennifer, and she quickly snatches it from Lee. "Jamie, now you can see the true colors of your friends; they befriended you for your richness, then stole from you. That is how low they are." Jennifer glares menacingly at Suzanne and glances at me with disgust before storming out of the room.

I swallow, my mouth suddenly a desert.

"I can explain! The ruby brooch was lying on the white rug beside the fireplace in the living room downstairs. I placed it in my bag temporarily to return to Jamie. But after seeing Jamie collapsed on the floor, I forgot about the brooch." Suzanne bows her head, tugging her lip between her teeth. "I am sorry, Mr. Henderson. Please forgive me," Suzanne begs.

Suzanne's hands are clutching each other tightly, and she shifts her weight while talking. I'm not sure if she is nervous about being accused or if she did take it. But she has been with us for ages. Why would she steal now?

"Ladies, since you have been Jamie's best friends for years, let us discuss this little, yet expensive, attempted robbery tomorrow. We will have a better understanding once the security footage is analyzed thoroughly. Then, my office personnel will contact you both." Mr. Henderson turns to look at Jamie and says, "And Jamie, please have a good rest." He frowns before continuing, "Tonight, God might have revealed the true nature of your two childhood friends. I would have put a stop to your friendship with them if I had known they would grow up this way." Mr. Henderson shakes his head, then walks out of the room.

"Out you go. Let me escort both of you to the exit and outside the gate," Lee says with a gesture.

I sigh and head toward the door. What a night for a celebration this turned out to be.

Chapter 4

"Hello, am I speaking to Alyssa Smith?" a man's voice asks through my phone while I walk toward the sofa in my apartment.

"Yes, speaking. Who is this?" I plop heavily into the cushion, fatigue pulling at my limbs.

"I am Dennis Lamberheart, Mr. Henderson's private secretary. You and Suzanne will come to discuss the attempted robbery of their valuable items last night at their mansion. Please be punctual today at Henderson Building & Construction Incorporation at three this afternoon."

"Yes, I will be there on time," I reply. I shift restlessly on the couch after I end the call, running my hands through my hair at the same time.

A few moments later, Suzanne's phone rings from where she sits across the room. "Yes, this is Suzanne speaking. Mr. Lamberheart. Aha." Her right hand grips her skirt while her jaw works. I listen numbly as the same message is relayed to her, looking over when she hangs up.

"You heard it, Suzanne; we are to meet Mr. Henderson and his lawyer for a discussion about last night's incident." I stand and start to pace, my arms behind my back as I inhale deeply and dig my nails into the palms of my hands.

"Let me call my father to see if I could get his legal representative to accompany us for today's discussion."

Suzanne nods at the suggestion.

I quickly dial my phone and speak before he can say more than hello. "Hello, Daddy, how are you? Something awful happened to Suzanne and me while we were at Mr. Henderson's mansion last night." I scratch the tip of my forehead.

"What? Let me know how I can help you, my girl. What happened?" he says, his voice filled with concern.

I reiterate to him what had happened the night before and the meeting we would be facing this afternoon.

"Let me get in touch with my company's lawyer to see if they have any representative that can accompany you," he says, full of confidence after listening to the predicament that we are in.

"OK, Daddy. I will be waiting for your call. Thank you," I reply emphatically before ending the call.

"Both of us are screwed big time this time. Ugh," Suzanne says while tousling her hair with one hand after my conversation with my father ends.

"You know what, Suzanne, once our discussion with Mr. Henderson is over, let's meet up with your uncle Samuel who owns the security company in this town. Hopefully, he can access the security footage of Mr. Henderson's mansion. I am not satisfied with taking the blame for this." I place my right fist on my left palm, determination shining in my eyes. "I want to know who framed me. As for you, you honestly forgot to return the items. In other words, while these were painful lessons, from now on, please, please ignore any valuables you come across, no matter what," I advise with my right index finger shaking left and right, facing Suzanne.

Suzanne nods, her forehead scrunching, and exhales noisily through pursed lips with her hands quivering.

My mobile vibrates, the screen indicating a return call from my dad. "Mr. William will meet you at the Henderson building to represent both of you. I will text you his contact information. I am busy directing a movie today, but if anything comes up, just message me. Good luck," he says with a shaky laugh.

"Thank you, Daddy," I reply with a smile, feeling more confident than I did fifteen minutes ago.

Later that day, two security guards escort us to the main meeting room at level 20, Block A. *I guess Mr. Henderson is taking the incident seriously.* We are being treated like convicts by having two security guards side by side with us. The treatment causes sadness to build up in my heart and squeeze my chest. I feel like crying, and I can feel my cheeks starting to boil.

Once our elevator door opens, Dennis is there to escort us. "Ladies, please follow me." After walking a bit down a hallway to the right after leaving the lift, Dennis places his staff card on the keypad just beside the door and pushes it wide open. We enter after him. Mr. Henderson, Jamie, a police inspector, and a man dressed in office attire stand up and shake our hands.

"Please have a seat, Alyssa and Suzanne," Mr. Henderson says our names while he sits back down in the head seat.

I clear my throat when Mr. Henderson's eyes look at my legal representative. "This is Mr. William, my legal representative."

Mr. Henderson nods and clears his throat. "This is a

discussion, and I didn't expect any legal representative from your side since we are not planning to file this case in court. But go ahead and have a seat, William." His right hand points to a seat on my left for William to sit.

Both of us nod and sit opposite Jamie, who is to Mr. Henderson's right. I sign subtly at Jamie, asking whether he is OK from last night. He smiles and nods at my silent question. I reciprocate with a smile and momentarily close my eyes, glad that he is better.

"Right then, we will start with the discussion and agreement at this very moment since I have other meetings to attend within the hour," Mr. Henderson says while checking his wristwatch and gestures for Dennis to get on with it.

I slip my hands inside my jacket pockets and wriggle my toes, waiting for Dennis to share the findings.

"Mr. Henderson's security team thoroughly reviewed the security video footage, and there is no evidence that Alyssa stole the items that were found in her handbag." Dennis looks at everyone in the room in turn.

Hearing this, I straighten my jacket, but my fingers play with each other since I feel nervous for Suzanne.

"As for Suzanne, the security video footage showed that you took the ruby brooch that was lying on the carpet and kept it in your purse. In the video, it showed Suzanne looking around nervously before placing the brooch into her pouch," he continues, switching on the video for everyone to view.

"From the findings and the fact that both of you are close childhood friends of Jamie, we will not press charges. Max Lincoln, my lawyer, has prepared a proposal to clear up last night's incident," Mr. Henderson says, looking from Suzanne's eyes to mine.

"Max, please read the terms for these two ladies." Mr. Henderson turns his head and nods in Max's direction.

Max turns to a two-page paper and reads it clearly for us to hear. "Ms. Suzanne Alberker—today, January 25, 2021, you will relinquish any form of friendship or relationship with Jamie Henderson. You are to work and move out of this town. Mr. Henderson's company will sign recommendation letters to support your pursuit to land a job in one of the several fashion design companies outlined in this agreement. If you are caught contacting Jamie and stepping foot in the Henderson mansion or this building, we will arrest you without any hesitation."

I quickly get up from my chair, my face turning red as I bang the table with my fists, ready to argue.

"Now, now. Alyssa, please remain calm," William advises me and pulls on my arm to remain seated.

"We managed to get a court restraining order for this," Max continues, showing off the restraining order. He slides the paper to William for him to read the terms thoroughly.

I push my chair back as I am about to stand again, rage filling my heart as I shake with fury. William taps my hand and whispers for me to sit and be objective. I breathe in and out deeply while staring at Max, barely holding my anger back.

Jamie slams the table with a loud bang and pushes his chair harshly back, which lets out a screeching sound.

"This is unfair, Father! She is not a thief. She just forgot to give the lost brooch back right away. Please give Suzanne another chance."

Jamie's face is red as he glares at his father, his jaw tightening.

Suzanne's eyes are red, trying to hold back tears from

falling but failing to do so. Tears begin to roll down her cheeks, and she looks at Jamie sadly.

"Please sign the agreement here," Dennis says to Suzanne, ignoring all of the outbursts.

Suzanne hesitates and looks at me for any signal of objection or glimmer of a way out of this.

"Wait, only Suzanne has to move, and her family remains as it is, right?" I ask, my right hand held out to keep Suzanne from signing.

"The restraining order only applies to Suzanne," Mr. Henderson confirms.

"Please make sure to indicate that clearly in the agreement," I reply with my fists on my hips. William whispers to me that it is best for both of us to agree, or else this will head to court.

"Dad, Suzanne has been my close friend since fourth grade; we have known each other's ups and downs for most of our lives. Please allow me to meet with and talk to her," Jamie pleads.

Mr. Henderson stares angrily and shouts at Jamie, slamming a pile of papers on the table. "Enough, Jamie. The decision is final."

"But, Father, please give Suzanne another chance. Jennifer should not have been careless and left her ruby brooch on the carpet. Jennifer is also at fault here. She should be punished for being ignorant," Jamie says angrily, with his fists trembling.

Suddenly, he grabs the agreement on the table and starts ripping it apart.

Mr. Henderson signals to Dennis, who immediately grabs Jamie and wrestles the papers from his grasp.

"Jamie, your behavior is outrageously rude. You were taught to not be so disrespectful to your father." Mr. Henderson runs his hands down his front, flattening his crumpled jacket.

"Max, please revise the agreement as agreed with the latest family arrangements. As for you, Ms. . . ." Mr. Henderson says slowly, trying to recall my last name as he looks at me.

"Alyssa Smith," Jamie spits my full name at his father with an annoyed tone. His eyes connect with mine and soften, a small smile pulling at his lips.

"Max has drafted an agreement that you are to fully cooperate with the police and private investigators on the possible shadow you saw at my mansion, and it has been determined that you are the victim, framed with those items. I have no objection to your continued friendship with Jamie."

"Please sign this agreement below." Max points to the line at the bottom after Mr. Henderson highlights the main terms.

I take the agreement and read through its entirety—even the terms and conditions, just in case any hidden items were not divulged during this discussion. I hand the paper over to William. Once he reads it and nods his approval, I sign the agreement.

With my agreement signed, Suzanne shifts her chair away from the table, more tears rolling down her cheeks and smudging her mascara, and walks nearer to Mr. Henderson's side. She kneels on the floor and bends her head down to the floor. "I am sorry for the incident. Please . . . Please allow me to remain friends with Jamie."

"Our decisions are final, Suzanne. We cannot abide the attempted robbery." Mr. Henderson's face turns sour, and his nose wrinkles as the words leave his mouth.

Suzanne snorts derisively, her eyes blazing momentarily before saying with a touch of defeat in her voice, "As you wish, Mr. Henderson. I will apply to those fashion design companies your company placed as a referral. I will come and go to this town, without living here, to see my family without stepping foot into your mansion or on your property or near your son," Suzanne finishes softly, her right hand fidgeting on the table.

Jamie clenches and unclenches his fists as his jaw ticks, his eyes jumping between the people in the room. Suzanne slouches for a moment more before looking up at Jamie, swallowing. They nod at each other as their eyes glaze with unshed tears. Suzanne pulls out a tissue from her handbag and wipes her cheeks.

"Very well. We agree upon that." Mr. Henderson smiles, leaning back in his chair, relaxing like a king.

Suzanne signs the indemnity agreement, sniffling.

"The meeting is adjourned. I have another meeting to attend now." Mr. Henderson gets up and walks to the entrance, leaving behind Dennis and Max to settle everything fully.

Jamie walks to Suzanne slowly. "Farewell, my dear Suzanne. We had many fun times together, year after year. Please take care of yourself, and I know you will do well in the fashion industry." Jamie hugs her tightly, giving her a sad smile when they pull away.

"Bye, Jamie. You have been a supportive best friend. I will miss your jokes and advice so much," Suzanne replies while wiping her tears away.

I walk toward them and open my arms widely to hug both of them, tears developing in my eyes as I pull them close with a burning sense of grief.

Chapter 5

One day after weeks pass by, I am in my apartment with my laptop open, checking for any Engineering vacancies. My phone rings, and I turn to look at the screen for the caller's number. My eyes open wide, seeing a number from one of many companies that I applied for. I scramble to answer, my heart beating quickly.

"Is this Alyssa Smith? I am Lisa from Beacons Tee Engineering. It is regarding your application for a position as Junior Project Engineer," a woman says matter-of-factly.

"Yes, this is Alyssa," I say, slightly breathless.

"I am pleased to invite you for the first round of interviews with our middle managers next Monday morning. Would you be available?"

"Of course. I would love to attend the interview." A flush of happiness resonates within me when I end the call after getting all the details. *Finally, a break*.

The interview day arrives, and I wait nervously for my turn in a lobby with ten other candidates.

The interview itself flies by, and by the time I get into the parking lot, I feel exhausted from the nonstop questions. All the interviewers were interested in was if I had any experience and if I had completed FE examinations. I slouch as I drag my legs toward my car. This just confirmed something for me; it will take longer than I plan to land a job. *Ugh.*

I am about to reverse my car when my phone vibrates.

I press the answer button, feeling suspense seeping into me for answering a telephone number I don't recognize.

"Hello, this is Alyssa speaking."

"Ms. Alyssa. Hi. I am calling to offer you an interview for the Assistant Project Engineer position you applied for a few weeks ago," the caller replies cheerfully.

I brush my hair over my shoulder, an excited flurry of nerves rushing through my stomach.

"I am interested in attending. May I have the details, please?"

"The interview will start at 9:00 in the morning. We are located just a few miles off the highway." I start imagining the location, nodding to myself.

"Yes, noted on the time. Thank you. I look forward to it." I grin to myself after the call ends. Another interview opportunity. I raise both of my arms and wiggle side to side as joy takes over the defeat from earlier.

I arrive at D&C Engineering at 9:00 am sharp the next day. Feeling confident that I will land a job today, I whistle on my journey to the interview floor.

Once the elevator door opens, I step out with a bounce but freeze just outside the doors. I gasp as I take in the many people sitting and waiting for their turn to enter the interview room.

I blink several times as I look over the interviewees again, most of them significantly older than me. *Am I at the correct interview venue?* Sweat appears on my fore-head, and I take out a tissue from my handbag to dab at it. I continue walking until I reach a table that has signage printed with "Administration Desk."

The receptionist looks up at me with a sheepish smile after I give her my name. "Hi, Alyssa. I am sorry, but the interviewer is looking for candidates with a minimum of three years' experience in project engineering. However, since you have been waiting downstairs, please go ahead and proceed to the interview room."

I blow my bangs away from my face upon hearing this and let out a sigh. I nod and proceed to the interview room. *Well, the more interviews I attend, the better. I will be better prepared for the next interview and land a job.* I smile at myself, thinking positively.

The next morning, my mobile vibrates in my pocket, and I quickly grab it, pressing the answer button. "Hello, Alyssa. I am from Beacons Tee Engineering. I am sorry to inform you that you were not successful, and we wish you all the best in your job search." The voice on the other end sounds bored.

"Did the interviewer gives any reasons?" I ask, tilting my head.

Click. I look at my phone screen and blink three times. *How rude!* Not waiting for me to respond. I huff and shake my head, tossing the phone aside.

I stand and walk to and fro in my kitchen, take out a soda from the fridge, gulp down a few sips, then jump onto the sofa closest to the kitchen in the living room.

I massage my forehead before pulling out my laptop and searching for FE courses.

Then I receive a message that brightens my morning. "It's Zoom time with Suzanne in Paris." Happiness shimmers inside my heart. I can't wait to talk to Suzanne, even though thinking of her still creates a lump of sadness in my chest.

"Bonjour, Alyssa!" Suzanne says as soon as the video connects, and she waves at me. "Woah, you look awful. What happened to my bubbly gal?" Suzanne points at me while she tilts her head slightly, and the smile falls from her face.

"I just received a call from Beacons Tee Engineering; they turned me down. This is the twentieth company I attended an interview at, yet I am still far from being an engineer." My shoulders slump, and I throw the empty can of soda into a waste bin across the room.

"Don't be sad, Alissa. Why not visit me in Paris? You never know; you may find a job here?" Suzanne chuckles and smiles at me.

"You know how to comfort me, huh." My mouth curves sideways. "That is a good idea, Suzanne. Maybe visiting you will bring me good luck." I give her a thumbs up.

"So, any chance you met any handsome guys while you were on job interviews?" Suzanne winks at me.

I shake my head from left to right. I start rubbing my neck, my thoughts turning to Jamie.

"That's too bad." Suzanne shrugs before sighing. "Speaking about guys, how is Jamie doing?"

I shrug while looking at my mobile phone screen momentarily. "We have not seen each other for two weeks, so I'm not sure how he is doing." I look down, staring at the floor. I flip through my messages from Jamie and read out the last one from two days ago to Suzanne. "I am busy, talk to you soon."

"We've never done that before. Why are you both

staying away from each other?" Suzanne rubs her chin, her eyebrows pulling together.

I sigh. "You know, a week after your restriction order was implemented, Jamie and I did not hang out that much. We realized that our friendship usually depends on you planning for us to meet up. Then when we did hang out, it was awkward to do things together since we have only ever been best friends, and we are male and female." Suzanne nods while placing both of her hands underneath her chin, understanding starting to light her eyes.

I continue, "Every time we go out, neighborhood friends say remarks like, You look like a perfect couple.' It was just making everything really weird because you know how I feel about him."

Suzanne interrupts, "Now I realize your predicament." She rubs the edge of her forehead.

I nod. "Every outing, I end up blushing and stammering, but Jamie's face surprisingly looks natural."

Suzanne makes a small, sad noise of sympathy, shaking her head.

"I guess he feels the same awkwardness every time we go out together, so both of us have just ended up Face-Timing each other weekly for updates."

I let out a loud sigh and lean back against the cushion, staring at the ceiling.

"He just updated me a few days ago that he is involuntary dating a rich girl from the nearby town of Lilyville. It is a punishment set by his stepmom for not accepting her proposal for him to fill in a position in Amsterdam." I roll my eyes before biting my cheek. I can feel the sadness filling my heart as a bolt of jealousy slices my chest.

"What? He did? You must be kidding me. He is such a coward, isn't he?" Suzanne scoffs, shaking her head in disgust.

I nod before shrugging. "I guess he has to respect his stepmom's decision, and you know him well. He doesn't like any form of confrontation."

"He will follow the suggestion from his parents, even though he dislikes it. Then, he will end up telling us all about his dissatisfaction and vent his anger into his soccer game," Suzanne mutters with a roll of her eyes.

Time to get off this sad subject. "How is your job search going? Hope you are having better luck than me." I smile.

"Let me show you the offer letters," she says as she shares her screen.

My face shifts closer to my laptop to read them.

While I read, Suzanne says, her voice brightening considerably, "I have two from different companies in Paris. They like my design portfolio. They said it was unique."

"Oh, that dress is lovely. I wish I could wear the clothes that you sew and design." I point at the furthest left designs on her sketch page—a pantsuit and dress.

"You can." Suzanne points her index finger at me. "You are slender, and I am searching for someone who can model my dresses at the Paris Fresh Minds Showcase. It will be held a month from today. Say you'll come. You only need to book a plane ticket, and the other expenses will be on me. I am sure you will like my apartment and neighborhood." She places her hands on her chest, her cheeks glowing with excitement.

I can't help the grin that spreads across my face. "That sounds perfect. See you next month. I can't wait to be with you in Paris."

I look down at my vibrating cell. "I have to get off

now. I have to take a call from my mother. Take care." I wave at her before ending the video call.

Chapter 6

"Hello, Alyssa. We will be having Lorraine's tenth birthday party at my house this Friday. I would like you to attend and introduce you to Lorraine properly. I didn't manage to introduce her after Dad's marriage to Jennifer last year," Jamie says over the phone while I am on my laptop in my apartment that evening.

I smile, remembering how sweet she looked a month ago. "Sure, I guess I will drop by. What have you been doing this week?" I ask while playing with a pen.

"Father has persuaded me to join his business, so this week is my first week in his office. There has been a lot of stuff to learn. Clients to meet. Sorry I haven't been talking to or texting you," he responds, his tone stressed.

"That's great that you finally landed a job. As for me, no job offers yet." My hand runs through my hair, and a sigh slips from my lips.

"Don't worry, Alyssa, you will eventually land an engineering job sooner or later."

"Thank you for trying to comfort me, Jamie." I smile.

"I miss you, Alyssa. Ever since I started working, I only return home at night, and I don't have time to call you, which makes my heart ache," Jamie says softly.

"Oh? And here I thought you were avoiding me," I tease, but my heart begins to race at his words.

"No. My silence doesn't mean that at all. Please know that, Alyssa," he responds, his tone nervous. I can hear what sounds like him tousling his hair through the phone.

"So . . . How is dating what's-her-name-again?" My voice sounds cheeky, even though my heart is burning with disgust.

"Rihana Spencer." Jamie snorts. "Apparently, she is my father's business counterpart's daughter. My stepmom insisted on me dating her so my father's business can gain more profitable and lucrative contracts. Father has been trying to get a contract from her dad for years and years, but nothing," Jamie says.

His voice sounds tense with annoyance.

"So Jennifer is suggesting you be your dad's spy, or if you marry Rihana, your father will have a share of her father's company. Indeed a cunning idea," I reply, doing my best to hide the bitterness from my voice as I slump on my couch.

"I suppose you can say that," Jamie responds in a sad tone.

"In another way, it is like an arranged marriage. Which may be good for you since you don't have a girl-friend yet. But I personally think that when it comes to relationships and marriage, love should prevail." My voice hardens, and I throw the pen that I was playing with on the floor out of anger.

Jamie falls silent. "Well, I don't have any feelings for her." He sighs heavily. "It is torture dating someone whose behavior irritates me." He pauses for a moment before continuing slightly hesitantly, "I have someone else in mind."

"Really?" A piece of me feels like it will curl into a ball and die. "You must tell me who has captured your heart and where you met this person. I would be delighted to meet her someday." I am trying my best to sound happy for him, though I'm not sure if my pain is hidden well. Deep in my heart, I feel a sudden pain thinking that I will lose him forever.

"Alyssa, are you alright?" Jamie asks worriedly after I'm silent for a moment.

My voice breaks when I try to reply. I swallow my saliva to clear my voice and try again.

"I am fine. Sure. I can't wait to see you and Lorraine. Lots of catching up to do."

"Sure." He doesn't sound convinced but drops it for now. "I will let you know on Friday the timing of things. I can't wait to see you. I miss you," Jamie says before we end the phone call.

The alarm on my clock rings. I yawn and toss on the bed, reluctant to open my eyes. Bright sunlight enters the thin layer of curtains, and I groan as the light pierces my lovely darkness. I rub my eyes and nose, sit up, and glance at the calendar on my side table. Suddenly, my eyes open widely, and I smile, realizing it's Friday and thinking of meeting Jamie and Lorraine.

I leave work earlier than usual to get ready for the party.

My fingers run through the hangers of dresses in my closet as I bite my lip, unsure of what to wear. I have not dressed up for a party since Suzanne left. My life is a bit boring without her.

While getting dressed up, adrenaline rushes through my body. I smile broadly, thinking of Jamie's dimple when he smiles. I have lots of interview blunders to share with Jamie.

I finally settle on an outfit of a sleeveless knee-length purple lace cocktail dress with my shoulder-length brunette hair with a tiny Swarovski clip to ensure my hair is in place. For the last touch-up, I swipe red lipstick on my lips.

"I am ready," I say before smiling at myself in the mirror.

Upon reaching the Henderson mansion, five luxury cars are parked near the fountain at the center before the mansion's entrance. The Hendersons' cars are parked at the designated owners' parking bay around the side.

After locking my car, I turn to look at myself in the car window, using it as a mirror to check my final look. Once done final checking and touching up my face, I turn and come eye to eye with Jamie. I nearly throw Lorraine's birthday gift at his face. "Oh! You startled me, Jamie," I say, placing a hand over my racing heart. Jamie reaches up and holds my bare arms to prevent me from falling backward. Once he is confident that I won't fall, he lets go of my arms. I smooth my skirt as a blush makes my cheeks flush. Jamie smiles widely before his gaze travels from my face down my body, and his lips drop open slightly. He immediately takes my hand and kisses it.

"You look gorgeous and sexy. I have not seen you in a dress in ages. Come in, and let me introduce you to Lorraine." Jamie pulls me into a hug and pecks my cheek.

I grin, my blush deepening. "Aw, thank you, Jamie. Sure. I can't wait to give Lorraine her birthday present." My head tilts a bit as I glance over at the other cars. "I noticed there are a few cars parked. Who else is here?"

"Jennifer's family and business acquaintances," Jamie answers while smiling. His eyes dart over the cars as well.

"Is that your new car?" Jamie asks, pointing in my car's direction.

I nod. "Dad was in town last week, and he dropped off this car for me to use. It is one of his extras."

Jamie chuckles. "Guess his business as a producer must be flourishing after joining Netflix's team?" Jamie asks as he pushes a strain of my hair behind my ear. His eyes twinkle while staring at me.

"He landed quite a good contract deal with a lucrative production company for the past few years, which makes Grandmother proud of him. He was a loser and alcoholic during his days with Mother, so it's good to see that he's finally financially stable." I shrug before scrunching my nose. "I only wish Father and Mother would talk and be friends. However, both seem to have a bone to pick with each other every time they meet or talk over the phone." I slouch momentarily, thinking of the fate of my parents.

Jamie smiles at me, pats my back, and leads the way to the party.

The party is in the backyard garden. Guests need to go through the main entrance past the living room with the fireplace and walk past a narrow corridor with a hall of family frames toward the sliding door. It is an automatic door that opens when we step through it.

The garden terrace looks vibrant with neon glow-in-the-dark balloons in different shapes with unicorns, circles, and stars at the back of a raised platform.

The tablecloths are embellished with stars and have spreads of a variety of foods. The guests' tables are beautified with plates and cups in glowing party colors.

A few steps away from us, Lorraine plays with her friends and cousins. A piñata in a unicorn shape is tied to a branch. We watch as they take turns hitting the piñata until it breaks open and all the candies and sweets fly out. All the children run in the direction of the candies to pick them up. While Lorraine looks and laughs at her friends gathering candies, we walk toward heJamie pats her shoulder. "Lorraine, I want to introduce you to my best friend, Alyssa."

Lorraine smiles, her hands full of candy which she immediately places in her dress pocket to shake my hand. "Hi, Alyssa. Do you like my party?"

"Hello, Lorraine. It is a pleasure to meet you." I smile and nod. "Your party looks fun, and I like the decorations." I hold out her present. "I brought a gift for you. I hope you like it." I hand her a long rectangular box wrapped in a colorful balloon design.

"Thank you!" Then, unexpectedly, she instantly unwraps the present.

I feel intense pressure in my stomach as my cheeks turn rosy red as she takes out the present. It was not pricy, and all of the guests are watching her unwrap it. All eyes are on my gift.

"Look! Look! I got a 'decorate your bottle.' I love it." She hugs my waist tightly, and I momentarily freeze at the action. Then I pat her back and peck a kiss on her head. She runs off, chattering excitedly to her friends.

"See, I told you she would like you instantly, especially since you are a warm person. I made a good choice for a best friend." Jamie's mouth curves to the side, showing off his white teeth, and he gives me a side hug as he leans forward to kiss my cheek. I tilt my head, moving nearer as his lips touch my cheek.

My eyes catch the gaze of a lady with wavy ash-blonde hair across the lawn. Her jaw tightens, and she walks toward us.

"Look who's here. This must be Ms. Alyssa that Jamie talks about a lot lately. From a broken family, if I recall." Rihana snorts while crossing her arms.

Hearing this, Jamie tenses but continues to kiss my cheek. He leans back and looks over at the woman, a plastic smile pasted across his face.

"Oh, Rihana, I thought you were not on the guest list." Jamie's eyes widen, and he scratches his temple. I feel his hands holding mine tighten, and he pulls me just a touch closer to his side.

Rihana is muscular with a curvy body and hair to her waist. She is dressed in a ruched bust spaghetti strap mini bodycon dress in red with a matching black Bvlgari clutch and stilettos. She pushes my hands aside roughly, leaving a scratch from her nails as she grabs Jamie's hand. Her face gets closer to Jamie, but as her lips are about to touch Jamie's, he moves backward, and her lips end up hitting air.

"Let me check on Lorraine," he says, grabbing my left hand. He makes eye contact with me to follow him. I follow his lead and walk hand-in-hand with him. Finally, he whispers after we are well away, "I don't know how long I can put up with Rihana's arrogance and possessive attitude. She checks all my phone calls and texts. I have no freedom."

"What?" My nose wrinkles while I tilt my head. "That is horrible. I would not be able to breathe that way. You should find an alternative for your father to get the contract than living a miserable life," I suggest as we walk away from the party. His left arm slides underneath my armpit, our bodies leaning against each other while we walk. My heart beats rapidly, feeling his body against mine, and my mouth curves from side to side.

"I wish I could find the solution to seal the business contract for Father without destroying my love life," he grumbles before ruffling the side of his hair, making it look messy.

He looks at me, something indecipherable in his eyes. "I feel at ease when I am with you." He tightens his arm around me, no longer tense.

I smile at him, reaching my hands up to flip some of his hair aside. His head tilts to rest against mine. Unconsciously, I part my lips, my breath growing shallow.

He leads me to the edge of the garden, where we turn to the corner, facing a poorly lit area. There are lamps in each well-trimmed bush, but none are lit. I narrow my eyes and glance sideways, my left hand feeling clammy against my bare knee.

"Jamie, where are you taking me? I have not been to this part of the house before," I ask while feeling puzzled since the area we are walking toward is further than the party area. The noise from the party is muted. I feel goosebumps rise along my skin as we walk in through the darkness.

After a few steps, a small garden hut painted white appears. It is dimly lit on its porch.

"It is my birth mum's tea painting room. She loves painting, and I want to show you some of her paintings."

I nod and smile before asking, "Wasn't this mansion bought after your father married Jennifer, though?"

Jamie's finger touches my lips to stop me from speaking. "Father bought it before that. Mother managed to stay here for a few months before he filed for divorce and remarried."

My head shakes, my index finger touching the tip of my chin. "Guess Suzanne and I got it wrong."

"Yeah, we often meet outside or at one of your houses. You both only visited this mansion recently." Jamie stops, turns to me, and smiles. "I was such a mess that I refused to bring you and Suzanne to my home for a while," he adds.

As we step into the tea painting room, automatic lights dimly light up the room.

I turn to look at Jamie. "The other day, you mentioned that you had a crush on someone. Don't forget to tell me about the woman you are head over heels for," I say with a wink and smile while releasing his arms. I sure hope my face isn't betraying my feelings.

Jamie takes my hand and massages it, smiling as his ice-blue eyes sparkle, looking right at me. I can't help the shudder that runs up my spine at his intensity.

"Let's see the paintings first," Jamie suggests after a moment, and we walk hand-in-hand. He explains the delicate details of each painting his mum drew as we slowly walk around the room. Once we reach the back of the painting room, which has neat cupboards and stacks of canvas with a tall white antique mirror leaning against two wide white frame windows, Jamie turns to face me and pulls me close to his chest. I can feel him breathing. His eyes are dreamy, gazing into my olive green ones before he abruptly opens his mouth to say something but hesitates.

His left hand rubs the tip of his collar as a bead of sweat rolls down the side of his forehead. Then his soft lips touch mine.

My eyes widen, surprised by his action. My heart races as my breathing accelerates. I am only frozen for a moment before I pull him closer into the kiss.

After a lovely minute, he leans back, his eyes dreamy as he looks at me. He says in a sweet tone, "You know, Alyssa, for years and years, we have known each other, and never once did you notice my feelings for you. It broke my heart whenever you confided with me about the guys you dated. I always wondered what I was lacking." His voice softened with each word.

"I know that I am often happy whenever we spend time together. My heart beats faster, and I long to kiss you deeply and hold you in my arms forever. I can't stop thinking of you. You are the person I have in mind that I told you about . . . So please stay with me all your life."

My eyes open widely upon hearing this, and I smile. I whisper, "I have the same feelings toward you, Jamie. I have for years. I cannot live without you."

After hearing my confession, he touches and skims my brunette hair. He tilts my head gently with his hand, leaning in and kissing me deeply. At the same time, his right hand pulls my waist closer to his body. My suppressed desire flashes through me. I want him to touch me more. I want him in me.

I lean against his broad chest, and he groans as more of our bodies touch. His left hand snakes around my hip to caress my butt. His tongue enters my mouth and slides against mine in a game of dominance.

I close my eyes, feeling his gentle touch smooth over my body.

My heart skips, never wanting this moment to end.

I finally open my eyes to catch my breath, looking at him with a twinkle in my eye.

I wrap my hands around his firm shoulders, my breasts leaning against his chest. His right hand drags up my side and squeezes my breast, and I let out a groan. His tongue touches my lips again, and I open my mouth to his exploration. He begins to open my dress zipper bit by bit, exposing my strapless bra. He licks and nips down my neck, stopping to lavish my collarbone with extra attention.

"More, please," I whisper breathlessly while gripping his hair. He looks up at me wickedly as he reaches around and unhooks my bra. I moan in pleasure as his tongue brushes my skin. My eyes catch on a silhouette in the window across the room behind Jamie, and my eyes open wide when I realize it's Rihana. She squints her eyes before they widen slightly with recognition. Her jaw tightens before she spins away, the sound of leaves crunching faintly entering the space. I tense and whisper, "I saw Rihana watching us at the window." Jamie's hand freezes.

He turns his head to face the window and whispers, "We will continue this later. Let's rejoin the party for now. Maybe we were away too long, and people started noticing our absence." I nod in agreement. He hooks my bra and zips my dress. After we straighten our clothes, he steals a last kiss on my lips and says, "I love you."

I grin back at him. My heart races wildly as I wrap my arms around him. *When did he fall in love with me?*

We step out of the tea painting room, passing by the kidney-shaped swimming pool as a shortcut to return to the party. Two of his helpers are walking through as well, carrying trays and gifts.

I expected to continue following them, but after a few steps, Jamie stops us, facing a white marble door. "Luckily, I have all the house keys with me." He presses the number on the keypad, then stands in front of the camera, and the door clicks open. Still holding my hand, he guides me into his house.

"Where are we going?" I whisper, looking puzzled.

"This is a shortcut. I need to get my guitar from the music room. I promised a surprise birthday song for Lorraine." We take a right, and he quickly presses a few numbers on the keypad. The room we step into is brightly lit, but noises emanate from the center of the room. We hear groaning and moaning. We both look at each other, eyebrows raised. Jamie and I look across at the Versace mirror on the wall. There is a reflection of wavy shoulder-length blonde hair—the same stature as Jennifer. Then, we see a man that's definitely not Mr. Henderson kiss the woman deeply as he pulls at her. The woman turns sideways, and I have to stifle the gasp that threatens to escape. From her profile, it is clear it's Jennifer. Jamie's face turns red, and I feel him clutching my hand firmly and trembling simultaneously. We watch as he kisses her neck, then her cleavage, as he unzips her dress. He licks down her chest—and a mobile phone alarm sounds through the air.

We look at each other and run out as fast as we can, heading toward the party area.

We are out of breath when we reach the garden terrace. We breathe in deeply, looking at each other, and burst into laughter.

We dare not turn to look back just in case we were caught sneaking by them.

Jamie whispers to me, "The lady's sapphire and diamond ring is the same design as Jennifer's. I am certain it is her."

Once we catch our breath, we move to the party scene.

Mr. Henderson is occupied with Lorraine, busy entertaining the children and their families.

Jamie pulls me aside near the punch table, pretending to refill our glasses. "It was Mr. Spencer, Rihana's dad, that we saw with Jennifer," he whispers in my ear before gulping at his drink. I can hear his voice shake, and Jamie's eyes are full of hatred. He clenches his teeth. "I was dead against Father marrying Jennifer. She's not a suitable mother or wife. Even Lorraine is adopted from her previous marriage. She must have married Father for his wealth."

A few minutes later, after Jamie finishes drinking his punch and a game of musical chairs is over, we hear Jennifer's voice shouting sweetly, "Jamie, come and let's take a family photo of the cake cutting."

His face looks tense, and his jaw tightens.

Seeing this reaction, I whisper, "Jamie, please act normal." I pat his shoulder softly, and he reluctantly lets go of my hand. He smiles and nods at me.

I move closer to the cake cutting, and just as we suspected, it was Jennifer that we saw in the music room. She has on the exact same dress as the lady from the music room, though this time, it is wrinkled. *I wonder where Mr. Spencer and Rihana are?*

Jennifer pulls Mr. Henderson close, kisses his lips, then leads the group in the Happy Birthday song before Lorraine blows out her candles and cuts her two-tiered unicorn cake. Since I am standing next to a helper holding several empty party plates, I quickly take the plates to Jennifer, who places pieces of cake onto them. I take them and place them on the tray that her other helper is holding. As the guests devour the birthday cake, a loud bang emanates through the serene night. Everyone freezes, blinking, then another bang sounds, lingering in our ears. Chaos follows; mothers run to find their crying children, and the crowd disperses in all directions, either looking for the source of the noise or for safety.

Lee and his assistant run by, quickly taking out their guns and yelling into a walkie-talkie to communicate with their main office for the backup team.

"Suspected shots fired. Proceed with caution," Lee gestures to the left side of the garden terrace. His assistant nods and leads the way for them.

A sudden panic shoots through me, and I whip around. *Where is Jamie? Where did he go? He was around a moment ago for the family photos. Where can he be?*

I turn around with my mouth slightly open, breathing shakily and prepared to yell his name. I scan from the left edge of the party scene to the right pathway toward the tea painting room. I run in that direction, straining my eyes and looking for Jamie. Sweat trickles down the back of my neck, and my breathing turns faster than usual. I grip my dress near my hips as intense fear threatens to choke me.

I start running to the tea painting room, but someone grabs my arm, swinging me off course, and I turn to see Jamie wide-eyed.

"What happened?" Jamie asks, looking intense. "I went to grab my guitar to play Lorraine's birthday song. Then I heard loud bangs coming from the swimming pool direction."

I quickly give him a short hug, relief filling my chest. "You're safe." He nods, and we both move toward the main party table.

Lee and his team arrive and update us, "We checked, and nothing could be found. We will be on guard, and the whole compound's lighting will be switched on as we continue to search elsewhere."

Mr. Henderson and Jamie nod in agreement with the suggestion.

"Let's get all of the guests into the house, which is safer at the moment," Jamie suggests.

The guests are gathered and guided into the main living room, leaving the party food, games, and decorations behind.

The murmuring in the room grows as parents work to calm their terrified children, and many people move to leave. Mr. Henderson stops them and speaks to the room, "Please, stay and try to calm down. For everyone's safety, please stay here in the living room until my security team has had a chance to confirm that it is safe to go out to the parking area." The parents nod reluctantly and settle uneasily around the room.

Suddenly, a loud scream comes from the swimming pool's direction.

Jamie and I look at each other, and he grips my hand harder.

"Jennifer, please stay with the guests and make them as comfortable as possible in the living room." Mr. Henderson waves to Jamie to follow him along with several other people.

Mr. Henderson starts to walk toward the swimming pool.

Lee and two security personnel move to lead the group.

As we near the location of the scream, we see Jamie's helper Marie standing frozen, her eyes staring and overlooking the swimming pool. Both of us stand still, my hands trembling, and my mouth falls at the sight before us. A pool of blood covers the swimming pool's surface. Jamie glances over and squeezes my hand. "You can stay here if you don't want to get closer."

Still holding his hand, I shake my head and tag along with him. I am a licensed PI, so I might be able to help with my knowledge. Before we take more than a few steps, we hear leaves shuffling in the nearby bushes. We turn our heads toward the sound, overlooking bushes of lush flowers. "Did you see? There are two bulky shadows running at top speed. Stay here!" Jamie looks at me, and before I can argue with him, he lets go of my hand. "I will try to catch them," he says, his feet already stepping forward.

"Be careful. It's dangerous, Jamie," I cry out as he runs off. Jamie uses his phone to alert the security team of the possible intruders, though I didn't see anything when he had. Even now, all I see is darkness and still brush. Chills run through my body as I take in the stillness around. *Was there someone? Or was it his imagination?* I step further forward and strain my neck and eyes, wrapping my arms around my torso.

One of the security members sprints past me to Jamie's aide, startling me. I move closer to the edge of the bushes, determined to be there to assist if I can. Maybe I will stumble into a weapon if I am lucky. But after a few moments, I give up. There is nothing in the bushes here.

Jamie and the security officer return, panting and shoulders slumped. "There is no one visible. Lee will check the video footage," Jamie explains.

He pulls my hand into his, and we both walk nearer to the pool. Mr. Henderson and Jamie's two uncles' faces look alarmed. Dread fills me as I turn my head, looking in the direction that their faces are staring. There is something like clothing floating on the pool's surface. Lee is using two skimmer nets to pull the items toward him. It doesn't seem heavy since there's no force in his movements. When the object reaches the side, he lifts the object out of the water with the skimmer and lays it on the ground. It is a gunny sack and a pair of men's trousers in black and splattered with patches of blood.

All of us sigh in relief but remain tense since this is an odd occurrence.

Mr. Henderson wipes sweat from his forehead, his brows furrowing. "Someone must be plotting a terrible joke, or did the butcher accidentally drop his gunny sacks here? Lee, please remove the items and send the blood specimen to a laboratory. I pray the blood is animal blood from the gunny sack. Dennis and Lee, please ensure my mansion and its surroundings are safe and ensure this pool gets cleaned," Mr. Henderson instructs. "Please call the police or an investigator to thoroughly check my mansion grounds tomorrow morning as well."

Jamie and I look at each other and slowly move nearer to the scene to get a better look. The smell is pungent, and I immediately throw a hand over my nose. I feel like vomiting, so I step back quickly. Jamie follows me only a moment later, also looking queasy.

His father and uncles continue talking to the security team as we leave the scene. Shudders wrack across my body. Deep in my bones, I can sense something fishy is happening. I have a bad feeling about what kind of blood that is. I am deep in my thoughts as Jamie leads me silently to the parking area.

"Are you fit to drive home?" he asks when we stop in front of my car. His hands run through my hair as he holds me close. I place my forehead on his chest, and I can hear his heart beating in a fast but steady rhythm. Slowly, I slide my head to his shoulder and whisper, "I have a hunch that the gunshots and blood on the gunny sack are the beginning of something awful yet to come."

Chapter 7

I just put some bread in the toaster and mix together coffee in my apartment kitchen the next morning when my phone rings with the tone set specifically for Jamie. I grin and skip quickly to grab my phone from the kitchen table.

"Hey, Alyssa, are you OK? Want to meet for breakfast at Tinsel Cafe?" Jamie's voice sounds cheerful.

"Sure, I would love to." As I am about to say more, I can hear Mr. Henderson in the background.

"We have not seen your dad, Rihana. I recall all of the guests leaving by midnight. I will alert our security to check my compound for your father. Please call me or Jamie if anything comes up." There is a small pause before he continues gently, "Rihana, please don't cry." There is another short silence before he calls out, "Hey, Jamie?"

"Hold on, Dad," Jamie replies.

"Got to go. Dad needs me urgently. I will see you soon, my love."

I blink at my phone as the screen goes black. Did I hear correctly? Mr. Spencer is missing? I focus on the empty space on the wall across from me. *With all that*

loud banging and his secret affair, I wonder if he is safe.
I place my right index finger below my chin and bite my
lip as my brain spins.

Within thirty minutes, I am ready for the day, and
Jamie calls me back. "There is a change of plans on the
venue. Lorraine insists on having breakfast and using the
bottle painting kit with you. Do you want to come to my
house for breakfast instead? It would be great for her as a
distraction from how her party ended last night."

I smile. "That is a good idea. I'd love to spend time
with you and Lorraine . . . But part of me feels uneasy.
Will Jennifer be fine with me spending time with you and
Lorraine instead of Rihana?" My voice shakes, and I gulp,
thinking of facing Jennifer.

"Don't worry. Jennifer is out until noon," Jamie reassures me.

I arrive at his mansion within another thirty minutes.
My heart beats faster as I park my car and hum as I lock
my car.

"You look beautiful." I turn my head to find Jamie's
sparkling eyes. He is standing a few steps away, and I
smile. He comes closer and kisses me, dropping me into
a small dip. I pull away, breathless, and my cheeks are
bright red.

"Alyssa! Alyssa! You are here!" Lorraine runs toward
me from the front entrance and hugs my waist. I kiss her
forehead, contentment radiating through me.

She pulls me by my hand, heading toward the garden terrace where a square table has a white tablecloth
decorated with a floral pattern lain over it. There are four
chairs surrounding it with three plates filled with sausages, sunny-side-up eggs, baked beans, and a salad with
yogurt on the side. I grin at Jamie, who returns my gaze

with a wink. *A full English breakfast.*

While we eat, Lorraine and I play riddle guessing games, and Jamie and I take turns telling her some fairy tales. Lorraine is all smiles and giggly childhood happiness. Out of the blue, she gets up and rests her head on my shoulder. "I wish that you could be with us every day, Alyssa. You make me feel happy." I smile and hug her tightly. Unexpectedly, she says, "Alyssa, I like you."

"I like you too, Lorraine," I say as I stroke her hair.

Lorraine returns to her seat, and we continue eating our breakfast. A few minutes later, Lorraine breaks the silence, "I hope you will be Jamie's girlfriend. Rihana often steps on my dolly and never apologizes." She wrinkles her nose cutely. "She brushes me aside and speaks in a harsh tone. She is rude."

Lorraine crosses her arms. I stop eating when I hear the statement. She catches me off guard, but I manage to smile at her and nod. *Me too.*

Jamie looks at me while smiling, his dimple visible. I smile back before taking a bite of my cereal. A breeze brushes my face and makes my hair blow to the side, causing me to close one of my eyes. Jamie's hand touches my hair to tuck it back, and we both smile at each other as I lean into the touch. I startle when Lorraine pats my hand. "Would you please cut my pancake, Alyssa?"

"Sure, Lorraine," I reply and reach to cut the pancake for her. Suddenly, a feminine scream cuts through the air. Lorraine drops her fork on the floor, pushing her hands over her ears as she cries. I hurry to her, hugging her to my chest.

"Alyssa, take Lorraine to her room while I check on the commotion." Jamie's eyes glance at me, then at Lorraine. Worry lines appear on his forehead, and his mouth pushes together tightly.

"Sure," I reply as I gently pull Lorraine toward the house. Her nanny appears at the doorway before we even get there and assures me that Lorraine will be safe with her.

I crouch down to look her in the eyes, wiping a trail of tears from her cheek. "Lorraine, I will accompany Jamie to check out the screaming. Please follow your nanny inside the house." I give her a squeeze and smile at her before placing her hand in the other woman's and watching them scurry inside.

I look around and realize that Jamie is already gone. I'm not sure how to get to where the scream seemed to have originated from, so I unconsciously walk in the swimming pool's direction. While walking there, I am astonished to see bloody fingerprints on the wall. My eyes widen, and I quickly snap a picture of it, just in case evidence is required, and someone cleans it up before the authorities come. I walk further forward, passing by the granite pavement swimming pool. *I hope I'm heading the right way.* While walking, I gasp at the sight of dried blood on the two wooden pool loungers with black cushions on them. I look around, ensuring no one else is around me before I snap a photo to show to Jamie.

I keep walking, and after a few steps, I recognize the marble door that Jamie and I entered last night. I let out a sigh of relief. The door is ajar this morning. I slip through the opening, not wanting to leave any fingerprints. I refuse to confuse the investigators about last night's events.

Across the room, a slight figure moves away from me. "Excuse me, wait!" I exclaim, wanting to ask where Jamie is. My attention is pulled away when a loud commotion comes from the opposite direction. I quicken my steps, approaching the noise. As my feet are on the threshold of the side sliding door overlooking the parking area, a firm hand presses on my shoulder. I gasp and turn to look, but there is no one. I swipe at the ghost of the feeling on my shoulder and shiver, glancing around the room behind. I shake my head, frowning. *I'm letting my imagination get the best of me.*

Once I arrive at the scene, the pungent smell of dried human blood hits my nose, and I gag before covering my nose with my sleeve. Jamie is soothing Jennifer, who is in tears with smudged makeup running down her cheeks. Her hands are trembling, and one of her shoes is missing a heel. I walk cautiously to the open red Ferrari's trunk. Lee stands beside the car, busy talking to Dennis. I inch forward, and I see the white and pink trimming of a Callaway golf bag spotted red. Curiosity takes over as I move even closer. I stop and blink; it looks like blood. I turn my gaze to the mouth of the bag, where a hand juts out, drenched with blood. I close my eyes, trying to shake off the vulgar image out of my mind. I open my eyes to find two eyeballs and an earlobe with some chopped flesh also spilling out of the bag. My left hand closes my mouth, preventing my scream from escaping. I feel my stomach churning. A rhythmic thumping fills both of my ears. My hands drop to my side, and my vision suddenly blurs. I backtrack away from the scene, breathing in and out rapidly. I can feel my hands shaking. Whoever killed the person has no remorse. The body looks like it has been made into meatballs and stuffed in the bag like a sub.

Jamie's eyes lock on mine when he sees me trying not to vomit. "Go inside, Alyssa. Police investigators will be coming soon," Jamie calls out from next to Jennifer.

I nod and wrap my arms around myself. I want to say

something to Jamie, but my voice comes out as a crackle. I walk closer to Jamie and try again. "Who was murdered, and who did it?"

"We don't have any clues at the moment." His arms pull my waist toward his chest, and within a few seconds, he hugs me. "Are you OK?" Jamie whispers. I shake my head, and he lets go of me, running his hands through his hair. "Jennifer returned to get something she left, and when she went to put something in her golf bag . . . that's what she found," Jamie continues, turning pale as he swallows.

"Maybe I stayed too long. I'll head home." As I turn to walk away from the scene, I feel a firm gripping hand on my shoulder. Lee clears his throat when I turn back to him. "Excuse me, ma'am. Returning home is not a good idea in this current situation. Police investigators are arriving within five minutes. Those who came last night and this morning are going to be asked here for questioning."

"Sure." I nod before giving Lee a tight smile. "I will stay here until the investigator does the questioning." I step backward to be away from the crime scene and stand near the door beside a huge brown vase with huge fern bushes half tall as I am. I notice a ring obtruding among the sand. Curious, I step closer, bending down and pretending to admire the leaves. I squat down to take a closer look and snap a picture with my phone camera. My eyebrows draw together. The ring is a pear shape similar to the one Jennifer was wearing last night. I need to see whether she is wearing it now. I get up and walk toward Jennifer's side—she is still sobbing.

"Jennifer, why don't I bring you to your room? You will feel better while waiting for the cops to arrive."

Jennifer and Jamie nod at the idea, and she gets to her

feet, sniffling.

I hold her hands and guide her to her room. I have to be observant of my surroundings on the way to her room just in case she is the culprit. She may leave evidence behind.

We move through the halls silently, stopping in front of her door. "Who opened my room?" Jennifer bends forward and massages her tummy. She looks pale as she grabs her phone and texts the 'Mansion Staff' WhatsApp group.

"Let me help you in, Jennifer," I say. She nods in agreement. Once we enter her room, an aroma of roses hits our nostrils. Her room is neatly arranged with a bunch of fresh flowers in a vase on a table near the door. "Let me tuck you in bed. Please lay down while I get you tea or something to eat?" Her hands tremble, and her feet drag slowly. Her gaze is unfocused, staring at the blank wall in front of her.

"Alyssa, I will take a shower. Please get me tea?" she says in a shaky voice.

"Sure, Jennifer." I smile and exit her room.

I am lucky. As I take a few steps after exiting her room, I bump into one of her four helpers. "Please get me calming camomile tea for Jennifer. I will be waiting for the drink in her room."

"Of course. I will be back with her usual tea." Her helper nods with a smile before leaving.

I take this opportunity to check on her ring. After closing her room door, the first piece of furniture I notice is an antique Italian sofa where her clutch is sitting. It is open with a compact and cigarette box jutting out. Curious, I walk toward her clutch, feeling the intensity in the pit of my stomach. I want to know the whereabouts of the pear-shaped ring. Upon reaching the sofa, I look at the side table for a pencil for me to flip it open more, not wanting to leave my fingerprints. I breathe in and out as my eyes skim here and there around the sofa area, but there is nothing for me to use to cover my hands. I turn to face her bed, and at her bedside table, there is a box of tissue. My eyes gleam, and I quickly tiptoe toward it. I take two of the tissues, then I quickly make my way to the sofa area opposite her bed, using the tissues to flip her pouch open widely. I rub my face with my hand, a groan of frustration fighting to get out. Her pouch has her credit cards and lipsticks, but no rings can be seen. Unconsciously, I sit on the sofa to think where is the most practical place to find her ring. My eyes catch on a glass cupboard. I move in that direction, and as I come closer, I notice that it is not a cupboard but a side room. My right hand reaches to touch the doorknob when I notice that the door is left ajar. I open it slowly in order to not make any sound. The first things I see are Jennifer's many designer clothes hanging on the hangers. Where does she keep her fine jewelry? It has to be a safe somewhere here.

While my eyes scan for a secret path to her safe, a Hermes crocodile skin bag with diamond trimmings catches my eye. It sits on a steel table covered with a French lace tablecloth. I walk to it, and to my surprise, all her fine jewelry is on this table as well. They are locked away with a combination number, but the top is thankfully see-through. My eyes skim from one end to another, looking for a pear-shaped sapphire ring. In the right-hand corner, in between other rings, there is one velvet ring holder without a ring. Realizing that I still have my phone in my hands, I quickly grab a photo of it.

"I notice you are interested in my jewelry collection,"

Jennifer says while standing by the sliding door of the room I am in. Goosebumps emerge at my neck, and I turn to her.

"Your jewelry collection reminds me of my grandmother's," I reply with a smile.

"You have a grandmother? I thought you only had your parents, who are not financially stable and are unable to support you in your higher education. You obtained a scholarship to study at the same university as Jamie," she says sarcastically.

A thundering rage fills my heart, and I can't stop my jaw from clenching at her remarks. My nose wrinkles with distaste.

Jennifer's arms fold over her chest. "And your father is a loser producer."

She lets out a scornful laugh while twisting the necklace on her neck. Her eyes stare at me from her spot while her head tilts. "So, tell me who your grandmother is. I may know her."

"Excuse me, ma'am, your tea is served," her helper's voice calls from her main room.

Hearing this, I walk out of the room and pass Jennifer. Her helper looks surprised to see me and accidentally drops a white hanky. I am quick to pick it up from the carpeted floor. I notice a spot of dried blood staining the hanky. "Here you go," I say to the helper as I hold it out. She smiles nervously at me and hurriedly tucks it in her apron before speeding off.

She didn't look like she had a cut, from what I could see. Another suspect on the list besides Jennifer?

My phone vibrates in my pocket and snaps me from my thoughts. I quickly pull it out to answer it. I smile when I see Jamie's name on the screen. I press the answer button.

"Hello, Jamie." I tilt my head as I look over at Jennifer. "Yes, Jennifer is just getting dressed."

"We are to meet the investigator in living room two now," he says.

I nod. "Sure, we will be there after Jennifer finishes her tea to calm down."

Jennifer stands across from me and, when I end the call, says, "I heard. Let me get dressed. You may wait for me just outside my room." Jennifer points at her entrance door.

I nod in agreement.

"Don't forget to drink your tea," I reply before exiting.

As I turn my body to walk out, I notice a white envelope with the Spencer Development Limited logo on a side table in the sitting area. *I wonder if Mr. Henderson or Jennifer finally got a business contract with Mr. Spencer?*

A few minutes later, Jennifer appears, her face fresh and serene. "I feel better with a warm bath and tea. Thank you, Alyssa, for accompanying me."

"It is my pleasure to ensure you are rested while Jamie is busy with the investigators," I respond while both of us walk toward the living room.

Jennifer stops as we descend the staircase, my hands sliding down the brass railing, her index finger firmly touching the top left side of my shoulder. She stares at me with a hostile glare. "My being nice to you does not mean I approve your relationship with Jamie. Jamie will marry Rihana at all costs!" Jennifer says sternly, her fist clenching beside her.

I blink at her, then continue walking, ignoring the implied threat for now.

I let go of the railing at the bottom before stepping

ahead to walk to the living room. My eyes open widely, seeing a familiar face from the police station in front of us.

I can hear from my spot a few steps away from the living room as he introduces himself. "Hi, I am Inspector Raven. It seems there has been a murder in this house." His eyes wander over those gathered before he walks toward Mr. Henderson and Jamie.

Mr. Henderson steps up. "I am Mr. Henderson, the owner of the house, Inspector Raven." He extends his right hand to shake hands with Inspector Raven.

"I would like you to conduct a thorough investigation of this case since my wife and I feel unsafe living here. Never know if the murderer is lurking around the compound," Mr. Henderson says to the Inspector while his eyes dart here and there. Finally, Jennifer and I step into the living room.

Eight of last night's guests have already arrived and are sitting on chairs, looking anxious. Some are fiddling with their fingers and toying with their handbag handles. I stand beside Jamie, and he whispers, "Rihana is stressed and crying because she has been unable to contact her father since last night. She will arrive in a few minutes with her driver." I nod and give him a tight smile.

"We will start questioning the visitors who attended last night's party. Please be informed no visitors will leave without giving their statement to me and my entourage." His eyes look at each visitor one by one while he straightens his pistol pouch at his waist. He points his pen at Mr. Henderson. "Mr. Henderson, please ask your security team to provide me with the security footage from yesterday morning until the time you found the body. Just in case any foul play was planned earlier," Inspector Raven demands, his eyes set firmly on Mr. Henderson.

Before the interrogations start and Dennis is about to close the sliding door, the helper who brought the tea for Jennifer arrives with a trolley full of drinks and snacks. She stands in the corner beside the antique clock. Dennis closes the sliding door for privacy.

Jennifer nods at her helper and smiles.

After two hours, it is finally my turn to provide my statement. Inspector Raven points at Jamie and me to step outside the living room. As we move, I whisper to him, "I have some photos as evidence that I want you to look at it." Jamie guides us to a corner where a see-through window with two armchairs are located.

"You are safe to show me anything you found, Alyssa," Inspector Raven says. I pull out my mobile and share the photos, bloody handprints, and sapphire ring.

With a hum, Inspector Raven speaks into his walkie-talkie, and his team goes to the designated locations where I found each item.

"Alyssa and Jamie, please wait for me with the others," Inspector Raven says while his hand gestures for us to leave.

Approximately thirty minutes later, I get up from my seat and begin pacing along the perimeter of the room. Inspector Raven finally steps into the living room and walks toward me. He shakes his head. "Negative, Alyssa. There was no blood, fingerprints, or red spots on any walls outside the swimming pool, garden terrace, or tennis court. Also, Tenny's team searched all of the landscaping. No ring or jewelry to be found," Inspector Raven whispers to me.

I can't believe my ears. I saw it, and I took pictures of it.

"Let me show your team where I saw them," I say as I start toward the entrance.

"Alyssa, wait, let me accompany you," Jamie shouts.

Before I can leave the living room, the helper walks hurriedly forward and accidentally knocks into me with her skinny elbow. "Oh, I'm so sorry. Excuse me," she utters while adjusting her apron. Her elbow brushes my face this time, poking my right eye.

"Ouch!" I drop my mobile and close my eyes, trying to withhold the pain.

"Are you alright?" Jamie asks as he runs his hands over my face and leans forward to quickly kiss my nose. I shrug and try not to glare at the woman as we leave the room. Jamie holds my hand as we walk to the designated locations. When I arrive at the corner wall of the swimming pool, I stop and stare. The wall is white, and not a spot is visible.

"I am sure I saw two bloody fingerprints, side by side. I can show you the photo I took again." As I grope around my pockets, my neck stretching to see where I put my phone in the back pocket, I gasp. "Oh, my!" Both of my hands hold my cheeks. "I dropped my phone in the living room and forgot to pick it up."

"It is OK, Miss. The most important evidence is we see it in reality, not via a picture," Inspector Tenny says at the same time he gestures to stop.

One of the investigators leads us to the next location, where I stumbled on the ring.

Upon reaching the vase, my mouth drops. "What, where is it? It was here this morning. I am positive I saw it." I dig into the vase to try and find the sapphire ring, swallowing hard at the panic growing in my throat.

"It is a sapphire ring similar to Jennifer's that was

buried in this vase. There was a stain of blood on the side of it. I dared not touch it since I believed it would be an investigation item." I pull my hands from digging through the sandy vase, not caring at the dirt smudge on them. My eyes look earnestly at the inspector, my chest moving up and down with my rapid breathing. I know my voice sounds strained and shaky, and sweat trickles down my neck. Both of my hands grip together when no items are hidden within the sand in the vase.

Suddenly, my head spins like a top, and my vision becomes blurry. I breathe in and out deeply, and my hands tighten on my jacket to regain my equilibrium.

Seeing my condition, the investigator says, "Don't worry, ma'am. Usually, in this situation, the item is buried deep inside. Let me assist you."

The investigator takes their detector machine and waves it over the vase. There is no sound or flashing indicator. It stays silent.

I stare at Jamie. "Maybe you were too stressed, and you may have seen something that looked like a ring with a bloodstain. It is OK, Alyssa," Jamie says in an attempt to soothe me, placing my head on his chest.

"I need to get my phone. I left it in the living room." I push away from Jamie's chest and start to run. However, still feeling nervous about the outcome of the evidence, I trip and fall, barely catching myself on the wall. Jamie speeds to my aide and takes my hand as we go back to the living room.

Our faces and palms are sweaty by the time we get back. We hear Inspector Raven say, his right hand holding onto his gun pouch, "All visitors' statements have been recorded; video footage and evidence have been collected." His head turns to look at his assistant standing beside him. He turns and smiles at the rest of the room. "Mr. Henderson and Dennis, we will be in touch to provide information on whose body is in the golf bag. Meanwhile, please tighten the security at your place." Inspector Raven continues talking while I grope around for my phone on the carpet.

"Hold on!" I raise my hand. "What about questioning the helpers that were around during the birthday party until this morning? I mean, they are people who were around during the event, so they can be of help to give you a clue to solve this investigation." I remain at my spot and shrug, my mouth tilted.

Inspector Raven and his team discuss for a while before he says, "That's a good idea. We will question and do spot checks of the helpers in this mansion today." His team starts walking out of the room. As they discuss the plan, Jennifer's face turns scornful from next to the door.

I begin to feel desperate and turn around at Jamie's voice. "Here's your phone." Jamie shows it to me. "It was on the side table beside the chair you sat in." Jamie smiles.

"Oh, thank you. Silly me for not picking it up when I dropped it. I better run along," I say to Jamie.

"Are you fit to drive in this condition? Would you like to rest a bit?" Jamie asks, his eyebrows meeting together, and he presses his lips into a thin line.

"I am fine to drive. Please send my hugs and kisses to Lorraine. Hope she is fine."

"I will check on her. Please drive carefully." Jamie smiles, pecks me on my cheek, and leaves me in haste.

An unyielding arm taps on my shoulder as I am about to open my car door.

I gasp and turn around, facing the person.

"Oh! Inspector Raven, anything?" My eyebrows pull

together.

"This is my contact number. If you recall anything, please let me know. I know I saw your photos and the video footage of you collecting that evidence." He pauses and shakes his head before he continues, "I find it suspicious those items have disappeared." He bites on a toothpick.

I nod and take his card. I move closer to him, pretending I am looking at the garden. "I saw spots of blood on the hanky of their helper that was at the food station in the living room. You may want to investigate that," I whisper. Then I turn, unlocking my car without looking at Inspector Raven. He walks away, searching around the parking area.

I sit in the car hastily, start the engine, and take out my phone from my pouch. I start scrolling through my album folder. Surprisingly, there are no pictures. My jaw clenches, and my expression hardens. All of the photos taken as evidence are deleted. I breathe in deeply, then I let out a loud huff. "Unbelievable!" I tousle my hair and wring the bottom of my top. Someone must have tampered with my phone when I left it behind. I am sure of this. Someone in that room must be the murderer or at least an accomplice who destroyed the evidence. "How rude."

After a moment, I smile to myself.

"Luckily, I forwarded those pictures to my email, and I copied it to Inspector Raven's."

Chapter 8

The ringing tone for Jamie resonates through my apartment, and I quickly press answer. "Hello, Jamie."

"How are you, Alyssa, my love? Are you feeling better from yesterday's interrogation?"

"Yes, I am." I walk toward my sofa and sit down, curling my feet under myself.

"I just need to update you . . . The body that Jennifer stumbled upon was Rihana's father." He speaks slowly, reluctant.

"What? Unbelievable."

"The investigators ran DNA, and it turns out that the chopped body in Jennifer's golf bag is Mr. Spencer. When Rihana got the news . . . It wasn't pretty." He sighs, then continues, "I heard from her cousin that she has a knife with her and tries to hurt anyone trying to get near to her."

"That is awful," I reply in a worried tone, shaking my head.

"Investigators are searching if Mr. Spencer and my father had any enemies via businesses," Jamie says while sighing.

"What? Why? We both saw him with Jennifer in your

music room that night. Who could frame your father and Mr. Spencer? Especially since he was with Jennifer before the gunshots." My voice is straining as I raise it.

"Was anyone who holds a grudge against Mr. Spencer aware of his whereabouts at your house that night? Maybe his secretary can check that information to assist with the inspectors' investigation." I shake my head and run a hand through my hair. "The murderer must have framed your father."

Jamie responds, "Maybe there is. As you know, there are two competitors trying to get hold of the contract with the late Mr. Spencer."

I jump up from the sofa, adrenaline flowing. "The envelope!"

"Are you OK, Alyssa? What envelope?"

I place the receiver closer to my mouth and lower my voice. "Jamie, I saw a white envelope with the Spencer Development Ltd logo on Jennifer's side table." My voice is barely more than a whisper.

"You pose good possibilities. I will inform Dennis about this. I will be with Rihana for a few weeks to help with things. I'll be in touch soon," Jamie responds.

"Hold on, Jamie. Let's keep it a secret regarding the envelope until we are certain what is contained inside." I pace from my sofa to my TV, unable to sit still any longer.

"Yes, you are right. We don't want to create any additional unnecessary headache, Alyssa," Jamie replies after thinking about my words for a moment.

"How is Lorraine coping with the recent incidents?" I ask suddenly, worried.

"She is clinging to Rosalind since Jennifer is also unstable. She will be sent to a psychiatrist just to be sure she is completely OK," Jamie replies with a stressed note in his voice.

"I am sure she will be fine soon. She looks like a brave girl," I comment.

Through the phone, I hear his door bang open. "Hi, Lorraine. Are you OK?" Jamie asks Lorraine on the other end. "Come give me a hug." I listen as she runs toward Jamie, her footsteps growing louder. "I am on the line with Alyssa."

Lorraine's voice suddenly sounds through the speaker. "Hi, Alyssa. I will be playing with my dolly and Jamie soon."

"Hi, Lorraine. That sounds fun. Maybe one day, I can come and play with you, too," I respond with a smile.

"Yes, you must!" she replies in her sweet soft voice.

"Look at the time. I better run along and play with Lorraine," Jamie says.

"Will text you if anything comes up," I respond with a smile before hanging up the phone.

We need to know what is inside the envelope from Spencer Development Ltd. Did Jennifer use her affair to gain access to the contract? It must be for her business and not Mr. Henderson's. Did Jennifer and her secretary plan for the murder once Jennifer got a contract with him? I pace around my living room while fidgeting with my fingers nervously. I stop on the spot and start texting Jamie.

Jamie replies, 'Will try to sneak into her room. It will be tough since she doesn't like me to go into her room."

'OK, sure,' I send him a reply.

Thirty minutes pass by, and a text from Jamie comes in.

"Disaster. Jennifer saw me entering her room. She pulled my ears and my shirt hard out of her room.' Crying emoji.

"Oh, my! It must have hurt. I feel for you. The pain must be throbbing. If only I was with you. I would place a cold pack on it to reduce the pain," I respond with a small smile.

"Aw, so touching. I am fortunate to have someone that cares for me. Anyway, the pain will eventually subside soon," he replies to my text.

"Since we need the information to clear my father's name for this murder, let me suggest that you do the sneaking when she is out of the house. I will get ahold of her schedule for today so that you can sneak in smoothly when she is out. You have a petite body, so I guess this job is easy for you." A chuckling emoji accompanies the text.

My eyes widen at this idea, and immediately, I dial his number. "But Jamie, I am not good at sneaking in people's houses, let alone your mansion," I protest before he has a chance to say more than hello. I crumple a blank paper and throw it in the nearby dustbin.

"Alyssa, this will be a training ground for you to become a certified PI," Jamie replies, pleading with me.

I rock on my heels as I debate, finally sighing. "Alright. I am only doing this because you are desperate to clear your father's name." I inhale slowly and let out a deep breath. "And please, Jamie, have your eyes open, just in case she brings the envelope with her. Then, we would have to go to Plan B."

"Right on."

"I suggest that you wait around at Le Petite Café just around the corner from my house so you will be within the vicinity to work quickly," Jamie suggests.

"That is a good idea," I respond while clicking my pen.

"I will text you about Jennifer's whereabouts for today soon. She probably will be with Dad or her secretary. She is a strong-willed lady, so my guess is that she won't stay in bed to recover from the incident for long," Jamie says before hanging up.

I make my way to the café and settle at a table near the windows. While I am sitting, having a cup of tea, I watch a dark blue chauffeur-driven Maserati drive by . . . *Wait, is that Rihana? What is she doing at Jamie's mansion?*

Instantly, I dial Jamie, chewing my lip. "Jamie, I just saw Rihana's car. Is she on the way to your house?"

"Yes, Jennifer invited her for tea." He sighs before he pulls the receiver closer to his mouth to whisper, "This is the best time for you to sneak in since Jennifer will be preoccupied with Rihana for at least thirty minutes. With that amount of time, you can come and sneak into her room easily. You know her room location and my room's for you to hide if you need to, right? Please use the back door entrance," Jamie advises.

"No worries. I will be as invisible as possible, and I remember her room location well," I reply. I breathe in deeply and shake my hands as I breathe out. I feel a nugget of panic rise in my throat.

I get up from the seat and quickly make my way out to the car.

As my car approaches his mansion, I text Jamie, and he uses his remote to open the main gate for me to enter without his security team stopping me for a security check. I gulp, thinking about what to say if his security checks me. Surprisingly, when I pass the gate, no security men are positioned at the gate. *Guess they must be busy with the investigators on the grounds of the mansion, and no one is left to guard the entrance.* Lucky for me, but this means that the security team is not tight, and a lot of crime could happen. I shake my head to brush aside the negative thoughts.

I park my car amongst the bushes near the cargo entrance as Jamie advised. Hopefully, no one would notice me this way.

Nerves flutter into my stomach as I stare up at the house. *Why am I so nervous?* I breathe in deeply to regain my composure.

I text Jamie, 'I am in.'

There is one white van parked in front of the kitchen entrance. I walk toward the van, my pace slow since my legs are wobbly. I try to get my breath to settle, but it's much easier said than done right now. "You can do this, Alyssa. For Jamie's sake," I whisper to myself. With that in mind, I am able to proceed without becoming too nervous. When I reach the van, I chew on my nail as I watch a helper carry shopping bags full of groceries around. I duck down behind one of the bushes beside the van and move slowly toward the back of the van while staying hidden. What feels like hours later but is, in reality, only a few minutes, the helper is finally out of sight for longer than a few seconds. I enter the kitchen, where there are lots of sacks of food supplies lying on the floor and on various trays. At the back of a cupboard hangs a helper's attire. I smile to myself while snatching up the apron, take a broom and duster, and toss Melludee on top of the pile. My rapid heartbeat makes my spine tingle with fear as I change to assimilate as one of their helpers to prevent any suspicion. I hope I don't get caught. I say a silent prayer and close my eyes momentarily before heaving one final sigh and moving from the room.

When I come out of the kitchen, I walk into their dining room. There are two doors connected to the room. I breathe in deeply and scratch the side of my head. *Which door should I choose?* Wobbling with shock, I bite my fingernails before scowling and shoving them into my pockets. Once I muster my courage, I open the door on my left. I see a snooker table. My eyes dart from the left of the room to the right, but there is no pathway toward the staircase to Jennifer's room that I can see from here. I backtrack to return to the dining room to enter the other door. *Guess I have no choice but to choose this door.* I open it slowly, my hands trembling. I can see a narrow pathway with an opening. I force my trembling legs to walk. Paintings of different types of yachts hung on the wall along the way. As the hallway ends, I start to hear ladies' voices; one is crying, and the other is soothing.

My heart jumps. I must be nearing the living room.

I rub my neck and walk closer to the wall. I inch step by step, momentarily stopping as I approach the end. I peek around quickly before stepping into the bare area that has an antique round table with huge roses in a vase on display. I turn my head to the left and smile, seeing the staircase.

This is the staircase that leads to Jennifer's room. I recognize it from the previous day.

I climb it quietly, passing a wall with Jennifer's portrait hung on it, and walk a few steps more before stopping at two wooden doors painted white. I touch the doorknob, and I am lucky; her room door is unlocked. I hope no one is in her room, and the envelope is attainable.

"1, 2, 3, 4 . . . You are my favorite dolly." It is Lorraine's voice that fills the air as I open the door.

I freeze momentarily as my throat squeezes shut, and I try to step forward. However, I can feel my muscles tighten. *Think. Think, Alyssa.* I breathe deeply, then in a dash, I put on my sunglasses, start dusting, and pretend to sweep without looking at Lorraine.

"Hi, good morning. Are you cleaning mummy's room already?" She clutches her doll tightly, her head leaning toward the doll protectively. "Is it alright with you if I continue playing with my dolly? I promised I will be quiet and not a nuisance to you," Lorraine asks.

I smile and nod. I don't dare to look into her eyes or speak, just in case she recognizes me. So I nod while looking at the carpet and place the dust cloth across my face. My forehead is sweaty, and my heart feels like it will beat out of my chest. Our mission will be worthless if my disguise is ruined.

"Thank you." She resumes talking to her dolls and hugging them. I freeze momentarily when Lorraine responds.

I shift my weight from one foot to the other, then I turn my head to face a sofa and spot the white envelope.

I blink and quickly think about what I should do to prevent Lorraine's suspicions. I resume my pretend sweeping activity, and I walk bit by bit straight to the side table surrounded by the two wing chairs. I smile to myself. *I am lucky the envelope remains untouched.* I start dusting, take the plunge and hide it in the pocket of my apron. I continue dusting, making my way slowly to the bathroom, and close the door behind me. I turn the water on, which flows into the sink. The sound of the water flowing should prevent any sounds that I will make from reaching Lorraine. Hopefully, she will just think I am washing the bathroom.

I quickly take out my phone and snap each page with my camera. This time, I use the scanner icon, so the document looks sharper. My eyes dart swiftly across the front page until the end page. My heart beats wildly seeing the contract signed between Spencer Development's directors and Jennifer Ahmed Shariff. Without wasting any time, I quickly tuck the contract in the envelope, slide it into my apron pocket, open the door, and move to wipe the side tables in the sofa area. With Lorraine in my periphery, I move to put the envelope back. A clatter from heels and voices sound from the door. I gulp, my face turning pale white, and panic booms inside my heart. I tense, my hands still in the pocket of the apron. *I better move out of this room before I get caught.* With that in mind, I instantly return the envelope to its original place by sliding it from my pocket and placing it gently on the table. I continue pretending to sweep, bit by bit, and I inch toward the door.

I hear Jamie's voice talking to Jennifer, and the footsteps retreat from her room. I smile to myself and take a calming breath. I wait to open the door, listening. Jamie's and Jennifer's voices rise in a heated discussion, and I quickly spring the door open. Jamie's eyes look directly at me, then shift to Jennifer's. He continues talking to her as I quietly close the door, not wanting to make any noise. Step by step, I walk toward the staircase, my heart pounding. I swallow and move as silently as a shadow, holding my breath.

I climb down the staircase as fast as I can, wishing to speed to the kitchen. Upon reaching the kitchen door, I push it inward. Empty space greets me. My breathing begins to slow, and my head turns to the right overlooking a passageway that has a signage indicating 'Helpers' Rooms.' This isn't part of our plans, but I can't help but get curious. I look behind me to see if there is anyone and satisfied that there is none, I step in that direction. My hands touch the wall as I walk. I need to know if the dried blood on the napkin yesterday has any connection with Mr. Spencer's murder.

My eyes dart around, not knowing where to start my search. I blow my hair bangs aside when I see each helper's room has their picture and name on it. I walk swiftly until the photo bearing the helper that dropped the napkin yesterday. Before I twist the doorknob, I place my ear on the door, straining to hear if anyone is in the room. Once I am satisfied that there is none, I push on the door. I am lucky the door is unlocked, and I slip into it. The first item that comes into view is a cupboard. I make my way toward it. I open the cupboard, and the first thing I see is a hanky. I take a tissue that was left in the apron I am wearing, flip it over, and sure enough, the blood stain remains. My jaw tightens, and I snap a picture with my camera, sending it immediately to Inspector Raven. As I am about to close the cupboard, I hear voices giggling in the hall. My pulse skyrockets, and I breathe in deeply, trying to hold my breath. I squat down to hide behind a chest of drawers. I quickly text a message to Jamie on my whereabouts. I don't want him to be worried about me.

A few minutes later, all sounds have faded, and I am confident that there is no one around. I get up, walk quietly to the door, open it, and walk straight to the kitchen. My breathing evens when no one is visible in the kitchen as I emerge. I pass by the long kitchen table just in front of me. A few steps before reaching the kitchen door, I notice an electronic meat-cutting machine at the side. I shiver and swallow. I hope Mr. Spencer's body was not chopped using that machine. I shake the thoughts away. Then I hear footsteps approaching the kitchen and check over my shoulder, my pounding heart sounding in my ears. My right leg starts trembling, and my right hand pinches my thigh. I walk as fast as my feet can carry me, stepping into my car in a whistle-stop, and drive out of the mansion compound. I look through the rear mirror for any vehicles pursuing me as unease unfurls in my chest. Once my car passes the mansion gate and down several streets, I park near some bushes, still looking over my shoulder for anyone. Once I am satisfied that no one has followed me, I pull off the apron and Melludee, hiding them in the glove compartment. I text Jamie with a smiley and heart emoticon. My shoulders relax as I throw the car into drive and step on the gas.

Mission accomplished.

Chapter 9

Drinking hot tea on the sofa with the television switched on as my companion, I shove the scanned photos of the agreements into a folder on my iPhone. I read the entire contract, forward it to my email for safety, and download it onto my laptop. My email dings with a message from the PI company I am attached to. I click it open, curious.

"Alyssa, there is an important case in town that we would like you to help with. I sent your name to Inspector Raven and Inspector Eleanor. They agree to use this case as your internship training. Please bring your PI license everywhere you go in connection to this investigation."

I reply, agreeing to these arrangements, and my eyes gleam with excitement. *I finally get to work with my cousin, Eleanor, who is known for her investigation skills and has won lots of recognition.* I clap my hands, rubbing them together.

An hour later, I switch the channel to get updates from the news when my phone rings. I answer it with a smile. "Hi, Jamie."

"Hi, how are you, my love? I wanted to let you know that Rihana will provide a statement at Mr. Spencer's office tomorrow at 10 am," Jamie says while I sip my tea.

"Finally, she wants to cooperate, huh?" I respond.

"Yeah. I would like you to accompany me. Please?" Jamie pleads.

"It will be awkward for me to be physically in the meeting. Especially since Jennifer already warned me that I must refrain from having any relationship with you." I bite my lip while shrugging.

"Alyssa, I feel more confident when you are around. Also, there will be a team of police investigators and reporters there. You can pretend to blend in with them in order not to look obvious? What do you think?" Jamie sounds hopeful, and I sigh.

"Well, I guess this will be a good training ground for me as a PI."

"So I will pick you up tomorrow." Jamie's voice sounds cheerful.

"Yes, I will be ready by 9:30 am. I will share my findings on the contract tomorrow too."

"Yes, sure. I can't wait to see you." He clicks his tongue. "You look cute in Melludee. My heart almost beat out of my chest when I saw you wearing it. I cannot stop thinking of you," Jamie says huskily.

I swallow. "See you." My heart skips a heartbeat, and I can feel a hot flush steal over my face.

At 9:30 the next morning, I wait for Jamie for five minutes before his car parks swiftly in front of my apartment's main entrance. I wave to the security guard on duty, then hop into his red sports car.

He smiles, then leans in, letting go of his steering wheel, and gently pulls my head toward his to peck a kiss on my lips. I sigh and deepen the kiss for a moment. He lets go of my lips and grins before driving off.

"Let me spill the beans on the contract." I wave my phone, the scanned contract up on the screen. "The contract is signed between Spencer Development Ltd and Ahmed Shariff Petroleum Inc. regarding oil and gas dealings between the two companies. And you know what, Jamie?" I smile crookedly. "One of the shareholders is Jennifer. She landed a lucrative business deal just before he died. It's worth billions of dollars." I flip my hair over my shoulder, touching the seat back and straighten my folded sleeve cuffs.

"Woah. That is news." Jamie points at my mobile screen, glancing down at it before looking back at the road.

"Tell me, Jamie, why did she marry your father? Is it because of love? Or did she use your dad for his connections to get contracts for her family business?" I look at Jamie and raise my eyebrows.

Jamie shrugs his shoulders, his left hand raising.

"One thing is sure; Father is definitely in love with her. They met on a luxury cruise ship vacation in Monte Carlo after Father caught Mother cheating on him since he goes abroad a lot on business trips. I was with him on the cruise, and I know the look of love at first sight." He runs a hand through his hair. "However, for Jennifer's love, I was skeptical. When Father met her, her family business was in shambles and on the verge of bankruptcy." His jaw clenches as his right hand grips the steering wheel, his knuckles turning white.

"With the contract, we can clear your father's name for any business rivalry that makes it seem like he murdered Mr. Spencer," I say, and Jamie nods in agreement.

Inspector Raven and his entourage interview Rihana for hours. I almost feel bad for her at their intensity. Her eyes turn red as tears continuously stream down her cheeks. She ends up wailing and sobbing when she gets overwhelmed, causing her makeup to smudge. A man in his thirties with dark brown hair, wearing a diamond stud on his left ear and a tattoo wrapping his hand and wrist, stands beside her through everything, hugging and consoling her as necessary.

"Her cousin," Jamie whispers next to me.

At some point in time, two brawny men with well-defined muscles push us aside, standing side by side next to Rihana and her cousin.

"Those are Rihana's bodyguards. Her father owned a casino hotel and felt she needed to have protection." My eyes are glued to the way the bodyguards are ensuring Rihana's safety. They look like thugs. *Definitely not people I want to tangle with.*

Once the meeting adjourns, there is a planned hour-long shareholders' discussion, and I am directed to sit outside of the room alone.

A few minutes after the meeting starts, Jennifer and Mr. Henderson stalk out of the room. Jennifer's almond-colored eyes are bloodshot and seem to protrude from her eye sockets. Her cheeks are cherry red, and her hands are in tight fists at her sides. When her gaze lands on me, she looks as though she wants to skin me alive.

In the blink of an eye, she is in front of me and punches my stomach. I tumble backward of my chair from surprise. Once I fall onto the floor, she steps on my hand without remorse. I cry out loudly in pain, tears springing from my eyes. Jamie appears with Rihana. She clutches his hand tightly, withholding him from moving forward to help me.

Jamie shouts from his spot, "Jennifer, stop it, don't you dare hit her. She is the love of my life."

Mr. Henderson, with his arms akimbo, streaks to Jamie and slaps his cheek hard. "You stupid boy! How could you love someone whose life is in shambles like her?" He grabs the sides of Jamie's shirt, purposely choking his neck in a threat. He whispers menacingly, "Do as I tell you for our family's business and sustainability that you are inheriting. You are to marry Rihana as planned by Jennifer, end of discussion." Jamie struggles against his hold to no avail. Mr. Henderson glares at him for another moment before letting go of Jamie's shirt in disgust and speeds off.

Jamie pants and shakes Rihana's hand hard, causing her to lose her grip on him. He hurries to my side and squats down, gently taking my hands, and helps me up. He tenderly slides aside the hair that covers part of my face.

"Jamie is mine!" Rihana shouts before snapping her fingers. "Jack, John, take Jamie away from her and teach Alyssa a lesson."

My muscles clench as one of Rihana's bodyguards pulls at my waist harshly in order to break Jamie's hug. I kick out, hitting the man's groin with my heel. He yells in pain, loosening his grip on me. The other bodyguard kicks me in the chest with a grunt. The impact is too much, and pain spikes through my body. I fall, hitting my head on the side of a chair. I feel a throbbing pain at the side of my head as hot blood rolls down my cheek. I touch my head, wince, and pull my hand away to see that it's covered with blood. My hands shake, seeing my blood, and my vision blurs. I breathe in and out rapidly, but I feel like I am choking. My eyes close as I tug at the collar of my shirt. From what sounds like a distance, I hear Jamie's voice shouting my name, growing fainter each second before nothingness embraces me.

Chapter 10

I open my eyes and try to move my hands. I wince at the small tug and look down at the wires attached to me and a machine. My vision is still somewhat blurry, but I can make out that the device is in a small box shape and has numbers. I lift my head slowly, and immediately, it is drowning with dizziness. Nausea threatens to expel everything in my stomach. I close my mouth and place my head on the soft pillow, groaning.

"Alyssa! Alyssa! Please, wake up. It's me, Jamie," says a panicked voice.

Hearing his pleading tone, I unconsciously open one eye, then the other. I attempt to smile, trying my best to prevent tears from falling. Tears of pain from the physical brutality and heartbreak. Deep inside my heart, I know this will be my last time seeing him for at least a while, if not forever.

"Are you OK? Speak to me. I am worried sick," he continues asking while kissing my forehead.

"Where am I?" I ask in a cracking tone. I sound like I smoke three packs a day.

"You are in the hospital. After being hit by Rihana's bodyguard, you were unconscious and bleeding from the side of your head." His finger points at my head.

Suddenly, the door slides open. "Jamie, you idiot, get over her. You are mine!"

My eyes open widely while my hands tremble. Jamie's eyebrows raise as his jaw drops at her shouts.

Jamie stands beside my hospital bed and turns his head to face Rihana, gripping the railing of the bed.

The flat of her hand hits Jamie's cheek hard, leaving a red mark. Jamie clenches his jaw, and his shoulders stiffen.

Rihana clenches her teeth, and her nostrils flare, trying to rein in her anger at Jamie.

"I will make sure she dies if you sneak out to meet her again!" she shrieks at Jamie while pointing her index finger at my face.

I gulp and feel my face turning white. Gradually, I pull my blanket toward my neck. *If only I could hide here.*

"Forget about us. You are wasting your time. I don't have any feelings toward you, Rihana," Jamie shouts, fists at his sides.

"I will get what I want. You are to marry me at all costs!" Harshly, she pulls Jamie's hand. Jamie resists, his left hand raising to slap her cheek, leaving a pink mark on it.

My room door opens again, and a muscular nurse appears. "Quiet, everyone. This is a hospital. Please let this patient rest and recuperate. I will call security if this commotion continues." His eyes stare firmly at Rihana and Jamie.

Rihana huffs and passes the nurse standing at the open door before giving a signal to her bodyguards just outside the room. They move in and pull Jamie away, even though he fights against them.

"You will share the same fate as her if you do not adhere to my command!" Rihana threatens from outside my room.

Hearing this, Jamie relaxes his body. "I can walk myself. Let go of me!" Jamie glares at her bodyguards, shaking his body to free himself from their grip.

He walks toward my bed and straightens the blanket to cover my chest. He strokes my hair, then places a kiss on my lips. "Whatever happens, remember that you are always in my heart. You are my true love," he whispers.

I smile, stare into his eyes, and whisper, "I love you, too."

One of the men pulls at his right hand. "Don't you dare touch me. I am going out now," he growls while roughly pushing the bodyguard aside.

The door slams shut with finality, and the sudden silence is pressing.

Tears roll down my cheeks like water flowing from the tap. I feel like a knife just struck my heart, seeing Jamie for the last time. Memories of the time we spent together as best friends, and the short time as more, flood my mind as I allow myself to wallow.

What feels like a few hours later, my phone rings non-stop. I muster my courage and get into a seated position. My head spins slightly as I grab it. The FaceTime icon blinks incessantly, and I press 'answer.'

"Hel—oh, my God, why are you in the hospital? Why are your head and hands all bandaged?" Suzanne frowns before continuing quickly. "I will punch the person who did this to you." She slaps her fist on the table beside her, and her lips quiver. She asks in a much quieter voice, "How can I help you while I am in Paris? I can call your father?"

"No. Please don't bother to call any of my family. This is a minor injury. I am not in ICU." I raise my hand connected to wires to show her.

"Minor?" Her tone is incredulous. "Wake up, girl. This is a massive injury. If I was you, I would charge whoever attacked you!"

I shake my head as tears fill my eyes again. My voice cracks as I reiterate to Suzanne what transpired.

"Let me get my hands on Mr. Henderson, Jennifer, and Rihana." Suzanne bears her teeth, and her face contorts with rage. "The three wicked pests!" She squeezes a can of soda beside her and throws it in the trash with a disgusted face. She cracks the knuckles of her fingers, and her ears turn red.

"Calm down, Suzanne. You cannot do much from Paris," I respond softly.

She breathes deeply, and soon her ears turn to a normal color.

"You are right. I will send someone to check on you. Your well-being is important to me. I will talk to you soon." Suzanne hangs up before I can protest.

I look at the heart rate monitor beside my bed and sigh. "Guess my heart is stable." I pull out the wires attached to my hand. "Ouch," I say as I shake it out. Bloodstains are visible around my skin, and I start wriggling my feet and hands to get the blood circulating. I get up from the bed slowly. My dizziness has died, and I feel confident enough to stand up from the bed. As I do, a surge of pain thunders at the side of my head. My tummy hurts from the kicking. I breathe in deeply to maintain my composure and slowly walk step by step, holding onto the chair. I grab my bag and jacket, cover myself, and grab the steel doorknob. I slide the door open, and the corridor is quiet.

I look at the directory pinned on the opposite wall for an exit.

I am momentarily stunned; why did they put me in the trauma department? My head injury is not severe. At most, I just have a concussion from hitting the chair. It must be Rihana trying to tarnish my reputation. I hope one day she will pay for this. I bare my teeth, and my hands curl into fists while shaking. My steps are slow since each step I take causes flashes of pain and nausea to sweep through me. I take a deep breath, then freeze, hearing voices behind me, and I instantly crouch, hoping no one notices me.

I gasp, tears rolling down my cheek as the pain intensifies in my head and stomach. I can't continue escaping at this rate.

I hear heavy footsteps stop beside me, and a concerned voice says, "Miss, let me call for help."

Within a few minutes, I am brought back to my room, and a doctor comes to examine me. He is silent until his exam is complete. From his findings, I may be suffering from vertigo due to the impact. He sighs. "Your condition, if it worsens, can turn to schizophrenia, a mental health illness." The doctor's forehead creases. I close my mouth with a snap as a feeling of sadness seeps into my heart.

"Please have a good rest to recover fully. No more running around the hospital, Miss." He chuckles with his index finger waggling left to right in a scold. "And I would advise you to prevent hitting your head again anytime soon."

With one eye open, I nod before closing my eyes and dozing off.

"She looks terrible. Doctor, can't you do something to make my granddaughter better? Please?" A familiar voice rings in my ears, but my mind is slow to place it. Curious to know who it is, my right eye, not blocked by the pillow, cracks open. My vision is still blurry, but I see the silhouette of a woman with wrinkles on her cheeks and a small mole near her eye. "Alyssa! Alyssa! My sweetheart. Please, wake up." *Grandmother.*

I tilt my head, rubbing my eyes to try and push aside the blurry vision.

"Alyssa, it's me, Eleanor." Her hand pats my shoulder. "I need your statement to kick off the investigation." Her voice is thick with anger.

Hearing her name and voice, my head lifts from the pillow. "My head!" It throbs with pain, and I wince. I rub my head and find that it is covered with bandages.

Eleanor continues, "Suzanne and Jamie texted me, saying you were in the hospital."

My eyes widen before I smile to myself. They are indeed my best friends.

Eleanor's face hardens, and she crosses her arms.

I reiterate the details from the beginning: the framing of stolen items, Mr. Spencer's brutal murder, and finally, Rihana and Jennifer's attitude toward me.

Eleanor lets out a disdainful noise and shakes her head, starting to pace.

Grandmother walks closer to my side, and her fingers push my hair behind my ear to look at my face clearly.

"You will recuperate under my care, Alyssa. Your parents agreed to my decision since I am the nearest blood relation in town. You are my only granddaughter. Nothing bad shall befall you under my watch." Grandmother's eyes stare into mine, and her skinny fingers stroke my hair gently. Her eyes are full of love with a touch of pity.

She faces Eleanor. "I want to implement a restraining

order on Jennifer Ahmed Shariff, Rihana Spencer, Ahmed Shariff Inc., and Spencer Development Ltd. If any of them try to get close to you, they will be put behind bars." She scoffs. "I am considering engaging a private secretary to tag along with you when you are up and running on your own." She looks out of the window with a hostile glare and curls her lips. Her voice shakes when she talks, and I can't help but feel sorry for Grandmother that she has to arrange this to ensure my safety. From her face and her hands, I can see how she has aged. My health and safety are not her responsibility; it's my parents'. Tears start rolling down my cheek, and I wipe them off with my bare hand.

The next day, after the doctor does a final check of my vitals, I am discharged and relocated to my grandmother's house, thirty-five miles away from my apartment.

Chapter 11

"Come, let's visit your apartment and bring some of your clothes and light stuff. Packing furniture will be done by the movers that I have engaged," Eleanor suggests while I sign the discharge papers in the hospital. I nod in agreement, relieved at the thought of grabbing some of my things.

We arrive an hour later. The windy breeze sweeps over my exposed skin, and goosebumps appear on my arms. I zip up my jacket. "Let's stretch our legs by taking the stairs. It's only to the fourth floor." Eleanor chuckles. I am grateful to have a cool cousin like her. She is like a sister to me. The only difference is that she is ten years older, so we don't use the same lingo.

When our feet land on the cement flooring of the fourth floor, I stop, and Eleanor pauses a moment later.

My apartment door is ajar.

I gulp. "I remember closing and locking my apartment door before accompanying Jamie to the discussion with Rihana and the police investigators. You know, before I was in the hospital." My voice quivers at the end. Trembles commence in my hands.

"Are you expecting anyone?" Eleanor whispers, her

hands in a questioning gesture at me. I shake my head and shrug. Eleanor narrows her eyes, and her brow creases.

"Please remain calm. The intruder may still be in your apartment." She takes out a Glock 19 gun from her side holster. I suppress a shiver as my eyes rove over it.

"Please remain behind my back. I will take the lead into your apartment." Her eyes dart behind us and back to the entrance of my apartment.

I nod.

My apartment's main entrance is located one door away from the staircase. Apparently, we are hiding behind the wall of the stairs. The one door before my entrance is my apartment's kitchenette, where the washer and dryer are located.

When Eleanor steps out from our hiding place and reaches the side of my apartment's back door, one masked man hastily runs out of the main entrance with a baton in his hand. "Freeze, police!" Eleanor shouts, pointing her gun in the man's direction.

The masked man quickly takes his own gun from his waist and points it in Eleanor's direction.

"No!" I shout to distract him, but I am late by a few seconds. He pulls the trigger, and Eleanor swiftly ducks down and hides behind a vase the same size as her. I can hear the bullet hit the vase, which breaks in half and exposes Eleanor.

The masked man jumps over the steel staircase railing at the end of my apartment floor. Eleanor follows at a safe distance as she can while I crouch at the edge of the landing to watch. I grab my phone from my sling handbag and quickly dial. "Hello, 911? This is an emergency. There is a firearm shootout."

I only manage to share my apartment address and turn

to look at my apartment's door when another masked man comes out, dragging a man out.

My hands tremble, and my throat feels dry. I can see the intruder's features from the spot I am hiding in, and his body is similar to Rihana's bodyguard's features. There is a long, deep scar on his left eyebrow. He holds the man harshly against the wall outside my apartment's main entrance. The man is hunched over from the pain, and the attacker firmly grabs the man by his jacket to pull him up.

I am still at my spot, crouching, and my heart starts palpitating like a machine. My hands shake as my thoughts take in the man . . . *Jamie?* His features fit him, and his shirt is torn, a line of blood dripping from his torn, bleeding mouth.

I look around, and luckily, there is a thick piece of wood lying beside the broken vase.

Without any hesitation, I run and grab it, staying in a crouch as I inch nearer and quietly hide just behind the broken vase. I feel unsafe since only part of my body is hidden, so I retrace my steps and quickly sneak to another place like a mouse would sneak into a house. I blow my fringe out of my face, feeling relieved that I am at the perfect hiding spot—close enough to see and hear everything.

"This is your last warning from my boss. You are not to visit that bitch Alyssa ever again if you want to live. We have eyes on you." He pushes Jamie hard against the wall. Jamie's eyes open widely from the impact of the hit, and his breath is driven from him. Jamie kicks the masked man. In return, the masked man kicks at his stomach before punching Jamie on the side of his face. A gush of blood streams from Jamie's mouth.

I cry, "No!" and run as fast as my legs can carry me

with the thick wood as my weapon. Hearing my voice, Jamie, his face covered with blood, turns in my direction and throws his hands up, trying to stop me from coming to his rescue. I throw the wood in the masked man's direction, hitting his nose with a satisfying crunch. The man groans, and his hand moves to his nose as it spurts blood. His other hand grabs blindly for the pistol at his waist.

Before he can take out his gun, the intruder shakes as a gunshot rings out. Excessive blood pours from his back. His eyebrows pull together, and he hisses as his hands rove over the injury. He finally pulls out his gun and shakily points it in my direction. Before he can pull the trigger, another bullet hits his forehead. The intruder freezes, and his eyes glaze as blood flows from his mouth. He shudders, and Jamie kicks him. His body flips over the railing, and he falls, landing on the cement floor below.

Tears fall from my eyes, and I rush to Jamie, panic threatening to choke me as I take in his state. I steady Jamie as he slides down the wall, panting. His face and hands are covered with blood. He looks at me and smiles weakly, reaching out to cup my cheek. He pulls my face closer and kisses me. I hug him, running my fingers through his hair to soothe him. In the background, sirens announce the arrival of an ambulance and police.

"It's Rihana's men. They were here to warn you not to have any relationship with me, otherwise, face deathly consequences," he says, his voice husky due to the pain. Fresh tears fill my eyes as I hug him closer, wishing I knew how to get rid of his pain.

"I owe you an explanation as to why I am at your apartment," Jamie says quietly. I hold his hands and look at his face. "I wanted to visit you, but the hospital said you were discharged earlier. I figured you will be at your apartment, so I drove here. I missed you." He coughs and wraps an arm around his torso. "When I got up here, the door was opened, and they were already inside." I smile sadly, kiss his cheek, and squeeze him.

Finally, help gets to us, and within a few minutes, the paramedics have him on a stretcher. I let go of his hand as he asks, "Please call my father," and hands a paramedic his phone. He closes his eyes as they do as he asks.

After seeing Jamie safe in the ambulance, I quickly search for Eleanor. I find her giving a statement to the police. Her feet were shot, but luckily her thick boots kept the bullets from hitting flesh. After being led on a goose chase, the masked man managed to escape on a motorcycle.

"It is either Jennifer or Rihana who paid them to destroy my belongings as a warning. Jamie was just unlucky to arrive after they came," I relay to Eleanor.

Eleanor waves at me and starts toward the building. "Let's get into your apartment and grab your clothes and important documents. Then we better run along." She readjusts her pistol belt that is hidden underneath her jacket.

"I am calling the other investigator's team to investigate and get the two men's fingerprints. They should be easily identifiable since they work for Rihana. My team will settle everything, and we will charge Rihana for destruction of private property," Eleanor adds with a fist in her other hand.

I push the door to my apartment open, and my mouth drops as I stare at the inside of my apartment. It's a total disaster. My anger thrums through my veins, and my hands shake from the effort it takes to contain my anger. My wooden dining table is broken in half, the chairs upturned. My chest of drawers is ransacked; papers and other documents are torn into pieces. The mirror in the bathroom is smashed, a crack down the center.

My hands cover my mouth as more tears roll down my cheeks. I can't stop them as they fall harder, seeing my family photo on the floor. The attackers did a thorough job of smashing it into the ground. I bend down with trembling hands and manage to grasp the photo, pulling it from the ruined frame. It is from when Mom and Dad were still together and I was ten. My body shakes with anger, and I throw my fist on the side table, making it shudder.

I wipe my tears with a tissue before getting up and walking toward my bedroom door. I push it open and breathe deeply. To my relief, my room is untouched by the intruders. I turn my head, facing Eleanor, who is looking around the living room. I say to her, "I am going to grab my laptop and pack some clothes, then we can go. I get the creeps up my spine just seeing this nasty mess." I wrap my arms around my body and shiver.

Eleanor nods and points a finger to gesture that she agrees with the suggestion. "Yup, that is what I was about to suggest." Her right hand waves at me. "Sundown within thirty minutes. Let's do it fast," Eleanor replies after looking through the window for her to gauge the sunset.

Chapter 12

My laptop dings with a notification that I received an email. I jump out of my bed, reaching for my laptop located on the table across the room. I unlock it, clasping both hands to say a little prayer before clicking the email to read the message.

Thank you for being so interested in our company, however, your application is unsuccessful after considering your application with other candidates.

We wish you all the best in your future endeavors.

I massage my forehead, then cup my hands over my face with a heavy sigh. Another day of rejection. I have to apply for more jobs, and maybe this time, outside my town. I huff as my brows touch each other.

Then I scroll and open another email from the PI company I am attached to that reads, *Dear Alyssa, Inspector Eleanor will be in touch with you for any cases now that you have been through the approval process. You are to follow her for any investigation and update us weekly using the attached form.*

I smile and type, *Noted, will do.*

"Alyssa! Alyssa!"

I quickly close the email, shut down my laptop, and

push my chair back. "Coming, Grandmother."

I wonder if she can hear me since my room is situated at the back, the fourth room, before reaching the living room at her villa.

"Alyssa, come and have breakfast with me." Her voice is loud and clear, even though I just came out of my room. "I have something to discuss with you."

When I reach the dining area, I smile and peck her cheek, looking at her radiant face. "Good morning, Grandma. You are looking good this Sunday morning. Do you have any plans today?"

She smiles in return and pats my hands when I sit opposite her at the table.

She tilts her head, then places her tea on the saucer, her eyes looking at me while smiling. "I have a brunch date with my university class today, and I would like you to join me. I want to introduce you to my circle of close friends." She smiles and shows me some old photos she keeps in a photo album on her phone.

"You do have a nice group of friends, Grandmother." I slide her phone to her side after looking at the photos.

"I am proud that you have graduated, and this is the time to be proud of my granddaughter." She grins. "These are my close friends that I will introduce to you during the luncheon afterward." She waves her phone, another picture now on the screen.

"Sure, I would be delighted to accompany you." Doubt squirms at the back of my mind, however. I graduated, but I've had many employment rejections. I guess I can count my blessings to have such a loving grandmother.

My fingers play with the teaspoon lying beside my plate absentmindedly, and the spoon accidentally clanks against my plate. I blink, realizing that I am lost in dark thoughts. I bite the lettuce protruding from my sandwich before munching the main part. My eyes close, and I hum in appreciation. "This tuna melt cheese sandwich is to die for. You are an amazing cook, Grandma." I smile at her and take another bite.

"Thank you, Alyssa." She takes a sip of her tea, smiles at me, and straightens in the chair. "It is not often that I get to have a quiet breakfast with you, Alyssa, and I would like to take the opportunity to bring up the topic of my business since you are a Smith." Her eyes look at me while she wipes off her mouth with a napkin. She continues, "You know my business owns conglomerates for several business ventures, yes?" Grandma stops and tilts her head, waiting for a cue about whether I am aware and listening to her.

I nod and smile, unsure of where this is going.

"Apparently, I have a new venture coming up in London within the next six months. I require a shareholder, an Assistant Director, who has an engineering background to overlook my business and report to the stakeholders quarterly on the progress." Her right hand smooths her napkin back into her lap. "So, I am suggesting that you can help me on this while waiting to land a job."

The sip of juice I had just taken gets stuck in my throat at her words, and I choke slightly. My eyes grow wide. I place my juice on the table, clear my throat finally, and say, "Grandma, would that mean my work base would be in London? I don't have any experience in management. How can I be of any help?" I tilt my head, looking directly at her, then look away at the dining area. Wrinkles form on my forehead. I shift my weight uncomfortably, waiting for Grandmother to respond.

"That is why after your trip to Paris to visit your best

friend in three weeks, you will be an Assistant Director at one of my offices in the US. You will learn the ins and outs of management and project management activities." She chuckles, then she reaches for my hands, squeezing both of them gently. I smile, feeling a bit more at ease, and my heartbeat regulates.

"Do Mama and Dad know about this arrangement?" My voice turns thick and unsteady.

"If you agree to this, I will inform both of them. It is a good opportunity to gain some knowledge and experience. Also, may I remind you that you are a Smith." Grandmother's mouth curves sideways, and her eyes twinkle. "You are the sole inheritor of my business since your dad's profession is inconsistent with the nature of my business. Also, don't forget to support your loving grandmother," she says as she winks at me.

I smile at her while stirring the juice. "Let me think about it?"

"This will also keep your mind on other things for a while, so things can clear up with Jamie." My nostrils flare in surprise, and the juice goes down the wrong pipe again. I nearly let go of the glass as I cough. My cheeks heat, and I see through the mirror across from the dining table that my cheeks are reddish. It takes a moment, but I recover without much more incident. *What Grandmother said is right. I will need to be busy to put my mind off Jamie momentarily.*

Chapter 13

Ten ladies are seated at a long oblong wooden table at Oakmont Pine Golf Valley's restaurant. I sit next to Grandma in my brand-new Nike golf outfit. Apparently, the ladies who attend the gatherings have high credentials, either themselves or from their families. From the mingling sessions, I realize the reason Grandma brought me along—to speed up my directorship, she wants to expose me to some directors.

In the car on the way to the golf course, Grandmother turns to look at me. "My dear Alyssa, the luncheon will be your first opportunity to get to know these influential ladies. Their connections will be important when you are appointed as Assistant Director." I nod slowly, digesting the information in my head.

"I guess the way they carry themselves is also important for me to take note of." I look at Grandmother, an eyebrow raised.

She nods. "You are exactly correct. As an Assistant Director, you need to carry yourself professionally." Grandmother buttons her jacket and adjusts her seat. The rest of the ride is silent as my mind wanders.

I am still deep in my thoughts about this whole deal

by Grandma as the meal progresses. It is a dream to be the next line in her empire. I smile to myself and take a deep breath, trying to push the worry back. *What if I don't do justice to her because of not having any prior experience in the project engineering line? Also, I need to adjust my time to continue my PI training. I really want to have time for both roles.* I press my lips together, and my fingers fiddle with the napkin lying on the table as I think over Grandmother's proposal.

"We have an engineering proposal at East London coming up in the next two months," I overhear one of the ladies say, and suddenly, her eyes catch mine. I blink at her and smile. I wonder if she asked me something. I gulp and grip the hem of my shirt.

Before I have a chance to say anything, the lady opposite me answers her. "It would be a good opportunity for newbies to oversee the projects." They continue discussing with each other while I eat my peas and carrots slowly, weighing the options. The other three ladies, further to my right, are laughing and eating their dessert.

I sigh. With Grandmother's connections, she should encourage me to work first, then maybe in three years, I can join her business. By that time, I would have sufficient training in both engineering and investigation. That sounds better. My mood perks at the thought, and I smile. "Are you agreeing with us on the proposed engineering project site in London, Alyssa?"

I pause, then blink, staring at the lady named Fanny Lorenzo. My mouth curves upward as I shrug. "Guess we need to see the site and the surroundings to determine its feasibility."

Fanny smiles at me brightly. "Very smart of you, Alyssa.'

Lady Jacqueline, who sits catty-corner to me, says, "Spot on," as she claps. I grab my napkin, wipe my mouth, and smile. My right foot jumps nervously under the table.

With the immediate attention off of me, I settle back into my thoughts. I will suggest the delay and hope she agrees with it. I hope she will not be angry as she has been with my father.

"Alyssa, you have a nice smile, just like your father. Though I cannot recall your mother's features well. The last time I saw her was on her wedding day," Lady Jacqueline says between bites of her carrot cake. Hearing this, I smile at her, then turn my head to face all of the ladies one by one.

I continue to stare at my food and get lost in my thoughts. My father's passion is in movie production, though he had countless failures when it came to acting. I smile before taking a drink. Suddenly, my phone chimes. I gasp and accidentally drop a knife on the floor. One of my hands tries to look at the message that just came in as the other stretches to get hold of the knife. Neither action is going very well.

"Excuse me, Miss. Here is a new knife for you. We will take care of the dirty one," a waiter says to me from just beyond my shoulder.

"Thank you," I reply with a smile as I straighten.

My eyes look over the ladies at the table, busy talking and laughing with each other. *Guess this is my chance to read and reply to my message quickly*. I sneak a look at my phone. I smile, seeing that the message is from Jamie. My heart races, and my palm start to sweat, feeling the adrenaline surge through me from his words. "I love you. I miss you," is written, followed by a heart emoji.

I respond to him with my own heart-shaped emoji

and start with the message, "I love you, too." Huge foot-steps near my side and a loud, glass-clinking sound sweep through the air. I quickly press send and shove my phone into my pocket.

The golf course manager, a man in his thirties with black hair and dark skin, appears at our table. "We are ready with three four-seater golf carts to take the ten of you to look around the green. This golf course is famous for its tranquility and has many lakes with a wonderful breeze." He shows some of the photos on the pamphlet he is holding. He grins widely, his mouth baring his white teeth. "So, enjoy the breathtaking view, ladies." He inclines his head in respect before walking to the front of the restaurant.

"Oh, why not start soon? The earlier we head over, the faster we get home," a lady from Grandma's company's subsidiary named Theresa Tan suggests. The other ladies agree and begin to gather themselves. Grandma's phone rings, and she grabs it, placing it at her ear.

"Hello, an urgent discussion via FaceTime now?" Her voice turns firm, and her eyes narrow. "Yes, sure. Just give me a minute to pull up my iPad. I need to switch to another device, Mr. Sauk." She quickly slips her hand into her bag and grabs her iPad.

She turns to the rest of the group, regret in her tone. "Sorry, ladies, please go ahead without me. I just received an urgent business call from Asia that I cannot decline." She waves her iPad, pushes her chair backward, and gets up.

Grandma waves at me to join the others. "Alyssa, please join on my behalf. I will be here waiting for you."

I nod in agreement. It won't hurt to look at the scenery. I quickly text Jamie, "I am off on a golf cart journey.

I hope it is not dull."

I hop on the third cart and settle into my seat, smiling at myself as the breeze already feels wonderful against my face.

We pass by lush greenery with a lake in the shape of an A in the middle of the golf course. We stop as ladies from the other two golf carts request time to snap some photos near the lake. While they take pictures, my eyes trail over the surroundings while I stand a few steps away from the lake. *Golfers must feel tranquil, with a lake and greenery encircling the golf course. No wonder so many working people join this game. I can believe it does relieve one's work stress.*

After about thirty minutes at the lake, we hop on the carts to move to the next stop. As we drive, the weather changes from sunny to brisk wind. Leaves on the nearby trees dance fiercely to and fro, and my light jacket flaps wildly. I quickly grab my jacket and zip it. "Weather changes fast at this golf course," one of the ladies says from upfront.

We stop at another lake, smaller than the other, with white lily bushes skirting the edge. It looks beautiful, and the other two golf carts stop for photos. I climb down from my cart, eager to snap some nice Instagram pics. This side of the course overlooks the mountains in the distance. I turn to face opposite the lake, and I quickly take out my mobile to take some selfies with the peaks as my background.

One of the caddies announces via the PA, "We have one mile to go before reaching the entrance, ladies. There is one last water feature after this lake. It's smaller, with some bushes, palm trees from Dubai are planted surrounding the corner of the lake, and nice camellia and azaleas flowers are blooming."

"Oh, that sounds beautiful. Come, let's go now, ladies," Teresa Tan suggests while waving at the other ladies, who smile at her and comply.

Upon sitting in the cart again, I close my eyes, letting the breeze wash over my cheeks and eyes. Serenity settles over my body, and I sigh contentedly before looking out again.

Oh, this is indeed a gorgeous lake. There is a lovely straight and unbranched stem of palm trees standing tall beside a small lake a few feet away.

I close my eyes again, enjoying the breeze brushing my face.

Suddenly, loud gunshots pierce the still afternoon, ringing in my ears. Instinctually, I cover my ears. I open my eyes, my heart skipping as I look around. I jolt from my seat as my eyes skim forward and stretch my neck to watch as the electric cart furthest front jerks. Their caddy driver slumps in the cart. A few seconds later, from my spot, I can see his head hanging at the side of the cart, a gory mess. My muscles stiffen, and his body gets thrown from the cart. Unconsciously, I start rubbing my neck.

What I am looking at is like a movie scene; I must be dreaming. I rub my eyes hard, sure they were playing tricks on me.

I strain my neck and squint my eyes to see clearer. Two men in black masks hold rifles in front of the stopped cart. One points their rifle at one of the ladies, Lady Jacqueline. She is wearing a blue checked button-down jacket with matching pants. She had invited me to visit her boutique when I visit Paris.

The other three ladies hold their hands up, and the other masked man shouts, pointing his rifle and forcing them to get down. On trembling hands, they place their faces on the grass. The man knocks their heads with the back of the gun, and they fall unconscious immediately. I breathe in deeply and swallow hard, only mild relief filling me as their chests move up and down.

The carts behind the first quickly swerve to the side to escape from the gunmen. However, the cart in front of us has its tires shot by the gunmen as it turns, causing it to screech, jostle, and topple. I watch from the corner of my eyes as the four ladies in the cart are thrown from the cart, their bodies landing a few feet away. Two land on their heads on the grass, the other two with their faces buried in the grass. I rock from side to side, my mind racing, trying to think of something to help.

Our driver is cunning. He makes a reversed turn as fast as possible. The woman sitting beside me quickly calls 911 as another calls the golf course management.

When she takes out her mobile to call for help, I see a pistol sitting in her purse.

"Does it have any bullets?"

"Yes, it is full," she replies in a shaky voice while her left hand pats the gun.

"I am borrowing." I snatch it and shake her hand to let go of her mobile once she is done talking. Without thinking thoroughly and though my heart is pounding as I fight the rising panic, I jump out of the cart, roll over three times, and hide in one of the white lily bushes. My eyes dart from the bushes and over the palm trees of odd sizes planted just beside the first cart. Seeing the two masked men busy focused on the ladies from the other two carts, I quickly run into the vast palm trees to hide. While running, I grab onto my left knee to ensure stability since I am trembling with fear.

"Who is Lady Jacqueline?" the taller masked man shouts.

Lady Jacqueline raises her right hand slowly. "I— it's me you are looking for. I'll do whatever you want as long as you spare my friends' lives," she replies in a shaky voice, her hand in the air, trembling.

"We only want you. You got what we want," the other man, still pointing his rifle at her forehead, says hoarsely behind his mask.

Seeing this, fury vibrates through my body. I slid my hand into my sling bag to take out my purse that has a picture of Lady Jacqueline and me from when I was nine years old. Tears develop in my eyes, and my index finger touches the photo. She took care of me for a year while my parents had a heated divorce and my grandmother was overseas for business dealings. *I have to save her.*

I am confident that I can shoot the men if required. My jaw tightens, thinking of this. *Thank God I had to take that gun handling class for my PI license. It will help me save some people, I hope.* I press my lips together tightly and breathe in deeply.

You can do it, Alyssa. You are going to be a heroine. All of them are Grandmother's best friends, and I need to save them.

I text Grandmother and Eleanor, "Please send help. I will follow the abductors if needed."

Once I press the send button, a sudden barrage of bullets sounds in the air. Immediately, I peer through the palm trees as I stuff my phone back into my pocket.

The two older ladies sitting in the same cart with Lady Jacqueline are moving quickly, their legs trembling and holding hands as tears roll down their cheeks. One trips and falls, and the other tries to pull her back to her feet.

Gunfire sounds in the sky again. My eyes dart in the direction of the attackers. *Did they shoot any of the ladies?* I strain my neck to look at the women. One of the ladies has frozen, her chest rising in irregular patterns upon hearing the gunshot. Her friend extends a hand and gives her a nudge to continue walking.

One of the masked men steps toward their direction, his right arm rising upward and shooting the sky again. He sneers and shouts harshly, "Run, old ladies. Run for your lives and hide away. I will shoot you if I can still see you after counting to ten." He laughs and throws a toothpick on the ground.

The man waves his pistol when the two ladies turn their heads to look at him. Their foreheads crease and both push each other to move faster. His mouth curves as he starts counting. "1, 2, 3, 4, 5 . . ." He stop talking as his head tilts. He shouts, "I can still see you." He rocks side to side and laughs with his free hand holding his belt.

One of the ladies turns her head, and I recognize her features as Teresa. She pulls the other lady to run faster.

The masked man continues counting. "6, 7 . . . You better hide, old ladies." He laughs again and starts pointing his pistol toward them.

My throat tightens at the predicament the 60-something women are facing. *How can I help them?* My head turns, and my eyes cast around the surroundings.

One of them runs in the direction of the palm trees where I am hiding. Theresa steps hurriedly in the direction of some lily bushes.

His harsh voice lingers in the air as he yells, "I can still see you, you old greedy lady." Hearing this, fear knots in my stomach, and I look at the source of the voice. His finger pulls the trigger of the pistol, and the bullet misses her by inches. Theresa ducks down and crawls, pushing her elbows into the grass with tears rolling down her cheeks.

The unhinged man steps closer as he says, "8, 9, 10," and shoots in their direction. The bullet sprays dirt near the bushes. He bends over as he releases a sinister laugh.

I wipe my sweat as Teresa hides in the bushes in the nick of time, surrounded by palm trees, before the masked man releases any more bullets. I blow my bangs aside and start breathing normally. The other lady makes it into hiding as well, just in time.

Seeing both of them are safe, I turn my head, and my eyes dart from one end of the course to another, searching for Lady Jacqueline. I'm too far away to do much without the attackers being able to see me. I visualize the plan to save her while my right hand lands on my right cheek.

As soon as an idea pops into my head, I leap and run as fast as my legs can carry me, hiding behind the overturned second cart. I pray that the masked men don't see me. Once I arrive at the back of the cart, I accidentally step on a branch, a slight cracking sound emitting in the air. I freeze momentarily as I feel my face turn pale. The overturned cart's four ladies are injured and cowering nearby. One of them looks at me frantically. I place a finger across my lips, and she lets out a wail in the direction of the masked man. *Hopefully, they don't suspect anything.* One of the masked men turns his head to look at the lady, his mouth moving in silent grumbles, and points his gun in her direction. Instantly, she stops wailing, remaining silent and crouching as she covers her head with her hands.

I can see the cart in front. One masked man has tied Jacqueline's hands, gagged her mouth, and blindfolded her. He looks around and grunts. "Damn, what is taking

Jojo so long?" He looks restless, his left leg bouncing, and he starts to pace a few steps.

His companion walks toward the overturned cart, still grumbling under his breath. I crouch further and try to make myself as invisible as possible. My eyes skim over the various types of golf clubs spilling from the cart.

When I turn my face to the right side, there is one club lying beside me.

As the man walks to my spot, I swing one of the iron clubs beside me in front of the man's leg. He trips and falls, clutching his rifle and shooting wildly; lucky for me, he shoots in the opposite direction.

"Who's there? Come and face me!" he says in a biting shriek. He looks down at the ground and quiets. "Oh, damn. It's just a club," he grumbles to himself, massaging his knee.

The sound of screeching tires emanates in the air, and police sirens sound from the opposite direction. I crouch and peek from behind the cart to watch a different vehicle appear before the police. It is a black Jeep Wrangler moving at top speed toward us. While I am looking at the vehicle, rustling grass catches my attention, and I turn my head, blinking at the man I knocked down with the golf club. He has gotten up and is patting his knees while looking at the Jeep. Quickly, I bang him with a golf stick on his butt, causing him to tumble to the ground again. His fingers are quick to pull the trigger in my direction, but my hands are faster. His thigh is hit by my bullet, and a pained grimace steals over his face. He limps and occasionally jumps as he moves toward the car, his jeans soaked with blood. Within a few steps, he turns his head, his jaw tightens, and his eyes lock on me. He swiftly pulls a pistol from his boot and pulls the trigger in my direction. I drop flat, and my hands cover my head, the shot just missing. I pant as ringing sounds in my ears.

He hobbles to the car, Lady Jaqueline being manhandled up by the other man. I scramble up and run at full speed to the Jeep. *If I don't follow, we will never be able to locate Lady Jacqueline.* The Jeep screeches to a stop next to the abductors, its trunk springing open suddenly as the car shudders slightly. Without thinking, I dive into the messy back. Breathing deeply with my collar sweating, I quickly pull a PVC cover over my head. I switch on my FindMy app tracker and send a message to Eleanor. "I am in the trunk of a black Wrangler. Help."

"Get in, you fool woman!" the man screams up front. A moment later, the car door slams shut.

Within seconds, the Wrangler is moving like a Formula One car. The ride is bumpy, and my body keeps knocking on the side of the trunk. I quickly cover my mouth with my left hand to prevent any noise from escaping. It's quiet for a few minutes, but eventually, I hear gunfire being exchanged between this car and what I presume is a police car. There is a loud crash, and metal groaning fills the air.

"Yeah, one down. Let's hurry," the kidnapper shouts.

The engine reeves, and the vehicle skids around a sharp bend, speeding away as fast as it can. The route is even bumpier, as though there isn't actually a road we are following.

My hands tremble, and I can feel sweat pooling on my neck, only occasional grunts or pained moans from the back seat piercing the silence throughout the journey to the unknown.

After what feels like an eternity but, in reality, is probably only ten minutes, the car screeches to a halt with a bang. The men start getting out of the car. One of the abductors tries to pull Lady Jacqueline from the backseat, and she fights him with all her might. I instantly open the trunk wider, roll over, fall to the ground, and close it. Seeing some bushes with huge worn tin barrels beside this car, I seek refuge there.

Lucky for me, when I jump out of the Jeep, the driver is busy speaking on the phone, and the others are occupied, ensuring Lady Jacqueline stops struggling and her arms are retied. They look sweaty, and I can't help but feel a fierce jolt of pride at her fight.

I quickly text Eleanor and Grandmother for backup. I remain quiet at my spot, snapping pictures of the place: a rundown warehouse with an attached house. The chimney is smoking. I guess someone lives here. Tons and tons of tin drums with worn-out tires and parts of damaged cars lie near the warehouse.

I inch a little nearer as they drag Lady Jacqueline toward the building. I muster my courage to peep through the broken window beside the door to gauge the surroundings for me to hide and plan an escape for Lady Jacqueline. Before I take another step, I check my messages.

"Right on. I know where you are," replies Eleanor.

"My security guys will work hand in hand with Eleanor to save both of you. Be extra careful," Grandmother writes.

I don't want to be caught, so I can only enter when the sun sets or when those guys leave her alone. While waiting, a tiny flicker of wind passes by my face. I hug myself, and my hand rubs my arm, impatiently waiting to be able to take some action.

I remain in my hiding place beside the broken window, thankful that I can hear their voices clearly. I stop rubbing my arm and step closer.

"Tell us where you keep the $100 billion gold bar!" The taller man pulls her silky black hair toward him. She whimpers, trying to withhold the pain. Lady Jacqueline's head is jerked to the left as the man slaps her. Red marks blossom on her cheek.

The sound of a car engine sounds at the back of my ears, and goose bumps glide over my skin, and I duck. The car door flings open, and a man in his forties wearing a golden chain around his neck with matching white trousers and a gelled crew cut appears from the chauffeur-driven car. I slink further into my hiding spot amongst the tin drums. My leg starts to tremble, and my body squeezes together to remain as small as possible. My right hand stabilizes my leg.

His fat palm is about to strike a blow on the wooden door when one of the kidnappers pushes it open. "She ain't talking, Boss."

"Let's go with Plan B." His mustache screws to the side as his hands rub together. He grins happily, and shivers run down my spine as they disappear inside.

The door is slow to close, and seeing my chance, I quickly slip in behind them. I spot some old steel cabinets and dart in their direction. As I move, I realize we are not in an abandoned warehouse. There are many worn medical appliances like Jolls thyroid retractors, Gigli saws, bone cutters and nibblers, ancient oxygen devices, heart and lungs machines, and Gatch beds. I gulp, and I recall seeing these as I was reading about criminals selling off body parts.

Are we in an abandoned hospital, or is this a place for the crooks to operate on people's organs and sell them? A sudden rush of shudders moves from the end of my neck and down my back, thinking that I can be their victim if I'm not careful. I pull the cupboard door to cover me but leave it ajar just enough to see.

"Lady Jacqueline, if you love your life, give me the $100 billion gold bar." The man in white gestures for Lady Jacqueline to hand it over. "Pull down her gag so she can speak clearly," the man says while pointing at her.

The blonde Jeep driver pulls down the cloth gag severely, hitting her chest, and she grimaces in pain. She breathes rapidly, and I watch as her chest moves up and down in a shallow beat. Tears roll from her eyes.

"Who are you? Please, I only have half the worth of the gold bar. Please, call my husband," she replies in a shaky voice, her head tilting to look at the man in white.

"Sounds perfect. I am your husband's friend. Unfortunately, he did not accept my business proposal." He walks opposite Lady Jacqueline, his hands clutching each other behind his back. He moves closer, his face next to her ear. "So here you are, the victim of his business failures. I am the famous Jake Kane." He steps backward, feet stomping, and snorts. She cries harder and rocks her body on the chair.

I gulp, and my throat tightens. *What is taking Eleanor so long to bring backup?*

The so-called boss punches Lady Jacqueline in her face suddenly, blood flying from her mouth, and one of her teeth falls from her mouth at the impact.

"Please, call my husband for the ransom! Please, spare my life," Lady Jacqueline pleads in pain, tears rolling down her cheeks.

"Very well." He places his hand in his pocket and takes out his phone.

"Duke Jacque Jules, it's me, Jake Kane." He stands

while looking at Lady Jacqueline, a cold smile taking over his face. "I spoke to you last month at the French Embassy festivals. You were wickedly cold-hearted and turned down my business proposal. You will pay for that." He pauses before continuing, "We have your wife captive." A moment of silence passes before he barks in laughter.

"You don't believe me?" Jake Kane immediately presses something on the screen, and Lord Jacque appears. Jake shifts his phone to show the bloody face of Lady Jacqueline.

"Please. Please do not harm my wife." Duke Jacque's voice shakes.

Jake smiles cruelly. "Bring me the $100 billion gold bar to Luxor Mint Hotel by tonight. If I see any suspicious activity from you or the police, I will not hesitate to end your wife's life and eventually yours." Jake flips his mobile to face him, his jaw tightening while he gives his warning.

"Jake! Please don't hurt Lady Jacqueline. I will find the gold bar. Give me a day. Please. Please!" Duke Jacque begs.

Jake Kane just stares with piercing eyes and ends the call.

"Lock her up immediately," Jake Kane shouts as he angrily rolls his sleeves, exposing a tattoo of a crescent and a uniquely designed knife.

The bald kidnapper harshly tugs Lady Jacqueline into his huge arms. Lady Jacqueline kicks her legs against his tummy, but he is undeterred. His muscular hand lands across her face, and a shudder runs through her. She quickly turns obedient. He pushes her onto the chair when he sees the boss gesture for him to follow.

Jake Kane walks by my spot, and I inhale deeply to ensure I don't make any noises. My pulse thunders when he stops directly beside my hiding spot. "Once we get everything we demand, kill her without remorse." He pulls the man's shirt roughly. "Understood, Joe?"

"Yes, Boss." He nods, giving him a thumbs-up.

"Meanwhile, let her live as our bait. You wait until I give you further instruction." A cigarette butt falls from his mouth, and he steps on it before walking away.

I release my breath slowly and silently. I can feel as my face turns pale.

The entrance to the abandoned hospital shuts, and the old wall made from mixed wood shudders.

The room grows silent, and I realize the men are with Jake Kane outside the hospital, taking for granted that Lady Jacqueline didn't need to be guarded. I quietly open the cabinet door, crouch down, and run to her while glancing at the entrance several times. My heart pounds, and I stay as quiet as possible. I am cautious of the path I take, not wishing to knock into anything while I hurry toward Lady Jacqueline.

When I am a few feet away from Lady Jacqueline's spot, I can see that she is tied to a steel chair with a new gag on her mouth. The gag has a blood spot coming from her mouth.

I crouch at her side and clear my throat to get her attention. "Lady Jacqueline, I am here to save you," I whisper with a look at the door. She opens her eyes and starts making noise when they land on my face. I place my index finger across my lips while facing her. Instantly, she turns quiet and nods once.

I quickly grab the bone cutter lying on the table two steps away. The bone cutter cuts into the thick rope that ties Lady Jacqueline's wrists tightly. My palm chokes up its handle several times, then begin to crush the material bit by bit.

I quickly place the phone I took from the woman next to me on the golf cart in Lady Jacqueline's jacket pocket. I hear the hinge of the door creak and freeze. Without looking at the entrance, I know that the abductors have entered, and I instantly change my position. I crawl on my hands and knees on the cold cement floor. I crawl as fast as I can to hide amongst the barrels behind the chair that Lady Jacqueline is sitting in. While hiding, I place my hands over my mouth, trying to quiet my breathing. *The cutter, where is it? Oh, my God, it's lying on the floor underneath Lady Jacqueline's chair. I must have thrown it on the floor in haste.* Sweat starts to soak underneath my armpit.

My hands tremble, and I start to panic, panting. My right hand covers my mouth tightly, and my vision grows fuzzy. *Please remain calm, Alyssa. You are here to help, not be a victim.*

"What in the world? Hey, Joe, you clumsy man, you dropped the cutter?" The masked man slaps Joe's bald head before he takes his mask off. This man is also blonde with a ship tattoo on his wrist.

"Hey, man, I didn't touch it. Wasn't me." He shakes his head vehemently.

"Then, who did?" Joe shrugs, touching his chin.

Suddenly, both twist at their waists, and their eyes move from one side then to the edge of the abandoned hospital.

'Is there anyone here?' the blonde shouts while loading his gun.

Butterflies flutter in my stomach, and a shudder runs

through me. I still my breath to maintain my composure. Dizziness creeps through my veins, and my vision blurs. I grip my jacket and close my eyes.

Two black cats run from between the barrels, hitting some hospital appliances on the steel table as they chase each other, sweeping the tools across the floor.

"Damn these cats. They must have hit those cutters under her chair," the blonde man says as he relaxes his stance. He flips his jacket open and holsters his pistol in one of the pockets.

Slowly, my dizziness disperses, and I stay crouching as quietly as possible. I breathe deeply. *I am safe for the moment.*

Chapter 14

Joe puffs smoke nearby.

The other abductor stands opposite Joe and says, "Bring her to ward Jupiter." He pats Joe's shoulder. Joe nods. The other abductor grabs his mobile from his pocket and walks away, holding it to his ear. He talks on the phone facing the entrance door, and a few minutes pass. Joe still smokes and fiddles with his phone.

Lady Jacqueline remains in the chair, sniffing. The blonde returns from his call and looks at Joe. Face turning red, he slaps Joe's bald head and sharply elbows him.

"What are you waiting for? Now! Now! Now!" he shouts, with both hands in tight fists at his sides.

Joe immediately throws his cigarette butt and massages his head. "OK, Jim. Geez."

Joe harshly pulls Lady Jacqueline from the chair, sending a glare over his shoulder at Jim. He pushes Lady Jacqueline forward with a rifle in one hand, guiding her toward a door on an inside wall. Jim lingers in the spot where Lady Jacqueline was tied, and it's too risky for me to follow. I remain at my spot, spying on him.

Once Joe leaves, Jim, with a cigarette in his mouth, turns his head to look around the abandoned hospital floor. His black boots squeak softly as he walks from one drum to the next. His eyes dart around before his eyes land on the supplies on the table and the cutter underneath the chair. His rifle is held tensely in his hand.

I freeze, not moving a muscle or breathing so as not to draw any attention to myself.

"I know you're hiding somewhere. Come out now!" He raises his voice and shouts to the empty air. The end of the rifle shifts from one drum to another.

Alyssa, keep still and do not utter a word. Jim is trying his luck to muddle with my confidence, I chant in my head as blood pounds in my ears.

His phone rings. He quickly pulls it from his pants pocket and looks at the screen before placing the receiver at his mouth. "Yes, Jake. I have Lady Jacqueline sorted out." He pauses, his eyebrows furrowing. "You need me to go to the shipment now?" His shoulders slouch as his free hand massages the side of his head. "Affirmative, Jake. I will be there in a jiffy." He ends the call and places his mobile back in his pocket.

Jim's eyes scan the room one last time before he walks away from my hiding spot and out the entrance.

A few moments later, a car door slams, and an engine ignites. He speeds off, and I breathe out in relief. Raising my head from the drum barrel to look at the entrance, my sight moves to the other parts of the abandoned hospital to ensure that I am safe to move from my hiding place to rescue Lady Jacqueline. Only two people are left for me to fight.

I text Eleanor that Jake Kane and Jim have left the building. I have two more men to handle to rescue Lady

Jacqueline.

"There will be two police cars nearing. Please be safe."

I scroll to my FindMy app and watch the blinking red light for a moment, the tracking device indicating that Lady Jacqueline is hidden near the exit. It must be the basement. I walk through the door Joe left through with Lady Jacqueline, tiptoeing to prevent loud noises.

Once I reach the landing, I raise my phone to get a better signal and find the exact location of Lady Jacqueline. As I raise my arms, the door on the left side of the stairs swings open. Hearing this, my heartbeat races again, and my mouth drops in a small gasp. I run back up the staircase. It's not a great hiding place since there is the other door that someone could enter through and see me easily, but I have to keep my hopes up that no one new has arrived. Well, I don't have any choices at the moment. My head, body, arms, and legs lean against the wall while I tuck my tummy in to ensure I am well hidden.

"Yes, Boss. I injected her with the sleeping pills and cuffed her to the bed. Dr. Lorenzo will remove her organs one by one once you give us the green light," Joe says over his phone.

My hand flies to my chest, and I freeze momentarily. *I must prevent this from happening.* I bare my teeth and clench my fists.

His footsteps are noisy, walking toward the staircase hallway where I am hiding.

I breathe in deeply, trying to hold my breath and think of something to do.

Where am I to hide without being caught? Shall I walk upstairs instead?

As the footsteps approach and I feel like I might faint

from stress, the footsteps recede, and the rasping sound of a rusty door hinge rings in my ears.

I sneak to the edge of the staircase to peek at the door and any electronic devices it might have attached to it. No sophisticated gadgets are attached to it, and I run a hand over my face as I release my breath.

I wait for two minutes, ensuring that Joe isn't returning. When I am confident that he is gone and no one is in the hallway, I tiptoe toward the room he came out of earlier.

I nudge the handle, but the heavy brass is locked. I shake the door, but it remains stable. I stomp my feet and kick the door. Nothing seems to be working.

My eyes dart around, searching for something sharp to unlock the door. I groan; the cement floor is clear of any sharp items. I search in my pockets for something sharp and thin. While ferreting around, I feel something thick and squarish. I pull it out and grin—my library card.

Quickly, I hold the doorknob in the normal direction for opening the door, slipping the card through the jamb. I wriggle it back and forth, finagling it until it bends into an S-shape.

Sweat drips from my forehead as I feel frantic to open the door and save Lady Jacqueline. I have a gut feeling the men will return for her any minute. My ears stay alert for any sound for me to run for cover.

I continue resolutely wriggling it in a sawing motion. I feel the card next to the latch bolt, which releases it from the strike plate.

Immediately, I kick the door with my muscular leg, the intensity strong enough to open it. The first thing I see is Lady Jacqueline half asleep from the sleeping drugs injected in her, with a gag full of blood, and her hands actually cuffed with handcuffs this time. She is lying on a decrepit mattress with holes at the edge.

Scanning the room quickly for any water to splash on her face to make her conscious, I spot a basin on a table next to a window with a rusty steel frame. The window is half a foot taller than me, and I stand on the balls of my feet to look through the window. I smile when I see a car; it's Eleanor and her colleague.

I sprinkle water on Lady Jacqueline's face, and her almond-colored eyes fly open, straining as though she sees a ghost. I smile and hold her hand gently. "It's me, Alyssa. I am rescuing you. Please remain alert and quiet," I whisper to her.

I find the edge of the gag and remove it from her mouth. I cast about the room and find steel scissors in one of the bare, dented chests of drawers. I close the drawer, and my gaze catches on two paperclips just barely underneath the drawer. I smile, grab them, and straighten them, accidentally breaking the first one. Being much more careful with the second, I fashion it at a 90-degree angle and fit it halfway into the cuffs. After a moment of fiddling, a click sounds, and they fall to the ground, unlocked.

Both of our mouths curve into smiles as hope fills my chest.

In the distance, faint footsteps can be heard.

I turn my head, looking at the door, and bite my lip. A sudden feeling of nausea seeps up my throat.

I swallow hard and use two fingers to gesture us running and point at the window, my heart sinking at Lady Jacqueline's doubtful expression.

Looking at the window causes fear to throb inside of me, but I have to try to break it.

As I am about to swing the steel scissors against the

glass, I step onto something that makes a dull clang and protrudes through the carpet. I wince in pain and hop. I push the dusty carpet aside and see a small handle. There isn't a lock, so I'm able to open it without problems. Dim light fills the passageway, and damp and dusty smells assault me. I thrust my sleeve to cover my nose, stopping a sneeze. The heavy footsteps are getting louder, just outside the door now. My heart beats faster as I glance over my shoulder. The only way to hide at this moment is this passageway. Otherwise, we are dead meat.

I point my index finger to the secret passageway direction, and Lady Jacqueline blinks at me. "Come, follow me into the secret passageway," I whisper to her. Her head shakes, and her arms cross her chest. I rub my shoulder, then tug her hands harshly. I whisper, "I will follow soon." She looks at the door, and tears roll down her cheeks as she jumps into it, landing clumsily on the damp floor.

I drag the heavy carpet, my sweat trickling across my forehead, and it takes more effort than I expect to move it back over the passage and me.

I place one foot hanging down in the hole, the other leg bending to remain on the floor beside the opening. I try to close the lid and struggle to pull the carpet to cover the secret passageway's entrance.

Time slows as the door's hinges open inch by inch, and my eyes widen while looking at the door. In the nick of time, I'm able to cover everything. I let go, and my body drops through the air and onto the damp floor.

My breath heaves, and I blink several times. I quickly get up and brush my pants to get rid of some of the mud.

Footsteps sound above our heads, the thumping sound of heavy boots signaling at least two people.

I gesture at Lady Jacqueline to follow me. The passage is dusty and damp, and both of us cover our noses, our eyes slowly adjusting to the dim light of the pathway.

I take out my phone, turning on the flashlight as we start on our journey. The voices of the men grow louder, and furniture crash to the floor above. We both look at each other, and Lady Jacqueline gulps. I gesture for her to hurry.

I blow my fringe and sigh. There is no network, and I can't message Eleanor about our whereabouts. We walk for a few minutes, and I nearly shout my head off when a rat passes by my leg. My eyes grow wide, and my left hand covers Lady Jacqueline's mouth just in time; only a gagging sound slips through her lips. I breathe out heavily and continue forward, biting my lip.

The tunnel eventually lightens, and we reach a bright opening with murky and muddy water rising just above our ankles. I place my index finger under my chin, wondering if the aperture leads to a river. As we step closer to the outside opening, water dripping can be heard, and we have to squint against the blinding sunlight. I place an arm just above my forehead to shade my eyes.

Chapter 15

The sound of bullets rings just outside the opening with blazing sunlight.

Lady Jacqueline, who is walking behind me, stops abruptly and accidentally hits my shoulder as she steps up next to me.

She turns her gaze, watching the fast-running water in the river.

I breathe rapidly, trying to maintain my composure. I turn my neck to look to the left, my mouth curving upward.

There are a few man-made wooden ladders crossing to the other bank of long unkempt grass.

I wave at Lady Jacqueline to tag along. She nods, her face tight and worried.

We reach the beginning of a ladder and turn our heads from one end to the other, getting an overall view of it.

"There are a few broken pieces and steps where we will have to jump to another ladder to get on the other side. This is the only way out of the abandoned hospital. You can jump?" My hands open in a questioning gesture.

"I will try my best." She nods, even though her forehead crinkles and her hands tremble.

I check my phone one last time and grin. "I have service; let me text Eleanor before we start. I need to inform her of our whereabouts." I quickly send the message before tucking my phone in my pocket.

I look at Lady Jacqueline's eyes and say, "I count to three, and we start. Whatever happens, do not look back." She nods and clasps her shaking hands together.

"You go first. Let me guard and guide you from behind." She smiles weakly and steps forward.

She puts her right foot on the first wooden step, then, feeling confident, her left foot lands on the same step. The steps are small and uneven in size, and she wobbles. One of her feet slips into the water. She is within reach of my arms, so I pull on her jacket to help balance her. She breathes quickly and gives me a quick nod of thanks.

My face shifts closer to her ear so she can hear me over the rushing water. "Open your arms out to the side to balance yourself." My arms open to show her what I mean.

Without hesitation, she sticks her arms out to her sides and steps from one ladder step to the next. Her steps are steady, and her body is balanced this time.

I walk directly behind her and say, "OK, good, go on to the next step. This time faster." I draw in a sharp breath when I glance back and can see two figures in the distance. A sudden panic blooms inside my heart. "They are nearing," I say loudly to Lady Jacqueline.

Hearing my last statement, Lady Jacqueline's face turns tense, and she quickens her steps, jumping to another wooden rung. I follow behind her. There is one step that gives way under her weight, but her reflexes are fast this time. Her shoe manages to barely sweep above the water, and I quickly grab her waist and steady her.

"Keep going."

She jumps and lands neatly on the next step.

We only have five more steps when a gunshot sounds in the air. I recognize the man from the corner of my eyes and gulp. Joe is at the foot of the opening.

"Quick!" My heart pounds, and I turn back to our task.

Lady Jacqueline trembles terribly, and tears start falling from her eyes, blurring her vision.

"Please be careful and hurry. Otherwise, we will be dead meat," I whisper.

I take the lead, moving with each foot on a different step, my weight balancing between the two.

"Lady Jacqueline, please do what I am doing. One foot on each step. This way is faster," I yell over the sound of the water.

I turn to raise my hands to assure her that she is safe and can do it.

From my spot, I have two steps to the other side and quickly cross to land. I raise my thumbs up and smile encouragingly. "Good, you are doing great."

When she's on solid ground as well, my eyes dart from left to right. We are surrounded by wild oat grass and bushes. I run a hand through my hair and rock on the balls of my feet. *Where to run and save our lives?*

Suddenly, the sound of bullets fills the air. My head turns, and Joe is halfway across the steps of the river.

My pulse skyrockets, and I gesture to Lady Jacqueline.

"Come on, let's go this way."

We shove through the long bushes with our bare hands, slipping on muddy land and getting tangled in the grass.

"Please leave without me," she cries and gestures at

me when she falls on the muddy ground for the fifteenth time, tears rolling down her cheeks.

"No! I am not going to leave you here. You have children who want their mother to be alive."

I move to her side and pull her up while holding her hands, guiding her through our escape route.

She rubs her eyes and breathes deeply, nodding to me after a moment.

We change our course of direction to further right. There are lots of unused drums lying around. I turn my head to check on Joe, and I gasp as my eyes lock with his menacing green eyes, barely forty feet from where we are.

He points his gun directly at my chest, and I grab Lady Jacqueline's hands, pulling her into a crouch and hiding in the tall grass. He yells in frustration as we disappear from sight, and a small sense of satisfaction fills my chest momentarily.

My eyebrows pull together, and sweat rolls down my temple. While this position makes it harder for us to move quickly, at least we are hidden. I peek over the top of the grass and point my gun, pulling the trigger and aiming for his leg.

His face grimaces, and he yells in pain, his hands holding his leg as blood becomes visible. He tears part of his shirt to wrap his bleeding leg. "Run, now," I whisper to her.

We get up, keeping our backs bent so that the long grass hides us. I urge us to move faster, and my jacket accidentally catches on a thicker reed, creating a small scratch on my jacket and jerking me out of balance for a second. We pass several barrels, and the scent of oil makes my nose wrinkle.

Even though one of Joe's legs is injured, it doesn't

deter him from chasing after us. He continues chasing while limping along with another guy, which must be the doctor that was mentioned. Joe's face is bright red and intense, whether from anger or pain, I can't tell.

My fear doubles when he points his gun at Lady Jacqueline, and I quickly jump onto her, trying to prevent her from getting hurt. We land on the ground, and the bullet passes just above my head. Even though it misses hitting us, the bullet smashes through a drum. Dark liquid pours through the holes that the bullet created.

My nose twitches as the smell grows overwhelming. My heartbeat ticks like the seconds of a wristwatch. *Are we safe hiding and walking around here where the ground is covered with flammable gasoline?*

As we run further, we spot four cars. One I recognize as Eleanor's, and another is a police vehicle.

Eleanor and her partners are within our sight, and she is cuffing the blonde man, Jim, who looks injured by the blood on his left hand.

Relief floods me at seeing Eleanor and her police colleagues nearby. Feeling confident that nothing can happen to Lady Jacqueline and me, both of us walk toward the gravel lot where the cars are parked.

Lady Jacqueline walks in front of me, her face gleaming with a relieved smile, and she walks confidently out of the grass and toward the car.

I am a few steps behind her, still among the grass. There are a few dirty barrels lying around, and I shudder. I lift my foot to follow her when an angry shout breaks through my thoughts. "You ain't going anywhere!"

I turn my head to look where Joe is standing approximately sixteen feet away. His body is hidden among the tall, thick grass bushes, and only his head is visible to me.

The other man standing beside him hands Joe something. I strain my neck to see the item clearly, my eyes drawing together on my forehead. My hands freeze as I take in the object Joe is holding. Is it a hand mower or a hand vacuum cleaner? I shake my head, disbelieving my eyes. I can't see it clearly, and I step further back into the grass to figure out what Joe is doing.

My stomach sinks as I take in more of the object, still not understanding what it is but not having a good feeling about it. I crumple my jacket, and my hands start to tremble as I back away toward the cars.

The aide beside him pushes over the drum that was shot by Joe before continuing and pushing over more barrels. Liquid spills from the tops as Joe points the item at the drums. I swallow as the area rapidly turns into flames. Bit by bit, like water running, the fire spreads from one drum to the next, rolling in my direction.

A sudden surge of adrenaline persuades me to duck down and run as fast as I can.

Flamethrower.

This is the first time I have seen one with my eyes. I turn my head and realize that there are many similar drums located on the grounds I am standing in.

I feel the heat lick at my back and the fiery flames flash.

"Run, Lady Jacqueline, to the police car!" I scream while waving my hands in the sky.

I am slightly slow, and the tip of my shoe catches fire. I wriggle my foot out of the burnt shoe, limping with one shoe still intact on the other. I run as fast as my feet can carry me.

Turning my head to see the next action from Joe, Joe's aide reaches my previous spot. He shoots three holes into the drums and pushes all the fuel drums that have yet to burn, rolling them toward me. Once they've rolled a few feet forward, Joe stands beside him and triggers the flamethrower. The three drums light with a roaring fire as they bounce in my direction.

Both of them jump backward to safety, laughing manically.

I turn my head to the left, trying to think of a plan. I see bare land next to where Eleanor's car is parked, and without any hesitation, I jump toward it, not going toward Eleanor's car.

I am lucky; my feet are two inches away from a blazing drum hitting on my leg. I yelp as I throw myself forward again, trying to put as much distance between me and the fire as I can.

I fall on the bare ground with some spots of grass opposite from the blazing drum, my head hitting the ground.

Luckily, my hands manage to cover my forehead to prevent a serious impact. I quickly turn my head to check the fate of the others, panting.

From my spot, I watch the three drums of blazing fire roll and roll. Nearing Eleanor's car, one drum hits a second drum. The fire explodes, eventually hitting Eleanor's car. The blazing drums fly in the air after hitting hard against the car. My shoulders stiffen as horror sweeps through me.

A massive flame bursts into the air, and thick smoke engulfs the car. Seconds later, an explosion fills the air, throwing fire wide like tiny droplets. Metal shrapnel from the barrels cascades down, and I cover my face as bits brush my skin.

Lady Jacqueline and Eleanor manage to run, jump,

and roll away from the car before the blazing drum hits the car, which is now just a burning husk.

Feeling the heat finally die some, I roll over further in the mud at my side before I get up in a crouch and look over the spot where I last saw the others.

Where is Lady Jacqueline? Why is she not with Eleanor? I inch nearer and slide the long grass apart for a better view. Eleanor moves with the blonde guy cuffed beside her.

A faint "Help! Help!" reaches my ears, and my blood turns to ice. The voice sounds like Lady Jacqueline's. I lift higher and strain my eyes, trying to find her. My heart stops as I spot her being dragged away, wailing and kicking, by a man. His huge arm with a crescent and uniquely designed knife tattoo wraps firmly at her waist, seemingly unbothered by her struggling.

I holler in Eleanor's direction, my hands waving and pointing in the Wrangler's direction.

"Eleanor, please look in the direction of 12 o'clock. Lady Jacqueline is being kidnapped again. I placed a tracker in her jacket, and I can view it via my mobile. We can . . ." my voice breaks as it gets higher and higher.

I clear my throat to yell again, yet before I do, the ground shivers beneath me, and I pause. Pebbles start rolling, and the land shudders again, more violently than the first. Sediment and rocks tumble off the furthest left side from me as I look around wildly. Seeing this, I blink several times, my mouth dropping. A sudden surge of panic envelops my heart, and unconsciously, I crumple my jacket tightly. *What is happening?*

Cracking sounds ring in my ears, and I instantly stand up from my crouching position, sweat beading on my forehead, and I face the left. I squint my eyes, straining to reason what is happening.

Fear hammers in my chest as my mouth opens wider and my shoulders tense. Bit by bit, cracks appear on the ground, and suddenly, the ground at the edge of the bare area, along with its tall, thick spots of grass, is sucked away from the vulnerable ground. My leg muscles wobble, and I turn quickly, wanting to run away from the edge. I pull up short when I realize the nearest barren land is engulfed with fire from the drums.

My lips tremble, and tears gather in my eyes as cracks emerge just two inches from where I'm standing. I cast around quickly and face the front. There is one bulky four-foot-high tree without leaves. The ground around it looks stable. I clear my throat, my shoulders pushing down my back, and I crack my knuckles.

"Jump, Alyssa! Jump!" Eleanor shouts from her spot as her hands wave and point at the tree.

I throw my phone in Eleanor's direction and shout, "It's tracking Lady Jacqueline!" I turn to my task, pushing my fear to the back.

My right arm stretches, trying to grab hold of the naked tree branch. Two of my fingers touch the branch, but the fragile branch breaks in half, and I let go, shaking out my fingers. "Oh, my God. Please save me," I say in silent prayer inside my heart as panic threatens to overwhelm my determination.

I clench my teeth and shake my head, determined to stay alive. My leg stretches toward the tree, lifting from the ground and hanging onto a different, sturdier branch. I push off with my other leg just as the ground shakes and vanishes below into the river. I quickly pull myself onto the branch, out of breath. Sweat trickles down my forehead as relief washes over me. I look at the vanished ground, shivering as a waterfall catches my eye. I can feel as my face pales how long of a fall it is. Without wasting any time, I shift my weight to turn and get back on stable ground.

I scream, and the tree groans and drops under my movement. "Help me!"

The tree's roots start to surface from the ground, and slowly the tree tilts, bit by bit, to a more extreme angle. My mouth widens, and I hold onto the tree for dear life.

I shift my weight to jump as far as possible forward, but the soil gives way, and both the tree and I are falling. Huge rocks line the blue water of the river feet below me. I hold onto the tree trunk tightly, squeezing my eyes as the icy wind rushes past my face.

The silhouettes of Mom, Dad, and Grandmother flash in my mind as tears freeze in tracks down my cheeks, my vision blurry. I don't dare let go, my arms still clutching to the tree branch as I bob in the water. The branch acts as a floatie, so only part of my body submerges, but the chill from the water seeps into all of my bones. Droplets of river water enter my nostrils, causing me to cough. I tilt my head slightly up to prevent more water from flowing into my mouth.

My chest moves faster up and down in shallow breaths as my body shivers, and numbness begins to pull at my limbs. Water splashes up my nose and into my mouth again, and I spit this time, not wanting to vomit. I strain to keep my head above the water as I am tossed about, the movement only gentling after what feels like hours.

Exhausted, my tree trunk bangs on something hard, and I raise my head tiredly to check it out. There is another, smaller trunk beside it, and I see sand approaching. I rest my head again and let the river guide me to the river bank. With all the strength I can gather, my arms push me from the river, and the tree trunk remains afloat at my side. I groan and roll to my back on the bank.

Chapter 16

"Alyssa! Alyssa! Please wake up!"

I cough and vomit water, lots of it coming out of my body. Some streams out through my nostrils. I feel like I'm choking.

There is numbness in my feet and hands, and I try to open my mouth to reply. It feels like there are tons of rocks in my mouth, and I groan, stopping the movements of my mouth.

Pain lances my hand that was gripping the tree. Maybe it cut my skin as I was thrown around while in the murky river.

A few minutes later, I open one eye, and the first sight I see is Eleanor.

"You're alive!" She smiles in relief with two people in wet diving suits beside her. A paramedic places an oxygen mask over my head, and they carry me to a gurney. Pain and dizziness streak through my body as I am taken to an ambulance.

"Grandmother will be with you at the hospital," Eleanor shouts, her hands waving my phone to and fro, showing me the tracking of Lady Jacqueline's whereabouts. She tucks it into my hand as we arrive at the vehicle.

"Here you go, Alyssa. I have connected your tracking device to mine. You can keep your mobile."

My mouth stays closed even though I try to move it; my muscles can't move to utter some words. *It is hard to move as though it is stuck with glue. Don't tell me I am mute. This cannot be.* I turn my head into the pillow and close my eyes tightly. I refuse to believe that. I groan as dizziness seeps in, and I pass out again.

———

Loud noises from many people's voices ring in my ears. My head tosses and turns like a rolling pin. After several times, my neck and shirt seem to get wet. I open my eyes, and the first thing I see is the ceiling. Its design differs from my room at Grandmother's. My hand touches my neck and my top as I try to sit up. "Ouch!" A drip line is attached to my inner elbow, preventing me from moving further. I turn my head and see my grandmother opening her eyes, and her mouth curves upwards at me.

"Alyssa, I was so worried about your safety. You are courageous to try to save one of my close friends." She hugs me and runs her fingers through my shoulder-length hair lovingly before she plants a kiss on my forehead.

"I missed you, Grandmother." My voice cracks, and a small blush fills my cheeks.

"It is a relief to hear your voice. The doctor mentioned that you may lose your voice for a day or two from the water current and wind pressure you endured during your fall. Don't worry too much, though. You will fully recover once you attend speech therapy." Grandmother smiles and pats my hand.

She continues, "I have it booked for you three times a week. So you are able to recover soon." I smile, looking at Grandmother as tears develop in my eyes.

"Now, now. Don't get too emotional. Save your energy for ample rest." She pats my hand again while sitting beside me on the bed.

My eyes droop, and a few minutes later, I open them slightly as the door hinges creak. There is a warm breath and a whisper in my right ear, "I am going home, Alyssa. I will drop by tomorrow morning." Grandmother's fingers tug my blanket up, and she kisses my forehead as I make a small noise of acknowledgement.

I shoot awake sometime later, my arms flailing, and the wires attached to my arm get tangled on my chest. My eyes fly open as a gasp slips past my lips. "Lady Jacqueline!" A trickle of sweat rolls down my forehead, and I wipe it away using my sleeve. I slowly pry the wires apart and away from my chest. I grab the TV remote and switch on the news. There is nothing on Lady Jacqueline, and my eyes gradually close. I semi-consciously open my eyes slightly to watch the news from time to time. When it turns to sports updates, my eyes slide fully shut.

The next day, I wake to the sound of the curtain being pushed aside hurriedly and the sun touching my face. I open my eyes gradually, my head groggy. I rub my temples and croak, "What time is it?"

"It is two in the afternoon." The nurse smiles at me. My mouth drops, leaving me speechless. "The doctor came to check on you before noon, and you are recuperating well. Please get some rest. If your results are better this afternoon, you can be discharged tomorrow." She smiles again and pushes the hospital table with a tray of food on it to my bed. I nod and smile weakly. Unbelievable I slept so long. I push the food table aside a while after she leaves, twist, and reach into the bedside drawer to pull out my phone to check for messages from Eleanor.

"The tracker stopped at a spot last night, then it went missing."

The hair on my arms stands on end, and I shudder. *What should we do to help her?* I switch on the TV, the news channel popping up from last night, and Lady Jacqueline's picture is on the screen. My eyes open wide, and I say a silent prayer as I chew on my lip. *I hope the police find her alive.*

"Police are still searching for Lady Jacqueline, who was abducted yesterday. There is a ransom of $100 billion from the abductors," the newscaster announces.

Sudden crackling sounds are followed by the picture blinking.

The screen goes blank, switching from the lady newscaster as she is about to utter some words to two men in masks. One stands with a long rifle in his arms, his build similar to Joe's. The other sits on an armchair lazily. His shape looks like Jake Kane. I blink multiple times, wondering briefly if I'm dreaming. Goosebumps appear on my skin, and my mouth and eyes open widely unconsciously.

"Listen! We will give you Lady Jacqueline's head and her chopped-up body if we do not get the $100 billion gold bar within 24 hours from right now." The man in the armchair leans forward, his eyes gleaming with greed and anger.

The camera moves to the side, showing a live Lady Jacqueline, her face covered in cuts and bruises.

The guy holding the rifle knocks the back of her head with the edge of the rifle, causing some blood to stream from the wound, and she cries out in pain. He pulls her hair and head toward the floor, making it hard for Lady Jacqueline to breathe, and her tongue juts out.

I clench the hospital blanket tightly, and I bite the edge of the blanket. "Argh! I was so close to saving her." Tears brim in my eyes.

"See this nation, the rich beyond avarice Lady and Duke," he trails off as the camera turns to show a monitor that plays a short real-life video showing the duke signing contracts worth billions. Another video shows of a blurred person being kicked and punched by the duke outside of a billion-dollar contracts dealings in Prague. The duke harshly tears the unsigned contract and speeds away, accompanied by two bodyguards.

Then the camera faces the abductor as he continues, "This kind of behavior of disrespect of his people comes to an end now!" He takes his gun from his pocket and shoots in the air.

"I am serious this time, Duke. Come and get your loving wife!" The abductor's camera focuses on Lady Jacqueline's terrified face.

The masked man with the rifle places it directly against the side of Lady Jacqueline's head. Her eyes become watery, and her jaw looks tense as she shakes.

"So hear this, high and mighty Duke. Your wife and you will be a lump of dead meat by 10 PM tomorrow if I don't get the gold bar and an apology letter to myself and my mate here for your wrongdoings."

A cracking sound resonates, and the television blinks several times before settling back on the newscaster's face, her mouth open wide as her jaw works to find words.

She presses her earpiece in her ear before saying, "Police did not manage to get hold of the masked men's whereabouts. If any viewers have information about the abductors, please come forward and call 1-888-888-8888."

I gasp, and my hands tangle in the bedsheets.

"Think. Think, Alyssa."

I bite my fingernails as I think of a way to rescue Lady Jacqueline. Unconsciously, I flip my phone around, and my eyes catch on a round red indicator blinking. I concentrate on the dot and its movement, and I click the icon to enter the application. The first thing that pops out is the FindMy app icon.

I squint my eyes to figure out where the location of the route is. It indicates a Hotel De Villa, a 5-star hotel.

I turn to look at the wall clock, which indicates six in the evening. Without wasting time, I pull the needle in my hand, grimacing in pain, and shake my hand out.

My phone vibrates, and I quickly answer it.

"Hi, Eleanor. I am feeling better. My tracker shows that Lady Jacqueline is at Hotel De Villa."

"We have been tracking her all day. The tracking seems to be wrong. Every time we near the tracking spot, the dot showing her location disappears." I hear Eleanor scratch her head, growling in frustration.

"We are not giving up," Eleanor says. "We are currently tracking her since the indicator is active. My colleague Jack is with me here. So you just stay there and recuperate. You hear me? . . . Hello? Hello! Alyssa? Are you there?"

I am already on my feet and groping through the table drawer to find my gun. I sigh; there is only my PI license and a pocketknife. No gun.

"I'll see you soon," I respond to Eleanor, who starts to raise her voice as I stuff them into my pocket.

"No. No! Stay put!" Eleanor screams.

I end the call abruptly and pull the heart rate monitor wires from my other hand.

Once free, I grab fresh clothes that Grandmother left

from the cupboard to change.

My phone vibrates again, and Eleanor's name appears on the screen.

I ignore it as I puff up the pillow and place sofa cushions on the bed in the semblance of my body under the blanket.

Footsteps scuff outside my room. I hide behind the door beside the cupboard. Then the door opens with a creak. Through the door gaps, I see a nurse standing at the entrance. She strains her neck to check my bed from her spot.

"Alyssa is in bed, Eleanor." A phone is at her ear.

She stays for a moment more as she listens before she turns and closes the door.

I drop my stiff posture and breathe out heavily. A few minutes later, I twist the doorknob and move my feet one at a time, not wanting to make any noises. With the door behind me, I see a directory stating "Exit" and other room numbers as I turn to face the right hall. While walking, I have to pass by the nurses' desk. There is one nurse at the desk having a hot drink while scrolling on her phone. I duck down and crawl past quickly. I hear footsteps and a man's voice faintly behind me. I suck in a breath. *Did I get caught?* I hide temporarily at the back of the chest of drawers filled with medicines, only moving again once I'm confident I wasn't seen. I continue crawling; the floor is cold, and my hands and feet grow numb. I get up once I am satisfied that the nurses can't catch me. I crouch and move quickly, abruptly stopping in front of a brown door with signage that reads "Emergency exit." I pull on the doorknob, the sound of the hinges squeaking. I hold my breath and momentarily freeze. My eyes dart from one corner to another, watching for any shadows or movement. I push the door further until there is a sufficient gap for me to slip through.

I run down a few steps as quickly as I can, skidding down some steps as I go, and get up with the assistance of the railing. I arrive at a door that indicates the lobby. My chest heaves, feeling exhausted. I clench my teeth and straighten my shoulders. *I must keep my strength, for Lady Jacqueline's life is at stake. I need to help Eleanor identify the abductor. I was there.* I hold my hands loosely behind my back, and my legs spread wide while walking smoothly and faster than earlier, feeling relief at the sight of the sliding glass door.

"Taxi! Taxi!" I wave at a taxi that is parked at the corner of the hospital's main entrance.

The taxi reverses to the spot I am standing in, and the driver rolls down the passenger window.

"Yes, Miss, are you calling for a taxi?"

I nod and smile.

"Have you been discharged, Miss?" the taxi driver asks as his eyes take in my disheveled appearance, gesturing from my hair to my wrinkled, dirty top.

The door slams behind me as I get into the taxi hurriedly. I nod and take out a compact mirror from my pouch to attempt a fix-up of my appearance.

"Mister, the journey is to follow the tracker on my phone. Also, wait for me to return once we get there. I will pay double for this with waiting time."

"OK, OK, Miss. Twist my arm," the taxi driver replies, looking at me with a crooked grin before he turns and buckles his seat belt, speeding off.

Chapter 17

Hotel De Villa is in a coastal area, and it's a windy route. The taxi smoothly navigates the sharp curves and bends, causing pebbles to fly off the cliff as we round sharp corners.

Driving for a few miles, we reach a stretch of barren land where the tracker dot flickers relentlessly. "The hotel or Lady Jacqueline must be here somewhere."

"Ain't no hotel here, Miss. Maps indicates the hotel is just around the corner," the taxi driver responds after seeing my confused expression.

"Hold on." I close the tracking app and dial Eleanor.

"Eleanor, where are you? I am in a taxi directly at the spot blinking on the tracker, but there's nothing here."

The car rocks suddenly, and I look around in fear.

My heart leaps into my throat, and my hands start trembling. I sigh in relief when I see it's Eleanor trying to open the door.

"Please wait for me," I inform the taxi driver before flinging the door open. I clamor out and hug Eleanor. Her body is tense, and she pins me with a glare.

"Unbelievable! I thought the nurse informed me that you were in bed." Eleanor sighs loudly, her right hand on her waist. "Please return to the hospital, Alyssa. It is my and my team's duty to be here." Her voice shakes as she tries to control her anger, pointing at me to leave.

"But, Eleanor, I am fine." I breathe in deeply and fake a smile. "You need my help to identify the abductor since I was in their trunk and saw them." I try to reason with Eleanor.

Eleanor shouts, creases appearing on her face, "You are not fully recovered!" Her hand points for me to get back into the taxi.

"I will be restless until she's safe, Eleanor." My hands massage the sides of my head as tears form in my eyes.

Eleanor heaves a sigh and stares at me for a moment before nodding. "Having you can be useful and good training. But still, only a day of rest in the hospital is not sufficient." Deep wrinkles form on her forehead, and her upper lip lifts.

With the tracker in her right hand, she looks at me and says, "We are unable to trace anything from Lady Jacqueline here." She shifts the tracker to face me and clenches her fist.

"Are you sure she didn't leave anything during her struggles? Since the hotel is nearby, could it be she is captive somewhere in the hotel?" I pose, tilting my head as I look at Eleanor.

She places her index finger on her chin before answering me. "Alyssa, the hotel is abandoned and rundown. There were financial difficulties by the management; I believe it was owned by a French family that fled a few years ago." Her head turns in the hotel's direction.

"What? There is no hotel, to begin with?" I exclaim and start pacing.

Eleanor holds the tracker up in the air, shaking her

head. "Nope, the network is fine," she says.

I stop abruptly, my left hand holding Eleanor's arm to stop her from doing anything.

"Wait, does this means that Lady Jacqueline is locked somewhere in the hotel while waiting for her husband to send the gold bar?" My eyes look into Eleanor's, excitement building in my chest.

"That is a good possibility, Alyssa," Eleanor responds as she looks around, thinking.

"What is her husband's plan to send in the ransom? Will there be any plain clothes police to escort him? This is a high-profile abduction case that should not be taken lightly." A fresh swell of rage rises in me, and I tighten my grip.

Eleanor stares at my hands, then lets out a forceful exhale through her pursed lips.

"Let me call the team that is handling the ransom side of this," Eleanor says, grabbing her phone to call the other team.

Eleanor steps forward, her eyes surveying the abandoned hotel while her left hand rests on her waist. A few minutes later, she turns to me and huffs. "Alyssa, the only reason I am bringing you for this case is because you were with Lady Jacqueline earlier. We may need you to identify certain things of hers." Eleanor looks serious, and I nod emphatically.

"Don't worry. I am determined to save her with your team." My hands are in fists at my side. "I saw how she was tortured at the abandoned hospital, and I cannot let her die this way. Let alone I need investigation experience." The muscles of my jaw tighten.

While I try to reason with Eleanor, she takes a small lipstick case lookalike from her waist pouch. When she flips it open, it contains two earpieces, one of which she puts on and pauses as she listens to what is being said.

"Roger. We are going nearer to the subject. We need backup ready. If we trigger an alarm, we will be in deep shit."

I hear a faint reply, and Eleanor nods. She passes me the other earpiece and signals me with her right hand to put it in. "Your main focus in this mission is to save Lady Jacqueline while my team and I bring down her abductors," Eleanor says to me.

I nod and smile grimly.

She lifts the hem of her jacket, her hand grabbing a pistol and handing it to me. "This is my spare. Please use this as a defense if needed."

I readily take the pistol, checking for bullets—full.

I tuck it away, and we move quietly but fast. We reach her partner, who has been watching the hotel. "Tom, you are to go in at the back of the hotel. Alyssa and I will enter via the front."

Tom nods in agreement, giving me a brief, tight smile.

The building is three-story high, and part of its roof looks caved in, leaving air and rain to enter.

There are cracks visible on its windows on the second floor, and the front door seems to be built with sturdy mahogany, still standing arrogantly and holding the fort.

Weird that there are no grass or rocks in front of it. The road is not tarred, and there are only two bushes with some dried leaves growing on both sides of the pathway leading toward the entrance.

We finally reach a row of broken bricks that once might have been a gated wall.

We stand just behind it for cover, gathering once more before the entrance. Both of our eyes dart from one end to the other to ensure no one lurks in front.

I raise my gaze to look at the second floor, and they catch sight of a dim light. "Eleanor, there is a flickering light at 3 o'clock," I whisper. "It just died down."

Eleanor nods, then gives a signal to follow her.

Adrenaline rushes into my heart, its beat like that of drums, and a sudden feeling of coldness envelops my arms. I quickly clutch them for warmth and confidence. *You can do it, Alyssa. This is your last chance to save Lady Jacqueline.*

"Coast is clear. Let's go in," Eleanor whispers.

I pull out my gun from my pocket and nod in agreement.

Eleanor pushes the mahogany door, but it doesn't budge. She kicks it with her heavy boots, grunting from the force, and the door gives way. Dust lingers in the dark space. I stand just behind her, straining my neck and eyes for any sudden appearance. There are half-broken, antique furniture and smashed mirrors littering the hallway.

Eleanor points at them, indicating not to step on any of the debris. I nod in agreement.

I step carefully, and we walk to the brick stairway. It winds in a tight circle before reaching the second floor. I tap on Eleanor's shoulder and show her the tracker. The dot has moved, and its location is now in this hotel on the third floor.

Eleanor gives me a thumbs-up and starts moving in that direction.

Holding firmly onto my mobile and watching the tracker dot, we move smoothly to the third floor. Surprisingly, the stairs are sturdy and don't creak as we walk.

A loud sound penetrates the surroundings, and I nearly throw my phone. My hands shake, and I let out a silent exhale. I thought it rang and blew our cover.

It is a relief it is not mine. Someone's phone is ringing. A man's voice hits our ears just behind the door. They must be on speaker since we can make out what the person on the other end is saying. "You better torture her to sign the order to release the gold bar and the revised will. Jacqueline controls all money and fortune, mate." The phone is quiet for a moment. Then the man in the room starts moving.

Eleanor and I look at each other, our eyes wide. Does this mean the Duke is behind this kidnapping for money and a new will or is he playing along?

Eleanor's finger taps on her watch, and a voice and video recorder on the wristband commences recording. Brilliant.

"Sign here, and I need you to put your password to release the $100 billion gold bar to Duke Jacque's account to save your life. He will hand it to our boss, then you can see the light of day." Paper rustling emanates within the quiet room, followed by the loud, sharp sound of smacking a table. "Your husband ain't got a dime. Cunning control freak!" the man's voice shouts.

I place my index finger under my chin and squint. The voice is familiar. . . Joe. It must be him.

"Yes, yes." Lady Jacqueline's voice is shaky and stressed as she responds.

"Promise me you will let me go once I transfer the gold bar, and your boss gets it from the duke," she says, barely getting the words out through her sobs.

"Affirmative." Finger tapping comes from within the room.

A heavy sigh rings in our ears. "Sign the revised will first." I shift and am able to peek through a crack in the door from my hiding spot. I can see a muscular hand pointing a rifle at Lady Jacqueline's face. Her eyes are red, and tears flow down her rosy cheeks. Her trembling right hand signs the will, and her left hand holds a hanky to wipe her tears.

"OK. OK, done." Her face tilts back to look at her abductor's face.

The sound of papers shuffling lingers in our ears, and I see Joe checking and flipping the document. His mouth curves into a wide smile when his eyes reach the signature page.

A creaking sound emits from the rusty door hinges across the room.

Eleanor and I move closer, peeking through the cracks of the door. We are lucky there is a huge vase just beside the door, which becomes our hiding place.

I close my mouth when I see her attorney, a man in his late 40s in matching office clothes, and his mouth is gagged and hands bound. Another of Joe's mates pushes him, using his rifle.

"Hey, you, Mr. Lawyer. Stamp this as an officially revised will." He turns his head, his eyes bulging, and I can only hear a muffled protest.

"Enough making weird noises," Joe indignantly roars while he pulls brusquely on the cloth covering his mouth.

The lawyer wets his lips and says, "Yes. Yes, provided Lady Jacqueline changes this of her own free will and not under duress."

There is silence for a moment before the click of the gun cocking echoes around the room, and the rifle is placed against his forehead.

Sweat trickles from his forehead, and his breathing becomes labored as he gasps for air.

"OK, I will do it." His eyes strain, looking at Lady Jacqueline. She nods to him and says, "Please proceed, Peter. It is money and company ownership and leadership that my husband wants."

Suddenly, the team handling the ransom updates us through our earpieces, "We cannot locate Duke Jacque anywhere. Not in the house, office, or villa, and his phone is switched off. We are unable to proceed with the ransom negotiation."

I tense, and Eleanor gives a thumbs-up to enter. I reach out to push the door, but she grabs my hand firmly. In the room, a live video of Duke Jacque appears on the screen of the laptop on the table. "Dear, for the past twenty-five years, I have had to bow to your demands. You make me feel useless as your shadow. Not even once have you acknowledged me as the man of our family." His ominous voice exudes through the room. Lady Jacqueline breathes shakily, her chest movements unsteady. "You control all our assets and money. Even my monthly income allowances." He scoffs and tosses his salt and pepper hair. "How do you think I feel as a man? You jeopardize my ego!" He clenches his fist and grits his teeth. Lady Jacqueline bursts into tears, sobs wracking her body.

The live video blinks and abruptly turns black.

A piercing gunshot fills the room, causing the crack on the wooden door to vibrate. My eyes momentarily shut, and goosebumps appear on my arms. We look at each other in horror before Eleanor pushes the door and shoots directly at Joe's colleague's chest. He falls with nothing more than a surprised grunt. I am behind Eleanor, my eyes scanning the room for Lady Jacqueline.

She lies on the floor, eyes looking lifeless and staring at the ceiling. Spots of blood are visible around her mouth and her top. Joe must have hit her with the back of his rifle. Her ankles are black and blue. I immediately yell into the earpiece, "Lady Jacqueline is down. Call backup, now!"

While I attend to her, placing my hands on her back, I push her to the side at the back of the room to avoid the heated fight between Joe and Eleanor.

I hear hurried steps from the hallway. Ignoring them, I continue pushing and halfway carry her to safety. I tilt the injured lady's face, and my mouth drops in shock. This isn't Lady Jacqueline. Her abductors must have switched who was wearing her clothes to throw us off. "Where is she?" I whisper in the injured woman's ear. "Where is Lady Jacqueline?" I ask sternly as I shake her. *Maybe the footsteps that I heard were the real Lady Jacqueline running away.*

She moans in pain before she croaks, "Lady Jacqueline was taken elsewhere."

"Where?" I demand, raising my voice impatiently while I pull her shirt toward me. Suddenly, the injured woman kicks my stomach with her stiletto. I tumble back, unprepared. The woman overpowers me, easily almost double my weight, and punches my stomach and face. Blood fills my mouth, and I struggle to throw her off. Suddenly, she gets up to run. My left hand grabs her ankle, and she stomps on my arm with her heel. "Ouch! You bitch!" I yell through gritted teeth.

She struggles to free her other foot and manages to shake herself free. She walks hurriedly, limping through the door and down the stairs before I can catch her.

An engine roars from outside.

Maybe Lady Jacqueline is there in the car.

I take off, leaving Eleanor behind with Joe and the

other abductor fighting. I climb down the three flights of stairs, limping in between as my stomach clenches in pain. By the time I reach the exit, the vehicle looks to be the size of an ant. I strain my eyes. It is the black Wrangler.

My attention is pulled away from the car by the sound of loud crashes from upstairs. I twist my body and tilt my head to look back, but I don't see anyone. There is a heavy *thud* on the floor. I suppress a shiver, my shoulder hunching. What if it's Eleanor? I have to help. I take my gun from my jacket and climb up the stairs, tying my hair into a ponytail.

I push the wooden door with my arms, my gun pointing in front of me. Eleanor kicks Joe's feet, making him grimace in pain, and his face reddens.

He grabs a pistol from a few steps away and fires a bullet in Eleanor's direction. Eleanor shifts aside, and it barely misses her. She jumps on him before he can pull the trigger again. Eleanor's muscular arms hold tight to Joe's hands to prevent him from moving. He thrashes around to release Eleanor's grip. Eleanor takes him to the ground, and he bends his knee to hit Eleanor's pelvis. She grunts and loosens her grip momentarily. Joe pushes away from Eleanor and rolls on the floor, aiming at Eleanor again. Fear washes over my body, and I instantly shoot at his right arm. He yells, and his breathing pulls in short intervals as he lets go of his gun. Blood flows under his sleeve from his shoulder, and he jumps onto a table just below the window. He takes out a small flamethrower from his shoulder bag, chucks liquid toward the center of the room, and ignites the flamethrower. It crackles alive, and fire sparks from the mouth. A gunshot rings, but before the bullet hits him, he jumps from the window. I turn my head toward Eleanor, her gun still pointing. She grits her teeth, and her hand clenches into a fist. Eleanor springs up, spitting blood from her lips.

Silence.

We both look at each other, our chests heaving, and I furrow my brows. Eleanor kicks a book on the floor that is in her way as she moves to the window. She wipes her forehead with her sleeve. I take a step forward, and together, we peer into the darkness.

"Where is he? He must have hit the ground by now," Eleanor exclaims.

"There should have been a loud thud," I continue as my eyes rove the stillness. Eleanor shrugs, at the same time, her gun pointing through the window to find a trace of Joe.

Popping fills our ears, and I look up at the ceiling. It groans, the red roof tiles developing cracks from the heat of the fire. My heart pounds. I move back, knocking into a wooden table. The fire is quickly dancing from object to object. Hissing vibrates from the brick walls.

Eleanor talks into her earpiece, "Tom. Roger, Tom."

The radio is silent. Her eyebrows pull together, and her lips press tightly.

Dust and debris accompany loud crashes as tiles start to fall. My mouth opens wide, and Eleanor blinks rapidly as part of the roof in front of the entrance gives way and hits the floor. My legs start to shake, and I cover my mouth. *Think. Think.* I look at Eleanor, and her eyes scan the room with furrowed brows. She looks at the open window. "We better hurry!" She pushes me, and we hurry back to the window within a few strides. "We jump and land on one of the bushes down there." She looks at me, and her hand nudges me to be quick.

I nod in agreement. Smoke is thickening in the air,

and my body wracks with coughs. My eyes sting.

"On the count of three," Eleanor shouts. She counts and jumps, but blind terror floods me as I look out the window. *The ground is too far. I will break my legs.* I notice the gutter on the trimming of the hotel and jump to the pipe. I hold on to it firmly and slide down it like a fireman's pole.

Unbeknownst to us, Eleanor's team is ready with an inflatable rescue cushion, and she lands with her hands and legs in a crouch.

Eleanor is still on the inflatable when she looks up at me, waving frantically. "Alyssa! Jump down. The building is collapsing. Hurry! There's a cushion here. Jump, now!" Eleanor shouts. I close my eyes and pry my fingers from the pipe. The wind rushes past me as I fall, and I open my eyes, seeing the black night sky with a star twinkling. I see a frail, leafless tree waving at me, and my body flushes cold with dread.

My fall ends abruptly as my body hits the cushion. I bounce on it and just lie there, my breath slowly turning to normal. I roll over the edge to be free of the rescue cushion. My surroundings spin, and I blink, suddenly nauseous. I inhale deeply with my arms out for balance.

A man runs to me, grasping my shaking hands.

He places an arm around my shoulder and helps me walk faster away from the building. Eleanor is beside us before she stops, turning her head back. "Where is Tom? Have you seen him?" Eleanor shouts into the radio.

"Negative. The last we heard from him was in the hotel's kitchen."

Eleanor spins back toward the building and yells, "Tom!" She takes a step, but a huge explosion engulfs it. Debris of window glass, wood, and other small and large materials mix with sparks of fire as heat batters us. A piece of glass strikes Eleanor, and one of her teammates stretches their arms, grabs her waist, and pulls her away, covering her body with his.

We reach the ambulance in the safe zone at the foot of the entrance, and paramedics reach for me. They cover me with a yellow blanket and place an oxygen mask over me. My eyes remain to stare at Eleanor and the team, overwhelming sadness spreading through my chest. My heart feels tightened, and I let go of the oxygen mask. I try to move toward them to help; however, the paramedic grabs my arms and shakes his head. My shoulders slump, and my lips press tightly at his action, but I follow his instructions. Within seconds, the ground shudders from another massive explosion. My hands grip the ambulance tightly, and I breathe in and out rapidly.

Sirens wail in the distance as a fire truck rushes to fight the fierce flames.

More paramedics arrive, carrying Eleanor to safety. Her face is blackened by the smoke and peppered with cuts, some deeper than others. Blood shows on her hands, feet, and face.

Tears fall from her dark brown eyes, her brows lowered, and her facial expression focused.

Chapter 18

Crackling sounds emanate from my earpiece. "Negative. There was no sighting of a vehicle coming from the direction of the hotel."

Once the fire is brought under control and dies, the firefighters enter the kitchen. A few tense minutes later, they bring out a body bag. Eleanor pushes past the firefighters as the paramedics move forward to take the body from the firemen. The body is placed on a stretcher, and she firmly holds onto the hand of one of the paramedics. She looks at him, and he nods and waves to his colleague to wait. Immediately, her hands reach out to unzip the bag, and one of the paramedics stops her. His words are too quiet for me to hear, but I watch as he speaks to her. Her feet shift an inch or so, and her jaw tightens. The paramedic unzips the pouch, revealing the head of a badly burnt body. She moves closer and looks at it in silence. Eleanor suddenly dissolves into tears. "It's Tom," she croaks, wrapping an arm around her torso. "Not another partner's death," she whispers, barely audible.

My mobile rings, and my focus shifts. I take it out of my pocket, surprised at the three bars on its battery life left. The dot tracker on my phone blinks and makes a sound again. The dot is no longer at this location. It seems the tracker is still active.

I look in Eleanor's direction. She is speaking with the paramedic, her face covered in grime. I hurriedly walk to her. My brows draw together, and I pat her shoulder. "Eleanor, the tracker is active." I flip my phone screen to face her, and I point at the moving dot.

"Also, I just realized that the car that abducted Lady Jacqueline must have made a turn and left at the back pathway." I turn to look in that direction. I stand on my tiptoes, stretching my neck. "I can just see a narrow clear route between the trees. Maybe that way leads to somewhere where she's being held captive. They won't kill her until they get everything since she controls it all," I say. Eleanor's eyes stare at the direction I am pointing in.

"Backup. I need backup," Eleanor shouts in the earpiece.

"Roger. Jason will be at your place within two minutes to join you with this mission."

With that, a car engine reeves in the night air.

"Alyssa, I see the taxi is still waiting for you. It is better for you to ride along with us." Eleanor pats my shoulder.

"OK, let me pay the taxi driver."

I run toward the waiting car a few steps away from the ambulance, parked behind a bare tree.

"Miss, I know it is not my business. However, I don't know if it will help you. I saw a black Jeep drive away from the building." His finger points in the direction, his gaze lost in memory. "There is an older lady with them." His right hand makes a circular motion around his mouth. "She was gagged, and there was some blood. Her hands were bound as well. I saw something blinking red covering the cuffs." His hands point at the location where I suggested they must have escaped.

"Thank you for the leads. Whatever you saw or heard tonight, you must forget and keep it a secret. It is a police investigation prerogative." I look into his eyes, hoping he understands.

He nods. "Yes, Miss. I will." He zips his mouth with an invisible zipper.

I hope they didn't see the taxi driver. Otherwise, he will be the next victim on the list. I place my right hand in my jacket pocket as I let out a long sigh and give him cash.

I watch until the taxi curves just out of sight and move back to Eleanor. A loud explosion envelops the quiet night sky. I turn my head, my heart hammering. Flames climb high into the sky from where the taxi just disappeared.

With my hands shaking and dizziness seeping through my head, I sink to the ground. "No! No!" Tears blur my vision as I hug myself and rock back and forth.

I spoke too soon.

The Wrangler's driver must have been outside of the hotel and noticed the taxi. I throw my fist against my leg and curl into myself.

Rushing footsteps reach me, and I turn my head toward the sound. Eleanor and her team look at me, bewildered. "What happened, Alyssa?"

"The taxi driver saw them put Lady Jacqueline in a black Wrangler and head that way." My eyes stare in the opposite direction of the burnt hotel while responding to Eleanor.

"There is no time to waste. Let's move . . . move!" Eleanor shouts.

Eleanor pulls me up, and we run to a waiting

167

car—Jason.

In minutes, we pass the ruins and take the bumpy back route surrounded by tall trees. I don't know why, but goosebumps develop on my skin. I grab hold of the handle just above the window to stop myself from slipping to the other side of the car as Jason takes a sharp turn. There are no seat belts in the back.

With one hand holding tightly to my phone for tracking, I watch as the dot stops and disappears. "Wait, I saw the dot stopping only a little further from here. There seems to be a log cabin on the left. But the dot's gone missing, and it was on the right side of the cabin. Does this mean we lost her again?" I ask in dismay.

"Nope. According to Maps, the log cabin is private property. There is vast empty land behind it. Let's check it out. Maybe she was hidden there temporarily until all funds are transferred," Eleanor replies.

Eleanor readjusts her earpiece. "We are at the log cabin, a private property at Leazy Street. Lots of trees with rundown material around. Be on standby. If we need, we will call. Roger." She looks at Jason, who nods at her instructions.

"Copy," someone else answers on the radio.

We park a few feet from the cabin, hiding in some bushes to prevent any suspicion. Then all three of us open our doors simultaneously, our guns in our hands. Eleanor gives the signal for me to hide in the bushes at the left-hand corner of the cabin, near the entrance.

She and Jason hide at the back of a mint green Honda Civic parked in front of the entrance. The cabin looks quiet and dark, and silence presses heavily on us. Eleanor signals me to stay put, pulls out her flashlight, and she and Jason head to the cabin.

Creaking sounds emanate from the wood floor steps at the front door. Eleanor quickly hides on the left side and Jason on the opposite. Jason hides behind an old wooden rocking chair. They are momentarily silent, then Eleanor raises her head, peeking through the window.

Ominous creaking looms on the still air nearby my hiding spot. I gasp and instantly close my mouth to prevent any other sounds from escaping.

I scan slowly for any intruders lurking, and my eyes start to strain from staring into the dark. Once I am confident that there is no one, my attention shifts to the front door. Eleanor and Jason have already opened the door, their bodies halfway in the cabin. Unease unfurls in my stomach, and I swiftly turn my head toward my back to double-check my surroundings. I don't see any movements, so I turn around.

Again the buzzing sound emerges. It's irritating, so I search for the source of the sound while covering my ears. It sounds like it's coming from behind the cabin.

I touch my earpiece. "I am walking toward a buzzing noise. Believe it's at the back of the cabin. Roger." My eyes shift from left to right on the lookout.

"Copy," one of the officers on the team answers.

Is someone's phone ringing? I rub the side of my forehead as a touch of dizziness hits.

My feet move forward, eyes swiveling as sweat causes my bangs to stick to my forehead. I step warily down the side of the cabin. I stop momentarily and look around me. The snap of a branch being stepped on cracks through me. I freeze, and my heart beats rapidly. From the same spot, my eyes dart all around, but I'm unable to see any shadows or silhouettes of humans or animals.

A minute passes by, and once I am confident there is

no one nearby, I resume inching further, approaching the empty backyard. I grin, seeing that the grass is tall enough to hide me. *No one can spot me,* I think to myself while smiling.

A gunshot rings in my ears as I take my first step into the yard. I cover my ears with both hands, my legs trembling, and I quickly turn to find where it came from. Figures tangled in a fight catch my gaze from the second-floor window, and I bite my lip. Eleanor kicks a heavily built man a few inches taller than her while Jason, who is of similar height as the man, punches another, smaller silhouette. *Is that the woman involved in Lady Jacqueline's abduction? Is she a mistress?* I place my index finger on the side of my chin as I watch.

I gasp as Eleanor's shadow falls, and I flinch, gulping as the silhouette of the man grabs and pulls her hair. They punch her chest. His arms drag her and throw her away, knocking her into furniture. I unconsciously straighten from my hiding place. I quickly duck down after realizing I am exposing myself.

"Oh no! Should I go in to help, or should I call for backup?' I bite my finger, and my jaw tightens.

I press my earpiece and speak into it, "Hello, we need backup. Eleanor is down. Location at the cabin. Roger." My voice sounds tense but firm.

"Copy. Backup is nearing."

"Alyssa, stay where you are. Do not enter!" another officer replies.

Hearing this, I gulp and crumple my pants in my fists. My left leg bounces slightly, making me nearly fall on my butt since I am crouching.

Sweet relief slides through me when Jason overpowers the woman and takes her to the ground.

I can't see anyone now. *Where did the man go? Did he escape?*

The door bangs open as the hinges squeak. The man is out back here. He runs as fast as his legs can carry him and stumbles as he looks back. *Who is he running away from?* I turn my head and spot Eleanor. Being tall, she can pursue at the same pace as he can run and quickly overtakes him. She jumps on him, both rolling on the ground, and a gun fires. I shake a little and remain hidden, breathing in and out rapidly as my eyes move over the space where Eleanor is rolling. Coming to a stop, Eleanor stands as a different man from amongst the trees extends his hand, holding a gun and shooting at Eleanor's thigh. Her nose wrinkles, squeezing her mouth in a grimace of pain. Blood flows from her thigh.

The other man steps forward toward Eleanor's direction. I can see him clearer and gasp. It's Joe.

"Jojo, get up, idiot!" Joe utters in a husky tone as he moves toward Eleanor.

Quickly, Jojo gets up after wriggling his leg and kicking Eleanor's grip from him.

Joe keeps his gun level at Eleanor's face, getting ready to shoot her. Without thinking, I come out from my hiding place, pointing my gun at Joe without any plan. I fire a shot at Joe's stomach. Jojo and Joe look in my direction, stunned at my sudden appearance. I quickly hide beside the side of the cabin and peer around the corner to watch.

I exhale in relief as a police siren can be heard nearing the cabin.

Joe scoffs and says, "Let's go. Let her live."

With the gun still in my hands, my hands shaking, I continue to aim in their direction just in case they decide to pull a surprise on Eleanor.

Jojo puts his hand around Joe, who is bleeding from his wound, and starts walking toward the long grass in the cabin's yard.

I walk toward Eleanor when I am satisfied that they are no longer in close proximity.

"Eleanor, you are bleeding heavily." Immediately, I squat down beside her, worry eating at my insides.

"Get the ambulance quick. Eleanor was shot. Roger," I shout via my earpiece.

"Copy. The ambulance is on its way."

My heart leaps into my throat as fear torments me at the amount of blood flowing from Eleanor's thigh. I grip my shirt. *Think, Alyssa, how do you stop blood flow?*

I use my hands and teeth to tear a strip from my long sleeve cotton blouse and cover her injured thigh, circling the piece of cloth over it and applying pressure. I tie it into a knot, and my hands flutter over it as I assess it.

"Go, Alyssa. Help Jason catch Lady Jacqueline's abductors. Be careful," Eleanor says, gritting her teeth.

Jason barrels out of the house. "You alright, El?"

Eleanor nods and waves him off, pressing down on the wound.

"Alyssa, come with me. What direction did they go in?" Jason asks, looking at me.

"They went to the right amongst the long grass, heading toward the trees," I respond, shakily pointing.

The sound of an engine grabs our attention. A motorbike appears from the road back to the hotel.

"Hey, Jason. Use this bike to catch them. You won't catch up to them without it," the police officer says as he hops off.

A grim smile appears on Jason's face as he nods.

Jason and I look at each other for a second before

172

both of us climb onto the bike, throwing on safety helmets and speeding away. I hug Jason's waist, holding on. I point him in the direction that I last saw Joe and Jojo flee.

After a few minutes, I shout over the engine, "Look, there are two fresh bootprints on this muddy pathway. Maybe it's theirs."

Jason stops the bike, hiding it among the bushes nearby.

"Let's follow the trail." Jason gestures to me.

"Roger. We are in the woods. Are you able to track me?" he whispers in his earpiece.

"Copy. Affirmative. You are nearing a private property. The owners are Duke Jacque and Lady Jacqueline. It is their weekend cabin."

"What?" I say in disbelief. I had to have heard that wrong.

Jason and I look at each other. Puzzlement takes over his face while I shrug, my hands up. Subconsciously, my hands touch my chin. "I guess it's confirmed that Duke Jacque is behind this all along. But why does he want us, the police force, to track him here?" I whisper.

"Only one way to find out the truth. Or maybe the abductors have trapped both of them and are trying to catch us, too," Jason says while shrugging.

"Backup will be arriving within ten minutes to the private property. Roger."

"Copy," Jason replies.

Both of us walk cautiously, and Jason signals to me to look out on the left side while he keeps watching the right and center. It's difficult to see much, as we only have the crescent moon's light to light our path.

Jason grabs my right hand, and my eyes widen as my heart starts to hammer. *What on earth is he doing?* Four bullets slide into my palm. I smile at him as my heart rate returns to normal. *What a relief; I only had one bullet left.*

We resume our walk, and within minutes, we are face to face with an old man with long a white beard and a straw cowboy hat neatly sitting on his head. His long rifle points in our direction. "You are trespassing on private property," he says in a husky voice.

"We are police. We are currently searching for a perpetrator, and they were heading this way. Please be cooperative," Jason replies, showing his badge.

The old man lowers his rifle to the ground as his head tilts. "I ain't seen anyone around here recently. This cabin's been empty since yesterday."

"Were there people before yesterday? Anything unusual that you saw or noticed?" I enquire.

"Nah. The usual. Duke Jacque was here with some guys. I believe they were repairing the cabin. They brought some duffle bag. I ain't see Lady Jacqueline anywhere. Usually, she is around hand in hand with Duke Jacque. A nice fine lady." His mouth curves into a smile.

"Since you are not a resident of this cabin, why are you here?" I ask.

"I am just a few feet next door. I saw the two of you, so I came out to look for any intruders. I better run along." He turns his back to us.

"Thank you. If you recall or see anything, please call the police," Jason says.

His head turns, and he nods at Jason.

We resume moving toward the cabin.

The cabin is pitch dark, and shivers run down my spine as I stare up at it. Jason signals me to follow him.

The wooden flooring squeaks when we step onto it, and I signal to Jason that I will follow slowly to prevent more noises. He nods and continues.

I breathe in. I tiptoe behind Jason while stepping on more stable flooring. Jason peers into a window as he passes, stopping for a moment. I walk ahead of him and sweep my eyes around the area when I reach the door. My shoulders relax, and I inhale deeply, seeing no suspicious activity or shadows looming. I place my other hand loosely on the side of my leg and confidently twist the doorknob. It doesn't budge. I shake it a little, wrinkles forming on my forehead. Jason readies his gun and nods. I take out a pocket door battering ram that was given to me by Jason earlier. After a moment, I push the door open. Jason steps in first, still pointing his gun, as he clears the area. I enter with my gun in my hand, ready.

Jason signals me to follow him, and I nod, squeezing my lips together.

We climb the antique wooden staircase. There still haven't been any movements or any suspicious activity, and my stomach clenches. We enter each of the three bedrooms, but all are neat and tidy, with no indication of other presence.

I leave those rooms and go to the back, where there's a window with see-through lace curtains. I turn my head toward the ceiling, standing on my toes to feel the ceiling for any openings for a hidden attic.

Jason joins me in the room and touches his palm to the wall and artwork for any clues or secret passageways.

I glance at my watch as I reach up again and watch as it ticks midnight. Instantaneously, a loud crash like broken glass sounds from downstairs.

Jason and I look at each other warily, and he gestures me closer to him, alert. I nod and walk to the spot quietly. He speaks quietly into his earpiece, "Broken glass.

Roger."

"Copy. Backup is nearing."

My jaw tightens as my hands tremble, and I squeeze the gun in my hands. Sweat beads on my forehead, and my breathing becomes uneven. *The intruders are here. Will I be able to shoot Joe or Jojo if needed?*

Before we walk downstairs, Jason pauses, glancing at me, and gives me a fist bump with a small smile. I smile hesitantly and put my hand against my chest, inhaling. *He's right. I can overthrow an intruder in case of emergency.* I nod at him and tilt my head to indicate to move.

On the ground floor, our eyes move around the surroundings for the broken glass. It is scattered across the floor on the right side of the door. I turn to look at the window above it, gasping at the jagged hole at the center.

My foot hits a light object, kicking it about a foot ahead of me. My right foot shifts slowly to the side as my body bends and my hands shake. I pick it up hesitantly and hold it up, unsure what it is I am holding. My eyes squeal when I realize that it's a man's finger with a rubber band tied around it. My nose immediately wrinkles, and I have to fight an urge to throw it far from me. I swallow and turn the finger over to look at a note tied to it.

"Don't poke your nose into this. Death is waiting for you." Dried blood stains the paper. The message is printed, not handwritten.

Jason steps closer to take the message, but he pauses as a ticking sound fills the room. We quickly turn our heads to find the source, looking down the kitchen hall, and the dim light reveals a long table and kitchen utensils hanging from the ceiling, shaking and rattling against each other.

"It is a bomb," Jason whispers and looks at me with

wide eyes. "Run!" he yells, his right hand gesturing frantically toward the entrance. My hands and legs freeze at his words, and my mouth hangs. He pulls my wrist harshly, yanking me into action. I stuff the note and attached finger into my pocket and take off, Jason hot on my heels as we race outside.

Ticking fills my head and beats all other thoughts from my mind. *We're about to die.*

Jason pushes me out the door, and together, we jump from the porch into the yard, landing hard and rolling on the grass. Jason's body surrounds me while his hands cover my head. I breathe in and out rapidly, and we tense, waiting. From the side of my eye, I watch the five police rescue team members rush toward us, wearing thick bulletproof jackets.

Jason and I scramble farther away as they enter the cabin. After several overwhelming minutes, the rescue team announces via the earpiece, "No bomb was detected or detonated."

Hearing this, Jason blows out a breath and squats. He turns his head to face the cabin door, a look of puzzlement on his face. His hand massages his chin, and his brows draw low.

"No explosion or bomb? What happened?" he asks his team, getting up from the ground as the team approaches us.

I rub my hands over my face and stand from where I am sitting on the ground, straightening my top and jacket as I stare at the doorway. My eyes dart to the second-floor windows for any intruders' whereabouts. I blink and squint my eyes, but nothing moves.

When my gaze moves to the furthest left side of the wooden cabin, rustling leaves pique my attention.

I hold my breath, my eyes straining to see into the surrounding darkness where the leaves are dancing. I stand on my tiptoes, putting my hand on Jason's shoulder for balance.

Unconsciously, my feet move in that direction, ignoring Jason calling my name.

There are many short bushes around, and my hand pushes back small leaves of lime tilia cordata. I sigh as a squirrel is revealed, munching something. He looks at me and runs off. I bend down, my hand extending to grab the item he was standing on.

This time, I remember to switch on a flashlight before I touch it. A tattered piece of thick cloth with a touch of blue. I gasp, my hand flying to cover my mouth. Lady Jacqueline's jacket.

"What are you looking at?" Jason says from beside me, my startled gaze meeting his.

"Take a look." I point at the tattered cloth on the grass with my chin. "It's from Lady Jacqueline's jacket. Is it a trail to find her?" I respond while my eyes dart around the cloth for any more pieces of evidence.

"The bomb squad is searching the whole house. While they are in there, we can wander around to find more clues?" Jason suggests, his head moving to the side.

"Sure." I hold up a thumb toward Jason.

"You look around the left, and I'll go right. If you find anything, buzz me," Jason says, and

I nod in agreement.

A few steps forward, I find a jacket button. Dread twists in my guts, and I bite my lip. *Is the next thing going to be Lady Jacqueline's body?* I squat to look closer at the ground for any footprints.

I take out a hand magnifying glass and shine my light

around, looking through it now. I turn my head from side to side, surprised the grasses are untouched. I walk further forward, adamantly wanting to find more clues. Several yards ahead, I still haven't found anything and decide to reverse, walking back to the spot where the button lay. I quickly unzip my sling bag to pull out a ziplock plastic bag, grab the button, and place it safely.

I stand up as Jason says in the earpiece, "Alyssa, let's return to the front."

"OK, sure," I respond and sigh.

I take one last look around. As I turn to join Jason, my eye catches something that causes me to double-take. A long silk cloth with the Gucci logo on it flaps in the breeze. *Is there someone else involved in this? I wonder who the woman is?*

Chapter 19

A few minutes later, I look at my watch, yawning as it tells me it is one in the morning. I run a hand through my hair, exhaustion dragging at my limbs. When I reach the front of the cabin, Jason extends his hand to show me a squarish object, about the size of his palm, with buttons on it. "I found this thrown in the unkept grass over there under a broken vase." He points his index fingers behind him. "This confirms that the bomb was controlled by a remote control. Someone must have stopped the bomb programming just moments before it detonated. Otherwise, it would have blown us up."

He pauses, tilting his head. "By the way, we received updates on Eleanor. She is in the hospital for the day, but she'll be discharged by tomorrow if all goes well." Jason smiles, relief and tiredness mixing on his face.

I nod, returning his smile. "I will speak to her later. Thank you for the updates." I glance at the cabin. "I wonder why the bomb was defused?" I ask, just loud enough for Jason to hear. "It was meant to chase us off to give them more time for something?" I place my right index finger on the side of my chin.

"Already posing questions like a full investigator," Jason says with a chuckle.

We are interrupted by the head bomb technician, Ben, before more can be said. He climbs down from the cabin, walks to Jason, and pats Jason's shoulder. He looks at him, then at me before he says, "The bomb squad has done a thorough search in the cabin and its surroundings. There are no clues about Lady Jacqueline's whereabouts or her abductors."

Jason nods to him, pats Ben's back, and thanks him. Ben turns, walking toward the patio of the cabin.

"Alyssa, according to my colleague on the negotiation team, Shawn, they are still unable to contact Duke Jacque." He shakes his head, worrying furrowing his brows.

I sigh and show Jason the ziplock plastic bag of items. "What is this?" he asks.

"You already saw the cloth, but there is a blue and gold trimming button as well, which I believe is also from her jacket. I recall she wore it the day of the kidnapping. I also stumbled upon a silk scarf with the Gucci logo printed all over it. Lady Jacqueline didn't wear it at all." I hold the bag in front of his face for him to see.

He squeezes my right shoulder, a small smile forming. "Wow, you are amazing. I'll pass this evidence to the forensic department to look for any DNA." He squeezes my shoulder again.

He sighs and drops his hand, rubbing his chin. "I don't know why, but I have an uneasy feeling that there is something to find in the house. We didn't really get to check out the kitchen and pantry, right?" He looks at me, his head cocked.

I nod. "Let's check out the kitchen before we do anything else," I say, already walking toward the cabin.

"Good idea," Jason says with a grin. "I'll follow in a minute."

I look around slowly as I step inside the cabin, just in case we missed any critical evidence in the first walk-through. I sniff for any peculiar smells, then I step in toward the kitchen. Nothing.

Someone touches my right shoulder, and I startle, quickly grabbing my gun at my waist and turning. "Here are gloves for you to wear if we find anything," Jason says, and I sigh in relief. I take them from him and put them on.

My nose twitches as I enter the kitchen, and I gag at the stench wafting within the kitchen. I quickly cover my nose with my sleeve. I walk from one cabinet to another, opening them one by one while wearing a glove, not wanting to confuse any fingerprints. My eyes scan the items arranged in the cabinet, and all appear ordinary, nothing peculiar. I close the cabinet and breathe in deeply, my fingers fidgeting on the cabinet handle while my head turns to look around the kitchen. *I can feel in my bones that there is something off in this cabin.* My eyes catch a small window with no curtain. I can see trashcans lying in the side garden through it. My hands press together as I walk steadily toward the window.

My eyes scan the outside while my left hand presses the earpiece. "Someone please check out the garbage bins in the garden near the kitchen. Roger." I stand beside the window sill, my body brushing the wall, and I look from one end to the other again. *There must be something. A clue.* I bite my lip and clear my throat.

"Copy," someone says through the earpiece.

I turn to walk back to the living room when I notice a

small room beside the kitchen with the door ajar. I swallow, and unease slides through me. It's pitch darkness inside. I reverse my steps, my eyes meeting Jason's, and I point toward the room with my head tilted. He nods and follows behind me, alert.

I use my elbow and boots to push the door wide, and a ray of moonlight glares through a small window above a washer and dryer set.

A round metallic item juts out from underneath the dryer, and I dash to it. I cringe and reach out my left hand to pull the item out.

Jason passes me a multipurpose steel pickup tool. "Thank you," I say gratefully.

I bend and pull the item toward me, causing it to roll across the floor. I pick it up—it is a blue and gold trimmed button. "It looks the same as the button that I found outside."

Jason presses his earpiece and says, "Hey, mate, please inform the forensic team to bring in the evidence bag from outside." I smile at him and move to stand fully.

My head naturally turns to the left, facing the washing machine, as I move. I gasp, my jaw working to find words.

"What? What did you see?" Jason asks from the side of the threshold. His eyebrows pull together.

He walks to me when all I can do is point. From my spot a few steps away from the machine, I can see dry blood stains splattered on and around the lid. I stare at his eyes, shivers running up my spine. He tightens his jaw and points his gun in the direction. I walk closer to the machine and grimace as the smell of iron registers. "It seems quite fresh, Jason," I say.

Jason walks nearer to the machine, bending his head

and staring at it. "Let's take the lid off." He gestures that he will open the lid.

I nod and take a step to give him space. "Maybe Lady Jacqueline's body is in here." My voice turns raspy as tears film my eyes.

Jason pushes the lid of the machine, and to our utter disgust, the pungent smell intensifies in the air. I instantly cover my nose with my sleeve, trying to keep from vomiting. The scent's like a ton of dead rats had been left in the sun to rot.

Jason quickly shines his flashlight on it, his face grim. "There's a chopped body stuffed in here. No way to identify visually." Within moments, the forensic team is at the door, everyone's faces in various stages of disgust.

"Argh," I scream as I glance at the washbasin and start to hyperventilate. My index finger shakes as I point at a soap dish. Two eyeballs stare at the ceiling, removed from their sockets, on the soap dish.

I walk woodenly from the room, approach the front door, and try to steady my breathing. I grab my phone as it vibrates in my pocket on reflex. I answer after seeing the screen with Jamie's name. "Hi, sweetheart. How was your day?"

In a shaky voice and with trembling hands holding my mobile, I try to find something to say. "Alyssa?" Jamie asks, his voice filled with concern.

A dam breaks in me, and a sob bursts from my chest. I drop to the ground, gripping my shirt as only whimpering comes out from my mouth.

Chapter 20

The next day in my bedroom, my phone rings on my bed. I run and grab it, pressing 'Answer.' "Hello, this is Unicornfire Engineering Enterprise. I am Sharon from the recruitment department. Am I talking to Alyssa Smith?"

Excitement runs through me as I reply, "Yes, speaking. Good morning, Sharon." I stand beside my bed, and my knee keeps knocking the mattress, feeling jittery.

Sharon's voice is cheerful. "Congratulations! Unicornfire Engineering Enterprise's management team has agreed to recruit you. I will send you our offer letter via email and require your acceptance."

I jump on my spot, my mouth curving broadly. "Oh my, this is good news." My eye looks at my table calendar opposite my bed. "Paris trip" is written over the next two weeks. I scratch the side of my forehead and hum softly. "However, I will be in Paris next week for two weeks to visit a friend," I say softly, my nerves on fire.

"It's not a problem. You can onboard a month from today," Sharon replies, oblivious to the relief that washes through my body at her words.

"That sounds great. Thank you, Sharon. You just

made my day," I respond and shut my phone, quickly texting Jamie regarding the good news.

I exit my room door, skipping and smiling, but I stop short. My grandmother sits on a couch watching the news. Her eyes are red as tears slide down her wrinkled cheeks, her hands wrapped around a tissue box.

My phone vibrates, and I realize there are missed calls from Eleanor and Jason, along with some messages. I check the messages first, just in case Grandmother already received bad news. I skim over the messages, closing my eyes with a deep inhale.

The body we found in the washing machine was confirmed as Lady Jacqueline.

"No wonder Grandmother is upset." Tears spill from my eyes, and I wipe them with my sleeve. I take a steadying breath and approach Grandmother.

"Grandmother," I say as softly as possible.

She turns her head, whimpering and sniveling. I move to hug her tightly. "She was my best friend. Like a sister to me. We were in the same college in England."

I squeeze her and kiss her forehead. "We were too late to save her. I am sure she will be in heaven. She was a nice lady." Grandmother nods and blows her nose loudly.

I console her for a few more minutes until she retreats from the room, and I watch her go with a deep ache in my chest. I walk to my room and call Eleanor. "How are you, 'cuz?"

"I am alright. Has the news hit Grandmother hard?"

I shake my head while answering, "Yes. She hasn't stopped crying."

Eleanor continues, "By the way, Duke Jacque is still missing. We have yet to fully determine his involvement in the case. Our team tracked the location where he demanded those valuables. Turns out that he was at the abandoned hospital where you and Lady Jacqueline were held captive. So we don't know whether he was forced to say those words to Lady Jacqueline or if he genuinely loathes her."

"What?" I raise my voice and scratch my head. "I thought the avalanche destroyed that place." I simmer with anger, my hands on my hips. "That is a great swindler, that Jake Kane guy. I wonder who the mastermind behind this kidnapping, murder, and robbery is." I stomp my leg onto the carpet.

"Apparently, the hospital grounds were firm," Eleanor responds in an annoyed tone.

After our conversation finishes, I open my door slightly and poke my head through the door. I glance around the living room to check if Grandmother has come back out. I don't see her, so I walk from my room to search for Grandmother. *Is she alright? I should keep her company today.*

I walk through the living room, dining area, and her office; however, there's no sign of her.

As my feet move on, Ms. Ann, Grandmother's helper, appears with a broom across from where I am standing.

She places the broom against a chair and heads to me.

"Miss, do you need any help?" she asks.

"Do you know where grandmother went?" My palm opens in a pleading gesture.

"She is in her room upstairs." Ms. Ann points at the staircase.

I nod and quickly turn toward the staircase.

When I reach her room, I twist the brass-colored doorknob. A light rose fragrance lingers in my nostrils, and small, intricately woven roses decorate her carpet.

A family portrait of my late grandfather with my mother hangs on the wall next to her dressing room. The room is gorgeous. I walk further in, then stop when I see Grandmother lying in bed with one of her hands covering her forehead. Her eyes looked swollen.

I tiptoe to her, cover her with a blanket, and kiss her forehead. She sleeps soundly, so I straighten my body to walk away. I will talk to her about my work opportunity later.

As I turn my body toward the door to leave, the side of my eyes snatches on several long scarves hanging neatly in a row in her dressing room, its door wide open. Interested to see my grandmother's collection, I walk into the room. The first items that I spot are her five long Gucci scarves, made of either silk or satin and with the same design as the one I saw at the cabin. I gasp and look closely from one scarf to another. All hang neatly, and I stop abruptly in front of a gap that looks like it should fit another scarf, and a scarf is hung beside it. I wonder where it is? I look at the floor for clues, but there are none. My left hand rubs my neck, and I bend down to look at the carpet to find the scarf. I rub my hands together, then shake my head to and fro and brush aside the thought that Grandmother is at the site. Lady Jacqueline must have a scarf similar to my grandmother's. Who doesn't? It is a common Gucci scarf.

———

During breakfast the next day at Grandmother's villa, I push a chair back for me to slide in at the dining table.

"Grandmother, I promised you I would work with an engineering company for two years while at the same time I would be a part-time Assistant Director at your company. The third year, I will fully be your Director. What do you think of my proposal?" I smile with a twinkle in my eyes, looking at Grandmother's grey eyes.

She stops sipping her cup of tea and places it shakily on the saucer on the table. Her eyebrows pull together as she stares at her untouched plate of breakfast.

She looks at me for a few minutes, blinking and thinking before she says, "Alright, it sounds good for you to be exposed to some real-life engineering work so that you can evaluate and analyze the proposal for the business accordingly." She smiles softly, looking at me.

My eyes sparkle, and my mouth curves widely into a grin. I stretch my hands out and pat her stacked hands. She shifts, her head turning to the right, and she extends her right hand to reach for an envelope. She grabs it and opens it slowly. She pushes the agreement paper to my side, laying it in a clear spot. "Yes, you are to sign here that you are taking over 70% of my shares. The remaining balance is 10% I will still hold, 10% is your father's shares, and 10% of shares being held by the Board members." Her finger taps the empty signature space for me. She watches my face as my eyes skim the contract, my fingers moving across the words.

"It has to be now, Grandmother?" My eyebrow quirks while flipping the pages.

"Yes, of course, dear. I am not getting any younger, and you are my sole inheritor with the brains to hold my company's strength. End of the discussion." She scoots back her chair, gets up, and puts her hand on her waist.

I nod and place my signature at the designated space on the agreement. "Done. It's official," I exclaim with a smile. I turn the contract to face her to see my signature.

I stand and move around the table. I kiss her temple and hug her tightly. "Thank you." Grandmother's eyes sparkle with joy.

My stomach knots as I hug her again, still wanting to know about her missing Gucci scarf.

Chapter 21

"Please have a nice and safe flight." The gate agent scans my ticket and checks my passport, handing them back to me at the boarding gate in the airport.

I smile at her and tuck them back into my bag as I walk toward the plane.

I cannot wait to reach Paris and see Suzanne. I miss her so much.

The ringing of my phone jerks me from my thoughts, and I pull it from my handbag. Jamie's name flashes on the screen, and I smile as I answer the FaceTime call.

"Hi, Jamie."

"I saw Suzanne's Instagram post that you will visit her and be her model." He grins and winks at me.

I nod as the PA system announces, "Final call for the flight to Paris. All passengers . . ."

"I need to get off now, Jamie." I adjust my saddlebag over my shoulder, stopping just out the door of the plane.

"Have a safe trip, Alyssa. I love you. I will find a way to be together, I promise."

I nod and smile at him, sadness seeping through me. With a heavy sigh, my lips press together, and I go find my seat. Once settled, I turn to look out the window. I smile at myself. *I will have a good time in Paris, and I will forget my troubled relationship for a while.*

———

A warm hand pats my arm, and I jolt awake. I yawn and blink when I see the flight attendant smiling at me. She says politely, "Please buckle your seat belt. We are getting ready to land." Her finger points at my unbuckled seatbelt. I nod and quickly turn my head to look through the window, and my hands clasp the belt tightly. I fasten the belt before looking at my phone to check the time. My eyes open widely, and I blink. I slept for ten hours. I straighten in my chair and smooth my outfit and hair. A warm glow envelops my body, and I smile to myself.

After collecting my luggage, I step through the automatic sliding door of the entrance. My eyes immediately land on Suzanne, and I grin. I wave at her, pushing the luggage cart in her direction. We hug as soon as I reach her. "Did you meet any handsome French guys on this flight?" Suzanne asks with a wink.

I shake my head and laugh. "I slept the entire way. I don't know what got into me." My hand squeezes Suzanne's right arm. "Anyway, I'm starving." I tap on my stomach with a pout. "I didn't have anything on the flight. Guess they didn't want to disturb me, or I refused to wake up." I look at Suzanne, and we both giggle.

A few minutes later, we are seated at a café overlooking the Seine riverboat tour start. The waiter serves us croissants, and we both sip on a cup of cappuccino. French cuisine at its finest.

We become so engrossed in talking and taking selfies that we don't realize the change in customers coming and going to the cafe. Our table faces a breathtaking view of the Seine River, and a pleasant light breeze stays constant over the hours. Small tour boats line the bank near the café as the sun sets, ferrying multiple trips of passengers. The boats and nearby buildings light up with bright lights as the sky darkens.

Suzanne and I are oblivious to the café patrons behind us as we catch up, our faces hurting from smiles and laughter. The merry atmosphere breaks when the sound of some plates and glasses crashing on the floor reaches us. Alarmed, I am about to turn my head toward the direction of the noises when I freeze. There is a mirror hanging on the wall above Suzanne's head, and I can see the reflection of the café interior. A huge man in his 30s, with a thick black mustache and a tattoo of a serpent, looms across the room. He overturns a few trays of glasses, which join the smashed mess on the floor. His eyebrows draw together, and his cheeks bloom red.

My eyes shift from the man and look at a metallic item flashing in his other hand under the lights. A red checked handkerchief lies on top of a gun, letting only bits of it show as he waves it around. My eyes widen, and my face creases, blinking several times as my mouth drops.

I crumple the tablecloth as my chest moves in rapid breaths.

"What?" Suzanne's eyes squint as she looks at me. Her hands gesture in question, and her eyes rove the changes in my facial expression.

"A gun—A man with a gun," I stutter and tighten my grip on the fabric.

Suzanne's jaw tightens, and her hands wring her used napkin beside her plate.

"Let's pretend we are not aware of what is happening," I say to Suzanne.

She nods in agreement.

I raise my cup to pretend that I am drinking, simultaneously facing Suzanne. "You've come to this cafe before? Is there an escape route from our table?"

Her face is tense, and her eyes dart here and there. "Yes, this is my usual table. I come here weekly. This café is situated strategically for visitors to wait for their tour ride."

"In other words, this is our escape route." I wink at her while putting on a confident smile as my head indicates the gate nearby. She nods in return, less confident in the plan.

"On the count of three, we jump over the wooden gate. It will be fine."

Suzanne's eyes widen. "We better go now," she whispers shakily while clutching her handbag.

"1, 2, 3."

I grab my saddle bag and pull it over my head. We push the steel garden chairs back quietly, trying not to make noise and attract attention.

We pause, standing as gunshots fire and scared voices yell from inside. "All stay put! All stay put!" a fierce masculine voice shouts.

"Please don't kill me. Please spare my life," the voice of a young lady resonates in the suddenly quiet café.

"Jump!" I whisper, pointing my finger at our escape route.

We crouch as we run, praying they are too busy to notice us. Suzanne places her foot on the railing, but her sandaled foot slips, and she falls over the wooden gate with a muffled grunt as she lands in the grass on the other side.

I hop over the fence a little more gracefully, shooting a worried glance over my shoulder before I help Suzanne to her feet.

I jerk as a man shouts in French behind us, and I turn my head to look. Suzanne grabs my hand, pulling me into motion. "Hurry!"

The man points the gun in our direction and pulls the trigger, a bullet hitting the gate with a wicked *thump*. I gasp, hunching and placing my bag at my back as I run after Suzanne.

More shots ring out, and angry French men trail after us.

We run to the other side of the road to avoid being shot, hiding amongst the neat bushes lining this side of the street.

I whisper between pants, "Since the gunman saw my face, we aren't safe to stay put. We can use the tour boats to hide and get away."

Suzanne nods and whispers, "Good idea. Let's speed there." Suzanne leads the way, and we take off.

We go as fast as our legs can carry us while crouching. We reach the end of the bushes and run on a cement pavement to climb down the few steps to the boats. We pass signage as we run past a wooden bridge that reads, "Seine Water Tour by Night."

Suzanne speaks in French on the phone, calling the police while she runs.

I look back and squeak, moving a bit faster. "Why are they chasing after us? What do they want from us?" I look at Suzanne, seeking an answer.

"I don't know. Stop talking and move fast," Suzanne responds, tucking her phone in her pocket.

"Wait!" I stop short and shove Suzanne to the side

of the bridge, hiding underneath close to the splashing river water. A small luxury boat docks underneath. "This looks like a good place to hide temporarily to try and lose them."

Fine lines appear on Suzanne's forehead, and her right hand firmly grips my right hand. "No, Alyssa. We join the cruise. It's safer," Suzanne suggests.

I bite my lip and nod, managing to smile at her.

Before we can do anything, a few bullets fly by our heads. We duck, crouching again, and have no choice but to hide here. We both look at each other, and understanding passes between us as we turn to the luxury boat.

Without wasting any more time, we scurry onto the boat. Still crouching, we move slowly further to the center of the boat. Lucky for us, the door to its inner area is not locked. I twist the doorknob, peep through it, and turn my head to face Suzanne, giving her a signal that we can enter. We creep into the room and quickly look around for a place to hide. It's messy, looking to be in the middle of a restock. There's a large wooden table on the far side of the cabin, and we move toward it. We grab a long canvas tarp from the floor as we run, covering ourselves with it as we slide under the table. There's a small gap between it and the floor, and I maneuver myself until I can just barely see the door.

A few seconds pass in heavy silence as we try to get control of our heaving chests before we hear a couple of footsteps land on the boat. The boat shakes and leans severely from the new weight.

"Must get them. They saw our faces!" an accented masculine voice growls outside.

"Yes, Boss."

We remain as still as mannequins, holding our breath.

Suzanne shakes next to me, and I slowly move my hand to squeeze her arm.

A few minutes pass, and none of them find our hiding spot. Grumbling trickles from the deck, and several people jump out of the boat. It rocks violently for a moment before settling. Quiet descends, and we strain for any additional noise or movement.

Suzanne pulls on my right arm and whispers, "We better run and get on the tour boat nearby. We will miss them completely, hopefully."

I nod, turning to look at her.

I place my index finger across my mouth, and I gradually get up, still bent over, and my right hand slides the canvas back cautiously. I pause, listening again for any intruder's footsteps. I push the gap wider and get up, raising my left hand toward Suzanne. I help her from under the table, hold her hand, and we run toward the water tour and freedom.

I turn my head back to look, and panic shoots through me. Hot on our heels about thirty feet away, the gunmen spot us and take off in our direction. My eyes open wide, and I gasp when I see one of the gunmen's arms. A tattoo on a broad, tanned skin, similar to Jake Kane's gang—a crescent and a uniquely designed knife.

The same people as the kidnappers back home. *What are they doing in Paris?*

Suzanne sees me slowing down and gives me a nudge. "Ouch!"

"Stop daydreaming and run faster! We are missing it." The tour boat's engine emits a churning sound in the still air.

Within a few steps, we jump onto the tour boat, out of breath, and we walk with quick steps toward the covered space. Moments later, the boat speeds off, leaving our pursuers behind. We duck down under a table to prevent them from noticing our hideout as we watch them race down the path and toward the tour operations counter.

The farther we move down the river, the more confident I become about having lost the gunmen, and our breath regulates. Once I am certain that we lost the gunmen, I text Eleanor, my palms still sweaty.

Immediately, she responds, "I will contact our counterpart in the National Police of Paris and work hand in hand with them. The murders of Lady Jacqueline and Mr. Spencer are high profile cases that everyone would benefit from concluding soon." I sigh in relief. "Someone from the National Police of Paris will be in touch with you, Alyssa."

I lean my head back against the wall and reply, "That sounds perfect."

I turn to look over the river, and a breeze blows on my face, causing me to shiver. Suzanne wraps her arms around her body, huddling into herself, and looks deep in thought.

Am I their target now too?

Chapter 22

Camera lights flash from every direction and partially blind me as I walk down the runway. My mouth curves into a broad smile while I strut in a pantsuit. It's a lilac and blue button-down, and shiny buttons trim the center of the pants. Suzanne's design for her entrance to Givenchy.

Crowds clap and cheer, a few wolf-whistles echoing when I make my entrance. I stop and shift on my feet to show off the clothes. The show is being held in Le Maurice Metiers Hotel's ballroom. Reporters, celebrities, and influencers surround the catwalk to the left and right. Many eyes sparkle at the outfit, and exhilaration makes me confident as I parade by.

There is a French Duchess, Lady Jessica, sitting at the VIP area in the left corner of the room, accompanied by an entourage. When I get to her corner, I walk gracefully, shifting side to side and circling slowly to show off the clothes for her, following the example of several other models in front of me. I turn to face her again, and a woman sitting beside her covers her mouth while screaming. I blink in confusion before my eyes notice the top of her evening dress is spattered with blood. I halt my movements as she jolts up from her seat.

I turn my head, searching for the reason she's causing the commotion.

"Argh! Argh!" I shout, breathing in and out shakily, my hands trembling. Blood flows from the Duchess's neck, and her eyes look blankly at the ceiling. Her head tilts to the side, and her body drops to the floor, lifeless. I quickly turn my head to the side, and the model beside me screams as well, pointing in Lady Jessica's direction. All of the models freeze, and some gasp, holding their sides in panic. My mascara smears as tears develop in my eyes, unable to get the look away from the horrific scene. I finally tear my gaze away and step back, accidentally stepping on another model's feet. Apologizing, I look at the ceiling where harsh lights are hung. Being on stage, I am higher than the guests, and I blink twice when I watch the shadow of a man move. I step nearer to them, my eyes trained on the spot. I lean from side to side, trying to catch a better view of the man. My eyes flare when the man's features register in my brain. Joe.

I shake my head and stare again in that direction, quickly taking my mobile from the pants' pocket and snapping a picture. I send the picture and a quick message to my message group with Jason and Eleanor. "I will chase."

The Duchess's security guard has covered her body with his large frame, shouting into an earpiece. Another security member runs after the suspected gunman. *Maybe Joe is the mastermind of this murder, but he had someone else do the dirty work for him. I must find out.*

Still feeling shaky, I muster my courage. I hurry backstage and turn to the narrow stairs on the right with a sign that identifies it as the backdrop and lights area. I jog up the stairs and look up when I hit the landing. I gasp, and my legs jam. My entire body shakes, and I come eye to eye with Joe, his right eye covered with a black eye patch. He had just landed from over the staircase railing. He stands, huffing and puffing after locking his eyes on me.

He casually straightens his black velvet jacket, pretending nothing has happened. We're so close that his chest rubs against my shoulder as he pushes me aside with his heavily built body. I try to avoid it, but it's too late. Knocked off balance, his vast arms wrap a soft cloth over my nose, and my eyes widen as he pulls me into his chest, holding me firm despite my struggling. I inhale instinctually as my body tries to scream. Panic floods me as the smell of chloroform fills my nostrils. He holds me there for several long moments before suddenly letting me go and pushing away. I flail and try to grab his collar, but my vision blurs, and my head spins. The floor shakes beneath me, and I breathe in and out deeply for clean air. I start to unbutton the top button of my blouse as I list against the wall for balance. My knees bend, and I slide to the floor, feeling weak. I turn my head to follow Joe's movements even though my head is heavy. Joe's silhouette is blurry, but I watch as he kicks the exit door and disappears outside.

I struggle to pull my phone out and dial. "Suzanne, he got away via the exit door. Call for help! He drugged me," I manage to spit out when she answers.

"OK, I'll call security," Suzanne answers in a quavering voice.

After the phone conversation, I look around, spotting a standing water filter a few feet away from me. I grit my teeth and stand, leaning against the wall, with my left hand pushing to move forward. Breathing heavily, I reach the filter and press the cold tap, which releases some water that splashes on my sleeve. I lift my sleeve to my nose and inhale. A few seconds pass before my vision gets somewhat better, and my spinning head stops. I stand straight, shake my head, and run wobbly toward the exit door. I push the door forcefully as I move onto the stairs. We're on the third level, and a *clink* echoes from below. I bite my lip as I try to think of how to get down quickly. My eyes snag on two service elevators, one of which is standing open. I jump into it, stabbing the ground floor button repeatedly.

I step out as soon as the doors open at the bottom, looking around wildly. My phone vibrates with a call from Suzanne. "A security guard noticed the guy you described walking toward a black Mercedes van out front. They tried to give chase, but he managed to stab their leg."

Hearing this, I run as fast as I can to the exit. I step onto the road, seeing Joe's silhouette about five hundred feet from where I am standing. He's pacing while waiting for his ride and on the phone. I take off toward him. While running, I pass by a few motorbikes. Joe's hand touches the door handle, and I jump onto a royal blue bike that is not locked. I throw on the safety helmet and hear from behind, "Salut, tu fais quoi?" A Frenchmen shouts angrily. "Only borrowing! I will return it," I reply, looking at the man with a smile and dipping my head down to show respect. I start the engine, squeeze the clutch, and speed off just in time to tail the Mercedes. The van speeds off to the left as soon as Joe closes the door. I ride the motorbike closely enough to follow their route. I say on the phone, "I am tailing them. Have Eleanor track my phone."

Suzanne replies worriedly, "You better be safe."

"Don't worry. I will follow until the Paris investigators collaborating with Eleanor have access to track the car."

"What do you mean?" she asks, sounding anxious, but I hang up without replying.

I speed the motorcycle closer to the rear bumper of the van, slapping an AirTag on its bumper while it stops at the red light. I reverse the motorbike and reduce my speed.

I press speed dial, and my phone connects me to Eleanor. "I just placed a tracker on the van. Can you see the tracking dot now?" I ask.

"Affirmative. Sending the information to my contact now," Eleanor replies gruffly. "Leave before you get into big trouble."

I hop off the bike at a bench on a street corner, grab a cigarette butt from the ground, and sit quickly. From the side of my eye, I watch the van, still waiting at the traffic light nearby. The driver rolls down the window, a gun pointing at me. My legs shake, and I hold the cigarette tightly, bringing it to my lips and keeping my face turned away. He watches me for a moment before he runs his tongue over his teeth, throws a cigarette on the road, rolls up his window, and speeds off as the light changes to green, the tires screeching in the night.

Chapter 23

I ride the motorcycle back the way I came, intent on returning the bike to the owner. As the bike passes by a garden next to the hotel, I notice the owner walking. I brake the bike beside a bench and take the helmet off. "Hello, I am returning the bike. Sorry for causing any inconvenience. Let me pay you for the ride." I take out some cash from my pocket. The French man smiles, checks his bike, and looks at the cash I am holding.

"I will take the money and consider it as if you rented it." We shake hands, and I smile, relieved he isn't angrier.

I make my way through the garden toward the hotel, and my phone vibrates in my pocket. I press to answer it without checking who is calling.

"Hello, Alyssa. One of the experienced Prefecture de Polis, Arthur Papon, an investigator in close association with us over there from the Gendarmerie Nationale Paris, will contact you to assist with the investigation." Eleanor sighs and continues talking. "I shared the tracker info with him as he is leading the case of the Duchess of France's murder."

"Alright. I'm happy to assist him." I chuckle and smile to myself before my head tilts. "Any luck on your side with tracing the abductors or Duke Jacque's whereabouts?"

Eleanor releases a long sigh, and her voice becomes tight. "No luck here for Lady Jacqueline's case. However, Inspector Raven, in charge of the murder case of Mr. Spencer, wants to talk to you about the evidence that you took pictures of. Nothing about locating them, though," Eleanor says before blowing a bubble with her chewing gum.

I stop walking, standing outside of the hotel, and my fingers shake as I talk, "Three murders within three months, all unresolved." My right hand clenches into a fist. "Two are confirmed to have Joe involved, and we have yet to find much about the mastermind that paid Joe and his gang to eliminate them." I pace, clenching my teeth at the thought of unresolved murders.

"We'll find them, Alyssa. I will piece together our records on the sequence of events. It will eventually lead somewhere," Eleanor responds with a thoughtful voice.

"OK. I have to go, for now, Eleanor. Talk to you later." I end the call and run a hand down my face.

A few moments later, my phone vibrates again, and I look at the screen. I blink at the unknown number before answering.

I place my phone to my ear and say, "Hello?"

"Salut. I am Inspecteur de Police Arthur Papon from the Paris police investigation team. Sorry to disturb you, Alyssa."

"Not at all," I respond cheerfully while I walk into the hotel. "Happy to help in any way."

"I believe you are the main person who followed the

murder suspect," he says, then clears his throat.

"Yes, Eleanor mentioned you would be calling." I smile to myself.

He continues speaking, "Let's meet up at the site of the incident in the hotel ballroom. It would be a great help if you could show me the suspect's exact location."

"Sure. I just got back to the hotel, so I will meet you soon." I end the call, keeping my phone in my hand.

When I reach the elevators, I notice Suzanne with furrowed brows and tapping her heels, looking around anxiously next to the seating area of the lobby. I wave at her and change directions. "Hi, Suzanne. I am required to meet an investigator upstairs to assist him. Please go home. I will call you once I am done and on my way to the apartment."

I hug her, and she pecks my cheek. She squeezes me before she pulls back to look at my face with tears rolling down her rosy cheek. "I nearly lost you." She holds my arms and looks into my eyes sternly. "Please be careful." I smile and nod before hugging her close again.

Minutes later, I am in the ballroom with Arthur Papon. After pleasant introductions, I show him where I saw Joe, as well as where I had my brief interaction with him. We then head back downstairs and to the exit.

"I am looking at the tracking device here." He glances at me, then focuses on the device that he is holding.

He shifts the tracker to face me, and my eyes watch the dots moving rapidly. Before I can speak, Arthur continues. "No time to lose. Let's track them down," Arthur Papon exclaims, his face looking anxious. I nod and walk side by side with him in long strides. He pulls out his keys and presses his car remote control, causing a nearby car's headlights to flash.

We get in a plain black Peugeot 308, and I connect the tracker to his dashboard digital map above the air vents. He turns his car 180 degrees from the hotel, and the car passes several buildings. The majority has beautiful architecture and various types of trees in front of them. Arthur Papon switches on the lights and sirens to speed through the traffic lights, and cars on the road yield to him.

He pulls an earpiece from his small glove compartment. He puts it on and says tensely, "Demander le renfort de la police."

The tracking dot is still moving fast, but Arthur seems familiar with the van's direction quickly, and our car heads to the motorway. His tires screech as we race on the dusty sand.

"Please open the glove compartment.'" He points with his right hand.

I push the lever overlooking a Sig Sauer SP22. Then I turned my head, looking at Arthur with confusion visible on my face.

"Take it. You may need it for protection once we reach the suspect's location." He momentarily looks at me, then looks back to the road.

"Sure." I take it and store it in my jacket.

I exclaim, "The tracker dot stopped at—"

"It is an abandoned fish storage warehouse. We are almost there," Inspector Papon interrupts.

He doesn't need to refer to the map as he swiftly presses the accelerator pedal and navigates us smoothly through several turns and traffic. Within moments, we arrive at the destination. *Amazing.* My mouth curves from side to side widely, adrenaline rushing through my veins. *This time, we will not miss catching Joe.* I breathe in deeply.

As the car reduces speed, Arthur leans closer to me and says, "Once we reach the warehouse, I will go in from the front." His head tilts, looking at the entrance from the car. I nod. He continues speaking, "Alyssa, go to the back entrance." His index finger points around the corner where long grass grows down the side, everything dimly lit. I gulp, seeing how unkept the grass is. "We will communicate via these earpieces. It connects to my team and me. Copy?"

"Yes, copy. Any backup?" I ask with my eyebrows pulling together.

"They are nearing. They are expected to arrive within a minute," he says with a chuckle.

He parks the car several feet away from the location, and I shut his car door quietly. A dull light emanates from the back of the warehouse through the front windows. As planned, I walk cautiously down the side, passing some varying-sized drums. They look similar to the ones back at the abandoned hospital. My eyes dart here and there down the path, and my breathing picks up. I point my gun at the ground, ready to pull the trigger if necessary.

I walk quietly, nearing the back entrance, and I feel sweat gather at the back of my neck, my stomach fluttering with butterflies. I inhale slowly to maintain my confidence.

I jump when Arthur Papon's voice suddenly sounds in the earpiece, "Alyssa, come to the front. I found the van. Repeat, Alyssa, come to the front immediately."

"Roger. Will be there soon," I whisper.

I am standing halfway to the back entrance, and my eyes roam from the back edge of the warehouse and its surroundings.

When I am satisfied that there is nothing of interest, I

step back a few steps and slowly twist my waist, turn my body, and scurry to the front entrance.

"The van is empty. I think they know they are being followed. They must have changed vehicles," Arthur reports.

"Interesting. Coming. I am nearing."

I pass dirty windows on the way with graffiti painted on the walls near the building's front.

I reach the front entrance and notice across the way and within the grass lie several durable, insulated fish containers. I quickly take out my gun and slowly open the door. I cautiously prod it with my gun as my feet step in, and I push the door wider so that my gun and my head have a clear view of the center, swinging to the right side to ensure no one lurks around the corner. From the corner of my eye, I can see Arthur Papon searching the van with his flashlight on, looking over every bit of the vehicle for clues.

"There are four fresh footprints, and it looks like they abandoned the van in haste. Roger," he says in the earpiece.

"I can see you. I am coming to assist," I respond.

Before I can step forward, a thunderous sound of rending metal envelops the warehouse. Goose bumps appear on my skin, and shivers run down my back, my stomach sinking.

Through the front door, I watch in horror as flames move like waves in the sea, hissing and sizzling, and engulf the van in a fierce fire.

Arthur Papon tries to run to safety as fast as he can, but the flames spread quickly like spilled water. When they mix with the materials and chemicals of the car, nothing can stop the explosion. The van's combustible materials, like dust and chemicals, evaporate, and the windows are shot up and sideways, shrapnel hitting his thigh and neck as he runs for cover. He limps before falling to the ground, crawling on the cement into the warehouse. He pushes himself to hide underneath a steel table located near the door. Unfortunately, the vibrations of the explosion are grave, causing the steel table to shake and drop, hitting Arthur.

The entrance door where I stand shivers, then jolts sideways. Its hinges rattle violently, cracking and pulling from their place. My feet freeze as my legs tremble from knees to feet. My hand pinches them, giving me the nudge to retrace my last several steps. A huge chunk of leftover window glass from the van flies further in the direction of the building's front entrance as another explosion rocks the shell of the van. I don't want to get hurt while holidaying in Paris.

I duck down while covering my head with one hand, the other hovering over my knees and legs, hobbling faster away from the warehouse.

"Call the ambulance and fire brigade quick," I yell into the earpiece. "Arthur needs help badly."

Once I am out of the warehouse, I hide near a bush. I watch as the warehouse also becomes engulfed in smoke and intense fire, moving quickly from one part of the dry roof to the next, windows breaking as the heat scorches everything inside.

How do I save Arthur without being burnt alive?

Thick smoke covers the surroundings of the warehouse as debris from bricks, pieces of broken glass, and other material flies through the air from the building's front and back.

The fire brigade and ambulance come screaming into

the lot, my jaw working as I watch on.

The firemen and paramedics spring from the cars running. I run to their side and speak with creases on my forehead, "Please, save Arthur Papon. Last I saw, he was at the center from this front entrance. Near the van." My fingers point at the location for the firemen. My brows pull together, and a small whimper slips from my lips. *I hope nothing serious has befallen Arthur.* I squeeze my eyes shut momentarily, then open them as I chew on my lip. I clasp my shirt above my heart and start pacing to and fro, hoping that any evidence that Arthur collected is safe along with him.

A paramedic approaches me and quickly hands me an oxygen mask after assessing me. I take the mask willingly, inhaling to neutralize any chemicals that I had inhaled earlier. At the same time, he places bandaids on both of my elbows as scratches are visible from me crawling on the cement floor and the rough ground outside.

Soon after, we hear heavy footsteps and voices. The paramedic turns his head as he steps backward.

"We need more help, quickly," someone shouts.

The paramedic that is attending to me quickly let go of everything he is holding in a flash, climbs from the van, and runs to the fireman to assist him in placing Arthur on a stretcher. Arthur is covered with a fire blanket when he receives him. Hurriedly, he puts an oxygen mask on him. Arthur's breathing is slow but deep, and another paramedic helps push the stretcher inside the ambulance.

Arthur is conscious, his face covered with thick ash, and he coughs non-stop. His hands move, and his eyes stare at me. I gasp and lean closer.

"Excuse me, I will accompany Arthur to the hospital." I hop into the ambulance and sit beside him.

His voice husky and short of breath, he tries to speak. The sound is not clear, and I lean my ear nearer to his mouth. "I have pieces of evidence. Please pass to forensic to identify."

My eyes grow wide at his words, and I pull back to stare at him. I open my mouth to ask about the evidence, but he stops me.

His right hand moves from his side, trembling as he shifts, and he clutches something tightly.

I extend my arm toward his, and his fist relaxes as something long is placed on my palm.

Knocking at the door rings in our ears, and an officer pops into the ambulance. I look at him with my hand clutching the item for dear life. "We are about to leave for the hospital. Please leave Arthur Papon with the team," the officer at the door says. I nod and smile at him.

"Of course."

Arthur's mouth moves slightly, and I place my ear near his mouth again. "Don't trust anyone, even Jerome." He tries to shake his head, but he grimaces in pain. I stare at him and breathe heavily. I pat his hand and jump off the ambulance.

While walking toward Arthur's car, I open my hand and look at the item, my mouth popping open. It's a mini spy camera the same size as my finger. There's another item, and I click it open. In a box the size of a matchbox, there is a hair specimen along with a cut fingernail. I slide it closed, my eyes looking around my surroundings while I slip them into my bag. My eyes continue darting within the vicinity while I zip up my bag.

I step back to allow more space for the paramedics to close the door, and I gasp as my body collides with a sturdy wall. I immediately turn my head, coming eye to eye with a man.

"Alyssa? I am Arthur Papon's partner, Jerome Gabriel." I smile at him. "Nice to meet you. Can I get a ride for you?" he asks as he holds out his hand. I shake it with my clammy hand.

"Certainly," I respond and nod.

Breathing deeply, I walk as confidently as I can master. Nerves run through my body as my thoughts run wild. I want to end this soon. I slap my fist on my other hand, determined to figure out the truth of everything.

Chapter 24

Back at Suzanne's apartment, and after cleaning up some, I dial Eleanor's mobile.

"Hi. I am positive that Arthur has information to share that leads to the suspects." I raise my voice while my hands shake, trying to control my temper. "Let me FaceTime you, Eleanor, to show you the items." I quickly tap on the screen, and Eleanor pops into view.

Eleanor raises her voice. "Woah!" Her face gets closer to her laptop, squinting. "It looks like a spy camera!" She points her finger at the item I am holding. "Please connect it to a laptop. Hopefully, there's something in the recordings."

I quickly switch on the laptop nearby, connecting the spy camera with a cord.

I blow on my bangs when I realize no password is required to access the camera and smile.

I click the icon for the spy camera, and a familiar face appears.

"It's Joe for sure,' I exclaim, jumping from my seat. I quickly turn my phone in the laptop's direction.

"So this is what Joe looks like," Eleanor responds and places her index finger on her chin.

I nod.

"But, wait. I can hear a faint voice." Eleanor waves for me to stay quiet and listen.

"Let's listen to the conversation and hope we see who the driver is too." A sudden flare of hopefulness seeps into my bones.

"The driver is French," Eleanor interrupts while folding her arms over her chest.

"We are to eliminate Lady Jacqueline's niece at all costs. Otherwise, our mission will be worthless. She knows too much."

A gigantic hand slams on the dashboard, causing a mini bobblehead's head to wobble wildly. Eventually, the vibrations cause the spy camera hidden in the doll to shudder, and the doll slides to the car floor.

My shoulder slouch as the view becomes only of the car's carpet.

The video recording of the conversation continues, however. It sounds like there is a phone conversation happening, as we can only hear Joe's side of the conversation. "Hey, it's me. Lady Jessica will be at Le Maurice Metiers Hotel's ballroom for a fashion show." He pauses. "Thanks, mate. You must distract her bodyguards while Mike and I take action." Another pause. "What? Shooting from the top near the stage lighting is the best position," he argues. We can hear him playing with a toothpick.

"Understood. Where is her reserved seat located?" His voice turns angry. "What? Idiot! Jason, you should have informed me of the process at the beginning." The sound of the van's door sliding can be heard.

He lets out a long sigh. "I am sending you the damn money now! Did you get it? Satisfied?" He grunts. "So blow the gaff now, mate." He laughs loudly after a moment. "So this is her VIP reserved seat in the corner. Perfect. If the seat changes, let us know." Joe whistles.

"Hey, Nate, you know what's the plan?"

Nate must be the driver, as another voice suddenly comes through. "Yeah. We will go in as cleaners in the afternoon to check the place out and store the rifle to eliminate Lady Jessica."

The sound of Joe clapping Nate's back is audible. "You understood well, Nate."

"Oh, here is her photo. So young. I believe she's in her twenties. She'll die young because she was never taught to not poke her nose into someone else's business." Joe chuckles lowly.

"Nate, we'll meet at noon to start our mission. Remember to get a fresh sponge for the chloroform."

Nate responds, confusion clear in his tone. "Joe, what's the sponge gonna do to help us?"

"Nate, use your brain, you fool. If our shooter misses Lady Jessica, the next best thing is to create a commotion and take her. We need to eliminate her at all costs. So we use it to knock her out. Then, we bring her into the van and finish her." He let out a hearty laugh.

"That's a good plan, Boss."

"Get the rifle ready and loaded with more bullets. And wear a mask and dark colors."

The car door opens and shuts with a slam.

The video goes silent, and I quickly press the pause button. "Wow, Eleanor, this murder was premeditated. I wonder who wanted her dead so badly, and what did she know they wanted to hide forever?" I run a hand through my hair, which becomes tousled.

"You are right, Alyssa. Is the recording finished? If the spy gadget remained in the same van the night of the murder, there might be some more conversations between Nate, Joe, and the mastermind?" Eleanor says, and I can hear her pacing.

I shrug and raise my palm, indicating no. "Let me continue playing it. I paused it just now." I press the 'play' button and rub my hands along my thighs, trying to ward off the chill in me.

Joe's voice echoes from the recording after a bit. "Hey, Nate, did you check everything?"

"Earlier, but let's go to the back and just double-check it again together."

We hear the van door open noisily.

There are no fully audible sounds for a bit, just stuff being picked up and placed down.

Finally, "Good, Nate. Everything is ready."

"Don't tell me I have to make the killing?" Nate's voice turns shaky. "I am not good at aiming, Boss. You know I have multiple sclerosis."

"No, you can't be the driver and the gunman. That's too much of a responsibility. You're more useful as a driver. Your knowledge of every street in Paris is awe-inspiring. I need you to get us out of there quickly."

A deep exhale can be heard. "Good. Kind of you." There's a pause. "Don't tell me you'll be in there alone."

"Definitely not." Joe snorts. "I will supervise. If the shooter misses their target, I cause a commotion so that they can kidnap her."

"Well thought plan, Joe. So who is your shooter?"

"Jake Kane appointed one. I will be meeting with her soon."

"A lady this time, huh? If plan B needs to happen, a woman is the most suitable way to prevent suspicion. Jake is damn good with strategies."

Joe chuckles. "See you in these clothes at 3 PM sharp. Here again." It sounds like he throws a bundle of clothes in the van.

"You can trust me. Everything will be perfect," Nate responds and whistles.

I pause it again and huff.

"There are lines on your forehead, Alyssa. What are you thinking?" Her right hand opens, facing me. "Spill the beans." Eleanor's gaze concentrates on me.

"We will be able to catch Jake Kane eventually, the mastermind that pays them to do the stinky job, once we capture this guy, Joe." I start pacing in front of my laptop. "However, I am also concerned about how we psychologically negotiate with or torture him once we catch him. He won't willingly share information about the mastermind." My fingers fidget on the table, lost in my thoughts.

We switch our FaceTime to our laptops, and as we discuss, a message beeps on both of our phones. I quickly look at the laptop, seeing Eleanor reading her message, and my finger presses to read the message. "Oh, it's a message from Grandmother." I frown as I read the first line, then continue. She says that her psychiatrist advised her to take a vacation out of the country. Therefore, she will be away for two weeks with Coco. I smile to myself.

I reply to her text, "Have a good rest, Grandmother. If anything comes up, please contact us. I am jealous of Coco. I wish I could just wag my tail, be cute, and accompany you everywhere." I roll my eyes.

"Don't be, Alyssa. When are you returning for my business, and when are you starting at the engineering company?" I scratch the side of my forehead, and my nose wrinkles. I pace within the sofa area, thinking of what to say.

"I will be back within a week's time to start at the engineering company. I am supposed to help Suzanne in Paris, but things have happened. Will discuss with you your business once we are both back. Take care, Grandmother."

I slouch, sitting on the couch as I close my lips tightly.

Eleanor's eyebrow tilts up at my reaction to Grandmother's question. I shake my head at her and sigh.

"Where was I? Oh, yeah. Eleanor, Arthur Papon's partner came to the site before the ambulance left. His name is Jerome Gabriel."

Eleanor nods and places her index finger on her chin. "Alyssa, I suggest you meet with Jerome and inform him of the findings in your possessions." Eleanor looks expectantly.

My mind goes temporarily blank, and I blink. I get up from the sofa and resume pacing.

"But, Eleanor, Arthur told me not to trust Jerome!" I shake my head. "He is definitely out, but I do require his forensic team to check the DNA of the hair and nail. But," My right palm faces forward, and I bite my lip. "Why does Arthur not trust Jerome?"

I hold my arms out to my sides, questioning Eleanor. I sit on the sofa and cuddle the cushion before continuing to share my thoughts with Eleanor. "Is he suspecting something? Is Jerome involved somehow?"

Eleanor hums in thought. "I understand your concerns, Alyssa. Let me search for the most reliable medical lab in Paris that can identify DNA. Meanwhile, go visit Arthur. Never know, he might be able to enlighten you." Eleanor's jaw tightens.

"Right on, Eleanor." I wave to her when she waves and the video disappears.

The sound of Suzanne's room door shutting echoes from the hall.

I power down the laptop, then walk toward her room. Her hair is tied up in a towel wrap, and she's wearing a fluffy white robe.

"Hey. Are you alright?" My eyes run over her, assessing for physical ailments.

"Yeah. I am happy that my clothing line was shown before the murder happened." Her voice is chipper.

I smile at her. "You are lucky. I heard the guests were excited about the line you made." I wink at her. My hands mime taking pictures before giving her a thumbs up, and we both laugh.

"What was the decision of the committee on the fashion show?" My palms lift in a questioning gesture.

"The committee approved me to design a summer collection for Givenchy since there were many guests that called to order the pantsuit that you modeled and the summer spaghetti strap dress another wore." Suzanne's cheeks glow as she smiles, and she hops on her spot.

I grin and clap my hands into hers.

"What! That is awesome news, Suzanne. Congratulations. I am so happy for your career," I say cheerfully while hugging her.

"Would you like to accompany me to the Centre Medical Saint Lazare Monte? I need to get something from Arthur Papon, then we can get a bite or something. It's been a long night," I suggest while tilting my head.

"Sure, OK. I would be delighted to follow you to the lobby of the Centre Medical," Suzanne responds. She looks at her robe and returns hastily to her room, her feet stepping in while her right hand pulls the door closed.

I walk to my room, deep in thought, and shut the door behind me. *I will get more information from Arthur.*

Chapter 25

We reach the hospital near midnight. I'm glad Suzanne accompanies me since she is wide awake from excitement; I'm starting to drag. We step out of the elevator quietly and walk for a bit before stopping at a door that says, "Arthur Papon."

We step inside, and I move to his side. "Arthur," I whisper in his ear to try and wake him. His face is peaceful even though a bandage circles his forehead, and there's an IV taped to his hand. The heart monitor beats out at a normal rhythm.

I say his name again, this time a little louder.

His eyes blink open, and his grey eyes stare blankly at the ceiling; then, he swiftly turns to face my emerald green eyes. His stiff posture relaxes, and his lips curve slightly upward. He clears his throat and opens his mouth to speak.

I smile at him and point to Suzanne. "My close friend Suzanne is the one in the fashion industry now attached to the House of Givenchy. Do you want her to step outside?" He nods with a small smile.

Suzanne whispers to me, "I will be at the nearby café, Au Depart Gare, since I am famished. See you there." She winks at me.

I nod, my mouth sliding into a lopsided smile.

I wait until the door shuts behind Suzanne before looking at him. "Arthur, do you want me to share my findings with you first?"

"Yes," he replies in a soft, shaky voice.

I report the video contents and tell him that Eleanor suggested submitting it to Jerome. His eyes open widely, and he has a sudden coughing fit. His left hand covers his face as it turns red, and he shakes his head in disagreement while his right hand waves no.

"You suspect he's a mole?" I ask him, tilting my head.

He nods. "I overheard his conversation to change the position of Lady Jessica's bodyguard. Her usual bodyguards went missing before the show too. I suspect he's being bribed to assist them." He rasps while his hands adjust the blanket.

He coughs again, then continues, "He just became a father, and they're having financial difficulties. He will do anything to get some cash right now." His gaze turns distant, and his mouth pulls tightly.

My jaw tightens at this information, and I exhale heavily through my nose.

"Guess the only way to find the culprit is for me to go to another forensic department to identify the DNA of the hair and fingernails." My heart pounds as excitement fills me at the idea of soon catching Joe.

He squeezes his eyes shut momentarily, then squints at me. His hand flashes me a thumbs-up at my suggestion before his gaze turns unfocused again. His index finger points to the side table's drawer, which has a get-well-soon basket sitting on top of it.

"You want me to open the drawer?" Lines form

between my eyebrows.

His head nods slowly. "Yes, Alyssa." Arthur clears his throat, followed by more coughing.

"Please take my phone and save everything I have in there on Jerome. I think it's related to this case," he manages between coughs, his voice cracking.

I extend my right hand and twist to face the drawer. I open it cautiously, wanting to make as little noise as possible since there is an officer on guard outside Arthur's room.

Suddenly, I feel unable to breathe normally, and my right leg starts to tremble. Arthur is giving me so much responsibility to end this case.

Why me?

I look down, and there are two phones and several trackers. I look at him, and his finger points at the one closest to me before placing his index finger across his lips. I grab the phone and a few trackers, placing them in my jacket's inner pocket for safety. I turn my head to study the door and bite my lip.

I pour a glass of water for him, and my head moves slightly to look at the guard stationed outside his room.

Arthur opens his mouth, and I lean closer to him, pressing the remote to tilt the bed, making it easier for him to drink. "I am entrusting you since we all want this case closed soon." He speaks slowly and quietly. "I also owe her from the Missing French diamond case." He sips the water from the cup I am holding to his lips. He coughs, and I hand him a tissue to wipe away the excess water.

"Thank you." He inhales deeply. "The only person you can trust is General Monte Alberque. His number is in my phone. My password is 461346." I nod, pretending to look for something in the basket and adjust the name card. "He is my boss, and I keep him updated frequently. Run along, Alyssa. And be careful." His eyes are serious as they meet mine.

"Get well soon, Arthur. It was nice working with you," I respond as I get up from the chair.

It's already half-past one when I leave his room. *I am lucky they allowed me to visit. The investigation is the only reason I was given a pass to visit him so late.* The hospital is still, and no one is around except for one nurse at the counter. I smile at them, passing by toward the main elevator. The normally bright lights are dim the entire hallway.

I dial Suzanne's number as the elevator doors chime open.

"Suzanne, I'm finished. Is the café still open? I'm starving." My right hand massages my stomach, hunger gnawing at it.

"Yeah. The café is just across the street. You leave the medical center's entrance, then turn to the right and walk until you see a traffic light where you're able to cross. I actually think Arthur's room overlooks it." Suzanne's voice says playfully.

Shortly afterward, I see Suzanne sitting with a steaming cup and move to join her. "You're right. You can see Arthur's room from here. I can see the police officer patrolling his hall through the window." I fall into the seat opposite Suzanne, facing the medical center.

My eyes dart from one table to another. Surprise flickers through me at the number of people here. I turn to look at Suzanne. "This café has odd hours." I narrow my eyes and look at the time on my wristwatch.

Suzanne twists her body to look around and shrugs before looking back at her cup of tea.

"They are a twenty-four-hour café. Their patrons are mostly from the medical center," she replies before sipping her drink.

"Here you are. Your croissants, ladies." I take the tray from the waitress's hands with a smile.

As we take our first bites, an ear-piercing screech of tires can be heard. Our jaws slacken as we look at the medical center's entrance to see the noise. Two men in tailored black jackets and sunglasses emerge from a car.

"No one wears sunglasses at night." Suzanne snorts, her eyes rolling as she watches the car.

"They look like they're late for something; though, I doubt they are hospital staff," I respond while munching my croissant.

Before long, the view of the Eiffel Tower nearby sparkling in the night pulls my attention from the men. I take out my camera from my handbag and snap some photos, enjoying the relative peace. A loud blast erupts in the night, which causes a shudder in my heart.

We instantly cover our ears, and scared gasps echo around the café. We look in the direction of the sound, and my stomach drops as I take in the sight of the hospital.

Thick smoke and fierce flames engulf the room that Suzanne and I assume is Arthur's. My eyebrows furrow, and my jaw hangs. The window has blown out, the frame dropping to the ground with a loud crashing sound. A body in a patient gown flies through the air not far behind the window casing. His arms flail while his hands work to find something to grab.

Suzanne drops her teacup, and we both jerk out of our seats instinctively. My heart races, and my hands shake as fear creeps under my skin. "No!" I scream.

The body hits the ground with a sickening *thud,* and

Suzanne and I quickly run over. The man's hands are splayed wide, his neck looks broken, and his eyes lifeless.

My mind finally processes the scene, and a whimper escapes my lips. "It's Arthur," I whisper, and I can't seem to stop my body from shaking. "Someone murdered him!" I shout with tears flowing down my cheeks, and I pull at my jacket.

Beside me, Suzanne's face looks like marble, and she's as still as a statue.

"How?" she utters in a shaky voice.

The sound of a message notification pulls my attention, and I fumble for the phone.

I take out Arthur's personal phone from my jacket pocket and read the message on the screen. "Stay Out. Or you will be next, Alyssa." The message is from an unknown number. My jaw tightens, and I grip my jacket hem.

"What's wrong, Alyssa?" Suzanne stretches her neck to peek at the phone in my hand. "Please share the message." I hold the phone out in her sight. Suzanne's eyes bulge from their sockets, and her right hand covers her mouth as a gasp slips past her lips. Tears brim, threatening to fall.

Screeching fills the air, and we turn to face the sound. A black van, similar to the one outside the warehouse, flies around the parking lot toward the exit.

My hand slides into my jacket pocket, and I smile when I pull out a tracker. "Suzanne, tell Eleanor to track my phone and call me."

Then, before she can say anything, I run as fast as I can after the van, sticking an AirTag in as I go. I was a national medallist sprinter in college, and I quickly gain ground as the van has to navigate traffic. I answer Eleanor's call as I run, and she tensely listens to me running.

The van stops with a shudder, waiting as an old lady with a walking stick crosses the street.

This is my chance. I dig deep and push harder, crouching to hide from the rear mirror's view. I reach underneath the van to place the tracker with one hand while the other holds onto the van's trunk handle. I fiddle with it until I am satisfied that it won't fall off. The driver accelerates suddenly, and the van takes off with my hands still latched to the van. I can't let go of the van while it's moving because of the angle my arm's in underneath it. I quickly jump, placing my feet on the bumper, and squeeze tightly with my arms, holding onto the van for dear life.

My heart thumps against my chest as the van continues. My AirPods are miraculously still in my ears, so I whisper to Eleanor about my tight situation.

"I will get help from General Monte Alberque immediately. Stay safe, Alyssa," she says in a tight voice.

The shrill sound of sirens fills the air after a few minutes, and the van swerves left, rocking as it hits something hard with a crashing bang. The vibrations shudder so powerfully through the van that I almost lose my grip. I gasp as smoke emerges from the front of the van. Another shudder runs through the body of the car, and I twist around to look. The van's front tires are wonky, one pulling loose and tipping over. The van jerks hard toward the unbalanced spot. With rapid breaths and sweat dripping down my temple, I let go of my grip, pushing my way into a back summersault away from the van. Panic turns my limbs to lead as an explosion booms, and blazing fire engulfs the van only a few feet in front of me. A man jumps from the driver's seat, scrambling away. The van is thrown high with a horrible rending. Thick, black smoke makes the air hazy, and the impact forces my body into a nearby garbage bin. Sharp stabbing surges down my back, and I massage it as I writhe in pain.

Sirens grow louder until there is a screeching of tires as a car skids to a stop nearby. A gunshot lingers in the air, making my heart skip a beat, and I inhale sharply. Quickly, I push off the ground and crouch, trying to make myself as small as possible.

Two policemen with guns and batons rush from their vehicle and chase after the van's driver. He is limping badly, blood gushes from his knee, and his skin is badly burned. Another police car races to the scene, the driver getting out to join the chase. It's Jerome, and he sprints, crossing the park filled with lots of benches parallel to his two counterparts. From his trajectory, he's going to make it to the driver first.

The injured driver turns his head, sees Jerome, and snorts as he glares at him. Jerome slows his pace, raising a gun at him. He shoots, dirt spraying from the ground several feet away from the man. The injured driver limps faster, heading to the corner of the garden.

My concentration gets interrupted when my phone vibrates, and I peek at the screen. There's a message from Eleanor that reads, "General Monte will be calling you soon."

Not even ten seconds later, my phone rings with an unknown number, and I press 'Accept.' "Hello, Alyssa. This is General Monte speaking. Eleanor informed me of the whole incident. Two of my trusted men will be there. They are in plain clothes, approaching from the north. They will be in light blue tops with sleeves bearing the French flag. Charles has an anchor tattoo on his right arm, and Jules has a birthmark on his forehead. Do not trust others within the police force."

"Copy," I respond with my head nodding.

My eyes dart back to the injured driver, not wanting to lose sight of him, while also stretching my neck to search for his men.

I walk several paces forward, not wanting to miss viewing the chase.

I gasp as a man with a light blue puffer jacket bearing a French flag on his shoulder climbs down the rope of a convenience store lot just beside the park. He lands smoothly and silently, then takes out a square blob from his backpack. He pushes a button, and the object grows longer sideways.

"Wow, that is cool," I can't help but say out loud. "Wait a minute . . ." I squint and burst out in disbelieving laughter. "It's a mini skateboard! Perfect!" I cry excitedly. Never in my life have I seen an officer use a skateboard to capture a criminal.

I make it to the entrance of the floral park closest to me, trailing closer to keep the group in sight. The injured driver fires in the direction of the two policemen, then Jerome's. A bullet hits the leg of one of the other officers, and he tumbles to the ground. His hands hold onto his leg, quickly tearing his sleeves and wrapping his leg. His partner continues the pursuit, calling for help over the radio.

General Monte's man, with the aid of the skateboard, reaches the injured driver in the nick of time. The man jerks away as a shadow falls over him. He stumbles, and the officer jumps on him, both hitting the ground near the road on the other side of the park. General Monte's man places a black baton on the injured driver's neck, not letting him move or talk. The agent skilfully cuffs the man.

A black Jeep appears, and the secret agent pulls the

injured driver up, shoving him roughly into the car. As the door shuts, Jerome curses and shoots at the Jeep.

I turn and head down the street, determined to get away as quickly as possible, but the car makes a turn and pulls up beside me.

"Get in, Alyssa. General Monte's instructions." He shifts to show the French flag on his sleeve and mutters, "I'm Jules."

I smile and get it. I have the spy camera recordings on Arthur's phone that I need to share with General Monte's men. Hopefully, this will help us catch Joe and Jake Kane.

The door slams shut once my legs are safely in. My left hand grips the handle above the door on the bumpy ride to avoid slipping and hitting Jules as the car speeds through the night.

I press Eleanor's name and send her a quick text. "I am in a Jeep with General Monte's men, Jules and Charles. We have the driver from the van. Will contact you later for any updates." I put my phone in my jacket pocket without waiting for her reply.

"Where are we heading?" My hand waves in an asking gesture.

"We are meeting General Monte for interrogation," Jules replies.

"Get ready to move soon. To cover our whereabouts, we are to leave via helicopter to a secret location," Jules shouts from upfront, his eyes meeting mine in the mirror.

The injured driver grumbles something, but he's gagged with a tight black cloth. He shakes his hands to adjust the grip of the cuffs, and his sleeves flip, flashing a tattoo of a crescent and an intricate knife.

I gasp, and my left hand massages my knee, which starts to shake slightly.

"This guy is connected to Joe and Jake Kane." I quickly text Eleanor. "He has the same tattoo as them. I wonder what gang they are in?"

The Jeep halts abruptly, just missing a truck that swerves into our lane.

"Move, now!" Charles shouts as lines wrinkle his forehead.

Jules instantly opens the door while pulling the injured driver, and I jump from my side's door, rolling toward the curb.

Charles jumps from the Jeep moments before a loud, piercing sound erupts in the air. The truck hits the Jeep, completely totaling it. The truck only suffers a minor dent and a broken right-side mirror; otherwise, it is still in good shape.

Jules whistles to signal me to follow him. Without any hesitation, I run to Jules, brushing dirt and street dust from my pants as I go. He takes two skateboards from his backpack and places them on the road.

My head swivels, looking for Charles, and I smile in relief as he approaches us.

"Run! The truck's heading toward us!" Charles screams.

Frozen, I stare for only a moment at the incoming truck before taking off with the others. We manage to dodge around several streets, the truck close on our heels. My chest heaves, and my legs burn, and I'm about ready to collapse when a rumbling sound echoes around us.

"General Monte!" Jules yells with a grin, and his eyes sparkle.

A silver sedan with wing doors that open upward breaks abruptly perpendicular to the corner ahead of us. Dust flies in the air, and I cover my nose with my sleeve.

"Get in. Let's be quick," he says while his hand gestures for us to get in the car.

I smile and dive into the sporty sedan.

The sedan driver takes off and swerves hard right as the truck barrels down the street, intent on us. This catches the driver by surprise, and I watch his jaw tighten as he struggles to maneuver the wheel. With a resounding squeal, the truck topples over, unable to navigate the sudden turn, and rolls over the cliff across the street.

We're all quiet for a few moments, trying to catch our breaths. General Monte dispatches a team to the site, and an ambulance is on the way as well. Finally, I'm able to drag my gaze from the cliffside and examine the interior of the car once we start moving. It's been built for rescue purposes with added wings and motor function to move underwater on the river. Once we reach the river bank, the driver presses a button which makes the vehicle morph, so we are floating on the river. There's a slight rocking sensation as the car glides through the waves.

From the side of my left eye, I strain to look at the injured driver. He is silent the whole journey but swallows excessively, biting his lips. He's jumpy, there's a distinctly worried look on his face, and his body looks uncomfortably stiff.

Within fifteen minutes, we park in front of the massive mouth of a cave. There's a mechanical sound as the car latches to a pad underneath. My heart thumps harder, and I start to grip my pants again. I feel jittery as the car descends from the top to the basement at a speed similar to a lift and dim lights welcome us.

Chapter 26

The door shuts noisily at a room in General Monte's hideout beneath the river.

"Interrogation will begin soon," I hear a rough voice say as I walk into a dark room set up with recording equipment. I move to the corner, planning to stay out of the way.

The table shudders as General Monte's huge palm smacks the table directly in front of the injured driver, causing him to flinch and grit his teeth.

"My name is Vermont," he provides in a shaky voice.

"Who sent you to kill Arthur Papon?"

His eyes open widely, and he shakes his head. "I only pick up the services without knowing who ordered them. I am only a driver for transporting humans, drugs, and expensive stolen goods." He shrugs. "I don't know the details. I need to feed my family, so I do whatever jobs come." He shakes his hand slightly to gesture no again.

"What was your role in the murder of Arthur Papon? You were always in the van, or you planted the grenade and returned to the van? Pressed the remote control to denote the bomb?" General Monte's face gets closer to his face with his after-smoke breath, and Vermont shifts back to avoid the smell. "Well?" General Monte asks him in a firm voice while gripping his shirt firmly at the neck so that his shirt collar only allows him a little space to breathe.

His mouth pulls into a grimace, and he draws back, remaining shut.

His hands are connected to a polygraph machine. A detection of stress will notify us if there is a sense of lying. So far, nothing.

The door to the room springs open, and Jules strolls in. It is his turn to interrogate him after watching through the glass. He shakes Vermont's chair hard. Vermont stares forward at the blank white wall. Jules leans closer to him, his arms pulling at Vermont's shirt harshly.

His forehead creases, and there are sweat marks visible under his arms. He raises a shaky hand.

Jules wipes his mouth as he lets go, waving his left hand at Vermont. "Speak. I need information on who murdered Arthur Papon and Lady Jessica. Who contacted you?"

His throat bobs as he swallows, and his upper lip curls before he lets out a sigh.

"There—There was a man, but I don't know his name," he says in a shaky voice. "He sends information and money to me."

"How do you contact him, or where do you meet him? How does he send the money?" Jules shouts. The driver shakes as he shrinks away from Jules.

I push my lips together and huff, then move to enter the room to ask him some of my own questions. "So you only met him once to exchange information and physical money?"

Vermont nods, glancing at me nervously.

I lean against the table in front of him, showing him Jake Kane's photo first. Vermont squints his eyes, confused. "Him?"

"No. I haven't seen him. He is not the one." He fidgets in his seat, looking down.

I push off the table and circle around to the other side, leaning closer. "What about this guy?" I ask as I hold up a picture of Joe.

He gasps, and his eyes open wide.

"So this is the guy who gave you the job?"

Sweat trickles down his temple. He plays with his fingers underneath the table, silent.

After a moment, he raises his hands, trembling, and his nails black from dirt, touching the photo. He yanks it from my hand and throws it on the floor, stomping on the photo. "I wish I hadn't met you or taken the job! You idiot!"

Jules grabs him and holds him as he regains his composure.

"Sit! Be calm," Jules shouts, concern on his face.

"Where can we find him?" I ask, opening my arms after he has quieted.

I lean nearer his face, asking, "Is he part of the Hornec brother gang?"

He responds while shaking his head firmly, "He is a private contract killer." He breathes in and out several times before continuing in a quavering voice. "He runs his own operation internationally." He rubs his sweaty forehead.

General Monte's phone rings, and we all look at him. General Monte listens, a look of concern sliding onto his face. "What? He escaped?" He clenches his jaw, and his posture stiffens. "Which part of Asia is he heading to? Shanghai . . ." he whispers, then his fist tightens on his phone. "Keep tracking him and keep me updated." He ends the call, his right hand resting on his waist.

General Monte signals me out of the room. We return to the viewing room, and he dials Eleanor's number. "Hello, I asked my other team to track Joe down. However, he's made it to Asia." His lips press closed tightly. "I will update as I can. Thank you."

I sigh and run a hand through my hair. "General Monte, I will be returning to the States tomorrow. Is there anything else I can help with before then?" I say with a small, tired smile.

He returns it with his own. "It was good having you here. Try to enjoy the rest of your visit." He pats my right shoulder. I nod, smile, and walk to the exit, where Jules waits to bring me to shore.

The next day, I take one last look at my room in Suzanne's apartment before closing the door. Sadness fills my heart. *I did not spend much time with Suzanne.* I sigh deeply. We head to the airport, and I squeeze Suzanne tightly before having to leave her at security. A tear tracks down her cheek, and my eyes fill with water. I take a tissue from my bag and hand it over to Suzanne, using another to dab at my own tears. She looks at my face, her makeup smudged, and blows her nose with the tissue. She pulls me closer and hugs me again. She lets go of me, her eyes red, and we wave at each other sadly before I turn and get in line.

Chapter 27

My phone rings noisily, and I push aside my messy clothes on the bed at Grandmother's villa to grab it.

"Alyssa," Dad's voice says in my ear.

"Hi, Dad. What's up?" I grin, not having talked to him in a while. I shift through my clothes.

"I have bad news . . . Are you driving?" he asks hesitantly.

"No. I am packing. What's wrong?" I put down the shirt I was getting ready to fold, sitting on the edge of my bed.

"When was the last time you talked to your mom?"

"Just last night before she went on a cruise," I say slowly as my heart starts to pound. "Why, Dad?" I ask as dread sits heavily in my stomach.

"A robber attacked her cruise boat. While chasing, your mom was accidentally shot and killed."

Ringing fills my ears, and my mouth drops. "What?" I whisper. "No. I just talked to her." Sobs wrack my chest, and my voice cracks. I wrap my arm around my waist, shaking.

"Officials are transporting her body, and she'll arrive

tomorrow." He pauses and audibly gulps. "Do you want to accompany me to identify her body at the hospital?" Dad's voice sounds intense.

I don't answer as another sob rocks my body.

He sighs softly and says, "I know it's hard to accept this news. But you are strong, my girl."

I swallow and manage to say, "Yes. Yes, Dad. I will be there." I hang up as a fresh wave of tears runs down my cheeks like a water tap was left open.

I slip from the bed to the floor, sitting curled in a ball with my knees close together as my soul breaks.

A few minutes later, someone knocks softly at my room door.

Jamie opens my door, and once his eyes find me, he moves to my side.

He tucks the hair hiding my face behind my ears and gently pulls my face up to face him. "Alyssa, I am so sorry to hear about your mother. If you need anything . . ." Fine lines crease Jamie's forehead, and a broad frown pulls at his lips. He sits beside me, rubbing my arm.

I look up with red eyes and nod before pulling myself into a tighter ball.

Jamie hands me a tissue, and I blow my nose before wiping uselessly at my nonstop tears.

He pulls me into a hug and pats my back as I sob.

A phone chime distracts me, and I look up, frowning. "It's Arthur Papon's phone. That was his message notification," I say, my voice cracking at the end.

"Let me look for you," Jamie suggests with his right palm up.

"It's in my top drawer on the left." I point with my chin.

He scurries to grab it. "What is the password?"

"461346," I respond in a quavering voice.

"Gotcha. I am in. Woah!" He presses his hand against his gaping mouth. "It's a threat to you." Jamie tousles his hair, and his jaw tightens.

"What do you mean?" I ask Jamie, and my hand grips the fabric of my pants. I bite my other hand's fingernails, my stare empty and distant.

Jamie moves closer to me and sighs heavily while holding out the phone.

I read out loud from an unknown number: "I warned you again and again, but you are stubborn. Look what you have done to your mother. When you called your mother last night, her phone activated the grenade in the boat that killed her. YOU MURDERED YOUR MOTHER!"

I turn my head to look at Jamie, and my throat feels thick as tears well in my eyes again. "No! That's not true. It wasn't me! It's you!" I shout in a croak at the phone. I snatch it from Jamie and throw it on my bed. Fresh tears fall.

He says in a low-pitched calming voice, "All of us know that he did it and not you. Your mother was shot, not blown up, as he claims. He's trying to manipulate your emotions and mind while you are in a fragile state." Jamie soothes me, hugging me and stroking my hair.

A few seconds later, his left arm moves, and a dial tone emits in the air near my ear.

I shift my head to look at him. "Jamie, what are you doing?" I grab Jamie's hand that is holding Arthur's phone. He shakes his head.

"I am warning the idiot not to disturb you." Jamie's cheeks glow red, and all of the fingers of his right hand are curled tightly.

The phone blinks with light, then goes blank.

"Is the coward not answering me?" Jamie raises his voice and frowns.

"He is using a burner phone. You can't reach him. The police in France and here is trying to catch him, but he keeps slipping away." I sigh, taking a tissue to wipe off more of my tears.

Jamie's shoulders slouch, and he pulls me close to hug me again. "You will be alright." He looks at me, concern in his eyes. "I will stay with you tomorrow." He smiles at me.

With an unsteady voice, I ask, "Will you get in trouble with Rihana for visiting me and accompanying me to the mortuary?" My eyebrows draw together.

He shakes his head and tucks me under his chin. "There was a death involved. Rihana's not fussy about it because she understands." We stay that way for a while, and my heartbeat slowly steadies. I lay my head against his sturdy shoulder, and a fragile peace settles over me that breaks every time grief stabs through my body.

The next day at the King's Hospital's mortuary, the morgue assistant pulls out my mom's body from a steel drawer. The three of us surround the moving stretcher, and the assistant pulls down the cover from her head. It is Mom, but she's too still. She's pale and peaceful. I start sobbing. "Why must you leave me so soon?"

Jamie wraps his hands around my waist, and my head leans against his broad chest.

The assistant breaks the silence. "The pathologist plans to perform an autopsy since the police suspected her death might be linked to Mr. Spencer's, Lady Jacqueline's, Lady Jessica's, and Arthur Papon's murders."

We nod solemnly, and my father asks, "When will the result be complete? And they will be reported to the police?" He reaches out and pats my hand.

"If it is simple and direct, the results will be out by noon tomorrow. Otherwise, it will take at least two days. All reports will be shared with Inspector Raven and Inspector Eleanor."

The mortuary assistant tilts her head, covers my mom's face, and pushes the gurney back into the steel drawer. She locks it, then shows us the way out.

Once we're home, I walk to my room, and my phone vibrates in my pocket. I pull it from my jacket and look at the caller ID, smiling wryly.

"Grandmother. How have you been?" I try to mask the sadness in my voice with excitement.

I take off my jacket, then plop on my bed.

"I've been trying to get some rest and peace of mind." She does sound refreshed, so I hope she's more at peace. "I've been to Malibu, Kuala Lumpur, Shanghai, and Thailand."

I gasp. *Wasn't Joe last heading to Shanghai?*

"Alyssa, my dear," she continues, oblivious to my inner turmoil, "I heard the dreadful news. I am sorry I cannot be at your mother's funeral." Her voice mellows.

I fall back and stare at the ceiling, unexpected tears falling from my eyes.

"It is alright, Grandmother. You have your own problems to settle." My voice quavers, and I get up to walk to the side table beside my closet to get a tissue box.

"Don't be too sad, my dear. She wouldn't want that." She pauses and sighs. "I will be home in three days' time."

I blow my nose with a tissue. "I heard you are actively packing and choosing which furniture to take to your new apartment at the Gold Luxe Luxury Apartments." Her voice turns cheerful. "I don't want you to feel pressured to move out, but I believe a lady your age requires some freedom now that you've healed." She chuckles.

"I understand your plans for me, Grandmother. I just wasn't aware that I owned two of the apartments and have 90% shares of the apartment building. Guess I didn't read close enough when I signed the contract." I rub my neck as the intense pressure of having 90% shares of the apartment slams through me.

"My mind must have been astray when you signed. Please forgive me for not informing you of the contract details fully, Alyssa," Grandmother asks in a sweetly soothing voice.

"It is alright, Grandmother." My right hand fiddles with a few strands of my hair. "I will do anything to make you happy and help your company flourish." I slump on the bed, feeling tired, and my eyes flutter closed.

"Aw, you are such a sweet, thoughtful woman, Alyssa." My eyes open at her voice, and I smile to myself.

"You sound sleepy, so I better run along. Try to rest, and don't be too sad."

"Have a safe flight and see you soon, Grandmother. I love you." I end the call and place my phone beside me. Soon after, I doze off.

Chapter 28

I stand in front of the entrance of Unicornfire Engineering Enterprise. The building must be at least twenty stories, and my floor is on the eleventh. The façade of the building is sleek and modern. The windows show shadowed silhouettes of chairs and workstations.

I gulp and look at the top of the building, raising my hand to block the sun and clouds. The skyscraper's façade is entirely tinted windows.

I straighten my blazer and walk through the glass sliding door. The lobby has a black office sofa set on the right side with some engineering magazines spread on a square glass table at the center. There is a pathway to a bank of six elevators in the corner from where I'm standing. On my furthest left sits a tall, rich mahogany desk with two female receptionists and two security guards behind it.

I swallow my nerves and approach them. "Good morning. I am Alyssa, a new employee for the Engineering Department. I guess I need a temporary pass to go to the eleventh floor?" One of the receptionists smiles while my left hand taps my left leg.

"Yes, your name is on our orientation day list." She

scrolls the list on her computer, then looks at me. "Welcome, and good luck. We're happy to have you join Unicornfire Engineering Enterprise. Let me get your pass." She grins brightly before turning her attention back to the computer, her hands flying across the keyboard.

A few minutes later, she places a staff ID card on the counter facing me. "This is your temporary card that gives you access to the elevators, utilities, and cafeteria. You will receive an email from security when your official card is ready to be collected." She smiles and gestures in the direction of the elevators. "This is the way to your department."

"Thank you." My mouth curves upward on both sides. My heartbeat is back to normal, comforted by the warm welcome from the receptionist. I walk past the gate and to my ride.

The door opens, and I step out onto the eleventh floor. Plants decorate the lobby area of the elevators, and a trash bin sits under the buttons. I turn and push the glass door that reads "Engineering" open and move inside the sleek office.

"Hi, good morning. Alyssa Smith. You are to join Team A. I'm Melissa Trey, your supervisor." A woman in her thirties with wavy black shoulder-length hair stands in front of me with a polite smile. She waves her hands. "Your workstation is at the edge here overlooking our Supply Chain Department that's headed by Albert Tan." Her finger points toward the desk.

"Hi, nice to meet you. I hope to learn and experience as much as I can," I reply while smiling, extending my right hand to shake hers. Ms. Trey nods and shakes my hand, and we continue my orientation day in a blur.

The next day at work, I just put down my bag and

jacket when Melissa stops by my desk with a smile. "Alyssa, we have a project in Dakota Jersey. You and Lucas, who is a senior project engineer, are to check out the site tomorrow morning and return to the office after lunch to write a report on your findings. This project will be for a month." She places her laptop on my desk, the project layout pulled up on the screen.

I nod and smile as I study the notes. "Sounds great."

A man with dark brown hair approaches, and he smiles warmly. Melissa introduces him to me as Lucas. He hands me a folder. "Alyssa, please read our client's information before we head out. Zarason Construction is a subsidiary of Spencer Limited." He pauses, making sure I understand. I nod, and he continues, "This project links to their plans to build yacht dock areas to cater to the rich and famous. We are to analyze the safety and profitability of the proposed area."

I nod and smooth down my clothes, grinning. *Real world experience. Fantastic.*

His eyes scan my attire, and he purses his lips. "I would advise you to wear pants and comfortable shoes for this project. Heels and skirts aren't great at a site."

"OK, will do. Should we meet at the site tomorrow morning at 9 AM?" I reconfirm.

"Exactly. You are OK to drive there alone?" He looks at me, and his head tilts in a questioning manner.

I nod. "Sure. The town is nearby, and I know the way there."

"Let's have a short discussion at 4 PM on your thoughts on the proposed development area." Lucas smiles, a dimple visible on his right cheek.

I return his smile with my own.

It's around lunchtime, and I am deep in numbers

crunching and research on the planning and size of the boat club. Phone notifications have been dinging nonstop from the Supply Chain department across from my cubicle. I roll my eyes and wrinkle my nose at the frequent loud sound. *Don't they have work to do other than messaging on their phones?*

I sigh and rest my chin on my hand. I turn my head slightly to my left to look at the Supply Chain desks. The side of my eye catches on a young man in his late twenties whose cubicle is just opposite mine as he rolls his shirt sleeves. I gasp as he reveals his forearm tattoo, and I shiver. My hands tremble, and I accidentally drop my pen. My gaze is far away as it rolls away on the floor. *It's the same shape and color Joe and his gang have.* I breathe in and out rapidly and shake my head.

He glances over and smiles at my carelessness. I smile at him woodenly, quickly grabbing the pen. Embarrassment turns my cheeks warm, and I look at my laptop, pretending nothing has happened. *Can he be spying on me, or does he coincidentally work here and with Joe?* All of a sudden, dizziness seeps into my head at the possibility. I swallow and inhale deeply.

I stand up and walk a few seats away to Lucas's cubicle.

"You look pale, Alyssa. Are you sick?" he asks, eyebrows meeting each other.

"Dizzy spell." My right hand rubs my forehead. "If it's alright, I will rest in the break room for a bit. I am halfway through writing my analysis and will be able to share as promised." I flash a quick smile to reassure him.

"Sure, go ahead," he mumbles as his brow furrows further in concern.

I walk to the elevators with my phone in hand, stabbing the down arrow impatiently. I step in, turning to look at the buttons, when a voice calls out, "Hold on!"

The man with the tattoo stops me from closing the lift door. Butterflies erupt in my stomach as he steps inside as well.

Oh my, it's only the two of us in the lift. Is he going to try to hurt me? I inhale deeply and can feel the color drain from my face.

My eyes stare forward at the floor button panel after giving him a polite nod. He presses the button for two floors below. His name card falls forward as he leans toward the buttons—Alistair. I blow out a silent breath and smile. We're not heading to the same place since the breakroom is four levels below.

He smiles at me and says, "I heard you are new here. Welcome. And as I'm sure they said, you need to be a top performer to be part of the Engineering Department." He grins and winks at me. "It is the fast track team, and without fail, they get the best bonus every year. So you're lucky." He chuckles and runs a hand through his hair before he extends it for me to fist bump. I hit his knuckles with mine while smiling at him. *He looks like an innocent guy, so why is he involved with Joe?* The doors open, and he gives me a small wave as he exits.

The elevator door opens on my floor, and I step out, turning to the right. I dial Eleanor's number as I find a seat in the corner and tell her the information in a whisper. There are only a few people across the room, but who knows how good their hearing is.

She hums, processing the information. "If possible, try to get to know him or follow him after work hours. Maybe he assists Joe, or he's Joe's relative?" Eleanor suggests.

"OK, Eleanor, will do," I reply softly.

Within a few minutes, I start to feel better, and I take the elevator back to my desk. I throw myself back into my work, wanting to forget about everything else outside of this building for at least some time.

I blink as my watch alarm chimes at four. I look at it, then continue typing, finishing up a paragraph.

I turn my head when a voice calls, "Alyssa, let's discuss in the small meeting room near the kitchen." Lucas looks at me as he gets up from his desk nearby. "I got your message, by the way." He smiles as he taps on his phone. "It's a good idea for the Supply Chain team to join us."

"Right on, Lucas." I push my chair back to join him. My mouth curves high on both sides before unplugging my charger from the socket. I gather my stuff on the workstation, bringing along a notebook, pencil box, laptop, and small projector. A shadow falls over my desk, and I shift my head slightly. Alistair is suddenly standing beside me. His hand takes hold of my laptop as it slips from my grip.

He chuckles. "We didn't officially introduce ourselves, did we? I am Alistair, and you are?" He smiles, his head falling to the side in a tilt.

He has the sweetest smile, and his sea-blue eyes are enchanting.

"Thank you. I'm Alyssa Smith." I tuck a strand of hair behind my ear.

"Ah, the Smiths." He smiles and, at the same time, winks at me. "Your grandparents and their businesses are very influential in this town." He walks beside me, and his hand gestures in a question. "Why are you working here when you can easily get a job with your grandparents?" He quirks an eyebrow as he looks at me.

"I just graduated. It doesn't seem right to work at their company without prior experience." I look at him while adjusting the projector bag on my shoulder.

He tilts his head, nodding thoughtfully. "Very wise granddaughter they have." He shakes his head and chuckles. "Shall we have a drink together after work?" he asks, pushing the glass door of the meeting room open and intently meeting my gaze.

I can't help the blush that washes over my cheeks. "That sounds perfect, provided I am not caught in this report for long." I shrug, smiling.

"OK. I will check back with you later then," he says with a grin.

Lucas turns his head as we enter the room and says, "Alistair! Come here." He taps a pencil in his hand. Alistair nods and puts my laptop down on the table before moving across the room. "We would like to extend an invitation to view our client's site tomorrow morning. Apologies for the short notice. My new teammate, Alyssa, here," his eyes look at me, and I nod, "highlighted a good point. Our Supply Chain Manager should share some of the input."

Alistair blinks at Lucas, lips pursing. "I have to check what is on my plate to see if it's possible."

"Not much for you to prepare, thankfully. We just need information on the cost of boats, berthing, membership, security, etc. You can email me the approximate cost before the visit?" Lucas takes off his glasses, and his jaw tightens, his fingers tapping on the table.

Alistair looks straight at the wall in thought, then replies, "Hm. Yes, mate, will do. I will send it to you and Alyssa by tonight. I will message you and Alyssa when it's done." He scratches the side of his forehead and looks at me. "I don't have Alyssa's number, though."

"I will pass the message to Alyssa once you text me. Thank you, Alistair, for your assistance. I owe you dinner once we win this project." Lucas laughs, smiling.

———

I pass Alistair's cubicle on my way back from the discussion, and he waves at me to stop. I stop at his desk, and he says, "We will have to postpone our drink to another day since I now have extra work," he says good-naturedly. I nod and smile.

How can I find out more about him? Unless I stay late at work with him . . .

My hands shake, and butterflies fill my stomach at the thought.

A few minutes pass before I work up the courage to put my plan into action. I approach him, and he's concentrating on the screen with a pencil stuck behind his right ear. "Alistair, since I am not doing anything tonight, and I have tons of amendments to make to the report before tomorrow's site visit, shall we go for a snack once we're done tonight?" I'm proud of the fact that my voice doesn't waver once.

"That's a good idea, Alyssa." He smiles, his dimple visible. He turns back to his computer, and his fingers resume their dance on the keyboard as I triumphantly walk to my desk.

At five in the afternoon, a phone rings loudly. I glance up and see Alistair pull two phones from his drawer. He places the Lenovo at his ear, "What do you want, Joe? I am damn busy." There's a pause, and he grunts. "It's a deal. The shipment is Friday night. Obviously, we can't make it faster." He tosses the other phone back into the drawer and slams it shut. He turns, and his eyes lock with mine. His sea-blue eyes look strained and stressed, but they sparkle when he sees me. He speeds away, still holding the Lenovo phone to his left ear.

I try my best to remain composed by smiling naturally as he leaves, but my pulse jumps. Is it Joe, the mastermind of the murders, or a coincidence? I need to befriend him to know. I press my lips together tightly.

I startle as an angry barbarous voice rings in my air. "You are too slow, Siew June. Look how long I have to wait for the report!" A hand slams a table, and the noise fills the quiet office. "No! No! No! This is a rubbish report, Siew June." I find the source of the commotion as the man throws the thick report harshly on the table. A woman who must be Siew June quickly gathers the papers into her arms.

Siew June looks like she is in her late twenties, and her face turns red as she breathes deeply. I guess she is trying her best to remain calm.

"I will email you the sample report. Submit it to me by ten tomorrow morning. I am off. I don't know why you are so stupid and slow." The superior places his index finger on the side of his forehead and shakes his head.

After her superior leaves, my eyes dart to the corner of her section. I prop my chin in my hand, curious to know the pair's department—Procurement. I sigh and turn, just noticing the sign above Alistair's cubicle that reads, "Head of Strategic Sourcing."

I whistle lowly. So he is the head of his section and can control and manipulate as needed to source materials. I shake my head, unconsciously letting my fingers fidget.

My head turns, and my eyes double-check my presentation. I clap my hands and click send to Lucas. I grab my phone from my drawer and type out a text to inform him to review my presentation. I look up as rushing foot-steps pass my desk. Siew June leaves her desk in haste, her phone at her ear. As I watch her, my sight catches Alistair's expression. His jaw and his hands are tight, and he looks stiff and slightly shaky as he returns to his seat. He releases a long breath and touches his mouse. The screen lights up, and he starts typing. He turns his head to face me, and I swing my eyes back to my computer screen. He calls from his desk, "Alyssa, I will be ready within thirty minutes if you are alright to wait. Otherwise, we can catch a bite after tomorrow." He shrugs, smiling. "Up to you."

I face him and return with a perfect smile. "I can wait. I can read more about our client while waiting."

He smiles, showing off his dimple. *He looks hand-some.* Warmth floods my cheeks.

Stop it, Alyssa. He may be an accomplice to the mur-ders, and you have Jamie. I pinch my hand to stop dream-ing. *I miss Jamie. I wish he were with me now.* My cheek leans into my hand while I sigh deeply. I switch hands and scroll the internet for news. My department's cubicles are still; all of my colleagues have either already left or are at a site. I am alone, and my eyes feel heavy as I yawn.

"Alyssa! Alyssa!" Someone touches my shoulder, and I open my eyes. I jump from my chair, my eyes wide and scared. Alistair holds my hand to balance me as I bump into my desk.

"It is just me. You must have dozed off while wait-ing." He smiles apologetically.

"Oh . . . I guess I must be tired." I yawn, covering my mouth before reaching out to grab my handbag and phone from the drawer.

He stands with a laptop bag on his broad back.

"Let's go. I'll make sure you make it home since it's late." He shows me the time on his watch. "I shouldn't be selfish and keep you waiting for me so long." He winks.

"Not at all. I had work to complete, and I wanted to chat with you too since we will be working on the same project," I respond with a smile.

The clock on my desk indicates that it's seven, and we switch off our computers, pushing our chairs in before we hop on the elevator.

In the lift, I start massaging the side of my head since I feel lightheaded. The last time I ate was breakfast; therefore, I can feel my stomach twisted into knots. I lose my balance, and my body falls aside; Alistair opens his arms and holds my hand and my left arm.

"You must be hungry," Alistair says while looking at my face.

I nod and smile.

Alistair smiles. "There is a café nearby that stays open until 9." He looks at his watch, then at me. "We could get a bite before leaving?" He grins, his dimple flashing.

I nod, my heart racing. I don't understand why his dimple makes me feel things.

I try to discreetly study his fingers for a wedding ring. "So, you have a family? You know, wife, parents?" I ask while we walk side by side to the café.

He shrugs his shoulders. "I am divorced with no children. I was an orphan, and I have been living with my uncle Joe." He lets out a loud sigh. "He is a grumpy old man who wants everything perfect, which gets on my nerves." He laughs, then unconsciously, he rolls his sleeves, baring the tattoo, and rubs his neck.

My mouth curves, and I nod. I gulp as I eye his tattoo.

He watches my reaction and looks at his arm. "Oh, this," he shows me his tattoo fully, "I was forced to get it by Uncle Joe. 'You ain't my child until you get the same.'" He sighs and smiles wryly while looking at me.

Immediately, my palms gesture no. "Oh, I'm sorry. I didn't mean anything by my reaction. I'm just surprised that you have such a unique-looking tattoo." I pat both of my cheeks as warmth surges into them.

"I don't mind at all. It happens every time." He scratches under his collar. "By the way, you're cute when you're blushing." He winks before pushing the café door open and strides in. Just as we step inside, a buzzing comes from his pocket. He slides the Lenovo phone out and checks the screen. After glancing at it, he pushes the phone back into his pocket, and I have to push back the questions crowding my mind.

Chapter 29

"**U**nbelievable. It's highly likely Alistair's uncle is our murderer. You must find a way to look at his picture," Eleanor advises me, her voice too loud through the speaker. I pull my phone away from my ear and push the door to my room at Grandmother's villa.

"That is a good idea. I will find out when we work together," I say as I hang my handbag from my dresser. I just returned from dinner with Alistair.

"By the way, Grandmother will be back today. Are you picking her up?" Eleanor asks me. I turn my head to look at the clock hung just above my bathroom door. I have some time before I need to pick her up. Her flight lands at eleven.

"Definitely. I wouldn't want to miss it." I clear my throat and shift. "Did you know that Grandmother went to Shanghai, too, along with other Southeast Asian countries?"

"Yes. You informed me of her whereabouts just in case." Eleanor pauses, and when she speaks again, it sounds as if she's pulled the mouthpiece closer. "Why? What is your concern, Alyssa? With that tone of yours,

I know you are thinking of something." She crunches an apple.

I clear my throat. "You know Joe was on the way to Shanghai on that boat, and suddenly Grandmother mentions she went to few places that included Shanghai. I was thunderstruck, that's all. Like, is that the famous place to go to nowadays?" My voice raises through my sentences.

"Ehmm, maybe," Eleanor responds.

"I don't know why, but I don't seem to sleep well nowadays since losing Mother." I sit on the vanity chair, slouching. "I feel Grandmother is keeping a secret or something." I crumple my top above my heart.

"You must be exhausted from everything that's happened," Eleanor tries to soothe me.

I turn to look at the clock and sigh. "I am off to pick Grandmother up now. Talk to you soon." I end the call, grab my car keys and purse, and head out.

I glance at the arrival times on the screen board above the sliding exit door of the arrival terminal before looking at my wristwatch.

I turn to look at the door, and I grin. My feet move automatically with open arms in Grandmother's direction. We hug each other, and I take her luggage from her hand. "You look refreshed and youthful. Did you get your much-needed tan and meet any men on your trip?" I wink at her, the side of my mouth curving upward teasingly.

Grandmother tries to suppress a laugh, sputtering like an old water faucet. "My dear Alyssa. Nothing new with you; always trying to make me happy." Grandmother grins with a twinkle in her eyes.

"I heard you have a crush on a manager at your workplace? What happened to Jamie?" Her eyebrows pull up, and she pinches the bridge of her nose. She shows the message she received from Eleanor.

I shift uncomfortably and see that she sent it not even five minutes ago.

I cross my arms against my chest and snort. *Of course, she had to tell Grandmother.* "I still love him. However, he asked me to wait for him for three years, which is when his marriage contract is complete." My shoulders slouch, and I shake my head. "By the way, Alistair is not my type. I am going out with him more for my investigation. His uncle Joe might be the Joe who abducted Lady—"

Grandmother instantly places a smooth, skinny index finger on my mouth, shaking her head at me.

I quickly stop talking and change the subject. A few minutes later, I look at her as she says, "When can the authorities catch the culprit? I want to give them a piece of my mind." Her voice is shaky, and all her fingers are folded.

I pat her back while we sit in the car. "Looks like it will be soon." I smile at Grandmother, then look out the window, saying a silent prayer to make that statement true.

Chapter 30

The next day, as I open the car door to drive to work, my phone suddenly rings.

I grab it from my handbag and place the receiver on my ear. "Alyssa, it's me, Inspector Raven. We require your assistance to identify certain things in connection to Mr. Spencer's death." His voice sounds tense.

I hope there's some progress in the findings.

He continues, "Please come to the police station this afternoon."

I place my phone in the phone holder on the dash and connect it to my Bluetooth. My leg presses the accelerator, and I'm on my way. "Yeah, sure. Once I am done with work, I'll head over. I will be slightly late since I will be in Dakota Jersey. I am on my way there now."

"It is 15 miles from here. Please message me when you are on the way," Inspector Raven says with a heavy sigh.

"Definitely, Inspector. Bye, and see you later," I reply.

Impatience runs through me. I can't wait to find out what Inspector Raven wants to talk about. In less than an hour, the project site is visible, and I turn into the lot, making my way to the designated parking. Lucas's loud voice is clear even though I am still in the car. "Alyssa! Over here!" He shouts once I've parked and gotten out.

I nod and walk in his and Alistair's direction.

"Here, Alyssa, this is the current layout. What are your suggestions to move forward?" Lucas asks while his right hand taps a pen.

"This is clean river water, to begin with. There is a spacious piece of land where we can place a gazebo and a nice transparent canopy as a membership club with a few luxury yachts for parties and sightseeing." My hands move around the air, miming the suggestions as I speak.

The two men grin, bearing straight white teeth.

"Brilliant idea, Alyssa." Lucas claps his hands.

"A good taste of luxury. Guess I know where it comes from," Alistair says with a laugh.

My hands smooth the front of my blouse, and I roll my eyes with a smile. Lucas hands me the original layout, and I hum away while sketching out the agreed proposal.

My car's engine starts, and I place my phone in the holder, pressing the call icon on Inspector Raven's contact.

"I am on the way, Inspector Raven. I will be there soon," I say via my Bluetooth on the way out of the lot.

"Great. I will be waiting," he responds.

Without too many traffic delays, I arrive safely at the police station. I scurry into Inspector Raven's office, which was pointed out to me by his subordinate. I smile as I enter, seeing another familiar face.

"Hi, Eleanor. You're here too?"

"We are working hand in hand since the pieces of evidence we have seem to be linked," Eleanor responds with a smile. She is sitting on one of the two chairs tucked in front of Inspector Raven's long desk.

Inspector Raven gets up from his chair, walks toward the door, and shuts it.

With a toothpick in his mouth, he says, "Let's start by sharing the evidence that we have both gathered." He gestures between Eleanor and himself.

We start with Mr. Spencer's murder. "The evidence and information that we have gathered are shown here," he points with a laser pointer at the projector display of the investigation. "Evidence identification at Exhibit 1, evidence location at Exhibit 2, evidence collection at Exhibit 3, and evidence protection/proper documentation is the last of the information. I managed to place it in one presentation for easy references," he says.

I nod, studying the screen intently.

"This slide represents the evidence identification." His laser points to the details which I am reading.

The pieces of evidence are gathered via interview, interrogation, and collection at the Henderson mansion, its compound, Mr. Spencer's two houses, his yacht, Spencer Limited's headquarters, and Henderson Building and Construction Incorporation's building.

"From the interviews, we gathered that Spencer and Henderson are not enemies when it comes to business and personal life. Mr. Henderson is unaware of Jennifer's affair with Spencer."

"Wait! How do you know that they don't hold any personal grudges?" I ask while opening my palm toward Inspector Raven.

"They have been best friends since college," Inspector Raven responds, pushing a college magazine and photos of them partying and vacationing together. My eyes widen at this statement, and I shake my head slowly.

Inspector Raven continues, "However, we interrogated Mr. Spencer's secretary. She said that he had several affairs, including a mistress before Jennifer. The lady is in her twenties. He was supposed to employ her in his office branch in Maineville. However, his daughter Rihana controls the employee placement. She disliked his mistress and didn't recruit her." My head leans back while my eyes roll.

He clears his throat before continuing, "The secretary named Beth overheard his heated conversation with the lady, Katherine, a month before he started an affair with Jennifer. Katherine barged into his office, crying, smashing vases on the floor, and took a golf club off a long steel stand behind his office door."

"Woah! She is one aggressive woman," I exclaim, rubbing my forehead and tapping the table.

He nods his head as he looks at me. "Luckily, Beth overheard the argument, and security came to his rescue. Katherine was mandated not to go near Mr. Spencer."

"Therefore, Katherine is one of the prime suspects in this case. This is her picture?" I point at a picture, and I study her appearance.

"Yes, correct, Alyssa," Inspector Raven confirms.

"I have never seen her before," I respond with a frown.

Inspector Raven clicks to the next slide. "Jennifer? Why is that?" I ask, my eyebrows raising. *I wonder if it's because of her ring.*

"With the cooperation of Mr. Spencer's lawyer, we were able to read in detail his revised official will. According to Beth, Mr. Spencer urgently requested a meeting with his lawyer once he found his new love, Jennifer."

"According to Beth, they were planning to propose a

better deal with Mr. Henderson, but in Asia. Meaning Mr. Henderson would be traveling to Asia most of the time, leaving Jennifer with Mr. Spencer. With that plan in mind, it materialized."

I jolt from my seat and look at Inspector Raven. "Wait! What do you mean the plan materialized?" I interrupt.

Inspector Raven squints, and at the same time, his index finger thumps on his table. "Mr. Henderson signed the agreement. He was busy traveling to Asia, which allowed Jennifer to have more time for the affair with Mr. Spencer."

"Now it makes sense when Jamie told me that his father had overseas business trips frequently. And why Mr. Spencer gave Spencer Limited shares to Jennifer," I exclaim.

"But why marry Mr. Henderson?" I stop pacing, facing Inspector Raven and Eleanor. "What are the benefits since she already had Mr. Spencer's wealth in her hands?"

He sighs as he leans forward. "A good question, Alyssa. According to our interview with Rihana Spencer, she was mad when she saw Jennifer's name in her father's will, especially since Jennifer has some shares and a few million were left under her name."

He shakes his head, disgusted. "She also threw a fit by saying, 'I never agreed to my father marrying the cheap woman!'"

My eyes narrow, and my hand scratches the side of my forehead.

His hands gesture for me to stop. "Before you ask, Alyssa, I have the answer. Rihana disagreed with Mr. Spencer's marriage to anyone else after her mother's death. The only way for Mr. Spencer to have a relationship was to have an affair." He straightens in his seat and continues, "Apparently, she nearly committed suicide every time Mr. Spencer had a serious relationship. To prevent her from doing so, he just had an affair."

"What a cunning bitch," I say. I circle around my chair and sit back down.

I nod and hum a bit. "Well, that explains it. The only way for Jennifer to sustain her business and be someone's rich wife was to marry Mr. Henderson as he was the only one available."

He claps his hand and chuckles. "Another wonderful conclusion made by Alyssa."

"With all the information here, the top suspect is Katherine?" I ask.

Inspector Raven takes out a photo from his drawer. "We found evidence that is similar to the blue ring that you found at the Henderson mansion. See this picture? Same design and color." He points before holding the picture out for me.

I study it intensely and nod. "Exactly the same." I look at the photo again, then at him. "Where did you find it?"

"It was found underneath Mr. Spencer's bedroom carpet."

I hold my hand up. "Hold on. What design is in the filigree?" I snatch the magnifying glass on top of a small table nearby.

I gasp, covering my mouth.

"What did you find, Alyssa?" Eleanor asks with her head tilted, looking at me.

I hold up a finger facing Eleanor. "Hang on."

I twist the ring on the paper, turning it from south to west. I stop moving the photo, and the ring faces north. My eyes widen, and my finger jabs at it. "Do you see that?

It's designed to be combined."

"Let me see. Is this a puzzle to something?" I take out my phone from my jacket and compare the ring photo that I took the morning of the murder.

"Look! Do you see how the ring at the murder site in my photo compares to the one found in Mr. Spencer's bedroom? The differences are the designs on the filigree." I rearrange the photo he took, laying it against the ones I snapped at Mr. Henderson's mansion. "It looks like a back of a boat shape when both are side by side."

"I wonder if there is a secret message or code," Eleanor exclaims as she leans forward.

I twist my wristwatch. Eleanor crosses her arms over her chest, and we look at each other.

"What about Mr. Henderson's helper? Did your team manage to find the bloody napkin she had?" Inspector Raven blinks at me and shakes his head.

"We went there to find it when the helper was out. Unfortunately, we were unable to find the napkin."

I slap the table hard, and the vibrations shudder through books and papers arranged neatly on his table. I stand again, pacing from one wall to the other.

I clasp my hands under my chin and smile. "We should be on the lookout for the next ring. Maybe that last piece will inform us of the item."

Inspector Raven grips the arms of his chair and stands, nodding. "We're already on it."

I wink at him, and Eleanor nods. Inspector Raven waves his hand, showing us his door. "Goodbye, and thank you." I nod and smile at him before I leave.

Chapter 31

Eleanor and I ride together and discuss further on the way to the villa. I just park my car when an unrecognized telephone number appears on my phone screen.

I am hesitant to pick it up, but when the same number calls me twice, I answer in speaker mode.

"Mrs. Smith was found unconscious on the floor of her bedroom. Her bedroom was ransacked." Grandmother's head helper's voice cracks nervously.

"What?" My jaw drops. "I will be there immediately," I reply. I remove my seat belt and burst from the car. With my legs trembling and my hands shaking, I manage to run to the entrance, Eleanor right behind me.

We arrive, panting, and the head helper's hands are trembling, and she stands near Grandmother's door.

"What am I to do?" she cries.

"Call her private doctor and do not touch anything. We will bring the police," I say confidently while I rub my throat. My hands unconsciously unfasten my collar button.

"I will call Jason to come take fingerprints and other shreds of evidence," Eleanor says as she grabs her jacket

266

and pulls out her phone.

There are footprints in the carpet of the hallway, and two vases are on the floor, broken into pieces. We reach the foot of the staircase, and Eleanor grabs my hand before I can hold the brass railing for balance. "There may be fingerprints that my team would like to gather since, obviously, the culprit climbed this staircase." I nod, retract my hand, and walk further in the center to avoid touching the handle.

Eleanor pushes Grandmother's room door with her elbow, not wanting to mix fingerprint evidence. "Grandmother! Wake up!" Eleanor shouts as she gently checks her pulse at her wrist.

Tears start flowing down my cheeks upon seeing my grandmother with fresh blood on her cheeks and a deep cut on her right hand. She must have defended herself with the Bohemia Czech crystal vase. Half of the Bohemia crystal is broken into tiny pieces beside her lifeless body. The attack must have happened after she sat at the vanity table.

Realizing that tears are rolling off my chin, I quickly take a few tissues from her dresser, accidentally knocking off a small half-empty ROJA perfume bottle. It crashes onto the floor, and the smell of strong, spicy musk envelops the air.

I sniff and sniff. *This smell is familiar. Where have I smelled this? Silly me,* I smile. *Obviously, Grandmother sprayed it during the get-together at the golf course luncheon.*

Wait . . . This is the odor that lingered in the cabin's kitchen, where Lady Jacqueline's body was stuffed in the washing machine. I suppress a shiver at the thought. I'm pulled to reality by the sound of a doorbell. I step back to look at the door, and a man in his forties with a Gladstone bag in his left hand and a statoscope around his neck appears at Grandmother's room entrance.

"Hi. I am Dr. Benedict, Mrs. Smith's private doctor. I brought my nurse to assist me." He nods with his chin, looking at Eleanor and me.

"Sure, please come in and check over and revive our grandmother," I reply in a shaky voice while I sniffle quietly.

Under Dr. Benedict's watchful eyes, her injuries and severe anxiety attacks are under control. He cleans her wound, and her head helper manages to change her into her nightgown. Dr. Benedict places Grandmother under an oxygen mask and lays her on the bed. Her heartbeat normalizes, and Eleanor and I resume searching for evidence of the break-in.

"Eleanor, let's split in order to work faster," I suggest while unconsciously wringing my hands and twisting my wristwatch.

Eleanor nods, gesturing for me to cover Grandmother's room. Jason stands outside the room, looking at Eleanor. She steps closer to the open door, her finger pointing to the areas. "Jason, let's dust for fingerprints on the windows of the ground floor."

Eleanor and Jason head from Grandmother's room and cover the search of the entire house, excluding her room. My legs carry me to the small garden-like parlor surrounded by fresh flowers and leaves. There's a small fountain beside a flamingo statue in pink studs. I step into the space and pull a pink armchair out. It is part of the investigative process that I learned from PI training that an investigator should consider checking the ceilings and windows first for any dubious assumptions. It is a known philosophy that intruders will try to enter from these two non-obvious locations.

With that in mind, my hands push the ceiling tiles one by one, trying to feel if there are any segments that are loose. Finally, at the edge of the ceiling near the window that has transparent pink lace curtains, I feel that the segment could move.

Click. I push another round, and another *click* sound emits in the still room.

I am momentarily thunderstruck, then I push it again. This time, it gives way, and some dust falls on my right shoulder as I am about to push upward.

"Alyssa, Eleanor," Grandmother's cracking voice echoes from the other room.

"Eleanor, Grandmother is calling us. Roger," I say via the investigators' team walkie-talkie.

"Coming," Eleanor answers in a strained tone.

I climb from the chair, and my sneakers and my weight step on the carpet. There's a squeaking sound on a particular flooring tile, and it feels like a spring instead of solid marble in comparison to the other floorings of the villa. I turn my head, slightly bending my head to look at it. It's beside a pot of flowers with a standing white statue in a ballet pose.

"Alyssa, Eleanor!"

Grandmother's faint voice brings me to a halt. Instead of squatting to figure it out, my legs run toward Grandmother's bed a few feet away from the parlor, which is covered by a glass sliding door with a thick curtain with frills.

We appear beside Grandmother concurrently.

Her face is pale, and her hands shake slightly. Wrinkles cover her skin while she clasps her blanket tightly.

She seems to have aged years in the last few hours. *Pity Grandmother has to endure this amount of pain at this golden age.*

I sit beside her and kiss her forehead. Eleanor clasps her hands. "Will I be safe living here after the incident?" Grandmother asks in a quiet voice.

Eleanor and I lock eyes, staring at each other until our shoulders rise. I whisper to her, "We never thought about that."

"Why not have Grandmother stay with me at the Luxe Gold Luxury Apartments while the investigation is ongoing? We engage 24-hour security, and we changed to the updated security system?" I ask while caressing her forehead. "What do you think, Eleanor?"

She walks to the other side of Grandmother's bed, placing her index finger on her chin, and nods.

"That's a good suggestion." She pauses and looks at me, then at Grandmother. "You should stay with Alyssa until security is intact here."

Dr. Benedict interrupts, "Excuse me for interrupting a family conversation, but I suggest that Mrs. Smith can only move starting tomorrow around lunch." His head turns to look at us. "Today, she is too weak, and I have given her IV drips to rejuvenate her energy." Dr. Benedict looks worried, his eyebrows meeting together.

My heart beats faster. "Does she require a more thorough check-up?"

Dr. Benedict nods and says, "We will bring her for a thorough check-up first thing tomorrow morning. As for now, Mrs. Smith needs to rest."

"Sure. I will stay with Grandmother in her room tonight," I say through tight lips.

Eleanor says, "I will also request for one police officer to be on guard tonight while I negotiate with Clare to stay overnight until Grandmother is fit to walk around."

I nod and squeeze Grandmother's hand.

About five minutes after our discussion with Dr. Benedict, we resume our investigation. On my way back to the garden parlor, I notice her cloakroom a few steps before the parlor door is wide open, and there is a mess of clothes scattered on the floor. Empty hangers sit on the rack, and her handbags are all thrown on the floor, some smashed against the locked mirrored cupboard.

My eyes dart from one corner of the cloakroom to the other, and the sound of heavy footsteps can be heard. I turn my head toward the room entrance, and Inspector Raven stands on the threshold wearing a hat. He nods at Grandmother with a small smile.

"Good evening, Mrs. Smith. I am Inspector Raven. Unfortunately, Eleanor cannot lead this case since she is related to you." Raven smiles again, placing his hat against his chest in respect.

I step out of the closet and move to Grandmother's side, nodding to Inspector Raven.

"Ah, Alyssa. You are here too. I will be interviewing your grandmother and Clare, the head helper, since both were around during the incident."

"Sure, please go ahead. I will recommence my investigation," I reply to him with a nod, walking back to the cloakroom.

I walk in further and let my eyes take in everything. I walk closer to the wall, pushing some of her designer coats aside, as I see one of her panties hanging. *Where's her other lingerie?* I place my finger beside my chin and push a red coat with black feather trim away. There at the center is a drawer full of underclothing. My hand touches the back of the mirrored cupboard, and a small hidden door opens slightly. I peek through it, and my eyes bulge. It's full of Grandmother's jewelry. Clever of her to place her thick coats in front. I let go of a long breath while patting the front of my blouse. Luckily, the intruder didn't find these.

I enter her jewelry room, my mouth dropping as I look around in wonder. *Woah!* Sparkles are thrown across the room everywhere from all of her diamonds and precious stones. There are all types of watches and bangles, and gold bars are stacked like a Christmas tree.

It is safer for Grandmother to keep these valuables in a bank vault.

I snap some photos and text them to Eleanor.

"Wow, how can we keep it safe when she is at your apartment?"

"Guess we require tighter security in place before we move her?" I suggest.

"Alyssa! Alyssa!" Inspector Raven shouts my name.

I run out, latching the cupboard and pushing the heavy winter coats to cover the door of her jewelry hideout. I am about to turn my body toward the door to her bedroom, but I step on something hard.

I look down, but before I can squat down to appraise the item, Clare, her face pale, approaches me and pulls my arm roughly.

Once my feet step from the cloakroom back into her main bedroom, Clare points at the modern standing floor mirror beside a white chest of drawers covered with fur scarves.

Clare, her hands trembling, pushes aside the fur

scarves with a long broomstick.

YOU ARE NEXT. UNLESS YOUR GRAND-DAUGHTERS STAY AWAY FROM THE INVESTIGA-TIONS. It is written in a deep red that looks suspiciously like fresh blood.

I cover my mouth, which unconsciously drops. My left hand wrinkles my jacket, and I start hyperventilating.

I jump as a hand touches my shoulder. "It's just me," Raven says. "Your grandmother's life is not safe until the two of you give up this case." His jaw tightens.

A sudden coldness creeps over my body, and my knees go numb. Eleanor's head pokes into the room, swallowing. "Wha—" I watch as fear grips her throat. She walks into the room and over to the standing mirror. Her eyes move from left to right, then she covers her mouth once she reads the warning scribbled on the mirror.

"That is what the murderer wants. Guess we are close to solving the mystery. Therefore, we will NOT stop." Eleanor's words are firm, and her eyes glare at Inspector Raven.

"We will resume indirectly. Officially on paper, you will be leading the investigations. We will be your invisible buddies," I add and smile in a fierce manner.

"A cunning way to trick him, huh." Inspector Raven places his fist on his palm. Eleanor stands with both hands in her pockets, and my head nods.

Inspector Raven looks at his wristwatch and sighs. "It's late. I better run along." He tilts his head to us, twists his body, and walks from the room.

"Thank you, Inspector Raven," I call after him, then move to change into PJs.

A soft scratching pulls me from my sleep.

I quickly open my eyes, turning my head to face Grandmother. She seems fine, sleeping peacefully.

"Clare, did you hear a sound?" I text Clare.

There is no reply from Clare after several minutes, so I get up. I grab a baton from inside Grandmother's top drawer. Breathing deeply, I gather my courage and head to the door.

I notice a wireless baby monitor on the bedside table and look at it in puzzlement before I recall Eleanor said to press this if there's an emergency. It connects to Eleanor's downstairs bedroom.

After pressing it, I exhale heavily and step out of the bedroom as quietly as I can. I hold the railing and climb down the stairs, alert for danger. A large shadow passes behind the wall fountain, and I tighten my grip on the baton. There is an intruder in the house.

I consciously steady my breathing, not wanting to give away my position.

At the bottom of the stairs, I quickly cross the living room and accidentally kick a stool, which emits a grating screech. I freeze and look around for the shadow, but there is none. I resume walking toward the wall where the fountain flows, my eyes taking in everything. I turn and walk barefoot to examine the fountain just beside the dining area. Once I reach the fountain, another shadow appears on the wall in front of me. I turn just in time to see a wooden bat heading toward my head.

───

I open my eyes, disoriented. My vision is blurry, and I rub my eyes. I try to raise my head, but it feels heavy. My hand massages my scalp, and I wince in pain. My fingers feel the tender skin, and there's liquid on my scalp. I pull my hand away and gasp at the blood coating my fingers.

A gunshot rings through the air. I jerk my head to face the staircase. My eyes widen, and I jolt up, holding my head.

Grandmother! A bolt of panic seeps into me, and fear threatens to choke me. I have to save her. Courage fills my limps, and I crawl toward the staircase while short of breath and groggy.

I must have been drugged too. Sudden tears develop, making my vision a little clearer. I hold onto the staircase handrail and pull myself up, determination fuelling my movement.

I move slowly up a few steps before stopping and spewing vomit. My stomach churns, and I wipe my mouth, panting. Weakness drags at me, yet I manage to continue my journey to the top. I freeze at the top when my eyes lock with a blonde guy's.

"Jim? Jim!" I stutter. "What did you do to my grandmother?" My eyes blur, and I rub my eyes again to see him clearly.

He jumps over the walkway railing and tumbles in a somersault. He stands, but Clare appears from the hall and knocks his head with a glass vase. He stumbles, and his hand rubs his bloody forehead. He blinks several times, then he quickly shifts and points his gun at Clare. She stiffens, not daring to move a muscle.

"Please don't shoot me," Clare stammers, her voice strained.

I stand helpless as my vision blurs yet again. My breath is rapid, and I am still unstable. I wrap my arms around my chest. All I want to do is to save my grandmother, but Clare is in trouble.

I turn my head to face the wall beside Grandmother's door, and I squeak at the sight of a panic button. I extend my arm, and two of my fingers press the button.

Blaring sounds and shining red lights erupt through the room.

Leaning against the wall, I shout, "Grandmother! Grandmother!" Tears flow down my cheeks as I fear the worst.

I strain my neck to check on Clare downstairs. I blink and breath in deeply as Clare runs away and hides behind a table, as Jim is distracted by the appearance of the lights.

Jim shoots at a variety of Bohemian glasses arranged in the living room, causing shrapnel to fly in the air. A shard hits Clare's cheek, and she ducks down with hands over her head to fend off other, more substantial injuries.

"Freeze, you are under arrest," Eleanor shouts from the hallway of her room, a gun pointing in Jim's direction. I smile to myself and start sliding down the wall. Jim takes his gun, pointing at Eleanor and Jason. His chest heaves, and he casts about, panicked. Eleanor chucks her baton and hits Jim's head, causing him to fall. He struggles to stand, and Eleanor's bullet hits his ankle. He yells, and his face creases in pain. He gets up, limping and hopping. Eleanor jumps and overpowers him quickly. She wrestles him to the ground and cuffs him.

Seeing this victory, I walk while bent as quickly as I can to Grandmother's room. She looks serene with her eyes closed and her chest falling in a regular rhythm.

I sigh in relief, then face a pillow beside her. "Argh! Argh!" I scream as blood drips from the pillow. I crawl further toward the other side. I puke on the floor, seeing a rooster's head and blood spotted on the pillow. The pungent smell wafts, and I cover my nose with my sleeve as my dizziness worsens. Heavy footsteps near in the hallway.

I sit on the carpet, staring, to maintain my composure as Eleanor and Jason appear.

Eleanor's voice penetrates the fog in my brain, and I rub my eyes to clear my vision.

"Grandmother! Grandmother, wake up." She sprinkles some water on her face. Grandmother's eyes blink open, and she smiles before frowning in confusion.

"Is it morning already, Eleanor? I had such a nice dream about a boat trip with you and Alyssa."

She curls her legs, then extends her right hand and strokes the lines on Eleanor's forehead gently. "Where is Alyssa?"

"There." She inclines her head to my position. "She's been drugged. Jason will bring her to the hospital for treatment while I take you to the nearby hotel," Eleanor says to Grandmother.

"No! No hotel for me." She shakes her head emphatically. "Just call Dr. Benedict to aid Alyssa and Clare. No one can go to the hospital. It will cause my business shares to plummet!" Grandmother instantly sits up, her hands shaking badly.

I can't withhold the dizziness anymore and flop on my side, my mouth open, as darkness pulls me under.

$\mathcal{C}hapter$ 32

"Are you OK, Alyssa?" Eleanor's brows crease, and she wrings her hands yet again. "I am fine. No more dizziness or nausea." I straighten myself on the bed. "Incidents are piling up. We are to move Grandmother somewhere safe today. Not even my place. I could be followed too." My hands tense, and worry lines appear on my forehead. I look at my wristwatch and bite my lip.

Eleanor's mouth opens halfway through my words, but it shuts upon hearing my statement.

"You want to say something, Eleanor?" My eyebrows rise.

She shakes her head, her eyes avoiding mine. *She is concealing something from me.* "Later, Alyssa," she replies softly.

Did Eleanor find something that she can only divulge when there is more concrete evidence? This is part of the investigation process. I press my lips tightly but nod.

<hr>

That evening after ensuring Grandmother is safe with Clare at the hotel nearby, Eleanor says, "Bring the blonde guy in. I wish to interrogate him." She cracks her fingers. I lean against a table located behind the interrogation table.

Jim's bulky form settles on a chair, and Jason puts the wire on his hand and chest to connect to a lie detector machine.

"You are being detained regarding the murder of Lady Jacqueline, Mr. Spencer, and breaking into Mrs. Smith's villa," Eleanor says while staring at his eyes.

Jason takes my baton from my hand and walks closer to Jim. "Speak up! Who sent you to the villa, and what is your purpose?" Jason knocks the baton on the side of the table.

Jim covers his ears, then blinks, his tongue tight.

Eleanor places a taser on his waist. Suddenly, his stomach, hands, legs, and face shudder, and his mouth wobbles. "Hold on! I will talk."

Eleanor disengages the taser, placing it at her side. "Speak up!"

"He is an Italian white man, balding." I stand beside him, watching his gestures. He touches his nose when he speaks.

"What is his name? More description, please," Eleanor adds in a firm voice, her eyes glaring at him.

"I got no clue." His eyes move to the top left.

I grab the chair, sitting backward in it, and flash a photo that fits his description. The first photo he stares at and shakes his head.

Then I pull out another photo, scrolling through several more. At the eighth photo, he blinks. "So this is the guy you mean?"

He gulps, and his fingers fidget, hidden under the table.

"Where is his location? Describe his features." Eleanor says firmly while she stares fiercely at him.

"I only met him once at the abandoned hospital. My main contact person does all other dealings."

"Who is your main contact person?"

"There are many. I don't work with just one." His eyes avoid us, and he bites his fingernails.

Eleanor and I look at each other with our eyebrows raised. He's lying; he knows.

"Who is your main contact person for Lady Jacqueline's murder and Mrs. Smith's villa break-in?" Eleanor asks as she stands beside him.

He tilts his head to look at Eleanor. "I never met him. We spoke by phone, and he pays well and on time. There are no requirements to know his name and meet face-to-face." His hands massage his neck, and sweat seems to crawl down the side of his forehead as he speaks.

"What is the purpose of breaking into Mrs. Smith's villa?" Eleanor asks in a calm tone.

"To give warnings." He shrugs, refusing to look at her.

"To her only?" Eleanor responds.

"To her two grandchildren especially." He points at Eleanor and me with his index finger, shuddering. "Too nosy. And a hindrance ever since Lady Jacqueline's kidnapping."

"So this guy," I point at the eighth picture, "called you to warn me?" I ask him in confusion.

"Yes. Yes," he says in a quivering tone and nods his head.

"This boss of yours, what is his name? Joe? I must have forgotten when you said it."

His eyes open widely. "Wait! I didn't mention any names." He starts scratching his head, and more sweat trickles down the side of his head.

I slam the photo on the table. He blinks, and his hands automatically cover his face.

Jason moves forward, extends his arms, and pulls his shirt collar, squeezing Jim's neck tightly. Approximately a minute passes before he lets go of Jim's collar, who wheezes.

"Joe is my boss. My main contact person. He deals with the white Italian bald guy." Jim inhales deeply, and his face returns to a normal color.

"Good. Do you know what you get if you cooperate with police investigators?"

"No. No." Jim's hands shake while his forehead is swamped with sweat.

"Your criminal offenses will be reduced in the court," Eleanor says, leaning closer to his ears.

Jim stares at Eleanor, blinking at the information. His fingers fidget with his shirt collar.

———

A few minutes later, Jim whispers, "I will help you." I stand at the opposite edge of the table, blink a few times, and turn my head. My eyes stare at Jim. He looks at me, sweat still heavy on his forehead.

Eleanor grabs Jim firmly, cuffs him, nudges him, and he gets up to walk out of the investigation room after her.

His head turns left and right at the door. "Where are you bringing me?" His face is puzzled, and his voice quivers.

"To Joe's place," Eleanor answers with a shrug.

His eyes narrow, and his hands tremble.

Jason and two other police officers grab his shoulders and push him forward. We get into two vehicles: a driver,

Jason, me, and Jim are in one Jeep, and Eleanor and two more officers are in another. Our Jeep is in the lead.

Jason points his gun at Jim. "Show us the way. I will pull the trigger if you play any tricks on us."

"Please spare my life. No tricks, OK, dude?" Jason's face stays serious, and Jim's legs shiver.

Vibration comes from my jacket pocket, and I grab my phone to look at the screen. It's a message from Grandmother, and worry overwhelms me as I open it.

"Alyssa! Where are you and Eleanor? I am not well. I am coughing badly. Why can't you be with me?" She includes a crying emoji.

"We are on the way to Joe's place. We caught the guy who broke into your house." I breathe in a sigh of relief.

"That is good news, Alyssa. Please come back instantly," Grandmother replies.

"I will be there within an hour," I send before putting my phone away.

Our vehicles glide along on the highway, passing several shops and discreetly arriving at a location that looks like a rundown car service center. It's dark with several broken windows.

"Where is this?" Jason asks with narrowed eyes, and his jaw tightens. He pulls Jim's collar tightly until his eyes bulge.

"Th—This is not a trick. This is where I meet him for jobs. I am supposed to meet him here tonight." Jim's hands flail, and sweat trickles down his forehead as he gasps for air.

Jason lifts a walkie-talkie and says, "Roger. This is the place. Jim is supposed to meet Joe tonight for another job from the same buyer." Jason signals to the other car where Eleanor is, giving them a thumbs-up that this is indeed the right place.

"We will go down to inspect. Jason and Todd, stay to guard Jim," Eleanor orders on the radio.

The Jeep rolls to a stop near some bushes, and I push the door open, creeping to meet up with Eleanor and the two other officers. All three are ready with a gun in hand. I bite my lip before I take out my black steel baton and clutch it tightly since I don't have any bullets.

Eleanor turns her head, her hands messing with her waist pouch, and she tosses something to me. "Alyssa, catch."

I smile, my left palm catching four bullets. I open my gun and place them in the compartment. I breathe in deeply, a fist on the side of my right leg. I feel a lot better now.

The two officers in front of us take out their flashlights, shining them on the ground to examine the service center while we hide amongst the bushes.

"Eleanor, there's nothing yet. No signs or clues of a living being."

"Roger," Eleanor responds tensely.

The officers move to return to our spot and open the main entrance door. One of them steps on a rugged welcome mat, and clicking envelops the area. They look at each other with wide eyes as sizzles and small sparks of fire like firecrackers move at lightning speed.

I look at Eleanor, and she meets my worried gaze. "Bomb! Out, now!" she yells, her reflexes fast. Her right-hand waves to get us to disperse as we start running.

Jason jumps from the Jeep that is parked near the door, rolling over the gravel, followed closely by Jim. The driver is opening the car door as an explosion erupts, their body shooting up as the Jeep is thrown by the blazing fire.

Jim trips as he runs, landing on his front, and yells, "Help! Help!" Jason turns to save Jim, but the debris and sparks dance around Jim's body, engulfing him fully and forcing Jason to back away from the heat.

Within a few minutes, sirens from the fire truck and ambulance fill the air, but they come too late.

Jason only suffers some bruises and cuts, and the paramedic manages to bandage his hand and shoulder as well since he landed weirdly on his left arm.

I dial Grandmother's number. "Hello, Grandmother," I say in a quavering voice.

"Alyssa, what happened?" she asks, concerned.

"Jim, the intruder, was killed when the car he was in exploded from a bomb." I speak slowly in a sad tone.

"What? Are we back to square one with no clue?" She raises her shaky voice.

"Yes." I try to hold back my tears, inhaling deeply.

"Alyssa, please hurry to stay with me in the hotel. I'm scared." Her voice becomes light and shakes more. In the background, I can hear her pulling at her clothes.

With a whimper, I say, "Yes, I will be there soon."

———

Eleanor remains silent beside me in the backseat of a taxi on the ride to the hotel. I glance at her, rubbing my pants at my knee.

Still, Eleanor ignores me.

I slip my hands into my jacket pockets, bouncing. "You have something that you wish to share with me? I know you do." I tilt my head just enough to look at her expression.

Her eyes meet mine as though she sees a ghost. My palms turn sweaty and cold.

She clears her throat. She twists toward my side, her right-hand waving at me. "Come closer," she whispers. She looks at the taxi driver in front of her nervously. I slide my butt a few inches closer and tilt my head for her to whisper.

Her eyes watch the road as she whispers, "The night of Grandmother's villa break-in, while Jason took you to the hospital, I overheard Grandmother on the phone. She said, 'You did not eliminate her!' then got off her phone." Eleanor turns her head to look at me, and I nod for her to continue, swallowing. "I backed away and hid. I recorded the things happening around me on my phone that night, so coincidentally, I recorded it." She moves her jacket aside and pats the inner pocket.

"Who do you think she wants to eliminate?" Eleanor shrugs, her eyes remaining on the road.

My mouth opens and shuts, and my eyes look everywhere in the taxi.

"Let's keep it secret and be watchful," she suggests while she looks at me from the corner of her eye.

My fists clench. "Maybe she has business rivals. I will attend the Shareholders' and Directors' meeting soon to gather some information." Eleanor nods her head and brings her left hand up to let her chin rest on it.

She gestures for me to come closer again. I tilt my head to her side. "Also, that night, how did she know Clare was injured? None of us told her, right?" Eleanor raises an eyebrow.

My head nods slowly, recalling the night of the tragedy. I place both of my hands on my cheeks, my gaze unfocused.

Chapter 33

We don't try to be quiet as we enter Grandmother's hotel room.

"Alyssa and Eleanor, come in quick." Grandmother's cheerful voice calls from the seating area of her room. "What do you think of this villa?" She holds up a pamphlet with a picture of a house and grounds, too far away still to see clearly. "Since there have been so many mishaps recently, I decided to acquire a new estate and sell the current property," she says excitedly, smiling from ear to ear.

"It looks nice and brand new." I smile at her and take the pamphlet to look at it closer. Eleanor nods as she looks at it with me over my shoulder.

"The estate is two miles from the Luxe Gold Luxury Apartments, so you will be in safe hands if anything happens," I say, then look at her face.

"It's settled then." She smiles and reclines on the sofa.

Her hand signals Eleanor and me to sit. I sit down beside her, and her hand pushes a strain of hair away from my face.

"Alyssa, with a lot of bad things having happened recently, I would like to accelerate your takeover of my business." Her eyes gleam.

I nod and smile. "As you wish, Grandmother." I hug her but can't help the stab of disappointment in my gut.

She leans forward and grabs papers from the table in front of the sofa. "So, Alyssa, here are the documents for Monday morning's meeting with the Directors. I will introduce you to the members. I hope your father will attend too." Grandmother's eyebrows touch as she speaks. She takes out her briefcase from underneath the table and places it on the table in front of us. She enters her passcode, and her briefcase clicks open, bearing some more documents.

I take those documents from her hands as well. I pat her shoulder and kiss her forehead.

"By the way, Grandmother, who will be staying at your current villa to protect your valuables while you're waiting to purchase the new one?" Eleanor asks while I flip through the documents. She shifts her body to the edge of the sofa in order to have a better view of Grandmother.

"You mean when I move my stuff to the new villa? I am already the proud owner of the Skyclouds residence." She chuckles, and Eleanor's jaw drops. I momentarily stop reading, and air rushes through my nose as I look at Grandmother, then at Eleanor.

"Alyssa, please be so kind as to stay there for at least a week to help Clare and the movers. Not to mention to keep an eye on my valuables. Guess you found out where I kept it." She sounds cheerful and winks at me.

I look at her and smile, just a touch hesitantly. As we start to get off the couch, she says, "And another thing, Eleanor and Alyssa." We both turn to face Grandmother. "I have spoken to the Attorney General so that both of you refrain from investigating the murder cases." Eleanor and I look at each other; her jaw looks tightened and her face firm. She continues talking, her eyes bouncing between our faces. "I cannot lose both of you." Grandmother crumples her clothes over her chest, and tears develop in her eyes.

We face Grandmother, standing together. Eleanor walks to her side and squats down, holding her right hand and rubbing the back of it gently.

"Grandmother, please, it is my duty to find the truth. We are close to uncovering it. You can stop Alyssa, but not me." Eleanor's eyes look into Grandmother's blue ones. Eleanor points her thumb to her chest. "It is my job, plus I will get a promotion if I settle this case." Eleanor lets go of Grandmother's hand, her hands turning into fists as her teeth grit.

Grandmother looks sadly at Eleanor's face, then she turns her head to face me.

"If that is the case, Alyssa will concentrate on her engineering work and being the director of my company. No more intervening in Eleanor's work." Grandmother's skinny index finger waggles at me. "Understand, young lady?" Her eyes are stern. I am wordless with rage, gripping the hem of my jacket as I try to come up with what to say.

After clearing my throat, I find my voice. "But, Grandmother, I have been involved from the start. Grandmother, this is my PI training case that I am working on with Eleanor. Eleanor is my mentor." I look at her with my hands clasped together, and I kneel on the carpet, rocking back and forth as I plead with her.

Her frail hands pat my hair and caress my cheeks.

"I cannot lose both of you. You both are precious to me." She kisses my forehead and gestures for Eleanor to come closer. She pulls Eleanor into a hug, kissing her forehead too.

Eleanor kisses Grandmother's cheek and says, "I will be extra careful."

"Alyssa, this will be your one and only case. Then you need to take a break, you understand?" Grandmother holds my hand, and my body moves toward her. We hug each other, and I squeeze her as tight as I can as tears threaten to fall.

Chapter 34

The next afternoon, I switch on the TV to watch the news at Grandmother's villa when my phone rings beside me on the bed.

I peek at the screen, and it flashes with Alistair's name. I slide to answer. "Hello?"

"Hi, Alyssa. Doing anything tonight?" My heart races, and my mouth curves into a smile.

"Not at all, Alistair." I turn the volume down on the TV and stand, one of my feet slightly swinging over the carpet.

"Want to meet up at the boardwalk at a corn dog café? We can discuss the landscaping of our client's project." I start playing with a strand of my hair and bite my lip.

"Sounds perfect. See you at seven." I end the call, suddenly feeling out of breath. *What will be my plan to gather more information about his uncle Joe?* I rub my neck and run a hand over my face.

I scratch the back of my head and start pacing, my arms clasp behind my back. I huff and call Eleanor.

I jump into it as soon as she says hello. "Eleanor, Alistair invited me to discuss the project this evening. I will take the opportunity to try to gather information about his uncle Joe. I have no clue how, though." There is an open notebook on the table, and I tear a blank sheet out, crumple it, and throw it into the trashcan nearby while waiting for her to reply.

There's a pause as she places the call on speaker. "Cool. Don't fall for his dimple and charm." Eleanor's voice is playful, and I can hear the same news channel in the background.

I smack my lips, frowning.

"I know you will find a way to find out about Joe. Play it by ear, Alyssa," Eleanor responds while chuckling.

"Alright . . . I guess." I sigh and slouch, then throw my mobile on the bed after ending the call.

I switch off the television, and my phone rings again. I walk to my bedside and grab it. This time, the screen indicates that Jamie is calling.

I smile to myself. *Finally*.

I press 'Answer.' "Jamie!"

"Hi, Alyssa, my love. What have you been up to these days?" His voice is deep with a husky edge to it, and I can hear him licking his lips. I can't help the butterflies that ripple through my stomach at his voice.

"How is it being married to Rihana Spencer?" I say without answering, tapping my fingers on the table, which I hope Jamie hears. My jaw tightens, thinking of Rihana with Jamie instead of me.

"A torture, I would say. A clearly spoiled brat." He sighs, and I can only imagine he's rubbing his neck right now. I smile.

"Can I see you tonight? I miss you so much." His voice pleads sweetly over the phone.

"Sorry, Jamie. My colleague has booked me for a discussion." My cheek leans against my hand on the table.

If only he had called me earlier, I would be able to spend time with him tonight. I speak through my teeth with forced restraint. "What about tomorrow?" My spirits lift with this idea, and hope flares through me.

He sighs heavily. "Can't you postpone your discussion with your colleague? For me? Please?" His voice becomes higher. There's a tapping of a pen and loud breathing that follows his request.

My heart sinks, and my lips press together. I collapse onto the bed, my shoulders slumping.

I sit up suddenly, grinning, as an idea pops into my head. "I will call you if I finish early, then you can stay with me at Grandmother's villa for the night? She has plenty of rooms, and after what's happened lately, I don't think I can sleep here alone." I gulp and look over my shoulder, even though I'm in my room.

He hums in pleasure. "That sounds perfect. See you later," he replies cheerfully.

The sea breeze blows my hair, and a strong gust washes over my face, making me shudder. I pull my jacket tight and continue walking to the café. My phone beeps, and I look at the message. It's Suzanne updating me that her clothing line is in high demand. I text back, "Congratulations. Keep it up. I am meeting Alistair now. Later, Jamie is coming to a sleepover." I roll my eyes at her response. "Love is in the air soon," with laughing and heart emojis.

A hand lands on my shoulder, and I jerk, turning to see Alistair. He smiles, his dimple visible. My heart skips a beat, and I fumble to come up with words. Automatically, my hand raises in a wave.

"It is cold tonight." He wraps his arm around his chest and massages his arms for warmth. "Let's grab a bite while we discuss the options for the yacht club." He smiles and tilts his head in the direction of the café.

I nod and follow him for a moment before speeding up my pace to walk side by side.

We order, and he carries our food tray of drinks to a table. He sets it down, and his phone rings. As he picks it up, my eyes catch on a photo of a man with grey hair standing beside Alistair.

He listens for a moment before his eyes meet mine, and he replies hesitantly, "Ehm, yes. I will transfer the money to you tonight." He waves his hand to me before stepping away.

He says as he walks away, "Yes, I will deliver the stuff by tomorrow." He tousles his hair, and the call continues for another minute. After, he returns to the table but remains standing.

He touches his chair, sits, and adjusts to move closer to me. I pretend to stretch as I peek at his phone. "Is that your uncle in the picture?" I point my finger at his phone screen, smiling.

"This?" He shows the lock screen to me. "Yeah. We caught a big catfish and won a trophy in Hawaii." He chuckles. I touch his phone to look closer, smile, and lean back.

"He looks Italian. Is he?" My head tilts as I look at his face.

"Yeah, he was adopted." Alistair's knee bounces. He continues, "I hardly see him nowadays. His business has been stationed in Asia ever since the Covid recession. I've been staying in his house, so it doesn't sit empty." He smiles and reaches for his drink. He takes a sip, his eyes locked on mine.

I smile and can feel my cheeks beginning to warm.

He shifts his phone from the table to his pocket, and his finger accidentally slides to the next photo of a man resembling the Joe we're after. My eyes widen, and I cover my mouth, trying to stifle my gasp. The photo shows his Uncle Joe as well, his arm adorned with an identical tattoo. Who is he to Alistair? Are there two Joes in his family? I look at him, my eyebrows raising as I ponder the possibilities.

A female waitress with a tray walks toward our table. "Here are your corn dogs." We both smile and thank her. He takes a bite of his corn dog and asks, "Why are you amazed by my photo?" He smiles, baring straight white teeth.

I swallow my drink and clear my throat. "I have never seen such a nice background, and before I met you, I didn't have any friends who fish. I am impressed. Did the fisherman or the organizer take the photo?" My eyes look again at the photo. "It looks neat," I say while smiling.

"It was my uncle's close friend. The funny part is that they have the same name." He chuckles and shakes his head, then he takes another bite of his corn dog.

I smile and turn to my sling bag, which has an envelope sticking from the front pocket. I wipe my hands with a napkin before reaching for the document and sliding it in front of him.

"So, about the project proposal, is it wise to propose cheaper materials or add another proposal for our clients to choose from?" My index finger touches my chin as I speak.

"Two options would be better, Alyssa. For any projects we undertake, we must provide some options for our clients to decide on. Since they are paying, they make the decision," he advises me before winking and taking another bite.

I swallow hard and nod. "Well, I guess I am ready to meet them this Monday." I fidget, discomfort with the intensity of his eye contact settling over me. My heart races every time he winks. *It's not right. I have Jamie.*

I take my last bite of the corn dog and wipe my hands before saying, "Woah! Look at the time." I raise my wrist-watch and look at it. "I better get going. My grandmother will be furious if I leave her for too long after the recent incident. See you on Monday," I exclaim before texting Jamie that I will be leaving soon.

I place my bag over my shoulder and push the chair in. He clears his throat, pulling my gaze to his. "Please drive carefully and text me when you arrive safely. It was a fruitful discussion. Have a nice weekend." He smiles, his dimple starting to appear, and my heart skips a beat, my cheeks flushing as I nod and rush out of the cafe.

"Hey, Alyssa, perfect timing." Jamie grins as we get out of our cars at the same time. "This villa is pitch black."

Jamie squeezes my shoulder, and my heart soars. His hand holds mine, a look of unspoken emotion pass-ing between us. I breathe in deeply and hug Jamie, and he pecks my cheek. I lead us to the door and open it. He pushes my butt forward gently, his other hand carrying his luggage.

I switch on the night alarm after both of us have brought in our stuff for the night.

"So you will be sleeping in my room downstairs here, and I will occupy my grandmother's to guard her valuable items." I walk with him side by side to show him to his room. He spins in a slow circle and winks at me when he faces me again. "I need to shower. I'll see you in a bit." I smile and leave.

Once we have gotten ready for bed, we sit in the living room watching the midnight news. Jamie shifts from sitting in another chair to sitting just beside me. I take in his scent with a deep breath, a calm settling over me. He caresses my hair as I lean into his side. Butterflies take flight in my chest as he wraps his arm around my body, pulling me closer.

His lips touch mine briefly before he pulls away. "You know what, Alyssa? Rihanna never loved or actually wanted me." His hand rubs my arm slowly. "The marriage was an arranged contract from the start," he says wryly.

My head raises, and I look at him in confusion. "What do you mean?" I tilt my head. "I thought all the while Rihana was obsessed with you." My eyes narrow, and my eyebrows touch.

His dreamy eyes stare into my soul as he shakes his head. "That was what we both thought. However, on the night of our wedding, Rihana introduced me to her girlfriend." Jamie shrugs, smiling.

I sit straight and face Jamie. "Woah! All this while she was acting? But why?" I ask. I rub my forehead, not understanding.

"She showed me Mr. Spencer's will and his wishes. Mr. Spencer wanted her to be married to Mrs. Henderson's son for three years. This was to give time for Spencer Limited to become a conglomerate with Henderson Building and Construction Incorporation successfully. It turns out that Mr. Spencer required my dad's connections to win a contract in Dubai and Shanghai." Jamie's voice turns hard.

"Henderson Building and Construction Incorporation's 10% shares owned by Jennifer transferred to Rihanna upon marriage to me, so Jennifer could own Spencer Limited with 60% of the shares." Jamie unbuttons his collar harshly, anger making his motions jerky.

"Wicked. A genius businessman and woman. I wonder who murdered him?" My index finger taps the tip of my head. "Anyway, you are lucky it is only for three years and not forever." My eyebrow raises as I smirk.

Jamie's eyes catch mine, and his mouth curves up on both sides, his eyes sparkling.

"Then I have you all to myself. I can't wait for this ordeal to end." His large hands start to massage my shoulders lovingly. I feel lightheaded at his soft touch. "We will have kids together." His eyes sparkle more, and he strokes my soft hair. His lips graze against mine in a teasing kiss. I close my eyes and press our lips together more firmly, and his hand caresses my back, pulling me closer. He kneads my breast as his hand trails down to slide my pants off, and my hand pulls down his shorts. Within moments, nothing is left between us, and he slips inside me. I groan, my heart, body, and soul brimming with happiness. We let our desire guide us, and I pray I never have to let him go again.

Chapter 35

The sound of drilling pulls me from a deep, satisfied sleep. I jolt in bed, my heart pounding. The sound dies, and I shake my head. It must be in my dreams. Feeling drowsy, I move the pillow to cover my ears and close my eyes to drift back to sleep. A few minutes pass before the sound pulsates through the wall again, and I open one eye in annoyance.

Grandmother's neighbor must be mad doing a renovation in the middle of the night. I punch the pillow beside me and groan.

Wait . . . This is not an apartment. My eyes gradually open as the realization dawns on me. There are no neighbors upstairs or beside us. The noise must have come from—I shoot up from the bed. My eyes are wide, and my hand grabs my phone on the bedside table. I stand still, adrenaline rushing through my veins as a memory slams me. During the investigation after the break-in, I landed on something soft and flimsy in the small parlor room. My eyes jump to the parlor room entrance, and I squint at the still darkness.

I shake my head. No. It can't be. I must be dreaming. There was no sound. I flop back on the soft but firm mattress, and the sound echoes again. I jump out of bed and grab my baton from underneath my pillow. I creep toward the room, a lamp brightly lighting a flamingo statue across the room. Maybe it is automatically on when it's dark.

I turn my ear to face the sliding door that separates the parlor from the main bedroom, trying to hear something. Yet, the parlor stands silent.

Maybe it is just a dream. I yawn and reverse my steps, pausing at a loud thud. Sudden shudders creep up my spine, and my legs tremble. I grip my left leg to ensure its stability. I swallow and take a deep breath before tightening my grip on the baton. I creep faster this time, not wanting to lose the sound again.

I push the lever, and the sliding door shifts, emitting a *thunk* as it hits the door panel. I gulp, not daring to breathe for a moment.

I feel as the blood drains from my face, my heart thumping. If there is an intruder, I am screwed. My right hand gropes my sweater pocket to find my phone. I retreat toward the bed and hide, calling Jamie. His voice is half asleep when he answers, and I harshly whisper, "I heard something peculiar in the parlor. Please hurry." My eyes stare at the half-open sliding door.

"Don't do anything. I will be there soon." Concern has replaced any trace of sleepiness.

Suddenly, feeling much better with Jamie on the way, I creep toward the door again.

Wait a minute, is the sound coming from the ceiling? I recall there being a loose tile near the window, but there was also that weird bit of flooring that was springy instead of solid marble.

I place my finger on my chin. *Where shall I look first?* There's a stool just beneath the ceiling, and I hop on it.

Now closer to the ceiling, I strain my left ear under the loose tile. Silence. I tilt my head toward the pot of flowers, the standing ballet statue creepy at this hour, with its eyes completely white.

Jamie appears in the doorway with a baton in his hands. My index finger points at the parlor, then raises to my lips. I wait until he nods before I slink forward. Before long, Jamie follows at the side. He signals to me that he will check the other side of the room. I give him a thumbs-up and smile before turning back to my task.

I squat, placing my right foot on the uneven flooring. If this is a door, the person would have to be pretty slim to fit through it. My hands press around the floor, and I hit a spot that gives a soft click as I lift my hand. It reveals a small panel with a combination keypad. I snap a picture of the secret doorway, then sit on my heels as I think about the password. I don't know if Grandmother even built this. I massage my chin, frowning. *Where could it be?* I close my eyes, trying to recall if Grandmother or Clare has mentioned anything before.

My heart lurches, and I nearly fall on my butt when I open my eyes. The statue's white eyes seem to be staring at me. Goosebumps appear on my skin, and my hands go icy and numb. "Don't you stare at me," I grumble at it before noticing a handkerchief on the floor, an elegant D embroidery on it. I toss it over the statue's eyes. *How does Grandmother stand its creepy eyes?* I rub my arms to warm myself and blink, refocusing on the figure. I inch forward, eyes narrow. The statue is tilted, exposing the ballerina's shoe. I must have knocked it when I covered it. Air rushes from my nose as I take in the numbers on the shoe. *Is this the code I need?* I shrug, biting my lip. *No harm in trying.* I snap a picture of the statue and its numbers.

I step back after trying the code, my eyes taking in the room and searching for an opening. A click rings in my ear, and I freeze as a secret hatch on the floor pops open to reveal a dark, narrow space. I shuffle forward and swallow the thick lump in my throat when I realize the opening is big enough for me to slip through. I place my Apple watch beside the statue just in case I am locked in. Someone will stumble upon the watch and look for me. *Right?*

I breathe in deeply and pat my arms, mustering my confidence.

I wriggle my body through the door, and within seconds, I hit the steps. It's dark, and it takes a minute for my foot to find support. I push my body in further, my hand sliding along the walls for some sort of switch. It's unnecessary because, within moments, automatic lights ignite the whole room.

My eyes open widely and dart around. Surprisingly, this place looks clean, and I walk further in once my feet are on the ground. My gaze roves the area in awe. It's wall-to-wall carpets in red with Gucci emblems in their corners. My nose twitches with the rich smell of coffee.

I swallow hard. "Hello, anyone here?" I place my hand against my cheek, my head swiveling.

There's the soft sound of footsteps running in the distance. I strain my ears to listen, but a click to the right distracts me. There's only a dark, narrow path that stretches that way. It's damp with ragged, worn stones on the wall, which I can't tell if they are basalt stones.

I let out a deep audible sigh. *Maybe it was a rat. I hope not.* I shake my head. *I will freak out if I see one.* I tighten my grip on the baton and bite my fingernails, imagining a rat running by my feet.

Alyssa. I pinch my hand. *Please do not lose your concentration.*

All of a sudden, my heart pounds in my chest as I walk into a nice Victorian-decorated room. There's a wooden sliding door, and many portraits, photos, and even a shining antique photograph sitting elegantly on an antique mahogany cabinet.

My heart skips a beat, and my right hand covers my slack jaw, flabbergasted. My eyes snag on a seated young woman flanked by two men. The man on the right I recognize as my grandfather. There's a small plaque that reads, "Son of the richest oil and gas tycoon, and John Lanvin, son of a French designer."

I look at the other portraits, and one photo sticks out to me. It's Grandmother and John Lanvin dancing with broad smiles. The date underneath reads 1965. Five years after Grandmother's marriage to Grandfather. I become engrossed in the treasure trove of pictures and captions, and I accidentally hit a chest of drawers. Its topmost center drawer juts out from the impact. A dusty old diary with yellowed paper protrudes from the drawer. I turn in a circle, alert for the presence of anyone else. I breathe in and out and hold my baton. A few minutes pass, and nothing new becomes apparent. My hand reaches out to the drawer to check Grandmother's diary. I find a glove in my PJ pants pocket. I use the glove to pull the diary from the antique drawer, placing it on my lap. I flip the front page and gasp. There's a picture of an old sonogram with the name Davies Lanvin jotted under it.

The next page holds a picture of a toddler in Grandmother's arms with John Lanvin holding her from behind. It reads in faded black ink, "My first child, sadly given away because of my arranged marriage to the oil and gas tycoon's son. I had no choice but to save my family's business from the brink of bankruptcy and regain my father's reputation."

I gasp, and my stomach flips. Tears well in my eyes, and I take a photo with shaky hands.

Suddenly, my skin prickles, and the silence grows oppressive. I turn my head to face the door, nerves jumping. I squint, searching for any shadows outside the room's entrance.

My hands shake, and I turn to face the sliding door. Maybe someone is hiding in the doorway of the room, waiting for me to leave. I peek at my mobile. 4:45 AM. I slip my phone into a hidden zipper of my sweater before placing the diary back in the drawer and grabbing the baton off the floor.

My breath is shaky, and my legs start to tremble, inching toward the sliding door. Upon reaching the sliding door, I push it open. My heart pounds, expecting someone, but the place is deserted. I step out of the tiny room and freeze when my eye catches a tall skinny shadow on the narrow pathway ahead, close to the wall.

"Jamie, is that you?" I tilt my head and blink. There's no response, but a clang comes from overhead. The sound must be coming from Grandmother's bed. I need to return to her room. *Is Jamie OK?*

With the baton in hand, I move bit by bit. My palms become sweaty, making my grip on the baton slippery. I breathe rapidly, yet try to do so quietly to give me strength and stealth. By the time I reach the area I believe the shadow to have come from, I am thrown off when there's a sharp pain in my neck. Blurry vision seeps in instantly, and dizziness develops in my brain. My right-hand latches onto my neck, grappling with a metallic item. I fumble with it, unfamiliar with the shape of the dart. My hands gripping the baton unwillingly relax as my eyes close tightly.

"Alyssa! Are you alright?" Jamie's face appears before my eyes. I groan, my head aching, and Jamie's massaging his head. I turn my face into the satin pillow, and the aroma of Grandmother's bedroom surrounds me.

Jamie's jaw looks tightened, and worry draws lines on his forehead.

I sit up slowly, feeling groggy, and rub at my eyes.

"Ah, my head," Jamie says with a wince as his fingers press on a tender spot. "Someone knocked me out while I was checking the bathroom." He pauses, frowning. "Are you OK?" He moves closer, his right hand gently stroking my hair. I lean against his chest and tilt my head to look at him.

"They tranqed me with a dart in my neck," I say in a soft voice.

"What?" His face turns anguished, and he clenches his fists.

I reiterate to him my night before pushing off of his chest and jumping out of bed. I hold his hand as we walk to the parlor.

"Here." I press on the particular tiles, but nothing happens.

My lips purse. "Hm."

I sigh. I'm sure it was here. I step around on the other tiles beside it. My fists ball at my sides. "No . . . No. The statue," I point at it with a frown, "was white. But today, it's pitch black." I tousle my hair. "Don't tell me someone changed the ballet statue." A flash of irritation seeps into me as my cheeks grow hot.

"I am positive that I saw my grandmother's picture with a man named John Lanvin and a baby." My jaw tightens, and my right-hand shakes as I try to control my anger. I look at Jamie. "In the diary, it said that she, unfortunately, had to give up her baby because of her arranged marriage to my grandfather," I whisper, my breathing turning rapidly.

Jamie strokes my hair gently and kisses my cheek. He nods. "I trust your words; however, right now, the passageway has vanished." He glances around the ground of the room with a worried wrinkle between his eyes. He wraps his arms around me, trying to pull me close.

I push Jamie aside, my hands in fists, and my eyes glare fire. "Where is my black baton?" I turn to look back at Grandmother's bed. I walk to it, searching beside the table and under the bed.

Sweat beads on my forehead, and my hands tremble.

"Alyssa. We will find it. Tonight, we will sleep here and keep watch for anything." His blue eyes are enchanting, looking deep into my eyes as he smiles, and his soft touch trails down my back.

I sigh and finally let him pull me into a hug. My eyes land on the black ballet statue over his shoulder, and a thought breaks through my mind. "My watch!"

I push Jamie away and run to the statue. The edge of a pink watch strap is buried in a flower pot next to the statue. I manage to pull it out, dusting it off as I hold it up.

"This is evidence that I did go down there. I placed this watch as a clue of how to find me, just in case I got trapped." I thrust the watch in front of Jamie's nose.

"The only way to find the secret passageway again is to wait for tonight," Jamie suggests, pulling me by my hand, then my waist.

Heavy footsteps clatter from the hall, and we turn to see Eleanor appear at the door. I wave at her. She pushes the door wider and steps into the room. She furrows her brows at us, and discomfort pricks up my spine. Jamie massages his head again as she walks to us.

We tell her of the entire ordeal, and I tilt my head to show the bruises on my neck.

She squats down, and her phone vibrates. She grabs it, and her eyes stare at the screen for a moment. She sighs and answers it. "Eleanor, your grandmother seems restless and wants you to stay with her tonight at the hotel," Clare says.

"What? Really?" She raises her voice and sighs loudly. 'OK, I will be there." Her voice is tired.

Eleanor looks at me, then at Jamie, as she hangs up. "Let me get any fingerprints on your Apple Watch now, and we can discuss tonight's incidents when we meet tomorrow." I hold out my watch. She pulls out a glove, putting it on before taking my watch. She pulls out a transparent plastic bag from her waist pouch and puts the watch inside.

"On second thought, I'll go with you, Eleanor." I gesture for her to wait and quickly go to change.

Chapter 36

We leave Jamie behind at Grandmother's old villa and head to the hotel after dropping off the watch.

Eleanor parks her car in the parking lot as her phone vibrates. She presses 'Answer,' and immediately, a voice comes through without a greeting. "There are fingerprints. One is Alyssa's, and the other is John Lanvin's."

"Good job. Thank you," Eleanor responds."

I sit beside Eleanor, and I can't help but eavesdrop on the conversation. "Who is he?"

The officer replies, "He's been dead for twenty years. Died in a car crash in Provins. He had a child but no marriage." Eleanor's eyes bulge.

"Where is his child? Maybe we can visit and interview him?" I ask curiously. Eleanor leans her head back, looking at me.

"Please check where his child is. Name is Davies Lanvin. We would like to have a word with him," Eleanor commands, then ends the call.

The evening of the next day, we sit and eat dinner

with Grandmother. She's unusually energetic and animated as she chatters away at us. Eleanor keeps looking at her wristwatch, her fingers tapping impatiently on a table beside the sofa. She walks quietly to the coffee maker, her head turning to look over her shoulder. She discreetly pulls something from her pouch and mixes it into Grandmother's drink.

Within ten minutes, Grandmother dozes off. Eleanor nudges me, and we quietly creep from the hotel room, leaving Clare to guard Grandmother.

We get in Eleanor's car, and she speaks before I have the chance to, "I know from your facial expression you require answers. I put Temasepam in Grandmother's drink to let her have a peaceful sleep while we investigate her old villa."

I nod my head slowly, still feeling a bit strange.

"Do you realize that Grandmother often calls us when we are investigating? I don't want her to disturb us this time." Eleanor raises an eyebrow at me.

I tilt my head and think for a moment before nodding.

We drive to Grandmother's old villa to spend another night. I hit my fist against my palm. "Eleanor, we better capture the culprit that hit Jamie and put a needle in my neck." I sit up straight in the passenger seat, looking at her intently.

Eleanor and I sleep in the bedroom next to Grandmother's. It used to be Dad's room. Tons of paper clippings are framed, and awards he received for producing some movies are hung on the wall.

His bed looks neat and comfy, so we snuggle together, and Eleanor places her gun on the side table along with a new baton I got this morning.

Jamie sleeps on the long sofa downstairs tonight.

My alarm buzzes after a few hours. I wake with a groan, my left eye cracking open to look at the time: three in the morning. My head falls back on the pillow before whispers come from the direction of Grandmother's room. I jolt from the bed, walk toward the wall, and place my ear against the wall separating us from her bedroom.

Two men's voices are muffled but still clear enough for me to understand their words. "Ouch! This is heavy."

"Shut up, you idiot." There's a muffled smack.

I scurry to Eleanor's side, shake her awake, and whisper in her ear, "There are two men in Grandmother's bedroom." She jumps out of bed and grabs her gun, shoving her earpiece in.

Fear tries to overwhelm me, but my determination to catch the culprit wins out, and I take my baton, adjusting my grip. Fear still churns in my stomach, but I swallow it back. I grab Grandmother's room key from the bedside table and put the extra earpiece in.

Eleanor signals for me to remain silent and walk behind her.

I nod, stepping around barefoot. Eleanor opens the room door with a soft squeak. I hold my breath, freezing at this sound.

Eleanor's hand waves for me to keep following her. We step into the room, and my head turns to the left to look at Grandmother's closet, where her valuables are hidden.

I shift my focus to look around the bed and notice a silhouette moving. I point at it as I tug on Eleanor's sleeve. It moves fast from the room, heading toward the cloakroom. Automatically, my left hand covers my mouth, preventing me from screaming.

Eleanor turns her head and runs toward the figure.

Another shape passes in front of my eyes, and my arms open wide with the baton in my right hand. My legs start trembling, and I breathe in and out deeply, suddenly striking out for the shadow. I growl as I miss my target.

"Second incoming," I whisper in the earpiece.

I pinch myself to get moving and run toward the shadow, this time passing the vanity table. It's a massive man. I throw my baton at his head, and it hits, dropping him to the floor. He quickly gets up, and his gold tooth flashes in the dim light from the hallway. I pursue him, and he knocks over tables and chairs behind him. Eleanor jumps on him, and he kicks her. He shoves his hand into her side, and Eleanor shudders from top to bottom as electricity zaps her. He pushes away and runs into the cloakroom, and I chase after him. He smashes the window of the cloakroom and jumps on the panel. I grab his shoe, and he wriggles his feet, kicking my face, and blood spurts from my nose. He jumps through the window as I cry out in pain.

I rub off the blood and look out the window, watching as a black Mercedes van shoots away, letting the man with a golden tooth escape.

I growl and clench my fists before another shadow darts into Grandmother's dressing room beside the cloakroom as I run to aid Eleanor.

"Eleanor is down. Mayday. Mayday!" I kneel, my right hand feeling for her pulse.

"Roger. We are coming from downstairs," the police respond immediately.

I am dying to know the culprit. I grab Eleanor's gun and run to follow the intruder. My chest moves up and down rapidly, and my thigh muscles burn as I push hard.

"I am in the dresser area where the vault is located.

Roger."

"Roger."

A gunshot echoes in the room. The man shoots in the direction of the sliding glass door. The door's glass shatters all over the floor, and I don't have time to avoid it. My bare left foot steps directly onto the pieces, and immediately, a thick flow of blood runs from my pale flesh. I stifle a scream and stop cold, my eyes trying to concentrate on the man. They disappear into the vault, and I limp and hop on my right leg to inch my way into the brightly lit vault. A man's hand disappears within the wallpapered walls as I enter. My mouth falls open, stunned. I just barely get a glimpse of his hands, bearing the crescent and knife tattoo. I swallow and limp forward.

"I am injured. I need help at the vault. Intruder escaped within the walls. Roger," I say while breathing deeply, my pulse heightened from the pain. I stare at the wall, frowning.

I press all around the wall for a hidden passageway, but I can't find anything.

"Alyssa! Shit, you need to go to the hospital." Jamie runs to me, pulling me into his arms.

"The intruder escaped within these walls," I cry. *I was so close to catching them.*

Three policemen run into the room and slide to a stop, gaping at the secret vault after looking at where I'm pointing at the wall.

A moment later, Eleanor rushes into the cloakroom, standing on the threshold. Her eyes are intense, and she looks as though she wants to eat someone alive. Breathing deeply, she says, "I am catching the culprit tonight. Show me where he disappeared?" She rolls her sleeves.

Jamie lets go of me but still holds my hand, and I

point at the wallpaper. There's a vintage white wall lamp with—I gasp. "There's a finger!" I scream in a rasp.

Eleanor moves closer, pulling on a glove before pulling a frozen, hacked-off finger from the lamp. *Mr. Spencer's missing finger?* She holds it up to examine it, and the wall shudders, sliding to the side and exposing a pitch-dark space.

"Jamie, wrap Alyssa's foot with some bandages and place Fucidin H on it quickly. Let her wear Grandmother's socks."

Eleanor stares at me as he does as she asks. "Jamie, please stay here. When Jason comes, please inform him to take fingerprints and check for further clues in here." Her hands run over her face, and she sighs tiredly. "Alyssa and I are going after the culprit. Let's go, Alyssa." She looks furious, and her jaw grits.

She turns her head to face me, and her eyes land on my empty hands. "Your gun. You need that." She quickly pulls a gun from her holster and smiles. "This is an extra." Eleanor chuckles and hands it to me.

Eleanor runs through the door, and I walk slowly behind her, still limping. Automatic lights illuminate the carpeted ground, and the lights obfuscate once we pass them. I inhale to calm my heart, and I smell the damp air as we move further into the narrow passage. I grow tired of the chase, panting and massaging my hamstring as everything compounds into pain. We halt abruptly, and my hands accidentally knock on Eleanor's back as we are greeted by a wall of red bricks. I step back and slant my head up, my eyes landing on a tiny window at the top.

I shift my head to look at the ground, but pain grips my body fiercely. I lean against the wall and bend to massage my leg. I tilt my head and hum softly to get Eleanor's attention, then nod to a shoe print on the old throw rug going under the wall.

"I assume it is another sliding wall," I whisper.

Eleanor starts pressing each brick. My eyes dart from one wall to another, trying to find any weird things that could be a hidden lever. I move backward and nearly fall as my knee gives out. I catch myself and lean against the wall. The brick beneath my shoulder shifts, and the wall in front of us shakes, causing dust to fly and land in Eleanor's hair.

Eleanor taps her feet and checks her watch while waiting for me to get back to her side. "You OK? Take your time. I'll go ahead," Eleanor says as I grimace in pain.

I nod to Eleanor, and she walks through the ajar wall alone.

She holds her earpiece as she says to her backup team, "Roger. I need backup. Alyssa should go to the hospital." Her tone is stressed, and she glances back at me before stepping in and disappearing through the brick wall.

I hobble to the doorway and stand on the threshold, watching Eleanor explore the next pathway from around the corner of the brick gateway. She hides behind a stack of boxes. I move back, and my eyes trail from one part of the area to the other. I gasp as water laps on the pavement. It looks like a loading bay with a stack of boxes piled up on the grey concrete and a small river to the right. There are two white and red striped floats hanging on the dull wall. I strain my neck to look over the river and see two motorboats. One's engine is running loudly, and the other is docked and floating like a peaceful ballet.

A loud gunshot emits and makes my body go numb. I

remain still in the same spot. *Oh, no. I hope nothing bad happened to Eleanor*. My hand cups my cheek, and I lean forward to peek at the surroundings.

Several people are standing on the boats, shooting in Eleanor's direction. There's a blare over a walkie-talkie, and someone shouts, "Run, run! If caught, suicide."

I cover my mouth and clutch my sweater. I tighten my grip on the gun. My spot is a blessing; I can see the intruders' locations clearly. I step out and shoot a guy at his feet as he faces Eleanor. Eleanor jumps back, and he falls forward, hitting his head against items in the boat, and more blood flows.

To ensure he is down, I shot his thigh. His face grimaces in pain, and he whimpers.

There's a clatter as lots of rushing footsteps come from behind me.

I turn to look over my shoulder, squinting, and I can see shadows with guns in their hands, out and ready. "We are nearing. Roger," The police backup responds via my earpiece.

"One man down in the motorboat. Hurry to cuff him. Roger," I say into the earpiece, then turn my head to peek at the same spot.

Jason, with his gun out and baton hanging on his waist, and three of his mates come. The four of them jump onto the motorboat in the nick of time. Before the intruder escapes, his hand is on the wheel, and the other twists the key. Jason throws a baton, causing him to winch in pain, letting go of the key.

Jason pulls him away from the outboard and cuffs him while the other three officers walk, their eyes moving around to find pieces of evidence and fingerprints.

Eleanor crawls to the side of the pavement. She sighs

and takes several cleansing breaths.

She smiles at me. "You are my heroine," she says with a chuckle.

I smile at her and whisper, "We caught someone. Hopefully, he will give us a hint for a solution."

Chapter 37

We are at Skyclouds residence, Grandmother's new villa, visiting her while we share with her our findings at the old villa.

"What? My vault has a hidden passageway? Probably the reason I lost one gold bar worth a million monthly lately," Grandmother exclaims, fists against her thighs.

"You did not inform us of your missing gold; otherwise, we could have investigated." Eleanor crosses her arms, and her lips press closed. Grandmother swallows hard. "Let alone not keeping it safely in the bank." Eleanor rolls her eyes, then looks into Grandmother's eyes.

"I was having Albert, my security guy, do the investigation, but he couldn't find anything. I also only realized it two months ago," Grandmother responds with an apologetic gesture.

"Do you know this guy, Grandmother? Have you seen him around the compound or your business deals?" Eleanor shows the video of him after she and her team interrogated him.

Grandmother blinks, then she places her spectacles on her nose from hanging around her neck. She strains her eyes and gasps, "Oh! My, he looks familiar. Was he the previous gardener we employed?" She gets up abruptly from sitting, breathing up and down rapidly. "However, he was rude, and I sacked him instantly." She places both of her hands on her waist.

Grandmother's security guy comes closer and views the video. "Affirmative, Mrs. Smith, he was your rude gardener of six months ago. We caught him luring Clare and stealing Mrs. Smith's golden bracelet, which ended his work contract."

"What punishment will befall him?" Grandmother asks with an eyebrow raised.

"Leonard will be put behind bars while we gather more information, just in case he was being paid to murder any of the victims," Eleanor responds.

Grandmother nods. "You are very right." She looks at Eleanor with a smile.

"Run along, you two. I have things to unpack with Clare." Grandmother kisses us both on each cheek, and I let go of her hands.

Eleanor and I head outside to the car, and I gasp, pausing with my hand on the door handle, as a thought occurs to me. "Argh, we missed it." I slap my hand against my forehead. "There was another idle boat behind the one Leonard was on. We should check it out, just in case there are others related to him." My hands run through my hair, and my hands fidget.

Eleanor nods and gestures for us to get in. She dials a number and places it on speaker. "Jason, apparently, there was another boat when the incident happened. Please check on it since you are there."

He's quiet for a bit before getting back on the line. "Negative. No boat is here. The motorboat must have left in the midst of the action. It's something we will investigate before we leave and close the passageway."

He pauses for a moment before sighing. "In addition, we have updates on John Lanvin and Davies Lanvin. John died in a car crash, whereas Davies Lanvin vanished during the accident. There's no trace of them. Therefore, John cannot be a suspect." My eyes widen, and I rub my neck in distress.

"Noted, Jason," Eleanor replies. Our eyes meet, and I shrug while Eleanor's hands clench on her steering wheel.

Chapter 38

I sip on some apple juice as Eleanor drives me to my apartment, and my phone on the cup holder rings, displaying Lucas's name on the screen.

"Alyssa, first thing Monday morning, we are to meet at the client's stock area. Two other senior engineers and five construction workers will work with us since the client requires completion within a month," he says, his voice firm but slightly shaky.

"A month? Woah, that's a limited timeline," I respond rapidly. We pull up in front of my apartment, and I wave at Eleanor in thanks as I hop out. I clench my fist and slouch, thinking of the project's safety.

The next morning, I'm looking over some architect's drawings at the waterfront location when someone taps my shoulder. The drawings slip from my grip as I jump at the contact. Alistair's hands are quick to save the papers.

"Guess we will be working here day and night for a month to ensure completion. This client is uber-rich, and they are paying 30% extra for the short notice." Alistair smiles wryly.

My mouth curves into a smile, and my eyebrow lifts. "We have no choice then, huh?" I rest my hand on my waist.

The work requires me to work hand in hand with Alistair, which is a blessing since I still need to figure out more about where his uncle's friend Joe is.

For two weeks, Eleanor stays with Grandmother at the new villa because I can't with work. I only return to my apartment at night to doze off for a few hours long after the sun sets each day to rise with it the next.

One evening after two weeks, several rooms and restaurants are complete with built-in furniture in the main building, but there's still so much left to do. My eyes slowly close during my lunch, and I doze off on one of the sofas in the site's construction headquarters.

A harsh voice abruptly pulls me back to consciousness. Curious, I remain in my position with only my right eye slightly opening. I readjust so that my ear is tilted toward the voice.

"Yes, Jake, we need to place John here once ready. It is better than the—what? The crazy lady sold off the villa?" the voice says angrily before the smell of smoke wafts from nearby.

I open my other eye to look around discreetly. *Is someone actually here, or am I just dreaming?* There's a man in a white shirt and blue jeans just outside the screened door, but they don't resemble anyone I recognize.

My heart beats faster, and I start to hyperventilate. I pull my jacket closed over my chest to stifle the shiver that runs down my spine.

I push from the sofa, grab my bag, and step forward to open the door, coming eye-to-eye with a guy I've never seen before. He is tan with a mole on the right side of his chin and a blonde crew cut. He quickly throws his cigarette butt on the ground, then runs to a blue Toyota sedan and speeds off.

"Who was that, Alistair?" I stretch both hands over my head, yawning.

"He's my friend. He's our supplier for certain exotic items that the client ordered." Alistair smiles and checks his watch while his other hand scrapes the top of his collar.

"It's late. You better go home and rest. See you tomorrow." He pats my shoulder and points to my car.

I smile at him and nod, then turn to walk to my car.

I use an alternative route back to my apartment due to road construction on the main street, and I spot a Toyota similar to the one the guy left in. I slow down to look at it a little closer, then smile to myself. It's the blonde.

I flip to my favorites in my phone contacts, dialing. "Eleanor, I am suspicious of a blonde guy in a blue Toyota sedan that met Alistair at the site. Do you think your team can run a check on who owns the car plate, 998-YDR, Colorado?" I ask while driving to my apartment. "I am tailing his car."

"Roger," Eleanor replies and ends the call.

I abruptly hit the brakes, not wanting the guy to realize that I am pursuing him. The seat belt cuts into my chest as my car jerks, and the blonde guy's car makes a turn at the corner of a playground. I park my car, switching off my engine and lights as I watch him in the fading light.

I gasp as a guy who looks like an older version of John Lanvin with white hair and wrinkled skin steps closer to the curb. He holds a dark briefcase and has on a long jacket covering his skinny frame.

He crosses the pedestrian crossing toward the playground and the waiting Toyota. Within moments, he's climbing into the car. I blink rapidly before quickly taking a picture of John Lanvin entering the blonde's car.

What's the connection between Alistair, Joe, the blonde guy in the Toyota, and 'John Lanvin'? I curl my right hand and smack it into my left.

Instantly, I redial Eleanor and inform her of what I saw. "Wicked. The blonde guy and John Lanvin? It seems like they are connected. John Lanvin is supposedly dead," I tap restlessly on my car wheel, "So, who is this guy that I just saw? Did he have an identical twin brother?" I ask Eleanor.

"You posed a good question, Alyssa. Let me request a further investigation on this John Lanvin," Eleanor responds, sounding just as troubled.

"Another thing, Eleanor. I can feel in my bones that this guy has a connection or illegal business dealings with Joe."

Chapter 39

"I don't have a good feeling about the passageway to the water at Grandmother's old villa. I think someone's living there." I rub my temples, a headache starting to form. "There should be another entrance to the small vintage room with photos of Grandmother's secret past." We are on FaceTime, and my forehead creases with work as my jaw tightens. I'm in the car, parked near my work site in Dakota Jersey, the next day.

Eleanor's eyebrows droop, and her hands cup both her cheeks.

"Alyssa! What are you doing on the phone? There's lots of work to do, and these are wrong." Lucas's face turns red as he folds his arms over his waist a few steps away from my car, the offending project papers on the table in front of him.

He tears the papers apart and throws the scraps on the ground. The wind blows the shreds across the lot, and I momentarily shut my eyes. My face feels hot, and I am unable to sit still any longer.

"Talk to you later, Eleanor." I turn back to finish my conversation, popping the car door open.

"Don't let your superior bully you, Alyssa," Eleanor

says with a frown.

Lucas stomps toward me. "Go to the office and do the paperwork properly, Alyssa. I want the report with the cost and benefits analysis by nine tomorrow morning!" He storms away, his fists swinging at his sides.

I huff angrily and slam my car door shut again. I try to start it, but the engine only makes clanking noises. A puff of smoke escapes into the air from under the hood, and I groan. *This is what happens when dad buys a used car.* I slouch, then sigh and get out. I slam the door shut in frustration and turn back around to the site. My eyes lock onto a pair of sea-blue pupils. Alistair. He puts down his duffle bag on the ground and walks to me.

He whispers, "Lucas had a rough day. Got chewed out by the client. Go ahead and ensure the paper is corrected." He holds out the car keys with a small smile. "You can borrow my car."

My mouth opens to speak, but he continues before I can. "Don't worry about me. I have friends here that I can ride with. Call the shop to repair your car. It will be like brand new tomorrow." He smiles again and swirls a toothpick in his mouth.

I hesitate for only a moment until I spot Lucas, his brows furrowed and his hands in fists at the sight of me still here. I bite my lip, grab the keys, and speed off before he can move.

On the way to the office, I slam on the brakes as the car in front of me stops abruptly. My breath is deep but fast, and my palms turn sweaty. There's a clatter as something big and heavy rolls around in the trunk. I lift an eyebrow, glancing in the rearview mirror. *What's that?* I quickly maneuver the car to the curb after the traffic light turns green.

I stand before the trunk and press the key to unlock it. It jumps open, and I narrow my eyes at the contents. There's a black scuba diving bag and two oxygen tanks sitting inside. *Interesting. Alistair must be into scuba diving.*

I push an oxygen tank to the side and relocate the bag to a wall to prevent it from rolling more. The zipper tangles with my open jacket's zipper, and it pulls harshly. "Ouch!" My face turns into a scowl.

I heave my jacket zipper, but it stays entangled. I sigh and decide to fight with the bag's zipper instead. It takes a few minutes to get them apart due to my jacket's thick fabric.

Finally, I manage to get them detangled, the bag becoming unzipped in the process. I gasp as my eyes focus on the inside of the bag. There's a frozen finger wearing a chunky ring on top of the rest of the items. I shiver, and unconsciously, my hands grip my jacket. I stumble back.

I should document this. I take out my phone with shaking hands while rummaging through my pockets. I pull out a latex glove and quickly take the picture. I gently push the finger over to look closely at the ring.

I squeal, and my hand covers my mouth. The ring is a pear-shaped sapphire ring similar to the one at the Henderson mansion where Mr. Spencer was murdered. My stomach roils, and I take a picture of this as well. I lean closer, studying it. The finger looks real, and I rotate it. It's been preserved, the nail still sparkling.

I jolt as my cell rings. Still wearing the latex glove, I slowly zip the bag and shut the trunk.

I text Eleanor and send her the photos. Numbly, I start the engine and pull back into traffic. I contemplate taking the car and everything in it to the nearest police station. However, if this has anything to do with Eleanor and Inspector Raven's cases, it would slow things down.

I make it back to work, and within an hour, Eleanor replies, "Meet me in the parking lot, Alyssa. We'll take those things to run fingerprint identification before Alistair collects his car."

"Coming," I reply. I press 'Save' on my analysis, then get up, pushing my chair in before leaving.

I reach the parking lot and look around, frowning when I don't see anyone. I nod at Eleanor, in plain clothes, upon finally seeing her, and she gestures for me to lead the way. We reach the car, and I pop the trunk. She quickly grabs the frozen finger from the bag, storing it in a small ziplock pouch, her hands already wearing gloves.

"It will take two hours. Then we will return it," Eleanor whispers.

I nod, pull the hatch shut, and lock the car, walking back to the building entrance.

"I have lots of paperwork to do. See you soon."

I finalize the analysis reports earlier than planned and lean back with a satisfied smile.

I FaceTime Eleanor while I walk to the entrance and grab a taxi since my car is out of commission.

"There are three rings altogether here. When connected, they form a half-shaped Viking boat. We need another, the last ring to complete the puzzle," Eleanor exclaims, showing the interconnected rings in front of her.

"Did you manage to get hold of Leonard? Were you able to gather any information from him?" I ask, and Eleanor shrugs.

"He's giving us false clues. I am so furious with

him. We wasted our time going to the beach and digging through the sand. You should have seen his face while we searched and dug. He was giggling." Eleanor's face turns sour, and her jaw tightens.

She adjusts her phone, and her voice gets louder. "I noticed you're no longer in the office. Care to help your cousin this evening to gather more information from Leonard?" She smacks her lips and smiles.

I laugh and nod. I switch the camera view to let Eleanor see the taxi seat. "See you soon," I say and get off the call.

In the interrogation room, I slam the table that Leonard is leaning on. My hand accidentally brushes his nose as I do. His mouth drops, and he sputters. "Yo—you nearly took off my nose." He scowls, rubbing it as he glares daggers at me.

"Tell us where Joe and Jake Kane are," I shout at him, angry lines appearing on both of my cheeks, which are beginning to turn red.

"I have no clue what you are asking." Leonard raises his shoulder, sliding back into his picture of nonchalance.

I stand beside him, take out photos of Joe and Jake Kane, and show them to Leonard.

He blinks and tilts his head as he looks at the photos again.

He shakes his head and releases a puff, breathing in and out to calm himself. His face smooths. "They will kill me if I tell you."

"If you tell us, your criminal sentences will be reduced to only three years in prison. Otherwise . . ." Eleanor trails off.

"Alright! Alright!" he shouts. "You promise only

three years, right? I have a 4-year-old kid," Leonard whispers as his eyes turn red and watery.

"It's a promise. We will submit the proposal to the judge. So no more playing. If caught, you'll be in prison for life." Eleanor replies matter-of-factly.

My phone vibrates, and I step back to peek at the screen. I signal to Eleanor that it's Grandmother. I run out of the room and to the nearest window to pick up the call. Feeling worried for her safety after receiving death threats, I insist on answering her calls. "Hello, Grandmother," I say cheerfully.

"Where are you and Eleanor? I am scared to stay alone with Clare." Her voice is thick with fear.

"Don't worry, Grandmother. Your new villa is fully guarded, and we installed a security alarm. We recruited a new security team for you. Mr. Lim and his team will ensure your safety. Please don't worry, and please sleep soundly. Eleanor will be there once she finishes her work. Love you, Grandmother," I say to soothe her, trying to sound convincing.

"Where are you? Are you still in the office?"

I suddenly feel uneasy about telling her where I am, so I reply, "Yes, I am still in the office. Take care, and if anything comes up, please call me or Eleanor."

I sigh as I walk toward the interrogation room, and its door swings open. "Alyssa!" Eleanor walks to me, gesturing for me to follow her to her office. I stare at her curiously as we walk, but she remains silent. As soon as the door shuts behind us, she turns to me with a grim expression. "Reports arrived. The suits were used by both Joes, and the preserved finger is Mr. Spencer's. It matches the other finger that was used as a lever in the hidden hallway at grandmother's cloakroom. Remember?"

I nod, working to suppress a shudder.

"The ring has another man's fingerprint. John Lanvin," Eleanor affirms. She rolls her sleeves, and creases appear on her forehead.

"What?" My eyes widen, and my jaw works for a moment before I can find words. "Does this means he's not dead? He must be in disguise. He did plastic surgery to look different or something. You can't really change your fingerprint, though."

"That's a good analysis, Alyssa," Eleanor says, and I respond with a quick thumbs-up.

Eleanor waves me back into the hall, and we head toward the conference room with the connected case evidence up. "At this juncture, there are three strong suspects," Eleanor states while looking at me. She grabs a marker, then circles and moves photos around on the whiteboard. I read over the list, biting my lip.

1)John Lanvin

2)Jake Kane

3)Joe

4)Katherine? (Is she connected?)

5)Joe M

6)Helper @ Mr. Henderson's?

7)Leonard – caught

8)Jim – dead

Then, the four victims' photos are pinned on the wall as well. Mr. Spencer, Lady Jacqueline, Lady Jessica, and Arthur Papon.

"Stop! Leonard's escaped!" someone shouts outside the room. Eleanor and I stare at each other, then spring the door open, and take in the site of the office, where chaos currently reigns. Eleanor spots Leonard's head bobbing over cubicle walls as he runs toward the basement.

She shouts wordlessly, pointing. There are several officers running behind Leonard, but he manages to stay ahead of them.

Eleanor quickly reaches for her walkie-talkie and says tensely, "Close all doors, suspect on the run. Roger."

Immediately, Eleanor takes off, jumping over the staircase railing and climbing down. Leonard climbs down another flight, and Eleanor shouts, "Freeze!" Leonard trembles as he looks at Eleanor, who is close enough for a good shot. She pulls the trigger, aiming at his feet. He falls, face grimacing in pain, and holds his foot while curling into his stomach.

Eleanor places her gun against his back, and Jason hurries to cuff him.

"I will not run again. I just miss my family," Leonard cries, his eyes turning red as tears develop.

A police officer that was chasing him bends with his hands on his knees, breathing heavily as he explains to Eleanor, "Leonard tricked me. He asked to use the bathroom and took off on the way."

Eleanor purses her lips and drags Leonard for a few feet, pressing a keypad to open a door. A gust of cold air swirls from the dark room, and lights turn on when Eleanor steps inside.

The room feels sterile and only contains a hospital bed with steel drawers. It looks like a surgery room. There are six surveillance cameras around the room, covering every inch. Jason pushes Leonard in after her, and the door closes with a foreboding bang after Jason.

It's midnight when Eleanor and Jason emerge from the room, grim-faced. "Leonard will be locked here for tonight. There will be further interrogation tomorrow."

I nod and walk to the entrance with my arms wrapped

around my torso. We will solve the case once we catch Joe or Jake Kane, I just know it.

Chapter 40

In the office the next day, Lucas is cheerful as he stops by my desk. "I'm impressed with the analytical reports you redid."

I smile. "That's good." He smiles back before walking to his own workstation.

I turn my head to look at Alistair's cubicle. His computer is dark, and his table is neat, without any traces of pens or paperclips. I frown and take out my phone from the drawer to call Alistair. "Thank you for your car. I filled the tank. I should hear something about my car this afternoon."

Alistair replies, a smile clear in his voice, "Anytime. I will only be by the office to grab the car this morning. It was an all-nighter for me. Things are moving fast here. The complex and other amenities will be ready by our project date." He munches on something and sighs.

"I'm glad the project is near completion," I reply, a wash of relief filling me.

He smacks his lips. "I heard you will be away for a couple of days," he says. My mouth opens slowly, my eyes narrowing. I start fidgeting with my pen, silent for a moment.

"Yes, I need to help settle my Grandmother. She's not been well since the break-in," I reply in a croak, and I swallow hard.

"Hope she will be in a good spirit soon. See you on Thursday at the site," Alistair replies energetically.

"Thank you. Sure. See you then," I reply automatically as my mind races.

How does he know I will be away for a day? I haven't put in the leave request yet. Goose bumps creep over my skin. *Is there an informant amongst Grandmother, Eleanor, Clare, and Albert?* My head tilts as my right hand continues to play with the pen.

"We are here to share news of the fate of the Board of Directors of Smith Corporation." All the board members' eyes are focused on Grandmother. "I hereby declare that due to my age, I will pass down 10% of my shares to Alyssa Smith, which makes her the majority shareholder with a total of 80%." She claps her hands, standing and beaming at me. The board members clap as well, smiling. "This morning, the remaining shares will be opened for voting on who retains or otherwise." Grandmother's voice is firm, and she smiles while addressing everyone.

Her eyes look from one Board member to the next while smiling, but a majority of them look troubled. Her hand waves, and she says, "I will remain the Advisor and appear for the signing ceremony." She chuckles, and everyone in the room claps as their faces relax.

The door bangs open and is thrown closed with an echoing slam.

Dad appears in front of the room in his cowboy hat and high boots. "I'm not too late to claim my shares, I hope." He chuckles, tilting his head, and laughter fills the room.

"You are most welcome. We need an artist on the team to move Smith hotels to further glory," a man named Benedict Fernsby responds while waving for Dad to come in.

Grandmother kisses his cheeks, then mine, smiling.

Discussions begin in earnest, but halfway through, my concentration is momentarily preoccupied when I notice a woman in her forties wearing a particular ring.

I squint, trying to make out the details from across the table. I believe if I were to place that ring with the other three rings that we found, it would complete the Viking boat.

I clap my hands without realizing it's so loud.

Suddenly, all the Board members turn to look at me expectantly.

I gulp and push my chair back to stand. "Hi, I'm Alyssa Smith. With my degree and background in engineering, I will lead Smith Corporation to glory. Your cooperation is much needed and appreciated." I smile, and the members clap, nodding approvingly.

A guy with brunette hair, a tiny mustache just above his lips, and a mole on his right hand stands from his seat. "Your private secretary at your service, Ms. Smith." He bows and smiles ear to ear.

Grandmother walks over the podium and speaks, "Alyssa will sit in during meetings as an Assistant Director while she is still working at an engineering company. Once she relinquishes her role at the current company in two years' time, she will join this office as a full-time Director." She smiles at me, and the Board members follow with cheers.

I put on a brave smile, standing tall beside Grandmother, even though my heart hammers rapidly and my knee hiding beneath the table shakes. "I hope I have sufficient experience to lead this Corporation by that time." Sweat develops in my armpits. I only wish Grandmother had given me some time to gain experience before announcing it. My hand starts tapping my leg as I hold my smile for the Board of Directors.

"You're moving to another project since the seafront project is finalizing, Alyssa."

I blink and stare at Lucas open-mouthed. I stand up and quickly counter. "But Lucas, I want to ensure the project is of the finest quality since I will be signing off as the Assistant Project Engineer. It would not be good for my reputation if anything happened." My fingers tap against my leg nervously.

Lucas folds his arms, and his face pulls into a frown.

His face turns red as he says, "Just do what I say; otherwise, you can get off my team." His hand points the door out to me, and he dumps some files on the edge of the desk.

I swallow and bite my tongue, jaw tightening. My body feels numb as humiliation burns through me, making my cheeks hot.

I close my eyes and sit again, looking at him with a hard glare. "What is the new project? Are these the files for it?"

Lucas nods. "It's a new project in the same town. Read them and provide me with your cost and benefit analysis and project options by the end of the week." He hums and walks away.

My eyes scan the pamphlets and layout of my next

project briefly, and I nod slowly. The location is indeed near my previous project. I lean back in my chair, smiling.

After two hours, my chair jolts, and I jerk back to my surroundings. Alistair's fingers tap on my filing cabinet. His eyes gleam with happiness as our gazes meet. "Don't be sad, Alyssa. The new project is nearby." His hands mime how close the project locations are. "We will definitely call you to drop by for your expert advice as the project wraps up in the next three weeks." He rolls a toothpick in his mouth. He leans his arm to rest on the top of my chair, looking at my screen over my shoulder. I smile at him and tilt my head.

"It's been extended by three weeks? Why?" My eyebrow quirks, and I turn fully to face him.

"Come to the site tonight. You'll know the answer." He smiles at me and plays with a pen in his hand. "I'll be waiting for you."

"I'm afraid I have to decline. I'll be with my grandmother tonight," I respond with a small shrug and smile.

He leans closer to me, and I can smell the mint from his gum as his breath washes over me. "I'm staying at a motel for three days, so give me a buzz when dropping by at night." He winks and moves to grab his bag before sauntering away while twirling his car keys around a finger.

Suddenly, my stomach knots. *Does he realize I found the things in his trunk? Is he trying to lure me to the site to kill me?* My forehead creases as worry consumes my thoughts.

I purse my lips and wrap an arm around my waist. *Only one way to find out. I have to go tonight.*

Chapter 41

That evening, I answer Eleanor's call on the first ring. "Luck is with us. This morning, Leonard shared with us his confidential information on the additional motorboat," she shares excitedly. I grin and jump in place.

"Come quickly to the old villa. Let's investigate together." Eleanor sounds as cheerful as I feel.

"Right on." I end Eleanor's call and help Clare in unpacking one of Grandmother's vases at her new villa. After ensuring Clare and the new head of security, Lim, will look out for Grandmother, I speed to Grandmother's BMW. *At least with this, Alistair won't recognize me if I have time to drop by.*

Goose bumps rise on my skin upon reaching her previous villa. It looks deserted and sad, as though there are hidden tragic stories taking place within.

Eleanor and Jason meet me in the driveway, and we make our way inside, heading straight for Grandmother's bedroom. I glance in the direction of the small parlor opposite of where I'm standing. I pause and gesture for Eleanor and Jason to follow me, heading for the room.

"Eleanor, Jason! Look at the hatch beside the black

statue! It's cemented and pinned all around with a hex-agonal-headed bolt," I whisper, my eyes darting around the room.

"Weird, there was none when we were here the night of the break-in. There's definitely someone staying here." Jason's fingers brush the dust from the cement, smelling it. "Fresh shoe shine." He sniffs again, his nose wrinkling, and takes out a transparent plastic back with his glove and scoops some dust in.

Eleanor hastily pulls my arm, pointing to the cloak-room that has the now empty hidden vault. We move together to the secret passage.

Eleanor pulls the installed lever in the lamp, and the wall shakes as it slides to the side, giving way to a pitch-black space. The automatic lights illuminate as we step down the hall.

I clasp a hand over my mouth, and unconsciously, my right-hand points at the ground. "Fresh shoe prints are visible on the ground," I whisper to Eleanor.

She bends her knees and takes a picture, sending it to the police team.

She nods for me to go ahead first. Eleanor is ready with a loaded gun, and I follow her lead, pulling a gun from my pocket to prepare.

I reach the brick wall and quickly push the wall I think leads to the river. Yet, even with force, the wall doesn't budge.

"Is that the correct spot?" Eleanor's head tilts.

I nod. Sweat gathers on my forehead, and I slide my hands over the wall, my breath becoming rapid as a feel-ing of desperation gnaws at my insides.

The sound of an engine is faint behind the brick wall. Both of us still and blink at each other.

"The intruder is getting away!" Eleanor, with her eyes wide, joins me in trying to find the correct spot. "It has to be here somewhere!"

Intense pressure to find the right spot churns in my gut, and I wipe sweat from my brow. All of a sudden, there's a loud crack as the wall starts to slide.

I smile and exhale sharply in relief.

Eleanor confidently runs through the wall with her gun already aiming. I follow behind her, then quickly duck down to hide behind some stacks of boxes. I creep along in a crouch to stay hidden. My hand grips my hem, and my breathing becomes irregular. Eleanor lets out a muffled shout, and I peek out just as a burlap sack is pulled over her head roughly. A muscular bald man grips her arms hard and binds her, a gun at his waist.

"One down. Urgent help is required. Roger." I stutter in the earpiece.

"Roger. I am on the way. More backup, please." Jason's voice sounds in my earpiece.

"I'll hide on the boat and follow," I whisper in response. A muffled sound comes from Eleanor's mouth. Even though she's gagged and can't respond, she can still hear everything.

I whisper, "I will save you, 'couz."

I jump onto the motorboat as the engine revs. I roll in a somersault across the deck before crawling to hide among insulated ice boxes of various sizes along the boat's edge.

Since the man is alone, he places Eleanor behind him and pulls the sack away from her face while directing the boat. The door that leads to the ignition and steering wheel is broken, hanging open by just the bottom hinge.

I creep as quietly as possible, hiding behind the broken door. Eleanor's pupils are dilated as she looks around wildly, muffled noise escaping from her gag occasionally.

The man turns his eyes to Eleanor, his face turning red. He shoots beside Eleanor's leg. Eleanor wheezes as she shies away. "Shut up, you bitch! Or I will shoot you," he shouts, pointing his gun at Eleanor's head.

I take cover underneath a raincoat between insulated ice boxes. A few minutes pass, and I slide the raincoat back to try and find clues about where we are as the boat slows.

"Three miles to Dakota Jersey." I blink twice and slowly pull the raincoat back over my head.

We're heading to Dakota Jersey? Are we heading to the project site? Is Alistair involved somehow? I tighten my jaw while thinking about how adamantly he wanted me to be in Dakota Jersey tonight.

The sound of an additional engine floats over the water, and I turn my head and slide the coat aside. There's a small motorboat a few feet behind and gaining speed. I strain my eyes to see Jason and the marine police. I grin.

"Slow your vessel, Duke Van Ville," a voice says over a loudspeaker from the small motorboat.

Suddenly, our boat speeds up, swiftly pulling a U-turn and facing the police boat.

"We are marine police. Your boat is out after hours."

The boat halts, and the driver pauses for only a moment before he quickly drags Eleanor to place her in one of the empty boxes. "I will kill you if you make any noise," he warns harshly.

"Hey, Captain." He tilts his white sailor hat in respect. "We ain't fishing. The boxes are empty. I'm warming up this baby since—"

Jason signals to me, and I stand, brushing the coat aside, and point my gun at the man.

His hand is quick to grab his gun, pulling the trigger and firing in my direction. I quickly duck down, and it misses me, sailing into the dark air over the water.

Jason jumps onto the boat, firing at the man in mid-air, and rolls over to my side.

The shot misses the man, and they both start kicking and punching each other. I race to the icebox where Eleanor is hidden.

I take off the cover without delay, and Eleanor's turning blue by the time I open the lid. She breathes in and out for a few seconds as her normal color returns. I look around to find something sharp to cut the rope.

A boat hook is on a barrel within my arms' reach. Without hesitation, I grab it and cleave the rope in two, which releases Eleanor's hands. I pull off her gag and help her stand.

I look out over the water to view a half-built Viking boat near the luxury boat clubhouse, the project site I was the Assistant Project Engineer for. I stare at it, shocked. It looks similar to the Viking boat of the rings!

There's a nudge on my shoulder, and I am pulled back to our current situation. "Don't just stand there, move!" Eleanor shouts at me.

A gunshot cracks through the air, and we turn at Jason's cry of pain. Blood flows from his thigh, and his right-hand presses on it as he grimaces in pain.

I look at the police boat and quickly cover my mouth as a wave of nausea hits me. "No!"

The captain's body is lifeless, covered with blood as a hook, nails him to the ground. The man is alone, but he must have incredible combat training to have landed that hit.

I clench my teeth and curl my hands into fists. The

boat is still for only a moment before the man comes out from his hiding place near Eleanor. He punches at her mouth, and blood flies from her torn lip.

I kick his butt hard, and he stumbles in surprise, landing on his nose. He quickly gets up, rubbing his face, which bears new scratches. "Let him live. He has information about the whereabouts of the others," a voice commands via the earpiece.

I quickly grab a long wooden plank from next to me. I wind up and swing it like a baseball bat against his legs. He grunts and grimaces in pain, holding his leg as he limps a few shuffling steps.

He's stuck. His eyes are panicked, and his Adam's apple bobs. He drops the gun he's still clutching in one hand, and it lands with a clatter on the deck.

Eleanor cuffs him, and he squeezes his eyes, biting his lip from the pain.

"You better tell me where are Joe and Jake Kane?" she shouts and shakes him.

Creaking footsteps echo from the marine boat, and I tense as we turn toward the sound. All I make out is the silhouette of a man before sharp, intense pain radiates from my neck. Instantly, I can't move or breathe, and my vision gets fuzzy. A long, feathered object protrudes from Eleanor's neck in front of me, and my hand itches to reach for her. But my limbs feel impossibly heavy, and they only lift a touch before falling back to my sides. Her eyes roll back into her head, and her limp body crashes to the floor, lifeless.

I fumble, pull the sharp needle from my neck, and look at the dart. I open my mouth, panting, and a rush of dizziness blurs my vision more. *Eleanor and I were shot with tranquilize*rs. I cough and cough, gasping to suck in fresh air, and my brows pull together as I struggle. My body grows light, and I fall, unable to do anything to catch myself. I can't move any of my body, and the last thing I hear before blackness pulls me under is a phone ring and a muffled voice saying, "Do not harm my grand-daughters. I'll give you another gold bar."

Chapter 42

" Alyssa! Alyssa!" The voice sounds distant, and my head swims in dizziness.

My eyes flutter, and sea-blue eyes and a dimple are the first things to register. Alistair squats beside me, and he pulls me into a hug.

Tears start rolling down my cheeks, and my heart hammers. *Can I trust him? Will he harm me or Eleanor, and is he pretending to care for me?*

"I thought you were gone," he says softly in a trembling voice.

"Where am I?" I croak.

"The older lady, your cousin? She is in a boat . . . a Viking boat," he says.

I sit up as quickly as I can, still blinking and massaging my head with a groan. "What happened? Where is Eleanor?" My eyes dart from one end to the other as I try to balance myself. I look to the side, and water greets my view. There's a boat in front of us, speeding away from ours. I know I shouldn't trust Alistair 100%, but I will only know the truth if I get him to chase the other boat.

I incline my head in the direction of the other boat. "You know how to drive a boat, Alistair?" I raise an eyebrow, looking at his face.

"Yes, of course," he replies, scratching the back of his head.

"Let's chase after the boat then! It's my cousin, Eleanor," I shout while waving my arms.

Alistair hesitates for only a moment before he nods and moves into action. The engine of our boat kicks in, and we speed after them.

I step back from Alistair and whisper into my earpiece, "Calling backup. I'm in a boat chasing after a motorboat heading east to Baltimore Karat. Eleanor's been abducted. Roger." I breathe in and out deeply, trying to think of a plan on how to rescue Eleanor.

"Roger. One police officer will attend to Jason while three of us will find a boat to reach you."

Thankfully, we aren't the only luxury boat cruising around the water tonight. Three other boats help camouflage our movements from the motorboat ahead.

I hide in the inside area as soon as I spot Joe in the distance, anger simmering through my body. *Where is Eleanor?* I can't see from my position, and frustration eats at me. I tilt my head and stand on my toes, trying to search for Eleanor in the darkening sky.

Water from the river splashes on my face, so I inch to the right side, still gazing at the front motorboat. I gasp and tremble as I see Eleanor. The hair covering her face has some blood on it, and she seems to be pinned to the floor through her hand.

My hands run down my face, and I twist my hair. I wince at the sight, biting my lip. Tears start rolling down my cheeks, and I can't stop my body from shaking.

Alistair turns his head to look at me, brows touching, and his head tilts in question.

"It's Eleanor. She is lying on the boat in a pool of blood," I say nervously while sobbing.

"Keep calm, Alyssa. We will save her in no time. I'm sure she's strong.' Alistair says, trying to calm me.

I step back, bend, and pull out a hidden gun from my thick socks. I straighten and aim at the driver's body.

"Don't shoot. Put your gun down," Alistair hisses at me, distress taking over his face.

He kicks my shin, and my gun slips from my grip. I'm suddenly flipped over, and his strong hand is pushing me to the ground.

"It's not a good idea to let the driver die while Eleanor is unconscious," he says, and his hands curl into fists. My chest heaves, and sweat builds on my forehead.

I cry out as pain bursts in my neck again, and dizziness seeps into my head. My hand reaches up to the long sharp syringe sticking from my neck. My vision blurs, and I can only see Alistair's lips move, but his face is unclear. Bit by bit, darkness takes over.

There's a loud smacking noise that wakes me this time.

"You idiot. Why did you injure her eldest granddaughter? She is as valuable as the young one. We ain't getting any gold if either is injured." A harsh voice racks in my ears.

"Bu—But Joe, I was saving your life," another man stutters.

"Enough! Call our doctor to revive her!" the first man shouts. This must be Alistair's uncle, as he doesn't sound like the Joe I know.

My eyes remain closed, but I strain my ears to listen.

I can't make out the third voice, but I can tell it's Alistair.

I fight a rising panic, and my heart hammers in my chest. Alistair is indeed part of the abductor scheme. They must have taken compensation from Grandmother. I feel like screaming. I start to wiggle my toes, trying to get the feeling to return to them and wake the rest of my body up.

"Alistair! Tie her up and take her to the other room now," the first voice shouts, another smack ringing.

"Ouch! Enough, Uncle Joe. I will hide her soon," Alistair says, his voice hard.

I try to open both eyes, slowly rubbing my head. Arms pick me up, and I freeze, going limp.

"I won't hurt you," Alistair murmurs in my ear. "My uncle's boss, Joe M, will kill my uncle's family if we go against him."

His sweat trickles from his face onto my neck as he holds me against his sturdy chest with chill hands. His chest moves up and down quickly, and he sighs heavily. In one more stride, his body tilts to push a door.

He gradually bends and places me on the floor of an empty room. He takes a cuff from his pocket and cuffs my hands.

My head still swims from the drugs and boat ride, so I can't open my eyes fully. They stay half-closed, and I can only see haystacks and iceboxes. My nose twitches at the earthy smell of hay that fills the air.

His breath brushes against my face, and he pushes my hair from my face to look at me. He adjusts my body to sit straight and whispers in my ear, "There are a few surveillance cameras, so I can't talk freely."

His gaze purposefully moves to where he smooths my jacket on the ground, sliding a tiny key under it. His lips touch my cheek, and he whispers about an escape route.

He wraps a black cloth around my eyes before standing.

"I am off to the office. I will inform Lucas you are on medical leave for a few days," he says softly.

My voice comes out muffled as my muscles still don't want to work fully. I suppress a shiver as the door shuts with a ringing finality. Panic swirls through me, with only the sounds of crickets and distant waves accompanying me in the eerie silence.

Where am I?

I take measured breaths, trying to calm my pulse. I work to wriggle my hands from the cuffs. Frustration overwhelms me, and I huff, trying to pull the blindfold off and failing.

I grope in the darkness, sliding my butt over the cold concrete floor, moving to the left where Alistair hid the cuffs key.

I scoot to the right and wince when I hit something. "Ouch!" I fumble on the floor, and my fingers touch my jacket. I stretch my hands to search under it. I catch the edge with my fingers but freeze when footsteps tap outside the door.

My fingers go numb, and my blood chills as they approach. The doorknob twists as someone whistles. In an instant, my fingers stumble over the key and slide it into my back pocket. I slide to the right, pretending to sleep as the door opens, casting a stream of light into the room.

"Hey, Joe, her breathing is normal," a husky voice calls from nearby. His breath reeks of alcohol. I twitch my nose, holding my breath.

"This will make her unconscious." A tin can squeaks open. Heavy footsteps approach me, and a huge hand touches my shoulder, tilting my neck back. He shoves a thick cloth over my mouth, just enough for me to inhale the chemical that is soaked into the cloth. Within seconds, splitting dizziness aches through my head, and tears fall as I can't breathe. My body starts to shake, then becomes light. I blink and gradually shut my eyes.

Chapter 43

Screeching tires and loud bangs ring in my ears. My eyes are heavy, and I am unable to open them. Two men's voices argue, but I can't understand their words. A short scuffle follows, then a crash. Someone is breathing.

My eyelids remain stubbornly shut, and I bit my lips, dizzy. I wiggle my fingers, then my hands, but they don't move much from being bound. I try again with my toes. Another crash, this time of wooden furniture and glass that most definitely shatter. I can't make out anything else, where I am, and what is happening around me.

There's a groan and then the sound of broken glass being crunched under weight.

"Give up!"

The voice. *Jamie.* I try to force my eyelids open, but still nothing. A loud gunshot lingers in the air, and my heart stops. A gentle touch slips its arms underneath my shoulders, and I feel him breathing heavily and his body warm. I'm held against a firm chest and lose consciousness until the rumble of a car engine pulls me back. A cool breeze caresses my face, and a wonderfully warm aroma enters my nose. A hand strokes my hair, and I relax, drifting into a deep sleep.

I wake in a bed what feels like days later, a floral scent surrounding me and my hands gripping the soft sheets.

Drowsiness and pain make it difficult to open my eyes, but I manage it. I kick a blanket from me, causing the chill air to creep over my skin.

I groan, feeling like someone is stabbing my head when I suddenly realize where I am. There is no scent of hay or fish. My nose twitches several times.

I rub my head and straighten my stiff legs from their curled position. The last thing I really remember is Alistair carrying me to a deserted room with my hands cuffed.

Suddenly, I bolt upright, holding my head, and look around in confusion at the plush room.

My eyes roam, and my mouth drops.

When did I get to my apartment? The wallpaper, the dressing table with its mirror . . . It's my bedroom. The smell, the bedsheets, and the family portrait hanging on the wall are all mine. *Am I home already? Did someone save us?* I tousle my hair and squint against the pain and confusion. I slap my cheek, which startles me, but the room stays intact. I am wide awake.

I inch forward, howling each time I move too quickly. My head is groggy, and it takes forever to make it to my door. I twist the doorknob, looking at my living room with the sofa, two armchairs, and table lamp sitting where they always have been.

Further into the kitchen, broken dishes are scattered over the floor, and there's a deep cut in the center of the portrait of Grandmother, Eleanor, and me with dried blood smeared on it that spells out, "BITCH."

A phone vibrates at my butt, making me jump. "Oh, it's my—" I blink twice. It's Arthur Papon's phone. A message flashes from an unknown again.

Two photos pop up. Duke Jacque and John Lanvin. Then Grandmother and Lady Jacqueline. Finally, two question marks.

I frown. What does this mean? The four connections don't make sense, especially since John Lanvin 'died.' My hand rubs my forehead.

"Wait!" *Where were Grandmother and Lady Jacqueline when he died?* Maybe this is a clue.

The phone in my hand vibrates again, this time with a call, and I almost throw it in surprise before hesitantly pressing the answer icon. "Alyssa. Alyssa? Are you in your apartment? It's Jason." His voice sounds pained, and he breathes heavily.

"How do you know that I am in the apartment?" I ask.

"We have a tracking device installed in your and Eleanor's phones and earpieces. Eleanor's tracking dot is stagnant in your apartment basement," Jason responds with a deep inhale. "I will save Eleanor."

"I need to go to the apartment library to check details on Duke Jacque and John Lanvin. I'll find you after, Jason." He mutters his agreement before we hang up, and I rush out of the door.

As the door shuts behind me, sudden tremors run down the walls. I nearly fall, thrown off balance. My head turns to the left to look through the window, and I freeze momentarily at the sight of trees being uprooted and waves of debris and muddy sand flowing toward my building.

I shake my head and turn back to the hall, pausing again when my eyes find the mirror hanging opposite me. My hands tremble while I pull my shirt closer to my nose to sniff.

The dark spot smells of dried blood.

My eyes scan my reflection from head to toe, searching for other spots. Only my top has blood dashed on my top right chest. There's also a deep scratch with dried blood visible on my left arm.

I take a step back, then a second, my eyes rapidly blinking.

I turn my head to the right, looking at the pathway, and I move, getting back to my task. *I don't have time to worry about this right now.*

At the emergency exit staircase, I stumble between steps, and someone's hand grabs my waist, holding me gently to balance myself. He hugs me hurriedly, then his hands tug me to move.

My eyes are wide as I stare eye-to-eye with Jamie.

"Jamie! Jamie! Please stop!"

His jaw is tight, and his hands are in fists. He says, "Alyssa, please stay in the lobby. I have to settle something." His eyes plead with me, and I swallow. I nod, and my legs start moving. He runs and jumps down a few steps at a time, leaving me behind. Worry eats at me as his hands noticeably shake. His shirt has spots of blood all over.

Why is Jamie here? And why is he also covered in blood? Did he save me?

Chapter 44

I step my feet into the lobby, and a loud bang echoes in the air. I jerk and swing to face the gunfire. I duck my head, and chaos is the best way to describe the rest of the lobby. Many residents are here, chattering nervously, their faces drawn with worry. I step forward but quickly change directions when I spot Jake Kane near the restaurant. I glance through the windows and doors as I pass them, my mouth dropping at the devastation and debris piled against the building. *Not now.*

I try to keep my breath steady as I press my earpiece, which is still miraculously in my ear and working. "Jake Kane is at the entrance of the restaurant. Need help."

"Help is on the way," comes the immediate response from a voice I recognize but don't know the name of. I quickly place my palm on the reception desk that I am standing beside. I breathe in and out, thinking of trapping Jake Kane for the police to put him in bars. I swallow and continue closer to him, finally seeing everything.

Jake Kane, with his enormous gold chain covering his hairy chest, is grinning at the sight of a man in a pool of blood. His right hand is in his pocket, grasping something that is definitely too long to be the shape of a man's wallet.

I turn to look over the crowd for a moment before looking back at the restaurant. I grit my teeth. In seconds, he's disappeared. I turn in a full circle, stretching my neck everywhere, to search for him but find nothing. I walk to his former spot, and there are several footprints on the marble floor, and my leg bounces.

Come on, which footprint is his shoe?

I blink several times, trying to recall the type of shoe he was wearing.

"He was wearing a white stripe red . . . I think it was an Adidas sneaker. Yes!" I smile when I pull up a picture via the internet. "Thank you, Suzanne, for your fashion training," I murmur.

I squat down to check the prints for the matching shoe and follow behind. Thanks to the commotion, the flooring is dirty, and it's not hard to follow. They lead to a small passageway to the ground floor residents.

I step into the hall just as a woman's screaming and the breaking of glass grabs my attention.

"Are you able to check whether she is breathing?" someone asks in a panicked voice. I raise my hand, step forward, and squat down beside the fainted lady. I extend my hands to her knees, bending them with her hips to the right angle, and my left hand holds her hips while my right slowly tilts her head back to open her airway. Within a few seconds, the lady coughs and opens her eyes. My arm slides under her shoulder blades to assist her to a seated position. I smile at her while the onlookers clap their hands, and a collective sigh of relief fills the room. I stand, and my eyes stare at the lifeless body at the foot of the Italian restaurant entrance.

I let go of a long sigh, placing my right hand on my

chest. *Luckily, it's not Jamie.* I speed to the passageway and see Jamie up ahead, walking toward the ground-floor residential area as well.

"Jamie! Wait for me," I yell, my palm raising at him to stop.

The lift door opens, and a beeping resonates. Jamie dashes into it, and the door closes behind him. I catch just a glimpse of something in his hands that looks like a long bat. I run as fast as I can toward the lift, panting by the time I get there.

The light stops at B4. I quickly press the lift button, but it remains at B4. Giving up on the elevator, I dash to the emergency exit staircase and make my way down several flights. I suck in air to regain my composure before pushing the door. Nevertheless, it remains shut. I shake the doorknob angrily. I run upstairs to B3 and kick the door, which flings open easily.

As my feet step in, a gunshot comes from B4.

Sweat trickles from my hairline, and my whole body shakes so bad I have trouble moving again. My hand crumples my top.

I hope Jamie is OK. I wonder who shoots whom.

I press the elevator button repeatedly until the door opens, and I ride it down to B4. The ceiling lights flash, and nausea returns quickly with a vengeance. I keep my hand against the wall for reassurance as I walk toward an electrical room.

Terror thunders down on me, and my scalp prickles with sweat thinking of Jamie. *I have to save him.* I clench my teeth, refusing to think of any other possibility.

A steel rod rolls across the floor as I peek in the door before slipping in.

A wooden baseball greets me on the ground, and I

snatch it up for protection.

There's a distorted image of a man through the glass cabinet to my left. His face has scratches and seeping gashes, and his hands are covered with blood. I walk around to reach him, crawling from one cabinet full of electrical items to another. The room buzzes from the central air, and steam occasionally swirls through the air. I trudge toward the motionless body, and I watch as a shadow other than mine grows on the ceiling and soft footfalls alert me.

I swallow and tighten my grip on the wooden baseball bat, my palms clammy.

A heavily-muscled body jumps from the top of a steel electrical cabinet, and I take off. He is faster and manages to yank my ankle when he lands on the floor.

I grab onto the edge of a wooden workbench, pulling against his grip as hard as I can. "Joe, why are you doing this?" I shout when I see who it is.

"Joe M will destroy me and Alistair if I don't eliminate you and Eleanor. All of this wouldn't have happened if you ignored Lady Jacqueline's death without getting involved," he utters in a hiss.

I bang his hands with the baseball bat and use my other foot to kick his face. He's thrown off guard when he answers my question, and I manage to land the blows, escaping his grip.

I run to Jamie's aid, panting. Jamie is breathing and conscious now, sitting against the cabinet. He holds his hand just higher than his thigh, showing the gun in his hand.

"Shoot him," he whispers.

I nod and grab the weapon in my right hand while my left wraps under his arm to get him up from the seated position.

His face grimaces in pain when his injured thigh releases a new wave of blood.

I look up, and Joe's eyes lock with mine, and my fingers pull the trigger without remorse as he points his own at me. His hand tries to fire his gun, but there's only a dull click. He throws it aside with a pained hiss as he falls.

I hoist Jamie up and take the brunt of his weight while walking out of the room. I look back to see the next move from Joe, even though his body is paralyzed as blood flows from his abdomen.

I refuse to be caught. I breathe in deeply, and determination tightens my jaw. We move slowly to the elevator with my strength and Jamie limping.

I grab my phone and press 'group favorite.' "Roger, Jamie is badly injured. Please get a paramedic or in-house doctor to see him at the library. I will bring him to the LG library as I need to find something in order to assist with the conclusion of the case."

"Roger. In-house medical assistance has been contacted."

"Jason, have you found Eleanor?" Dead silence greets my question.

Chapter 45

Shrieks emanate from the ground floor. I lay Jamie over two chairs in the library. "I will return. I need to check out what happened in the lobby."

Jamie smiles softly and pulls me in for a kiss before I leave.

Upon reaching the ground floor, my breathing grows ragged, and a shiver runs down my spine when my eyes land on a young woman in a yellow dress trembling as she points in the direction of the carpeted staircase. Her mouth drops in a horrified gasp. Her shaky finger points at the centerpiece of the luxury apartment building, the most expensive Parisian painting, sprayed with graffiti that looks an awful lot like blood.

"The End of Mrs. Smith."

My left-hand lands on my chest and grips my top as I hyperventilate. I turn to run to the library, and standing beside Jamie once more, I manage to reiterate what had happened in the lobby to Jamie while I search for a paper from twenty years ago. "Aha!" I exclaim when I find it. The headline reads, "John Lanvin - the son of the ill-fated designer." I read the article out loud.

"John Lanvin and his son meet with a car crash, many

believe to be an arranged accident. Unfortunately, the bodies of both have gone missing from the site after the crash. Witnesses managed to snap photos of the injured but alive. Both were reported missing as the ambulance and police arrived.

"A passer-by named Marie Lemons saw a black car with two gentlemen in suits carrying the injured away. There were no plates. A week later, there was a funeral held for John Lanvin.

Davies is still reported missing."

I firmly hold onto the computer mouse, shaking it and making a lot of sounds while I breathe noisily.

Jamie's voice crackles as he calls out, "Alyssa?" I turn my head to him and smile.

"Yes, Jamie? Is the pain worsening?" I ask as worry pulls my face into a frown. I push the chair out and walk to him.

"I want to let you know that my driver and I fought some guys who we saw coming out from the Viking ship clubhouse under construction, carrying you tied and blindfolded."

"What?" I stand beside him and hold his hand, my free hand massaging my neck. "So the crashing sounds and car engines were real. You were the one who fought and carried me to my apartment?" My brows lift in surprise.

Jamie nods and smiles.

I bend to kiss Jamie, only pulling away when Arthur Papon's phone chimes. I slip my hand into my pocket and bring it to the front of my face.

A message comes in from the same unknown number. "Mrs. Smith has been naughty. I will seek revenge." There are several photos of Grandmother being romantically involved with Duke Jacque that follow.

I scroll through all the photos I receive, and my eyes bulge from my sockets. Why is Duke Jacque in my Grandmother's life?

I step back and look down when I step on something small but hard. I shift my foot and squat, squinting at the chair's four legs. I smile; an iPod. I snatch it, rub the headphone, and place it in my ear, connecting it to my phone. "Hello, can someone run the thumbprint of Duke Jacque against John Lanvin? I suspect they are the same person with different faces after the accident."

"Roger. Right on," Eleanor's voice crackles through.

"Eleanor!" Relief makes my knees weak. "Thank God you are saved." I clap my hands.

"I am at Luxe's sickbay while Jason is searching for Jake Kane. We believe him to be Grandmother's out-of-wedlock son with John Lanvin since one of our team members has an informant from the registration department that provided the information on the change of name from Davies Lanvin to Jake Kane."

I gasp when I hear the particulars from Eleanor. My lips curl back in disgust.

A message comes in again on Arthur Papon's phone. There are two photos this time. Jake Kane with his face half blotched with blood, his hands with a blood-splattered chef's knife dripping on the floor, and Grandmother smiling alone in a room.

What is the message? Is Grandmother in trouble? I pinch the phone screen to enlarge the photo. Then my eyes catch on the room's background that Grandmother is in. The furniture and wallpaper designs look familiar. *Where have I seen it before?* My fingers massage my chin.

I cover my mouth with my hand as I shoot up. My hands fidget on the library table, and I re-examine the photo's surroundings, then say into the earpiece:

"Grandmother is being held captive in Luxe Gold! At her penthouse," I shout in the earpiece, breath rushing through my nose.

My eyes look at Jamie, and I say firmly, "Jamie, stay here until the medical staff arrives. I need to help the police save Grandmother."

I'm so sucked into a fog of fear that I run into a chair in front of me, accidentally flipping it onto the floor noisily.

"Go! Run, and be safe, Alyssa!" Jamie shouts to give encouragement.

Chapter 46

How am I going to get into Grandmother's penthouse without a key? My hand scratches my arm, and I frown.

"Ugh!" I shake the doorknob and kick out the door with my leg.

My face fills with concern, and my heart stops beating momentarily as I feel steel prod against my back. Shudders creep up my spine, and my hands freeze.

Before I can turn to look at my assailant, a brawny arm hugs my neck and stomach strongly to prevent me from fighting. I manage to kick my assailant's thigh, and he lets go of my neck with a muffled sound.

He strengthens his grip on my waist as I wriggle to break free. He loses his grip on me, and I quickly pull away, ready to run. I turn my head, his cap covers his face, and he holds a baseball bat. He is fast and hits the side of my head. I rub my head, groaning, when suddenly, my assailant pulls my legs, and I crash on the floor. My hands flail, grabbing hold of books and glassware from the side table on the way and throwing them at his face. It doesn't deter him. Instead, it only angers him, and he punches my stomach, tossing me over his shoulder like a ragdoll before picking me up and pushing me forward. My legs kick at him.

My vision turns blurry, and with the last of my will-power, my legs curl back to kick at my assailant.

"Ouch. You idiot!" he grumbles in a fury.

He punches my stomach again, this time knocking the wind out of me and leaving me feeling like I'm suffocating. I twist and thrash, making it almost impossible to hold onto me.

An agonizing pain batters my head. His strong arms push me harshly forward again.

Dizziness seeps into my head, and I have to close my eyes to stay upright.

I passively allow my assailant to lead me as I try to recover. He pushes a door open as my ears hear the hinges squeak. His footsteps are behind me, and he pushes me once again onto a hard but smooth surface. A wooden door closes, and no light seeps into my eyes. The last thing I remember before passing out is the smell of perfume persistent in my nostrils.

It's Grandmother's Nina Ricci.

I return to reality with groans of excitement, licking, and laughter ringing in my ears.

I try to open my eyes, but my body is exhausted. It's like there is glue stuck on my eyes. I breathe in and out slowly, and the air feels misty and damp. Small, straight lines of light illuminate my spot weakly. *Where am I?*

Two people are conversing, and Grandmother is one of them with her soft, sweet voice, and a man's booming laugh joins her. The sound of kissing fills the quiet place I am locked inside.

His voice is familiar. Where have I heard it, and who is it? My head pounds, and I close my eyelids, dozing off again.

The same voices surround the room, and I open my eyes. My head is still heavy, and I barely open my eyes, though it doesn't take as much effort as before. I turn my head and strain my ears to hear their conversation.

"We finally are as one again after fifty years of waiting, John," Grandmother says with a groan.

"You make fireworks glow inside me from the touch of your lips," John replies huskily.

"What took you so long to plan the murder of my non-love wife, Lady Jacqueline? Day and night, I had to spend heartsick seeing you from afar while you should have been in my arms."

My dreamy thoughts are disturbed by the man's soft-spoken voice. My eyes open widely as my brain makes the connection.

Duke Jacques. His voice is the same voice that threatened Lady Jacqueline in the abandoned hotel. A sudden cold shivers up my spine, and I continue listening to their conversation.

"Our son finally mustered the courage to plot the murder of your wife with the gold bars that I gave him," Grandmother replies.

"Jake Kane finally has the guts to help us reunite as a family," the man says, a slight disappointment in his tone.

I force my eyes open, and they dart around the dark space, finally actually absorbing my surroundings. I'm in my grandmother's closet.

I'm crouching with my knees bent, and I realize only my hands are tied with a green ribbon, and the rest are free.

I wriggle my hands to lose the knot, biting the ribbon. Once free from the ribbon, I remain quietly in the closet. Suddenly, I recall the assailant, and I peek through the closet holes to see where they may have gone. *Where is the bulky guy who hit my head? He's not in this room. Where is he hiding?* I breathe in shallowly. I hope he is not a danger to my grandmother and her lover.

As I look through the hole, I freeze when my eyes snag on Grandmother's clothes thrown on the carpet. Unbidden, my eyes flick up. She is naked under a man who resembles Duke Jacques. His pants are down, and he's thrusting inside Grandmother. Grandmother is groaning, her hands roaming over his back. He gropes Grandmother's breasts before his hands move to his collar.

He unbuttons his shirt while scrubbing at his neck. In chunks, prosthetic rubber silicon falls off, which reveals—

I blink twice and rub my eyes for good measure. It's John Lanvin. Exactly the guy in the photos in Grandmother's diary in the secret room. My breath moves quickly, coming in pants.

"John, my love. Let's abscond and stay in Malibu," Grandmother groans in a pleasure-filled voice.

"Yes, my dear." He caresses Grandmother's hair and leans down to kiss her. I gasp, quickly closing my mouth. I finally am able to pull my stupefied gaze from the couple and resume my search for the assailant. My hands accidentally push the closet door, and I fall out of the closet, Grandmother's scarf fluttering to land on top of my face.

Grandmother and John Lanvin are staring at me.

"Alyssa?" Why are you hiding in my closet? And who brought you here?" Grandmother asks, hugging the man.

I look up and wince. "Sorry to disturb you, Grandmother, but there was a guy who knocked me out when

I was knocking at the penthouse door. I passed out and found myself hidden in this closet of yours." I massage my head where I still feel immense pain.

I climb from the floor, smoothing my jacket with my hands, and my eyes land on the Viking ship picture that resembles the Viking ship from my first project with the engineering company. My mouth starts to move, and Grandmother pulls a bathrobe on to cover her body.

Grandmother, now dressed, hums and clutches John Lanvin, tossing a sheet over his waist. "I can see you have a lot of questions. I'm the owner of the project completion; the Viking ship at the members' complex was meant for my lover, John Lanvin, to reside in and conduct businesses. It's part of our plans for union and the reason I relinquished my shares and roles in my businesses to you, Alyssa."

I nod slowly as I process everything. I poke my tongue against my cheek and exhale forcefully.

"We had no choice but to end Lady Jacqueline's life. That bitch! Since she adamantly refused a divorce. We are both old, and we want to spend our remaining life together," John Lanvin says softly, glancing lovingly at Grandmother.

As my mouth opens to respond, a loud gunshot breaks the silence of the room.

My eyes widen, then, in a flash, I turn my head to face the shooter. A person who resembles Jake Kane holds a gun and stands before the couple.

It's Jake's face, but that is not his overall shape.

Grandmother holds tightly onto John while he takes out a gun, pointing it at the imposter.

"Who are you? You are not my son!" John's jaw tightens, and he pushes Grandmother behind him as he stands, the blanket around him.

My mouth drops, and I turn, grabbing a sharp wire hanger, and twisting it into a shape more weapon-like as I turn back to the group.

"Freeze!" Jason's voice emanates in the air, pointing his gun at the fake Jake Kane from the foot of the door.

The person scratches their neck, pulling bits of the rubber silicon off to reveal the beautiful face of Jennifer Henderson.

I step forward, tears flowing down my cheeks as my eyes turn red.

"Why, Jennifer? Why do you plan to kill my grand-mother?" I ask, my hands trembling with anger.

"Mr. Spencer, whose murder I planned on the night of Lorraine's birthday, in his will, indicated that Mrs. Smith would get 10% of his estates in Australia, Asia, and Amer-ica. They had an affair before me due to a business pro-posal that your grandmother helped him win." She bares her teeth, her chin tilting high.

"Please don't get me wrong, I only murdered Mr. Spencer to get my share of his company, and tonight, because of the will, I plan to kill her, too," Jennifer utters in conviction as she steps closer gracefully with her high heels. Jason moves slowly while Jennifer is talking to me, and he jumps at her, capturing her immediately. Jennifer is in tears, and her makeup smudges as she sobs.

"Who planned the murders of Lady Jacqueline, Lady Jessica, and Arthur Papon?" I shout, my face turning red and my hands in fists. I look from Grandmother to John and Jennifer.

Unexpectedly, Jennifer readies her leg to strike at Jason's navel, but Eleanor steps into the room, her gun drawn. "I wouldn't do that if I were you." She growls and lowers her foot, and Jason cuffs her.

I walk closer to Jennifer and narrow my eyes at her. "Did you frame your helper with the blood-spotted hanky?"

She lets out a loud snort. "She was my guinea pig. I was using her and the hanky to mislead Inspector Raven and you." She nods at me. "The helper was the one who placed the spots of blood on the wall near the swimming pool and my ring in the huge vase. Once she saw you take a photo of it, she removed them so that when investigators went looking for the items, none were available." Her mouth curves to the side in a cocky smirk.

My right hand turns into a fist, and I am breathless, with anger exuding from my skin.

The room door is thrown open again, and the real Jake Kane storms into the room. He stares at me from his spot and inches further toward Grandmother and John.

"Your Grandmother . . . she paid me, her out-of-wedlock son, to do the dirty job for her. Lady Jessica and Arthur Papon were not in their initial plans. I had to dispose of them since they were our hindrances. Lady Jessica overheard your grandmother's plan and saw her give me the gold bar." He inhales deeply with fists on his hips. He continues, "Lady Jessica wanted to report your grandmother and me to Arthur Papon, thus the reason I had to eliminate both of them since I wasn't sure what she had already told him."

Jake turns his head to Jason, whose police badge is out and against his chest. Then he shoots in rapid fire. The first is at Grandmother, who drops on the bed, then at John's head, where he falls on the carpet. Finally, as Jason moves to jump on him, he pulls the trigger on himself.

In the end, they reunited in a blood bath.

Tears fall from my eyes in thick sheets, and my hands grip my jacket as I walk to the lifeless body of Grandmother. I take her hand in mine, squat down, and kiss it while sobbing. Eleanor is crying, her hand squeezing my shoulder. She shakes as we stare at Grandmother's eyes looking at the ceiling.

A week later, it's a dreary morning with drizzle, and my hand clutches a hanky, and the other holds Jamie's tightly. My eyes have been red-rimmed and misty the last few days. We are standing at the burial site, giving our last respects to Grandmother. She is buried beside her lover, John Lanvin, and her son, Jake Kane.

Chapter 47

Two months later, we have finally settled everything with Grandmother's villas.

Eleanor is conferred a promotion for settling the most challenging high-profile murder, while Inspector Raven is given a medal for his bravery.

As for me . . .

Jamie smiles at me while holding my hands, and he pulls me in by my waist for a kiss.

Max Lincoln, Mr. Henderson's lawyer, waves at Jamie and smiles as he approaches.

He pushes a chair aside to sit beside Jamie on the boardwalk leading to multiple cruise ships.

He pulls out an agreement, sliding it to Jamie, and I peek over his shoulder to read each line. We both look at each other and smile. I place my head on his shoulder with a twinkle in my eye, and he kisses my right hand. Max hands him a black ink pen, and Jamie signs the agreement of his contract marriage with Rihana Spencer being canceled and voided.

Then, he shoves another contract in front of us, which we both read, nodding and smiling.

Max's finger points at the end of the page where it's

missing two signatures. A marriage contract for us.

He hands me his pen, and I sign before passing the pen to Jamie to sign.

Jamie's hand strokes my hair, and I shift to look up at him, his eyes melting my soul. I lean in, and we kiss.

Max clears his throat, and we separate. "Congratulations, Jamie and Alyssa." He winks and leaves.

We both walk on the pavement toward the cruise ship, standing at the railing, and Jamie pulls me to his chest. He kisses me, and my hands lock around his firm body with one of my feet rising.

Once the cruise ship starts its engines, a waiter approaches us with a tray of drinks and a yellow envelope. He looks at me and tilts his head curiously. I look at him and take the envelope slowly. Jamie looks around while I open the envelope, and my heart beats rapidly, my mouth falling open. The letter is written in blood.

"Wait!" I call out at the same time the waiter waves and jumps from the ship into the water.

My eyebrows lift, looking at Jamie. "Guess we're into another mystery sooner than expected." Jamie chuckles and winks at me, kissing my forehead.

"Whatever mystery comes our way, you'll always get to the bottom of it."

**MORE GRIPPING FANTASIES AND THRILLERS
FROM SHERLINA IDID**

MIDDLE GRADE

Mystical Adventure of Ashley Sprinkler

Ashley Sprinkler: Ancient Sacred Twisted Journey

YOUNG ADULT

Today, Tomorrow & Never

ABOUT THE AUTHOR

Sherlina Idid studied in Coventry University, United Kingdom and graduated with a BA Hons in International Relations & Politics. She has been working in the human resource management line.

Her love for reading adventure, fantasy and mystery books and her interest in traveling exposed her to other cultures, environments, and sightseeing which eventually sparked her to write her first novel *Mystical Adventure of Ashley Sprinkler (Book Series).* In due course, her interest in writing expanded into horror and thriller genre. She can be reached on @sherlinaididauthor on Instagram and as Sherry Ina on facebook.

Printed in Great Britain
by Amazon

20310755R00217